John Park

Evil Lurking

Book One of the Nixland Saga

Snowy Range Press

Evil Lurking
Book One of The Nixland Saga
Copyright 2023 by John Park

ISBN 979-8-9866376-1-7: All rights reserved.
Printed in the United States of America

This book is a work of fiction. Names, characters, places, and incidents are either a product of the author's imagination or are used fictitiously. Any resemblance to actual events, or persons or locales living or dead, is purely coincidental.

Published by
Snowy Range Press
Laramie, Wyoming

To my mother, who fostered in me a lifelong love of books. Moving from country to country was especially difficult when we didn't speak the local language. As we moved frequently, books made my mother and I feel less isolated. The wonderful characters became our friends who we could turn to no matter where we were.

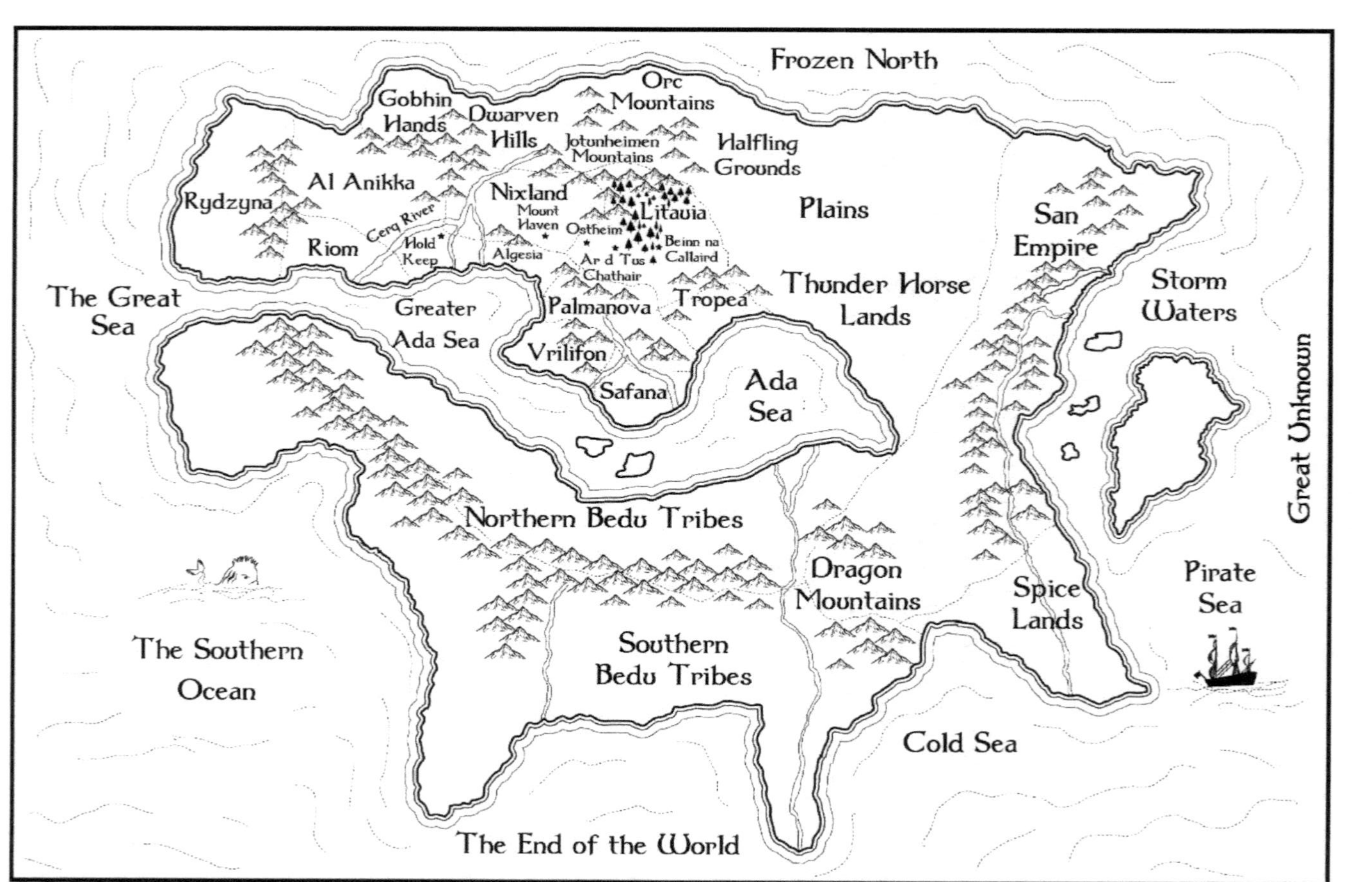

Frozen North
Orc Mountains
Gobhin Hands
Dwarven Hills
Jotunheimen Mountains
Halfling Grounds
Al Anikka
Rydzyna
Nixland
Litauia
Plains
San Empire
Mount Haven
Ostheim
Beinn na Callaird
Riom
Cerq River
Hold Keep
Algesia
Ar d Tus
Chathair
Thunder Horse Lands
Storm Waters
The Great Sea
Greater Ada Sea
Palmanova
Tropea
Vrilifon
Safana
Ada Sea
Great Unknown
Northern Bedu Tribes
Dragon Mountains
Spice Lands
Pirate Sea
The Southern Ocean
Southern Bedu Tribes
Cold Sea
The End of the World

The Inhabitants of Nixland
(In Order of Appearance)

Andanir Noldorin: elf boy

Aide: elf female maid loyal to Andanir's mother

Ututur Bunour: half-orc male soldier in charge of the baggage train/logistics train

Manfred Bohm: human councilor of Nixland and a captain in the Nixland army

Aurelio Tommaso: human male, Bohm's guard

Jen Hiskia: human male, Bohm's guard

Aldous Lorenz: human Consul leader of the Nixland army and a member of the high council

Leandro Campagna: human male, aide to Lorenz

Ilina Kuhn: human female healer

Sigmund Becker: Ututur's friend, works for him in the baggage train

Adala Mann: human female works in the baggage train

Larvarnis: trickster goddess

Clodagh of clan Sioban: elf female, Andanir's stepmother and high priestess/dark sorceress

Aoife Sioban: elf male, Clodagh's son from an unknown father

Eithne Sioban: elf female, Clodagh's daughter from an unknown father

Doireann Noldorin: elf female, Andanirs's deceased mother

Osin Noldorin: elf male, Andanir's father and chief of the southern elves

Bandit: male dog, large hunting hound, Doireann's and Andanir's dog

Eoin Clomin: elf male, Second to the warlord of the Southern elven army

Kiley Saoirse: elf female, another Second to the Southern elf warlord

Dowan Eachmhile: elf male, warlord of the Southern elven army

Roisin Heenan: elf female, Clodagh's helper

Avar Trahern: elf male

Rianor Enid: elf female, dark sorceress

Balor Ayden: elf male, dark sorcerer

Maeve Fiadl: elf female, dark sorcerer

Cadnael: elf male warrior an aide to Eoin
Meliore: human general goods and clothing merchant
Galdino Di Bartolo: human male, head of Nixland high council
Sergio Salce: human male, member of the Nixland high council
Ursula Schwertfeger: human female, member of the Nixland high council
Astrid Moretto: human female, Nixland council member
Birger Dybdahl: dwarf male, member of the Nixland high council
Ronaldo Viccari: Sergeant at arms of the Nixland high council
Niccolo Eufrasio: human male, spice merchant
Emile Vogt: human male, captain in the Nixland army
Max Pfeiffer: human male, captain in the Nixland army
Rosanella Bianco: human female, captain in the Nixland army
Rialta Bianco: human female, Rosanella's niece
Emiliana Westlan: human female, worker at the Iron Caldron
Venturi Westlan: human female, worker at the Iron Caldron Emiliana's mother
Eleonora Bohm: human female, Manfred's mother
Timoteus Bohm: human male, Eleonora's husband
Joacim Bohm: human male, Eleonora's other son
Enni Bohm: human female, Eleonora's daughter
Horch Klaus: human male, soldier of fortune/guard
Rolando Fulvio: human male soldier of fortune
Ateos Bastina: human male, sheriff of Nixland, Ututur's friend
Ridolfo Parisi: human male Vigiles
Greta Albrecht: human female Vigiles
Harun Faheem: human male Vigiles
Azmi Issawi: human male, grand master of the Vigiles
Wilhelm Martel: human male, captain in Nixland army
Ingrid Netland: human female, sergeant in Nixland army
Biagio Pierluigi: human male, sergeant in the Nixland army
Lucio Cociarelli: human male, sword master and Ututur's friend
Ovidio Villasana: gnome wizard, scholar and Ututur's friend
Rolf Helfgot: human male, works with Ututur in the store
Birger Dybdhal: dwarven high council member
Dodek: half dwarf half human, sells weapons and other metal goods

Caden, Aodh, Clom, and Maoilios: four elves sent to kill Captain
Wilhelm Martel and Kiley Saoirse
Neeiv Bronwen: elf female, priestess of the Huntress
Marco Savin: human male, ballista crew chief
Dario: human male, ballista crew member
Ahern: human male soldier in the Nixland army
Bacstair: elf male, leader of a small village
Catguallaun: elf male leader of the northern dark elves
Wulfnoth: human male, sergeant in the Nixland army

PROLOGUE

The noonday sun warmed Andanir Noldorin's face and reminded him of his dead mother in her beloved garden in the spring, her lovely face glowing in the sun as she tended her garden. He had been knocked to the ground and didn't know how long he had lost consciousness, but he still held onto his tampa, a medium-framed drum with a shallow body and a single-skin head. The drum was still in his left hand, but he didn't have his drumstick. Andanir felt around for the drumstick. He couldn't find it and he felt his mind drifting. *I hope I don't get yelled at for losing the drumstick. I could lie here in the sun forever, it's so peaceful and soothing.*

Andanir's mind faded back to his mother's garden as he thought about the events that had led to this day. Even though he was frightened and in pain, he was glad he hadn't been killed in the battle. As one of the drummers, he had to stay close to the commander and the soldiers so they could hear the musical signals given by the Second. He had never been in battle before and never seen anyone get killed. His only experiences of death were at a funeral of an old seer of their tribe and again when his mother passed away from illness. The old seer was supposed to be four hundred years old and looked like he was asleep. His mother was in pain from her illness, and when she passed, she looked peaceful and at rest. But on the battlefield, he saw the savagery of men and elves. Blood flowed as elves were cut down while crying for their mothers.

He started to cry and asked the goddess of the hunt for help, thinking to himself, *why was my mother ill for so many years, and why did my father have to send me away less than a year after her death?*

His older stepbrother and stepsister, children of the woman his father took to his bed when his mother had become ill, had cornered him days before he was sent away to the army. They teased him, and bullied him as they were accustomed to doing.

Aoife Sioban, was almost an adult and his wavey short blonde hair was always messy. By outward appearances the two males could have been real brothers. But his older stepbrother liked to beat him. He would often push the younger elf boy to the ground and punch him in the stomach; making sure that so there were no visible bruises. "My mother is going to make sure you're sent away to the army forever," Aoife told him.

Eithne Sioban, who was a little younger than his stepbrother, added, "If you're lucky, you might live to tell us about how you peed your pants in battle. I hope the humans catch you and eat you."

When he started to cry, his stepsister laughed. "Look! He's crying like a baby."

The older boy slapped Andanir's head again and said, "Real elves don't go crying to their mothers. I bet you made her sick, so she died." Then they both laughed and left Andanir sobbing in his dead mother's garden.

The small elf boy thought about his mother's death. He had no idea why she died and hoped it wasn't because of anything he did. He just remembered feeling helpless at her side when she was vomiting in pain. His mother had become ill two years prior to her death, and all of the healers had been helpless. The priests and priestess at the temple had refused to ask the gods to intercede on her behalf. He tried to comfort her, but there was nothing he could do. At nine he could barely help her in and out of bed.

The day after her death he was summoned to his family's meeting hall. The hall was filled with servants and a couple of older cousins who lived there while attending the Academy of higher learning. His father, Chieftain Osin Noldorin, once a tall and proud warrior and hunter sat there ill, too weak to stand. His tall stepmother stood towering over his father; her long blonde hair flowing to her waist her blue eyes staring into him with a hateful look. His stepbrother and stepsister stood to his father's left. He remembered that day clearly. His stepmother talked while everyone listened, her high-pitched voice reverberating in the great hall.

"Andanir, my children have been telling me for over the last two years about your bad behavior and your ill temper. My daughter told me how you tried to hit her with a stick and spied on her during her baths. If you were a stranger I would banish you, but because of my love for your father, I asked for mercy. He has decided that you'll leave this hall today to join Eoin Clomin and our warriors. You'll remain there as an apprentice to the musicians for no less than thirty years. Perhaps the disciplined life of a soldier will teach you respect. May the Huntress forgive you."

Lady Sioban hated pretending to follow the Huntress, a weak and uncaring goddess, who had let humans dominate her people and the known world. The Huntress answered no one's prayers; not like the goddess she prayed to.

Tears rolled down his face as she finished addressing the hall. His father remained passive and looked slightly ill as he opened his mouth to speak and tried to sit up. But his stepmother pushed him back down and said in a small voice, "Darling, you aren't well, and Andanir is already nine years old. He must be sent away to help us feel safe."

His father looked up at his stepmother and just managed to nod. "So be it." Andanir remembered his father looked at him as if his mind were elsewhere, his eyes unfocused.

His stepbrother and stepsister told him he would never come home again. One of the new servants brought out a small bundle of his belongings tied in a square cloth. An old elf gave Andanir the bundle and said, "Follow me."

He started to walk out of the only house he had known. As he was about to exit the great hall Andanir looked back and saw his father. He seemed so old and frail even though he was only 147. Another new servant girl was holding onto the family wolf hound, who tried to go to Andanir for a last hug. The servant had a muzzle on Bandit and pulled the leash hard to keep the dog from going to him. He turned to the door and left all he knew behind. As he walked out, he blamed himself for his mother's death and for being a bad son.

As he was leaving, his mother's personal servant, Aide, ran up to him and hugged him. "Your mother loved you. Here, I took this; it was in your mother's family for generations." It was a solid gold torc armband, but she placed it on Andanir's small neck. "I'm sorry. Be safe and come home to help us."

"Thank you," he said and drifted into unconsciousness with this last memory of his former home and the mother he had lost.

CHAPTER 1

"You ugly lazy half-orc! Get up and help clean the battlefield. Take all of your camp follower scum, make sure to plunder the valuables, and help the healers sort out the wounded," yelled Captain Bohm who was also part of the elected High Council which governed the free Cantons of Nixland. The inexperienced human was temporarily appointed as the second in command of Nixland's expeditionary army.

"But I was ordered by the Consul General to guard the baggage train and prepare the evening meal for the army," Ututur protested.

"Are you talking back to me? I'm a Lord Captain of the council," said Manfred Bohm. "I should have you flogged for insubordination, you stupid immigrant half-orc."

Ututur Bunour was used to these insults. "Yes sir," he replied without showing his anger.

Captain Bohm wheeled his horse and left the baggage area flanked by two horsemen in light plate mail and conical helmets. They all wore yellow sashes on their waists.

Ututur stood up, stretched to his full height of twenty hands, each hand being the width of an average man's hand. He shouted to his men and women, "You heard the captain. Bank all of the fires, and take the ten large cauldrons off the flame and move the pigs off of the coals. Let's go!" It was an early summer morning and the pigs needed to roast the whole day for supper. Now these freshly butchered pigs would rot in the summer heat. The army had been hastily assembled when news of an elven army arrived at Mount Haven, their capital city. To meet the enemy far away from the cities, the Consul force marched the army for three days, only stopping to eat dry double baked bread soaked in water, and dried fruit. This was the first camp they had been able to set up and slaughter some of the animals they brought with them.

Ututur took his axe and led his crew to the battlefield where a company of Nixland soldiers stood guarding the healers as they walked among the fallen. As Bohm had ordered, his company striped the dead of valuables and helped the healers as best they could. The half-orc saw the healers struggling with the wounded. "Help load the wounded onto the carts first, help strip the dead of the valuables, and then start gathering wood for the funeral pyres."

He recognized Ilina Kuhn right away. Her long black hair stood out in the sun even as she bent over a moaning man. He strode up to her and noticed her green eyes. "Hello, Mistress Kuhn."

She looked up at the giant and smiled. The half-orc stood head and shoulders above even the tallest human, but had a gentle smile and soft brown eyes. He also had bronze skin which was darker than many pale skinned humans from the mountain region. "I wish we could've met under better circumstances. Just call me Ilina. Help me set his leg; I'll hold him down, and you pull straight."

The half-orc said, "Please call me Ututur. I'm ready." He hated seeing anyone hurt this way but serving in the army was part of his duty as a citizen. Ututur had come to Nixland from the northern mountains to be free of the traditional tribal hunting and gathering life of orcs living in a war band. He didn't want to be treated as an inferior because he was a half-orc, he wanted to be a free voting citizen of the United Cantons of Nixland, own a business, and be free. Like so many other races, he had come for opportunities that were not available in their places of origin. Nixland was rare among the kingdoms where other races were tolerated but couldn't practice a trade or join a guild. In contrast, Nixland was a powerful commercial free state that thrived partly because of its openness. To remain a citizen, everyone was required to join the militia until they were deemed too old to fight in the field and pay taxes.

The man he held was awake and was sweating. Ilina held him down. "Now, quickly."

The man screamed in pain and passed out as Ututur straightened the man's leg and Ilina stabilized it with wooden sticks, wrapping them into place with a long strips of cloth. She stood up and wiped sweat from her brow. "It felt like a clean break, and I didn't feel any small shards. This should heal well."

"I'll take him to the cart and be right back."

"Take your time, I need a little rest," she replied, moving a stray lock of dark hair out of her green eyes.

Ututur deposited the man in one of the healers' carts and hurried back; he loved being around Ilina, who always treated him with kindness. If only he was younger and not a half-orc. He grabbed a clean water bladder as he walked back to her. He offered her the water and she took it with a smile, asking, "How come you aren't back setting up the kitchen for the evening meal?"

"I was ordered by Captain Bohm to come here."

"Did you leave anyone behind at the camp?"

"No, he made me bring the entire baggage train."

Ilina took another sip of water and offered it to Ututur. "What a fool."

He was happy she was willing to share a drink with him; so many others wouldn't. "I tried to tell him that the Consul wanted the meal ready for the soldiers after they finished pursuing the elves to the edge of the forest. I didn't even have time to find hard bread."

Ilina turned back to the field of bodies. All of the walking wounded were already headed back to the camp, and around a hundred elven prisoners were held under guard. Ututur's group of male and female workers were busy gathering weapons, armor, and other valuables, or preparing the funeral pyre. They walked a little ways and saw a dying elven soldier; a spear had pierced his side, protruding all the way through his body. She looked under the armor and noticed a large amount of blood and intestinal contents on the ground. "You are gravely wounded and cannot be healed," she told the elf. "We have no healing monks here, and even they cannot heal this type of wound. Do you wish to take the passing potion?"

The young-looking elf couldn't speak; he coughed some blood and nodded his head several times. She reached into her leather bag and produced a glass bottle of dark liquid. "Ututur, hold him up a little so he can swallow." She put the bottle to his mouth and brushed his long hair back from his face. The elf visibly relaxed as the potion took effect.

The half-orc laid the elf back down gently and asked, "How long will it take?"

"The potion will ease the pain immediately, and the poison will take as long as it takes for bread to bake, but not longer. Let him rest; we have more work to do. Why did the elves attack? We've been at peace my entire life. There hasn't been a major war among the different races or even among the human kingdoms in such a long time."

"I don't know; the elves just came across the neutral border. During my time in the militia, I've only been called out ten times. Twice against the human kingdoms to our western border over trade disputes, once against the dwarves over a border dispute, the rest were against small groups of brigands. But with all of those we had some warning. This elven attack was a total surprise. The elves, goblins, giants, and ogres have been quiet since their defeat in the Goblin Wars over hundred years ago. They were soundly defeated by the combined army of humans, orcs, dwarves, halflings, and gnomes," said Ututur.

The two worked in silence. He admired her skill and kindness toward the fallen Nixlanders and elves alike. What he didn't like was his people being used to strip the dead; they were supposed to be building the camp.

They walked past a dead horse in tall grass, skewered by a ballista bolt. The bolt was as tall as a small man and as thick as a child's forearm. Nixlanders used this wagon mounted weapon behind the shield wall to target enemy leaders and horsemen. The half-orc heard a small whimper. "Did you hear that, Ilina?"

She looked around and pointed to the horse. "I think someone is under the horse."

They pushed the grass away and saw a small elven boy. Ututur knelt down; the boy opened his eyes and tried to scream, but only a small yelp came out.

"Get out of the way you're scaring him."

"Why? because I'm a half-orc?"

"No, because you look like a soldier." The healer placed a kind hand on his shoulder, moved him gently aside, and said, "Don't worry. We're here to help you." She brushed the dirty blonde hair out of the boy's clear, amber colored eyes.

The boy nodded once.

Ilina quickly assessed the situation. "Half his body is under the horse. We need to free him."

Ututur said, "I've seen men crushed by fallen horses; many do not live long after the weight is taken off of them. Here, let me move the horse as you pull him out." For the giant half-orc the horse was heavy but easy enough to lift off the boy.

Ilina put her arms around the boy's armpits and dragged him clear. The boy tried to sit up but she put her hand on his chest. "Stay still. Let me check your limbs to make sure nothing is broken."

The boy held a drum in his left hand and said, "I need to find my drumstick." He spoke in the common tongue, as most of the races did since the Goblin Wars. No one really spoke elvish anymore and even the priestesses reserved the dead language for ceremonial occasions. The different races were forced to set aside long disputes in order to fight the elves and their evil allies. During that long-forgotten war, the elves used dark magic to summon all manner of evil creatures and other races to their cause, including humans to prevent the death of their decaying empire and serve the dark gods. Now the elves lived in poverty, some as shepherds while others made trinkets for trade. Because of the poverty in their homeland, Elven women worked as entertainers and courtesans throughout the known lands.

Ututur looked around the area and found an intricately carved stick about the length the boy's forearm. "Here it is."

The boy took the stick and asked, "Is he going to eat me, pretty lady?"

Ilina smiled. "No, he'll take good care of you." She finished checking all of the boys' limbs. "Well, nothing is broken, and you aren't coughing blood. I think you'll be fine. We can take you to where they are holding the other elven prisoners. By the end of summer, you'll be taken back home."

The boy shook his head as fast as he could, "No. I don't want to go back. I can't go back. There's nothing left for me."

The healer gently stroked the boy's hair. "Calm down; you don't have to do anything. You can stay with Ututur here." She pointed at Ututur with a gentle smile.

"Yes, you don't have to do anything you don't want to." The half-orc turned to the healer and said, "What do you mean he can stay with Ututur? That's me."

"The boy can't stay with a witch. That's what people think I am, you know. Some would think I'd use him for evil. But you have a business, and people respect you. He can join your group as an apprentice," she added while she continued to look over the boy.

"But he's an elf."

She put a reassuring arm around the boy as she said, "There are other free elves in Nixland. All are welcome to live there under the rules of the council."

"But he's so little."

She smiled. "And you're so big."

The elven-boy started to smile a little, looked at the two, and asked, "Are you husband and wife? Or lovers?"

Both turned to the boy and said, "No!"

Ututur didn't know how to argue with her. He simply stood and said, "Let's go back to camp. It's getting late and looks like the field has been cleared."

The half-orc was already tired when he got to camp and it was too late for the healer to walk back to town; all of the carts for the wounded had left for the city of Ostheim. "You can stay here in my tent with the boy."

The healer said is a coy voice. "What will they think about me?"

"Nothing, there's lots of work, and I have a feeling I'm going to get yelled at. It's too dark to start cooking, and the pigs have spoiled out in the sun. There's nothing prepared to eat."

Chapter 2

Consul Aldous Lorenz, also known as Lorenz the Black, rode at the front of the small Nixlander army of one hundred mounted and five hundred infantry, supported by a hundred crossbowmen. His war banner was a black flag with a white star. At his side another rider carried the banner of Nixland, a rectangular flag with a yellow field and black divisions with a sun on the yellow charge. His soldiers harried the fleeing elves to the edge of the Great Eastern Forest. It took the whole afternoon to march back to the camp. The men, tired and hungry, had fought the decisive battle before midday and the cavalry pursued the enemy at a fast march for most of the afternoon. The infantry kept pace as best as they could after dropping their spears and circular shields. They had fought skirmishes all along the way to the forest edge.

Nixland was the only sovereign human nation to allow non-humans to serve in the professional army and the militia. The Consul, tired from the battle, expected camp to be ready for his mixed band of soldiers when they returned. Instead, the baggage was barely unpacked, and his tent was set up but not entirely ready. He had an attendant help him take his breastplate off and changed out of his sweaty arming clothes into comfortable, clean dry ones. When he came out of his tent, his aide Leandro ran to his side. They strode into the main camp as the Consul greeted and praised his soldiers who were sprawled tiredly on the ground.

As they reached Ututur's tent area they found the half-orc trying to unpack the wagon train in torch-lit darkness. "What's the meaning of this?" the Consul demanded. "You had all afternoon to prepare the camp and the food!"

The giant half-orc turned and said, "I'm sorry my Lord."

Before the Consul could say anything more Ilina came out of the tent speaking loudly. "Ututur was ordered by Captain Bohm to work clearing the battlefield and help with the wounded."

The Consul asked, "Did you tell Captain Bohm that you were ordered by me to prepare and guard the camp?"

"Yes, I did, and he told me he didn't care, and that I was clearly not doing anything important," the half-orc replied with a bitter note to his voice.

"Leandro, get Captain Bohm here right now," Consul Lorenz said as he looked around the ill-prepared camp. The Consul's face didn't betray his anger. The army was central to Nixland's continued independence and survival. No one was allowed to undermine the army's effectiveness, not even its wealthy citizens.

They waited in uncomfortable silence. Lorenz looked curiously at Ututur. "So, is this your woman, Master Bunour? She's a noted healer."

The half-orc and the dark-haired beauty looked at each other and said nothing as Leandro ran back. "My Lord, Captain Bohm will be here shortly." The group continued to wait in awkward silence for Bohm's arrival. He finally strolled up at a leisurely pace with his two bodyguards. "Consul Lorenz, how may I help?" His words were solicitous, but his tone was not.

The Consul, not one for ceremony, asked, "Did you order Master Bunour here to stop preparing the camp and disobey my direct orders?" He hated these kinds of rich fools who didn't understand the importance of maintaining good camp and kitchen for the morale in a citizen army.

"I told him to stop being lazy and get back to work; we can't have a bunch of lazy people lounging around camp while real men of Nixland fight," Bohm said in a dismissive tone.

"Do you have any witnesses?" asked the Consul with a deepening frown on his face.

"Yes, my bodyguards were with me and will swear oaths to back up my story." He pointed to his two men. They looked uneasy; they knew the seriousness of any insubordination in the army.

"Captain Bohm, you are new member of the High Council, and this is your first military campaign, but Master Bunour has been with the army for over fifteen summers now as a fighter and as quartermaster. There is a reason I left him in charge of the baggage train. His expertise is crucial to these expeditions to the border regions. I've never known him to lie. We've forced marched here for several days to battle the enemy with little to eat. The soldiers fought and marched all day; now they have no food." Leandro whispered something into the Consul's ear. "And where were you during the battle and the ensuing pursuit?"

The inexperienced captain said, "The men can eat the rations we gave them. I was feeling slightly unwell and stayed back to guard the camp with my personal guards."

Lorenz the Black said in a loud voice. "Leandro, send for all the other captains right now."

Not being good at judging the severity of any situation, Bohm turned to leave, but the Consul stopped him. "Where do you think you're going?"

"Back to my tent."

"No, you will wait here for the other captains. I don't think you realize how much trouble you're in." He was almost glad this had happened; Bohm was a bully, a self-serving son of a bitch. He only became a member of the council to serve himself, not his fellow Nixlanders.

The three other captains arrived quickly, Captain Vogt of the infantry, Captain Pfeiffer of the cavalry, and Captain Bianco of the crossbowmen. Bohm smiled and joked with his men as he waited, not realizing the seriousness of the situation despite Lorenz's warning. When the three other captains were before him, the Consul gave a quick summary of events. "Manfred Bohm, you are charged with insubordination and failure to present yourself for battle. You have failed to look after the welfare of the citizens of Nixland and its armed forces during a time of conflict. I strip you of your military rank and privileges. This is an offense punishable by death, but your rank and family saved you from that. By show of hands, who is in agreement with this judgement? What say you, captains?"

Rosanella Bianco said, "I, as Captain of the crossbowmen agree with the Consul."

"I, Captain Emile Vogt also agree with the Consul."

Before Captain Pfeiffer could speak Bohm said, "This is

ridiculous, to take the word of a half-orc over mine. I demand a fair trial by *pugna judicialis*, as is my right under the laws of men and the gods."

"Under normal circumstances this would be your right, since all intelligent races in the now known world allow trial by combat. However, under *jus militaris*, during an active military campaign, the consul and the other captains will adjudicate matters," Aldous told him. "Judgement is final, and the full council is required to accept the judgement. You have the right to challenge Master Bunour to trial by combat, but the outcome will not change your status in the army. It might make you feel better but it won't change the outcome."

Captain Bohm edged closer to Master Bunour. "I insist that this half-orc accept my challenge, and I'll take my fourteen days to train for this fight."

Leandro spoke up. "Normally that is the case, but on campaign this has to be resolved immediately."

Consul Lorenz smiled. "There is no shame in backing down, Manfred."

The demoted captain looked slightly pale but he stepped up to Ututur, slapped his face, and with a slight tremor in his voice said, "I demand a trial by combat to show my innocence and expose your lies. Since I'm the accused, I'll choose the weapons."

Trial by combat was popular and was often misused by powerful and well-trained individuals of the world. Even women used it to further their personal ambitions or exact vengeance upon another woman in judicial combat. Additionally, men and women were also allowed to fight each other in judicial combat but the rules were different for trials between men and women.

The half-orc straightened his posture and looked even more imposing as his cheeks became slightly red. "I accept this challenge. I was only doing what I was ordered to do. I did nothing wrong."

The Consul spoke the formal words clearly for all to hear. "The accused has invoked his right to *pugna judicialis*. This trial by arms will determine the righteousness of the accused as is the right of all sentient races. The challenger being over the age of sixteen, a male with no disability, being of sound mind and body, will not be allowed to nominate a champion to fight by proxy. Make ready the ring. Combatants make ready and pray for the strength of the righteous."

Leandro walked through the camp until he found a flat piece of ground and pushed back the growing number of onlookers as more soldiers gathered to witness the combat. He paced off a circle with a diameter of thirty paces.

❃❃❃

Ilina heard the last bits of the Consul's formal declaration of the trial as Ututur walked toward the tent. She quickly checked on the boy asleep on the makeshift bed.

Worried, she walked up to the half-orc. "What is this foolishness? Hasn't there been enough blood shed today?"

"Yes, I'm sorry; too much has been shed today. It wasn't up to me. I did nothing wrong. I didn't even say anything. He ordered me to stop making camp for the soldiers. What was I supposed to do?"

The healer's face softened, the wealthy always got their way in this world even in Nixland where the sovereign citizens both male and female had the right to vote. "Look, I'm sorry, but do you know who that is?"

"No. I don't keep up with the high society crowd."

"He's dangerous, and he was able to get on the council not only because of his father's money, but also because he used trial by combat to intimidate his opponents. He's a vicious swordsman."

"I'll keep that in mind. I must go now," said Ututur.

She hugged him unexpectantly. "Be careful."

She was surprised to see the tough half-orc turn slightly red. He smiled and replied, "I'll be fine," then awkwardly hugged her back and changed the subject. "How's the little elf boy?"

"He's fine; just focus on what you're doing." She hoped that the boy didn't harbor any of the general racists attitudes elves had toward other races, especially orcs.

❃❃❃

The half-orc walked out of his tent with Ilina and approached the ring. The Consul waited, seated on a campstool while the captains stood at his side. The ring was surrounded by a huge crowd including the men and women of the baggage train. Consul Lorenz stood. "Enter the ring! Captain Bohm, will you withdraw your challenge?"

Bohm was wearing a finely crafted black gambeson, with red brigandine armor and nothing on his arms. On his head he wore a finely crafted open-faced helmet. "I'm ready to show that I'm innocent and that this half-orc is lying."

Lorenz turned to the half-orc. "Will you accept this trial to show that your words are true?"

Ututur had been in two other trials by combat. Both occurred when he first immigrated to Nixland; his victories had discouraged further challenges. He nodded his acceptance. "Yes, I accept!"

Lorenz pointed to a table next to the ring where there were a variety of matched weapons. "Captain Bohm, as the challenger you may choose the weapons."

Bohm felt sure of himself as he went to the table and picked an arming sword. He had trained since early childhood with the best sword masters and street fighters. He wouldn't give the orc any advantages by picking a mace or any weapon that just depended on brute strength and not finesse.

Ututur went to the table still wearing his cotton pants and linen work shirt and picked up the second arming sword. A double edge blade with a small hilt, it was twice as long as a man's forearm. He knew how to use all manner of weapons but he preferred a hefty axe or poll axe because those weapons felt better in his large hands.

"Pray to your god or gods for strength; may the righteous be victorious, and the truth will prevail," Lorenz pronounced ceremoniously. "None may leave the ring until the trial is over on pain of death. You may commence when ready."

All of the other captains knew Bohm's reputation as a swordsman, but they had never seen the half-orc fight before. Captain Vogt said, "I'll wager a gold coin the half-orc doesn't last more than sixty heartbeats."

Captain Pfeiffer turned to Vogt. "I've heard the half-orc was a good fighter in his day."

"I agree with Captain Vogt, I saw Manfred fight last year; he's a superb swordsman. What do you think Consul Lorenz?" asked Captain Pfeiffer.

Consul Lorenz replied without hesitation, "I'll take that bet against all of you; I've seen them both fight. Bohm may be fancy, but Ututur is a great fighter, a real killer, and his strength is incredible even at his age."

✹✹✹

Bohm tuned out the noise of the crowd and focused on the ugly half-orc. He got into a good fighting stance and circled the giant, who stood still at the center of the ring. Bohm wanted to end this as quickly as possible. He circled, and as fast he could, executed a feint from the classic long tail guard with the point of his sword to the face followed by a straight thrust to the belly. The half-orc easily stepped back, unfazed. Bohm recovered and used all his strength to deliver a heavy swing to the top of the head, but the half-orc blocked the downward swing.

Bohm felt as if his sword had hit an anvil. A jarring sensation radiated up his sword arm and he almost lost his grip. He'd heard that half-orcs were almost as strong as full-blooded orcs but his opponent's strength surprised him. He began to sweat, and for the first time since stepping into the ring, Captain Bohm was unsure about his victory. It was time to use his speed to his advantage. He attacked as fast as he could and delivered a classic full lunging thrust to the orc's unarmored chest. The sword tip barely touched the half-orc's chest, but Bohm felt elated; he had scored the first blow. That feeling didn't last long. Ututur got into a half-sword stance. He gripped the top part of the blade of his arming sword in his left hand and swung it hilt first. The hilt hit like a mace and struck Bohm's helmet squarely on the top of the head denting the steel helm. The captain was stunned, his whole-body reverberating from the strike.

The half-orc recovered and grabbed the handle with his right hand, keeping his left hand on the sword blade. He hooked his leg behind Bohm's, used the sword and wrestled him to the ground, straddling the stunned Bohm. He used his weight pin the human to the ground. Growling, he exposed two small tusks in his lower jaw that were normally invisible and used both hands on his sword to sever Bohm's head.

✹✹✹

Captain Pfeiffer gagged and almost threw up. "Wow! I've never seen that before." She took out a gold coin.

The Consul stood and declared, "By combat Master Ututur Bunour has proven his innocence and did not falsely accuse Captain Manfred Bohm." He turned to Vogt, "I think you three owe me some coins."

"The half-orc is still very strong but I'm glad I don't have to tell Bohm's father," said Captain Vogt, handing the Consul the gold coins.

Captain Pfeiffer handed over some money as well and added, "From what I have heard, it's the mother you have to watch out for."

Lorenz put the gold coins in his purse and faced the crowd. "Get some rest, all of you, and tomorrow after a hardy breakfast, we'll head back home." The crowd cheered and broke up. Some gathered into small groups to chat as they walked back to their individual sleeping areas.

Bohm's two guards stood near the dead body. Consul Lorenz beckoned them to him and said, "Look, I don't want any trouble out of you two. Take care of the body now. Leave the camp in the morning and tell the truth about what happened here. If I get word that you lied about this trial, I'll have both your heads. Now go." He turned to his captains. "Stay a while; I have a question to ask."

When the witnesses to the trial dispersed, Lorenz addressed his captains. "I don't want any answers right now, but what do you all think of changing the way our army is formed? This expedition took too long to organize; we need to move faster. I've been reading about how the Southern City States organize their armies.

"We should break up the army into three groups: the vanguard, the center, and the rearguard. The vanguard would be comprised of mobile units. The center force would be the main heavy infantry with long spears, pikes, and crossbows be backed by a squadron of heavy cavalry. The rearguard will have a small contingent of irregular troops and the supply train, the composition of which can be changed depending on the duration and nature of the campaign. I would like a short, written answer from each of you. This will be shared with the full council. Thank you all for today's victory and thank your troops tomorrow."

Ilina pointed to a spot outside of Ututur's tent. "Come here, closer to the lantern so I can see what I'm doing."

The half-orc sat; he wasn't even breathing heavily. "It's nothing; I've had worse."

"Sit! Take off your shirt. Hold still; this might sting." She had already washed her hands, now she used the same vinegar water to wash and clean his wound. "I'll use this silver needle and silk to close your wound."

"But it will heal by itself." The half-orc tried to sound brave as he watched her approach him with the needle.

"Yes, but it could become contaminated and make you ill with fever."

He tried not to flinch as Ilina sewed the wound closed. He also tried to ignore her sweet smell with her head right under his chin. Her hair smelled of spring flowers.

"There, all done. I only used four stitches. I'll also rub some of this raw honey on the wound and let it breathe now, but tomorrow let's bandage it. Come to my farm in three days and I'll see if we can take the silk out."

"Thank you. I won't forget. What about the boy?" He pointed to his tent.

"You can take him to the elf prisoner's camp at daybreak." She put the tiny silver needle into the little cup of vinegar and threw away the rest of the silk.

"But you heard the boy. He doesn't want to go to his people."

"You can take him back to Nixland and speak to some of the elves that live in Mount Haven," she said.

"I thought you would take the boy."

"No, not me. I'm too busy, and besides you found him." The healer packed up her wound kit and stood. "I'm tired, and I have to find a place to stay."

"Stay here," the half-orc spoke quickly before he realized what he said.

"Sure, but don't try anything," without any seriousness she put her hand on her dagger. "Or I'll really give you a cut to worry about."

"I wouldn't try anything with you." As soon as he said it, he regretted the way it sounded.

"Why, am I not attractive enough for you?" She turned and went inside the large tent.

The half-orc sat outside for a while and drank some water from his bladder and touched the wound. *This hurts more than I thought. Bohm was fast, but I got lucky with the hit to his helmet. Getting old,* Ututur thought as he took another swig and went inside to find the boy asleep next to the dark-haired woman on his woolen blanket and fur. He covered her with the blanket. He put on a clean shirt, put out the lantern, and went to sleep using his jacket to cover his massive shoulders. Before falling asleep he remembered one of his grandfather's wise sayings, "You can only fight with the axe if you practice with it." He vowed to practice more with his weapons. Bohm shouldn't have wounded him.

Chapter 3

Andanir was exhausted from the aftermath of the battle, even his fear of the giant orc couldn't keep his eyes open. Most of his people believed that orcs were evil and that all other races were inferior to elves. Although his mother had taught him that deeds separated the good people from those who serve evil. After eating the tasty oat and dried fruit cake she gave him, his eyes started to close of their own accord. The human female made the bed for him inside a huge tent and covered him with her woolen travel cloak.

As he drifted to sleep, his thoughts returned to his former home.

He was walking alone in a place that felt familiar. The flowers made him think of his mother's garden. He heard his mother's gentle voice. "Be brave; don't be afraid and don't prejudge others. You can build a new life." Andanir felt calm as a gentle hand held his. At first, he was confused; his mother's hands were small and soft. The hand he was holding felt huge and calloused. He looked up and saw the giant half-orc smiling at him. His mother's voice returned, "Don't be afraid. Stay with him. Don't go back."

Ututur woke up at his customary hour right before the break of dawn and opened his eyes to see Ilina and the elf boy sound asleep. He imagined what having a family like this would be like. But as quickly as he entertained the thought, he brushed it away. He got out of his tent quietly to prepare the morning meal for the soldiers. While he washed his face with the clean bucket of water outside his tent, he did some quick calculations in his head. Normally he would make one mug of oat porridge each for the troops. For that he would have Sigmund use ten sacks of oats for a thousand people. Today he wanted to make sure the men had more to eat since all they had had the previous night was a hard biscuit and water.

Ututur saw Sigmund, his trusted friend, stretch his arms in the air as he approached.

"Good morning, Sigmund."

"Quite a night you had. Good morning. I think today we should make fourteen bags of oats instead of ten. Many did not eat last night," Sigmund said flexing his arms to get out the morning stiffness.

"Let's forget about last night. I agree, and since we're headed home, we should finish the dried fruit as well. We have four bags of mixed dried fruit and five clay jugs of honey." He did more mental calculations as he watched his workers wake up and begin their preparations to feed the army. "Give each of the soldiers one and a half mugs of oat porridge with a spoonful of dried fruit and a spoonful of the honey. If there is any leftover, mix the fruit and honey, and we'll have it as a snack on the road. We shouldn't have any porridge left over."

Sigmund asked, "What are you going to do with the elf boy?"

"I don't know. I don't know anything about raising a child. I'm just a simple old warrior. Maybe I can convince the boy to find some elves to live with."

"You're more than just a sword hand, you're a fine cook, a good leader, and a loyal friend. If you need help, I'll help you as much as I can, and so will my wife. We've had five children you know." Sigmund grinned showing a broad smile which was missing a couple of teeth.

The horsemen came first with the bowls to get their oat porridge with fruit and honey. Ututur stood near the servers to make sure that the line moved quickly. The crossbowmen came next, this time led by Captain Bianco; she stood by and watched the men and women under her command get their breakfast. She then came over to him and asked, "Where did you learn how to fight?"

He gave her a short bow. "I learned how to use an axe, spear, and hammer in my homeland in the Northern Mountains. Everyone is expected to know how to fight and hunt. The other things I learned from Lucio Cociarelli while serving in the army."

Captain Bianco looked at the half-orc in surprise, "The great sword master?"

"Yes, but he was just a young swordsman back then. He was still very good, but his name was unknown."

"I think he became famous after one his students won a trial by combat against a well-trained professional swordsman who took the place of an injured party."

The half-orc gave her short bow again. "Yes, that was long ago. Excuse me. I must get new water for cleaning. Have a safe journey back, and we can talk further when we're back in the city."

"Yes, I would like to hear more of your stories about going on campaign. This is my first since I was named Captain and I have a lot more to learn more. Have a good day."

"Good day to you too," he said as he walked toward two cleaning cauldrons that stood on the other side of the cooking area. He took the cold water cauldron which normally took at least three men, walked away from the main area, dumped the water, and refilled it from a nearby barrel.

The foot soldiers were almost done with their breakfast when Ilina came to the kitchen area and got two bowls of porridge. He noticed that the men treated her with reverence, especially those who had had their wounds treated by her. While others received treatment when someone from their family was sick. She saw him and gave a quick wave before getting food and returning to his tent. The half-orc smiled and waved back.

Sigmund said, "She's pretty, that one. You need a woman like her in your life my friend. She's been a healer since she was young. Her mother, who passed away a few summers ago was also a noted healer and taught her everything."

"What? I didn't notice." The giant lied to keep his mind on the work they had to do after the meals were served. For the small force they had twenty wagons with three dedicated field kitchens. "Sigmund, as soon as the last section of footmen receive their food, start breaking down the kitchen and pack up as soon as possible."

"Yes, sir. About the trial. If they treated us more like an equal part of the army, things would have been different."

"Maybe if I weren't a half-orc, things would've been different."

"Perhaps. I have to go; I think that's the last group to eat. I'm going give the boys more if there're any leftovers."

Ututur felt a little hungry himself. He got his bowl and went to one of the serving lines. Young Constantino, an apprentice to the leathermaker filled his bowl. "How did breakfast go?"

"Ututur, the soldiers didn't complain, and we only have a little leftover. Here you go, master." Costantino gave him some extra honey and dried fruit.

"Make sure the others working in the baggage train get a little extra food; it's likely that that the Consul will order us to march a long distance today to get as close to home as possible. We'll be home in three days."

"Yes, master. Any thoughts on what we're going to cook for supper?"

"I'll have to think on that. Thank you and I'll pass the word as soon as I've talked to Master Sigmund." He finished his porridge; as he walked to the wash station, he thought about what to do about supper. If the men ate the pigs yesterday for supper, he wouldn't have to worry about a hungry army tonight. The porridge was good, but after a full day of marching everyone would be hungry.

❁ ❁ ❁

Andanir was awake by the time the human healer returned with the porridge. "Are you hungry?"

Andanir nodded his head. "Yes, and thirsty."

She gave him the bowl and found the water skin. She took a drink to show how to drink from the skin without touching the spout. As he ate, Ilina cleaned the tent as best as she could, but didn't put anything away because she didn't know how Ututur liked to pack his things. She made a small fire outside the tent to boil the needles she had used to sew wounds.

After Andanir finished eating he came out to return the bowl and water skin. "Thank you."

She was looking at her little cauldron. "What should we do with you? We can send you to camp where the elven prisoners are being held."

Andanir remembered his dream, "No, I do not want to go to the elven camp. I don't want to return to the Great Forest."

"All right. Don't be afraid; I won't send you back. Rest while I finish cleaning these. We'll be breaking camp soon."

"Yes, mistress."

"Just call me Ilina."

"Yes. Ilina," Andanir said as he returned to the interior of the tent.

She placed the small flat clay bowl on the ground, took the small cauldron off the fire, and poured out the contents onto the clay. There were nine curved silver alloy needles and four straight ones. She would put them back after she let them dry on the clay. She could see the muscular half-orc walking toward the tent; he looked tan and handsome in a rugged way. His amber eyes were bright and lively. Too bad most men were afraid of her as a healer.

"Good morning, how are you feeling?" she asked as soon as he was close enough.

"I'm feeling fine. We'll be leaving as soon as we get packed; the horsemen already left with the crossbowmen. We'll leave next, and the infantry will start moving after us. What should we do with the boy?"

"Well, I spoke to him briefly, and he still doesn't want to go back to the Great Eastern Forest."

"I'll talk to him," he said thinking he should convince the boy to go back to his homeland.

"Be gentle," Ilina said, looking up at him.

"Boy! Get out here!" Ututur regretted being so loud.

Andanir came out, looking at the ground. He walked up to the boy, towering over him. "Why don't you want to go back to your people?"

Andanir's head was bowed low. "I just can't go back."

"Your parents must love you and miss you," said Ilina from behind the giant.

Ututur saw tear drops fall to the ground as the little boy spoke, "My mother is dead. My stepmother sent me here to die, and my father does not want me back home."

In a surprisingly gently voice Ututur said, "All right. We'll find you a place to stay. Maybe one of the elven families can take you in once we reach Mount Haven. Or Ilina can find you a place."

"No, I'll stay with you." Andanir's eyes were filled with tears as he looked up at him. The small boy reached out and took the giant half-orc's left hand.

The half-orc held the boy's small hand and squeezed it a little. As he looked into the boy's eyes, he said, "You can stay if you want."

Ilina looked at the two and started to cry. "I'll help you as much as I can, Ututur."

The half-orc finally let the boy's hand go and said, "You'll have to work hard and earn your keep." Ututur didn't know what came over him to invite the boy to stay.

The little elf smiled, wiped his tears away. "I won't disappoint you, master." He pointed to a gold necklace. "You can have this to pay for my keep. I'll do my best to please you, and you can punish me for any mistakes."

He placed his large hand on the boy's shoulder. "It's yours. You keep it; you're not a slave. We'll talk to each other if there are problems. Now let's pack up and get ready to go. You help Mistress Ilina with her things. I'll take the tent down." The half-orc watched the two talk quietly as Ilina and the boy washed their hands. Then she showed Andanir how she packed her healing equipment.

When Andanir held his hand, Ututur remembered his own loneliness. He thought back to his own childhood as an orphan in his rugged mountain community in the far north and how his gentle aging orc grandfather did his best to raise him as a real, traditional orc warrior. Although orcs and humans lived together, full blooded orcs didn't welcome many half-orcs or humans into their war bands. Many of the older warriors thought that humans and half-orcs were not strong enough or tough enough. Ututur had to prove himself over and over again as part of a large warband. He looked at the sad elf boy and vowed, *I'll raise the boy gently, I promise, grandfather.*

The men and women of the baggage train took turns driving the wagons and walking along the dirt road. The battle had taken them five miles off the main paved road; it would take them the entire morning to reach it. Once on the stone road they would be able to cover at least twenty-five miles in the afternoon. Master Ututur walked up and down the caravan as he checked on his people and the wagons.

Sigmund walked over and asked, "So, what should we feed this rabble for supper? We didn't have time to get organized."

"I don't know; the loss of the pigs makes it hard. I think we can make a vegetable stew and put in some salted dried beef.

Sigmund said, "I'm glad this campaign was short. I hate being away from home. I'll only have to serve two more years after this, and then I'll be too old to go out on campaign."

"What will you do for fun?" the half-orc joked. He knew that every citizen of Nixland had to serve in some capacity for the common defense of the confederation of free cantons in exchange for the right to vote and equal treatment under the laws. However, the wealthiest somehow always managed to get the lightest duties.

"Do you have a replacement in mind when you retire?"

"Well, yes. There is the blacksmith's apprentice, Adala Mann. She's seventeen and has good basic smithy skills. In addition, she's good at organizing and knows how to set up the kitchen equipment."

While listening, the half-orc scanned the area for any trouble. A habit he formed while he was part of a fast-moving orc war band. "I've seen her work. She's a good choice. Give her more duties and talk with her after we get back home."

Lady Sioban threw her wine goblet at the messenger. "What do you mean the scouting party was defeated?" Her beautiful face wrinkled in an angry frown.

"Once the scouts crossed the disputed lands bordering Nixland, a large army met our warriors as they came out of the woods. Out of the five hundred, only three hundred and thirty-two returned. We don't know how many were captured."

"Send an envoy to negotiate for their return."

The elven warrior hesitated and looked at the two other warriors. "The Chieftain should be giving the commands."

She stood and looked at the three warriors in the council chambers where the Chieftain normally conducted official business. "The Chieftain is not well and has given written permission for me to do his bidding while he is sick. I'm also a Priestess of the Huntress. Are you questioning my authority?"

"No, I shall tell the Warlord. Will the council meet to approve of the negotiations?"

"Yes, the council will endorse this decision at the regular meeting." Lady Sioban dismissed the messengers with a wave of her right hand. She frowned when she noticed another wrinkle. She hated the idea of getting old.

"I have one more piece of news. I was hoping to tell the Chieftain personally."

Lady Sioban said, "What is it? Tell me."

"Please, it is about his son. I insist that I be allowed to speak with him directly."

"What is your name?" she asked with disapproval in her voice.

"I'm called Eoin of clan Clomin."

"You're the Warlord's Second, come with me. The rest of you stay here!" She turned and walked quickly to a bed chamber not far from the office. She felt her exasperation growing, but she controlled her emotions and smoothed her face.

"My dear husband, you have a guest. Eoin has news for you. Can you sit up and listen?"

Osin Noldron sat up. He looked old and his skin had a yellowish tint with pinkish splotches. "Yes, what is it?" the Chieftain asked in a weak low voice.

"Be quick," added Sioban, hovering over the sick Chieftain.

Eoin bowed his head. "The scouting party was defeated, and your son Andanir was not among the warriors who returned this morning after marching all night." He waited for some kind of response from the chieftain.

Lady Sioban stood by the Chieftain and stared disapprovingly at the Second. "Finish your message and let my husband rest."

"We do not know if Andanir was killed or captured in battle."

The Chieftain raised his head and looked as if he wanted to get out of bed. Instead, he lay back down. "I understand. I need to rest. You may leave." He waved his trembling hand in a vague gesture.

Lady Sioban smiled at her husband and spoke. "Now that you've delivered your message, go back to the Warlord and work on getting our soldiers back."

Eoin bowed and left the chamber, his anger growing with each quickening step.

❋ ❋ ❋

Lady Sioban stood naked in the moonlight and waited for the witching hour as the moon broke through the clouds, reflecting on her journey from innocence to power. Once she was a Priestess of the Huntress, just going through the motions of the empty rituals. How had she gotten here? It began when it became apparent that her prayers to the Huntress were futile, she turned her prayers to more ancient deities she had found through her research. One answered her and she was directed here. Elves from Beinn na Callaird avoided this part of the woods, and she never would have found the ancient stone altar in the old forest if she had not seen the place in her dreams. She had ignored the visions at first, but the dreams became more insistent as the years passed. When the voice first came to her, she had just given the customary offerings of fruit, grain, and a portion of wild game meat. The voice made it clear that she was not the Huntress. In recent months the voice had grown, not just in her mind but she could converse with it. The voice demanded a living sacrifice, so she had offered live chickens. She believed that this ancient goddess, long ignored, was speaking to her directly, calling her to revive her worship.

Lady Sioban listened to the goddess. She made a potion with ingredients that came to her in a dream. She gave the potion to Doireann Noldorin to make her ill and removed her from serving actively as a Priestess of the Huntress. Sioban was jealous of Doireann's beauty and the respect she commanded. When Doireann died from the poison, she was sure people would suspect her. But nothing happened; no one suspected any foul play.

She had always wanted to become High Priestess and wanted her son to become the Chieftain. The dreams had told her to marry Osin Noldorin and use other potions gifted to her through the dreams to make him want her and later, to control him. She had gotten rid of Andanir. Now her goddess revealed her name as Larvarnis and demanded a greater sacrifice. She'd brought a baby goat and tied it to the ancient stone alter; the goat was shaking with fear and didn't make a noise.

It was near the middle of the night; The full moon's beams bathed the stone altar in faint light. She chanted and prayed to Larvarnis, the goddess of the underworld, a trickster. She quickly slit the kid's throat in one quick motion. As the warm blood flowed onto the altar, she felt the ground around her feet hum with power. She opened the goat's stomach, took out the organs, and placed them in the pattern she remembered from her dream. As she stood chanting in the moonlight, the altar began absorbing the blood and the organs. After a dozen heartbeats the altar was empty, and she felt the power of the goddess course through her, leaving her refreshed.

Over the next few days, the voice told her to meet Roisin Heenan, a 270-year-old maiden who lived alone on a farm on the outskirts of the city. The goddess told her that the old crone would help her gain more power.

On the appointed night, Lady Sioban snuck out of the keep, got a horse from the stable, and made her way to Roisin's small farmhouse. She hoped no one saw her; the stable boy would know better than to say anything.

From a distance she saw the windows of the farmhouse glowing yellow from a lantern inside. Lady Sioban took a deep breath while she walked toward the house and squashed any second thoughts. She paused at the front door when she heard her goddess' voice whisper softly in her ear. "Do not be afraid my child. You must continue on this path. You'll find the power you crave. You'll bring back the glory your people deserve and the reverence you need."

"Yes, my mistress," she said as she knocked on the door. An old female elf with a hunched back opened the door and let her in. In the middle of the floor a young elf child lay on the dirt floor, gagged and tied. She looked at the two of them from the floor with tear-filled eyes.

"I'm Roisin Heenan, and I know you, Clodagh Sioban. I took this pauper's child from the city; she'll not be missed." Roisin never followed the Huntress. She had been praying to Larvarnis all her life; she had almost given up hope when the answer came in a dream. For her faithfulness the goddess had promised her a new young body and power over others. The older elf believed Larvanis would finally reward her for her faithfulness. "Start the fire, and let's get her on the table and undress her."

The two of them managed to strip the struggling girl and tied her spread eagled on the small kitchen table. The two elven females undressed and began chanting the words that came from their dream. Sioban got her knife, cut her left palm, and used the blood to draw runes of power on the girl's belly, then on Roisin. Lastly, she drew the same symbols on herself. Sioban stood next to the naked girl's head, and for a moment a flash of doubt went through her mind. But before she could dwell on it, she cut the little child's neck on the side and, as the blood slowly drained out, she cut open the struggling girl's belly. She had to use both hands and dumped out all of the intestines onto the floor. The girl's muffled gurgling screams were an annoyance to ignore as she used all her strength to reach into her chest and gripped the beating heart. Then she used her right hand, held the beating heart, and began reciting more incantations. Both elven women could feel the power growing underneath their feet. As the girl's heart stopped, the power grew. The younger female took out the heart, the liver, the kidneys, and the uterus and gave them to the crone. Afterward, she cleaned her knife and watched the other elf roast the heart, liver, and kidneys. Roisin offered the cooked meat to her.

Sioban took a bite of the heart and felt even more power surge through her as she watched Roisin's body change into that of a young elven maiden.

"I'm young again," cried Roisin with a wild smile as she examined her arms and her firm breasts.

"I also feel young again." Sioban said, her wrinkles had faded and her belly flattened. Her muscles felt strong. "Praise the goddess."

A thundering voice filled the room. "Now listen, both of you. This is but a small taste of what is possible. Obey, and I'll send you warriors and other acolytes to use as you please. You must continue these sacrifices for me to gain strength to fulfill our desires."

"Yes, my goddess," said the two elves as they gorged on the sacrificial meat.

✹✹✹✹

The Second did his best to look confident as he walked to the Warlord's house. Along the way he stopped and talked to some of the wounded survivors of the battle against the Nixlanders. The wounded were resting alongside the guard's stables, and he could smell the stench from their festering wounds. The priestesses would not come and use their healing powers on the commoners. He looked down on a young elf barely an adult; he was sweating, and his arm wound was not healing. The bandage was soaked with pus. He felt the wounded elf's head; it was hot with fever. The young elf looked up and tried to sit up straighter. "My Lord Second."

"Rest easy. Save your strength. You've fought bravely." He didn't know this young one, but the lies were easy enough. Those who could walk had already left for their homes after collecting their pay: a bag of grain, a small measure of salt, and a copper for each day of service not including days of captivity. With each step his anger grew. He entered the Warlord's house without knocking. "We were set up to fail, my Lord."

Dowan Eachmhile was two hundred years old and kept his greying blond hair in long braids. In contrast his younger Second kept his hair very short, unlike the majority of elves. The Warlord was seated behind a small desk with a letter in his hand. "I know. It's good to see you're alive my friend. I disagreed with the council's plan, but they insisted that we start scouting the edge of the disputed lands bordering Nixland. I told them their army was powerful and would respond the moment we crossed the border. The covenants with Nixland creating a neutral area between us could only be patrolled by a joint group of elves and Nixlanders. There was no reason to provoke them."

"But, why didn't they listen? We have been at peace with our neighbors to the west for so long. What we need to do is increase our patrols on the eastern edge of the Great Forest and stop any more incursions by the Thunder Horse Tribes. They've been getting bolder each passing year," he said as he sat down in front of the Warlord.

"I told them you could lead a group of five warriors posing as hunters to enter the disputed lands. You could've scouted the territory, and if you're caught…"

The Second finished the Warlord's sentence. "I would've told them my hunting party got lost chasing forest game. But what of the eastern border?"

"I was told that the council is well aware of the Thunder Horse Tribes, and they believe these incursions were typical of their spring raids; nothing out of the ordinary."

"What about the Chieftain?"

"I'm no longer welcome to visit my friend. I have to make an appointment just to see Osin."

Eoin chose his words carefully. "The Chieftain looked old and frail. I know he is not much older than 190 years, but he looked four hundred years old, like an elf well past his prime. He didn't react when I told him the news about his son. I also didn't like the way his wife seemed to be in charge. She ordered me to tell you to get the prisoners back."

"Be careful my friend. Clodagh Sioban is a powerful priestess, and her influence is growing. From what I've heard; she's the one who convinced the council to send you on the foolish mission. Do not talk openly about her. Tell me more about Osin's son, Andanir. I tried to get him to be your apprentice, but Lady Sioban forbade any arms training for the boy. She made him go to work as a servant and drummer boy."

"I didn't speak to him much, as far as I could tell, he worked hard. The musicians are an independent lot."

The Warlord asked, "Did you see him fall in battle?"

"No, he was with the musicians near me as I gave orders; they played the music for us to march forward. But once our line broke, our warriors fled in panic. It was a miracle that more of us weren't killed in the pursuit. We were lucky many of us made it to the woods so their horsemen couldn't cut us down so easily."

"You'll lead the mission to Nixland and negotiate for the release of the prisoners. Get the boy back if he lives. It's the least I can do for my friend."

The Second nodded his head, "I'll do my best. I need to rest for a few days first."

The old Warlord stood and came around to put his hand on his shoulder. "Can you leave tomorrow? I don't want our warriors to be prisoners for too long."

The Second looked up at his friend and commander. "Yes, of course. I'll leave after I pick up the ransom gold from the treasury, I'll take ten warriors for the mission. But my Lord, you must send a larger scouting party to the east and set up a few long-range patrols."

The Warlord warmed his hands by the fire. "I have chosen another Second. With so many problems on the horizon, you cannot do everything I need; she'll lead the scouting party of two hundred warriors. A priestess will accompany them. I'm also sending out three smaller long-range patrols to the east today."

"I welcome any help, my Lord. Who's the other Second?" Eoin was curious and hopeful, he had too many duties and welcomed all the help he could get.

"I chose Kiley Saoirse. She's a little young at 68, but she's skilled and comes from a noble family."

He smiled and said, "A great choice my Lord."

"Don't forget; make sure a Vigiles is present during your negotiations. You have my full authority and the authority of the elven council to negotiate with the Nixlanders. Now leave me; I have letters to read and things I need to consider before my next meeting with the council."

Lady Sioban was angry as she waited for her daughter Eithne to come to her sitting room. The room was larger than most commoners' entire houses, and there was a fire there to warm the room. Eithne's reddish-blonde hair flowed around her head as she walked; her pale skin looked radiant in the firelight. "Good. You're here. I have a mission for you," Lady Sioban said, not even looking at her daughter. She felt jealous every time she was in the presence of her beautiful young daughter. The older elf didn't like being reminded of her age and fading looks. But now with the power of the goddess her beauty was returning.

"Yes, Mother, what can I do? And who is she?" Eithne pointed at Roisin Hennan.

"This is my new assistant and a fellow priestess. Her name is Roisin. I'm sending you with the Second to Nixland. You'll watch him while he negotiates with the mongrels. Report back to me everything you see and hear."

"But they'll treat me like a child. Why not send Aoife? He's older?"

"I know you are only nineteen, but I'm sending you as an initiate of the temple and its direct representative of the High Priestesses. Besides, your brother's already on a mission for me. He'll be busy helping me."

"But Mother, only the High Priestess can appoint initiates."

"Don't worry child. I'll be High Priestess by the end of the day." She smiled and looked at Roisin.

Eithne bowed her head. "Yes, Mother."

CHAPTER 4

The group left Beinn na Callaird and travelled through Ar d'Tus Chathair at a leisurely pace. Eoin's little group rode slowly west and arrived at the border-fortified town of Ostheim, which belonged to Nixland. This town controlled the main trade route East to West. He was bothered by the inclusion of Eithne Sioban in his group, but he had little choice after the hectic naming of Lady Sioban as the new High Priestess of the Golden Rose, no other religious leader could challenge her. The other candidate had passed away suddenly from an apoplexy. The Second knew older elves and humans sometimes had seizures where they could not speak nor see, and their face sometimes looked paralyzed. This malady was rare but not unheard of in elves who lived much longer. What made him uneasy was the fact that deceased priestess was only 158 years old. When Lady Sioban was elevated, she promised an era of piety and renewal of elven traditions. She quickly appointed fifty new initiates and sent them to observe the council and other officials throughout the Elven lands. She also forced many older priestesses to retire from the temple. Now he had The High Priestess' daughter watching him. She was only supposed to observe and learn. The Second knew when he was being spied upon.

The journey west was uneventful and Eoin ignored the High Priestess' daughter as much as possible. As the group approached Ostheim, an alarm bell rang out from one of the towers. He continued leading his group forward.

Eithne rode up next to him and asked, "What's going on?"

"They are sounding the alarm," he said shrugging his shoulders.

"Why? We come in peace," Eithne huffed as she moved closer to the Second.

"We fought a battle just north of here five days ago. From their perspective, how would you view a group of armed riders approaching?"

Eithne let out another huff and refrained from further comment.

As they got closer, he saw dozens of crossbowmen along the parapet and sixty warriors forming a line across the main gate, standing in three ranks of twenty.

He could see Eithne's already pale face become paler. "Are you alright?"

"How can you be so calm? These mongrels mean to kill us."

"I want you to take deep breaths and stay calm. I know you're afraid and you have never been out of the elven lands."

"I'm not afraid." But even Eithne's horse could sense the nervousness of the rider and whinnied in protest.

"Go to the back of the warriors and don't say anything. Is that understood?" The Second commanded.

Eithne looked like she wanted to argue but bit her lip, nodded, and rode to the back of the column.

As they drew closer a single rider in armor with a conical helmet rode out at a trot and approached the party.

He used his right hand to halt the group, noticing the crossbowmen had their weapons aimed at them. He rode out by himself, and they met in the middle.

"Hello. I'm Captain Martel, leader of the town garrison."

"Hello," the Second said as he bowed slightly on his saddle. "I'm Eoin of clan Clomin, the Second to the elven Warlord."

"Why are you here?" the human asked in a clipped tone.

"I was sent by our Chieftain and council to negotiate the release of the elves captured in battle."

"I have strict orders not to let elves pass; any caught will be imprisoned," the human Captain said, but began to visible relax as they spoke.

"What about the merchants along this border?" asked the Second.

Wilhelm replied. "They must conduct trade here; they cannot be allowed to pass. We also told our merchants they cannot travel into elven lands until this dispute is over."

"May we pass?" Eoin asked, hoping to be able to follow his leaders' orders without delay or further bloodshed. "You can send a few guards to escort us to Mount Haven."

Wilhelm sat back on his horse for a moment. "I have to go to

Mount Haven today. You alone can travel with me. The rest of your men can camp in the field outside of the town wall over there and wait for your return."

The elf regarded the captain for a moment and nodded. "Agreed. I'll tell my warriors to wait here for no more than seven days. That should give me plenty of time to complete the negotiations and then return."

"I'll get my traveling kit. If we ride at a good pace and camp near the road, we can reach Mount Haven before midday tomorrow."

"Done." The elf reached out his right hand to shake hands.

Wilhelm took his hand and said, "Agreed. I'll meet you back here before the end of one hour."

"What do you mean you will continue alone?" The young elf girl stomped her feet and folded her arms in front of her chest.

Eoin said, "Look, it's not up to me. The Wilhelm said he had orders not to let anyone pass. Even regular trade is being blocked. We must do as they wish; we can't make them any angrier. It was our fault for crossing the border with the warriors."

"What! The elves have every right to those lands. The humans and other races of Nixland can't stop us from using our ancestral lands."

"The treaty that was negotiated after the Luna War, which they call the Goblin Wars, was fair. We can't build settlements there but we're allowed us to use the lands. Now we don't have to constantly worry about our western borders, which is actually good for our strategic position. We should be focused on the Thunder Horse clan's incursions in the east. Now we may have to worry about both borders again."

"I'll tell my mother that you are a defeatist and do not see the importance of freeing our ancestral lands," Lady Sioban's daughter threatened.

"Do as you will. War is not a trivial thing. The choice was not mine," he replied trying to sound confident.

Wilhelm didn't like being called back to Mount Haven while the tensions along the border remained high. He rode out to meet the elf and brought two extra horses so that they could ride quickly and not abuse the animals. He saw Eoin standing by the dirt road, a young elf girl standing next to him.

Wilhelm raised his hand. "Hello, aren't you ready to go?"

"I'm ready to travel. My gear and horse are ready. But she has something to say."

"I'm an initiate of the High Priestess and was ordered to observe these negotiations and must travel with Eoin," the delicate female elf said.

"Eoin, are you not fully authorized to negotiate on behalf of your government?"

"Yes, I'm the Second to the Warlord. This is an order from our council and Chieftain. She's here because the High Priestess wants to be kept informed."

Wilhelm stroked his dark brown beard with his free hand. He liked the young female's assertiveness. "Fine, but let's not delay much longer. You'll need extra horses. I don't intend to slow down because of you, girl. If I have to, I'll leave you at the next village with one of the local headmen and have you imprisoned till someone can bring you back here."

"I'll keep up. I'll go get an extra horse from one of the warriors," she said as she walked back to the camp site as fast as she could.

Eoin yelled at her retreating form, "Bring my horse and an extra for me as well!"

The girl waved her right hand and just kept going.

The captian said, "You can call me Wilhelm. Your attack has created a great deal of chaos along the border."

The Second stood and looked at the young, well-muscled warrior. "Yes, and you can call me Eoin. I hope we can reestablish peace. The warriors did what they were told to do. There was no malice."

"I see," said Wilhelm as he paused to think about his lot in life. "I have to follow orders as well."

After the High Priestess' daughter fetched the horses, the three traveled in silence. The small group moved quickly as they alternated between walking their horses and riding at a trot. The captain would have loved to pick the Second's mind but not while the girl spy was there. He looked at his horses. "Eoin, I am determined to reach Mount Haven by nightfall tomorrow."

The Second rode closer to the captain and so did the girl. "How far do we ride today?"

"I was planning to ride at least sixty miles today and almost ninety tomorrow."

"How far is a mile?" she asked.

Wilhelm kept his focused on the road but replied in a friendly tone. "We calculate a mile to be three hundred and forty double paces. A double pace is about five of my feet."

"We use that as well since we trade with everyone. That mile is eight furlongs, Eithne," added Eoin.

"Since we have four extra horses, this distance should not be difficult for them, although it might be a little uncomfortable for us," Wilhelm said as he urged his horse into a trot. They traveled until the sun hung low on the horizon, riding in silence, each immersed in their own thoughts as they passed through the lush forest. Wilhelm called a halt before the light of day faded completely. As they set up camp for the evening in the open air, the captain asked the girl, "Can you help me take care of the horses while Eoin gathers firewood?"

Eoin nodded and left the camp area to look for firewood while the human showed the girl how to care for the horses. When he returned, the human had finished making a small fire pit using stones to create a small ring. He dropped the wood and went to gather more for the night. The human used his small axe to cut thin wood shavings to start the fire and waited for the elven warrior, who soon returned with another armload of wood.

"Wilhelm, do you want me to start the fire?" Eoin asked. "I have flint and steel."

"No, this dwarven device will be faster," he said as he took out a small wooden box. "It works with a mechanism that spins the steel wheel on a piece of flint and creates lots of sparks. Here, let me show you." He wound the spring and got close to his fire bundle. He pressed a brass lever device a few times, and the nest caught and began to smolder.

"That is nice. May I have a look?" The elven warrior asked, amazed that such a clever device existed.

Wilhelm handed the elf the little box and picked up the tinder and blew on the coals. When the tinder lit, he placed it under the kindling and waited for the fire to grow before taking out his cooking kit. "What did you bring to eat?"

The young girl joined them by the small growing fire as Eoin handed the device back. "We have some travel cakes and water."

Wilhelm took out his small iron pot and set it up to heat water. "I have some dried vegetables with herbs and spices for soup. Do you want some?"

Eoin took out three travel cakes. "Yes, and you can try our travel cakes. They're made of toasted oats, barley, dried fruit, and honey."

Wilhelm took out a small silk cloth sack from his waterproof leather travel bag and poured the dry contents into the small pot, using his metal spoon to stir the soup. "I'm going to wash up a little." He stood and took off his brigandine vest and placed it near his blanket.

The elven warrior looked closely at the vest and noticed that the inside of the velvet exterior was made up of small metal plates tied together to form a protective garment for the torso. When the human returned, he said, "Your vest is very nice. I didn't realize that it was so well constructed."

Wilhelm picked it up and handed it to the elf. "It's made for travel. The metal is thinner than the ones used for battle, but this will still stop an arrow or a sword."

The elf handed the vest back and felt jealous. The priestesses over the last two hundred years had been growing in power and influence and prevented the adoption of many foreign devices and practices. Goods from dwarven lands were frowned upon, and priestesses argued that these foreign influences were eroding elven cultural purity and advocated isolationism. Eoin still wore an old chain mail that was poorly made by elven smiths who struggled to make good armor because they did not have access to good quality ore and only produced a limited amount of high quality steel. "I wish we could have armor like that, and the dwarven box is clever."

Wilhelm noticed a strange tone to the elven warrior's voice. "I always thought that elven warriors just didn't like armor. I have never really seen your people wear any."

"No, my young friend. We like our parts protected, but we just don't make anything this good. I'm not sure my chainmail could stop anything but a shallow cut. I know it would not stop a spear thrust, and definitely not a crossbow bolt."

"Eoin. The armorer that sold me this vest said they test all of their light armor against a battle crossbow of at least ten talens of draw strength. The point may penetrate, but the armor will stop it from going deep."

The girl listened to the conversation with growing anger. She sat up proudly. "Our elven warriors do not need such modern things. They fight with the courage of our ancestors and the knowledge that the goddess protects them."

Wilhelm looked at the girl and the warrior, trying to find a response. He had heard about how the elves of the east were religious fanatics, but this was the first time he had encountered it firsthand, although Eoin seemed reasonable.

Eoin just looked at the girl and held his tongue. Too many elves had turned away from basic progress and just focused on religious customs and rituals. Many of the pure bloods had stopped eating meat even from the annual spring hunting festival that was held to honor the Huntress. They never ate meat raised by farmers and herders, saying that eating meat was unclean. Eoin just pointed to the boiling soup. "Looks like the soup is done, and since it doesn't have meat, we can share this."

"I'm going to pray before I eat," said girl in a serious tone. "Will you join me in devotion, Eoin?"

"I'm tired and hungry; I'll pray later."

"Fine, excuse me," she said snippily as she stood and stepped into the woods to pray. As soon as the girl was gone, Wilhelm had to ask, "Are most of your people like her?"

"Religious? Her kind are growing in number, and their influence has growning for over fifty years. Now that the Horse Clans of the far east have been raiding our eastern border regions the religious sects are even more influential." Eoin knew he had said too much.

"Wilhelm, I'll go get some bowls for us."

Wilhelm made a mental note to tell the Consul when they had their meeting while the elf fetched the bowls.

While they were eating the elven warrior said, "This soup is very good."

Wilhelm took a bite of the elven travel cake. "I like this cake. It goes well with the soup. It's made by a half-orc who lives in Mount Haven. He owns a store that sells travel provisions. If you need supplies, maybe you can get some for your journey back."

The High Priestess' daughter, who had returned from her prayers, coughed and stopped eating the soup. "No, we will not take food from unclean hands."

"It is only food," Eoin said. "I'm sorry, Wilhelm."

"I'm going to sleep." The priestess' daughter stood and moved to her sleeping blanket.

The Second kept his face neutral, looked at the human captain, and shrugged his shoulders. "I like the soup." They sat by the fire in comfortable silence and watched the flames for a while before they retired.

Consul Lorenz knew today would be important. He had been back in town for a week when the emergency meeting of the High Council and the full council was called because an elven emissary had arrived. The full council was made up of fifty members, two elected from each canton. The full council nominated the members of the five-person High Council from among council members. In turn, citizens of Nixland, both men and women voted for their candidate. Each High Council member served eight years, and each council member served four years.

It was Consul Aldous Lorenz's second term on the High Council and his first as the leader of the military. He had gone on campaign with the previous consul numerous times as second in command, earning high praise. When the previous consul died, Lorenz was appointed to fill the vacant position. The successful battle against the eastern elves was his second campaign as Consul and reassured everyone that he was the right person for the job.

Galdino di Bartolo, the head of the High Council said, "I'm glad you're back, my friend."

The five members of the High Council sat together in a small antechamber with richly carved, wood-paneled walls lit by smokeless oil lamps. The full council chambers were adjacent to the antechamber, separated by another ornately carved door. There was also a public gallery, and the whole chamber was guarded by ten armed, professional soldiers.

"Welcome home, Aldous," added Councilor Salce, a local banker. "But what are we going to do about Bohm's seat?"

"Congratulations on another victory, Consul Lorenz," Ursula Schwertfeger added. Turning to Master di Bartolo she added, "The laws are clear. We shall appoint Mistress Astrid Moretto to the High Council since she only lost to Bohm by twenty votes."

Consul Lorenz took a sip of his tea and said, "Thank you, ladies and gentlemen. The business with Bohm was unfortunate, especially since his election victory was suspect. After all, he had originally lost to Mistress Astrid Moretto by three votes, and after a recount, he ended up winning by twenty." Lorenz placed his mug of tea down on a side table. "I have a written proposal on changing the organization of the army, and I have included statements from the other captains. I fear we need to be better prepared for other conflicts in the future. The army needs to be more mobile and better organized."

"We also have an elven emissary here asking for the release of the prisoners," added Councilor Salce. "I suggest we stay with the traditional price of one gold piece of at least 1,000 grains of wheat in weight, or our own Vreneli coin equivalent in weight and purity for each captive. We should also charge the elves for reparations for the fallen."

"I second that," said di Bartolo. "We must take care of the families of the fallen and wounded. How much should we ask?"

"I think we need at least twenty Vreneli coins for each of the fifty dead citizens and five coins for each of the wounded. There should be special compensation for any who are permanently crippled," added Councilor Schwertfeger. As the members nodded their heads in agreement di Bartolo rose from his chair. "Let's go to the full assembly."

As soon as the antechamber's door opened, the Sergeant-at-Arms Ronaldo Vicari rose and shouted, "Quiet in the chamber; all rise."

The murmured conversations ceased and all fifty council members from the twenty-five free cantons rose to greet the High Council. A voice called out, "All hail the victorious Aldous." The chamber was filled with loud cheering that did not cease till the members of the High Council took their seats. The Sergeant-at-Arms called the meeting to order.

Everyone cheered except Eleonora Bohm, who remained seated in the upper gallery. As the cheering died down, the Sergeant-at-Arms, readied himself to call the meeting to order when Lady Bohm stood and called out. "I demand an investigation of my son's death."

The Sergeant-at-Arms stood. "Order; the meeting will begin, and this is not the time nor place for grievances."

"Are you hiding something?" she called out.

Councilor Salce, the banker and the only ally of the Bohm's stood. "I assure everyone that the matter of Manfred Bohm's death will be looked into."

Consul Lorenz stood and looked around the room and at Leonora Bohm. "I too welcome a thorough investigation of this matter, although it's unnecessary. I'll call upon the Vigiles to investigate and present their findings, and I will allow them to follow their leads to anything they want to investigate." There was a loud mummer in the council chamber and the upper observational gallery. The Vigiles were known for their honesty; people respected and feared them. Once they made a finding of fact no one could challenge it. The Consul thought they might even find election irregularities and link the Bohm family to the crime.

Over one hundred years ago when several brigand bands disrupted trade among the twelve known kingdoms, the rulers of those kingdoms agreed to meet regularly to solve these common problems under the auspices of a neutral party. To this end they founded the Vigiles as independent watchmen with the power to investigate crime throughout the different lands. They also were given the power to force all parties to a binding arbitration of disputes among the different kingdoms and races. Every race, even the dwarves, elves, goblins, and giants contributed to building the citadel where all could meet and discuss common problems.

These men and women became respected and feared. They were scholars and great warriors who had strongholds throughout the lands. Over time more non-human races used the Vigiles to investigate unsolved crimes and they were allowed to travel freely. They could arrest anyone, including a ruler. Once an arrest was made, they would present their findings to a local jury for trial. The accused did not have the right to ask for a trial by combat. The council of twelve realized that the Vigiles could become a threat to any kingdom if allowed to grow in size, so their numbers were permanently limited to one thousand active members.

Lady Bhom turned a little pale at mention of the Vigiles. She had hoped to recruit some of her trusted friends on the council to conduct the investigation internally. If she withdrew the request now, she would look weak, with something to hide. "Thank you, Consul Lorenz, for looking into my son's death and I accept your findings."

The Sergeant-at-Arms called the meeting to order and the regular business of the united cantons of Nixland began.

CHAPTER 5

Eoin had asked for a Vigiles to be present at the council meeting where he would negotiate for the release of the prisoners. He sat with the high priestess' daughter observing how the Nixlanders conducted their business and found them efficient and orderly. There were a mix of humans, dwarves, gnomes, halflings and a few orcs, half-orcs and even a few elves. They seemed able to live together. He recognized Greta Albrecht, the leader of the Vigiles in Mount Haven, as she took a seat next to Eithne, who instantly moved closer to him so as not to have any part of her body touch a human. "Thank you for coming," he said to Vigiles Albrecht.

"You're welcome; your case should be next." She looked around and nodded to various council members. She had stood in the back to observe the meeting and joined the elf as the council was about to discuss the battle.

Consul Lorenz stood and gave a brief summary of the battle and the trial by combat. He also gave a written report on his recommendation to change the organization of the Nixland army. He wanted to divide the army into three groups; Vorhut (vanguard), Gewalthut (center), and Nachhut (rearguard); to facilitate better command and control of the army in the field and also help the army maneuver and respond to threats faster. When his speech ended it was met with a chorus of yeas.

The Sergeant-at-Arms stood and spoke loudly, asking for silence to hear the elven emissary. Even though Eoin knew this was coming, he felt unready. He stood uncomfortably; his palms sweaty. He had never liked big crowds, and he disliked speaking in public even more.

"Gentle beings, I am Eoin Clomin, the Second to our Warlord. I was sent here to present a humble request. I know the memories of battle are fresh, but I ask this council to release the elven prisoners to return home to their families. We did not mean to provoke a war."

There were a few low boos in the chamber. The Sergeant-at-

Arms instantly stood and said, "Silence, we shall hear the emissary's words."

"Thank you." The Second acknowledged the Sergeant-at-Arms. "I'm willing to pay ransom for the release of all the prisoners. Please have mercy and let us start the process of mending our relationship and prevent any further hostilities."

Councilor Schwertfeger spoke as soon as the Second stopped. "Why hasn't your Chieftain sent other emissaries to negotiate peace? Do your people intend to continue this border war? If you aren't here for peace, why should we swell the size of your army by releasing your warriors?"

"Please, we did not intend to start a war. I was asked to scout the neutral border area to make sure that the area was secure. I also bring a letter to your High Council from our Warlord."

Councilor Schwertfeger said, "If I may, you knew the treaty between our peoples forbade any armed force from marching into the disputed territories. So, if you didn't mean to start a war why did you violate the treaty? Should we treat these captives as brigands and sentence them to death?"

"No, please, the release of the prisoners will be a sign that Nixlanders and elves can still find common ground and continue to live in peace."

"Well, the price will be as in the past, but since this was an unprovoked attack, we shall have to add the cost incurred by the army and find compensation for our wounded soldiers. For each prisoner we demand a 1,000-grain gold coin or one of our Vreneli. For each of our wounded three gold coins, and for the permanently crippled twenty gold coins. For the costs to the army, I recommend that we collect at least five hundred gold coins for the cost of supplying the army. So, by my rough calculations, the return of the prisoners we shall require eight hundred and thirty-one gold coins," said Sergio Salce.

The High Priestess' daughter gasped and opened her mouth to speak. The Second quickly touched her and shook his head. He spoke quickly. "I think that is fair under the circumstances. But I would like the opinion of Vigiles Albrecht."

"Yes, what does the Vigiles have to say?" asked Salce. His tone seemed to suggest that he didn't need her opinion.

The Vigiles stood and spoke, "I thank the council for allowing me to speak and give my opinion. The money for the individual elves has been agreed to in the treaty, so it is fair. The compensation for the wounded and crippled is also fair." There was a general mummer of agreement on her pronouncements.

"But asking so much for the army's expenses seems a little excessive. Do not make future peace more difficult by profiting off one victory and sowing the seeds of anger and distrust."

"Thank you, Mistress Albrecht; the services the Vigiles provide throughout the known lands is worthy of respect. I agree that we should be prudent and fair in the amount demanded from the elves," added Lorenz.

"I'm disappointed, but I understand the Vigiles' wisdom in this matter; I feel that a total compensation of six hundred and fifty-two coins will be adequate," Councilor Salce said, looking at his fellow High Council members. He felt slighted but what could he do? No one appreciated his wisdom.

The Head of the High Council di Bartolo asked, "Does that seem fair to you, Eoin?"

The Second bowed low with his right hand over his chest, "Yes, my lord, thank you."

"Good, the matter is settled. I will ask you to carry a message from the High Council to your Chieftain," added di Bartolo.

"Yes, I'll take the message and begin preparations to travel home as soon as we can."

Councilor Salce asked, "How will you pay?"

"My warriors are at the border, and they have sufficient gold to pay," Eoin said.

"So, you will have us wait?" asked Salce.

"You can have the border guards collect the gold," said Vigiles Albrecht.

Councilor Di Bartolo faced the Second. "Done. You are free to enjoy our city while you stay here. I'll send the letter to you by the end of the day tomorrow."

The Sergeant-at-Arms rose. "The meeting is now closed. All rise!" The High Council retired into the smaller chamber, as the larger chamber began to empty.

Eoin turned to Vigiles Albrecht, "Do you think that this was a fair deal?"

"Yes, under the circumstances they could have asked for more. They want this to end as soon as possible; they don't want war with your people."

"I agree; I don't want a war at all. Thank you for coming."

"You're welcome," she said and left him with the fuming Eithne standing next to the elven warrior.

As Eoin walked out of the large stone council building, the high priestess' daughter moved closer. "I can't believe you agreed to pay such a high price to these grubby merchants and common tradespeople. You should have demanded that our warriors be set free immediately, or we would take them back by force if necessary."

Eoin tried to keep the growing anger out of his voice. "You're young and foolish. We were wrong to violate the treaty. Threatening people with violence and war wouldn't have gotten our warriors back. Besides, our entire host would not be able to defeat the well-trained and equipped Nixlander army. If they attacked us with their entire army, they could conquer us in a matter of days. And if our warriors were set free at this moment, how would they eat, and where would they stay? They only have the clothes on their backs." He had gotten the address of the half-orc food merchant from Wilhelm and wanted to see if he could purchase some travel rations for the hundred and seven elves. If they had to walk, it would take four to five days to reach the border, and once he reached the border, he could send riders ahead to arrange for assistance from his Warlord. He stopped and asked a passerby the location of the food store. The human knew of the place but did not know the exact location, but a passing halfling was able to show him exactly where to go and added that the food was particularly well-prepared.

The elven girl walked in silence, absorbed in her own thoughts. *I hate cowards, I hate this smelly city, and I hate these mongrels mixing with each other. I hate feeling so lonely. No one around here thinks like I do, not even Eoin.* She finally emerged from her reflections and realized she did not recognize the street. "Where are we going?"

"I want to see if I can purchase some traveling rations for our warriors once they are released. It'll take many days on foot to get back to the border."

"Yes, I suppose we'll need rations." She looked suspiciously at the bustling city street.

"Here we are." Eoin pointed to a wooden sign above the door with a hand painted sign of a crossed wooden spoon and ladle on top of an iron pot. The shop had a well-organized window display of cheese and charcuterie. He walked in and a young human girl greeted him.

"Welcome to the Iron Cauldron, I'm Emiliana. How can I help you?"

Eoin smiled at the charming girl. He took a deep breath and was rewarded with a mixture of fine herbs and spices. He looked around the well-stocked store and his smile deepened. "I'm Eoin and I need to purchase some travel rations for a large number of people."

"Hold on; I'll call Master Ututur." She went toward the back and called out. "Master Ututur, a customer wants to inquire about travel rations."

"I'll be right there," a deep voice came from the back.

As soon as his dark olive skin and tall frame came into view, the high priestess' daughter gasped at the sight of the huge half-orc. She had covered her nose from the food smells. "I'll wait outside. Don't take too long."

Eoin shook his head and looked around in amazement at the store. He recognized some of the herbs and spices but others he had never seen before. He turned his attention to the giant half-orc who was a good four hands taller than he. "Good morning. I would like to purchase some travel rations."

The half-orc asked, "I'll do my best to fill your needs. Are you from the East?"

"Yes, I'm from Litauia."

❋❋❋

In the backroom the little elf boy was finishing his oat porridge and was about to clean the bowl when he heard the unmistakable voice of the Warlord's Second. *What is he doing here?* He didn't want to go back and face his stepmother. He quickly left the shop through the back door. *Is the Second here for me?* Once he got to the alley, he ran without looking where he was going and he collided with a female.

The boy got off the ground and dusted himself off as the female with the head covering got up from the cobblestone road. "I'm so sorry. I wasn't looking."

She finally got up. "You clumsy, reckless brat!" Her face became visible, and the little boy froze.

Eithne finally looked at the small form and grabbed his arm. "Why it's you!" she said, surprise, anger, and shock warring for supremacy in her voice. "Andanir, what are you doing here? Did you run away from the army? I bet you ran away and told these people how to defeat the elven warriors."

"No, I was there the whole time. I got captured."

"Liar. You are free while brave warriors are in prison."

"The warriors broke and ran when the Nixlanders attacked; they were too fierce," he said as he started to pull away from her grip.

Eithne slapped Andanir. "How can you stand there and lie to me, your sister."

"You aren't my real sister," he said and looked at the girl with defiance.

As soon as the words left his mouth, she slapped him again. I'm going to tell everyone that you are a coward, deserter, and a spy."

"Please, I didn't run away."

She smirked and thought, *what a perfect opportunity to get rid of him forever.* He would not be able to lay a claim to the title of Chieftain once his father died; her mother would be pleased. "If you promise to never return to Litauia or try to become the Chieftain, I won't tell anyone I ran into you."

"Yes, I promise. I'll never go home again."

"Now be off with you before the Second sees you," she said as she gave little Andanir a shove.

He ran to a park nearby and sat crying under a small tree, feeling helpless.

The Second came out in time to see a small boy run away from Eithne. "What was that?"

Eithne brushed dirt off her dress. "It was nothing; some clumsy street urchin bumped into me and knocked me over. I yelled at him, and he ran off without apologizing. Well, is your business done with that creature?"

"Yes, Master Ututur was fair, and he can provide me with at least six meals for each warrior for the journey back. I'll get some travel bread from a baker he recommended. He also told me where I can get a few pack mules to transport the food. We'll have to get some cooking utensils and bowls as well."

"I'm tired and need to rest. I'll go back to the inn," she said.

"I'll be back before supper."

Eithne turned and started to walk back to the inn, pleased with herself. Getting rid of Andanir had been easy; her mother was going to be satisfied. At the same time she felt sorry for the little boy.

❊ ❊ ❊

By the time the boy returned, Ututur had done the dishes and put away everything in the kitchen. "If you are going to stay, you have to help out with the chores."

The boy stared at the ground. "I will; please don't send me away."

"Look at me, boy." Ututur could see a handprint on the boy's face. "What happened?"

Andanir couldn't tell the whole truth and be sent back to be punished as a coward and a deserter. "I was outside and ran into someone. She slapped me. It was my fault; I wasn't looking where I was going."

"I'm not going to punish you. But we do have to work out a schedule for you. You need to be educated; there's much to learn. You can also help out at the Iron Cauldron and work in the garden."

Andanir wiped his face. "I'll do anything, master."

Ututur felt a little guilty after hearing and seeing the desperation in the young boy's pale face. "You can sweep the front area of the store and sidewalk. After that we'll take a break and go see Master

Lucio Cociarelli at his school of arms, then we'll go see Master Ovidio at his home and see if he has time to tutor you."

"Yes, master." He promised himself and the Huntress that he would do everything right and not create problems for Master Ututur. He wanted to prove that he was not a cowardly good-for-nothing, like his stepmother thought.

"Oh, and you should go to Mistress Ilina's and help her with some of her chores." Ututur was trying his best to figure out a way to keep the boy busy. *What did Grandfather use to say? Your sword should always be sharp, but without a sharp mind, spirit, and body, you might as well be holding straw.* "When you're done come back here and help me before supper.

CHAPTER 6

Ututur finished his morning chores and supervised the preparation of the kitchen to make at least two hundred dried spiced sausages of different flavors. He made sure all the surfaces were cleaned at least twice and the metal equipment was cleaned with a mild vinegar solution. He told Andanir to stay by his side and observe the work.

"Andanir, have you tried the spiced dried sausage?"

"No, master."

Ututur reached up to the drying rack, grabbed one, went to a tall wooden table, cut several slices, and gave one to Andanir. "We'll eat the rest of this for our midday meal. Now let's go to Lucio's. Rolf, I'm leaving you in charge of the kitchen, and if Emiliana or her mother needs anything…" Andanir took a bite and was amazed by the savory taste of the dried sausage.

"We'll be fine, Master," said Rolf, who had been working in the kitchen for over ten years. He had started late at age thirteen, and the half-orc had been the only one willing to give him a chance after he had been accused of stealing from his previous apprenticeship. He had taken extra food for his hungry mother and little sister; without the half-orc's compassion, his family would have starved.

"What are the instructors like, Master Ututur?" asked the elf boy.

"Master Lucio tries to be strict but is a softy; he'll teach you all that you'll ever need to know about fighting. Master Ovidio is old, wise, and a little forgetful. People say he is a wizard, but I've never seen him do much. You already know Mistress Ilina; she's kind and a skilled healer. She is very knowledgeable about herbs."

"She's also beautiful, like my mother."

"Hmm. I suppose. What happened to your mother?"

"She died of an illness." He didn't want Master Ututur to find out how he was responsible for her not getting better. Andanir thought, *if only I was a good boy, she would be alive.*

"I'm sorry boy; I lost both of my parents when I was young, too."

The boy looked up and took the giant's hand; they walked in silence the rest of the way to the arms master's training ground. They approached a large building with both indoor and outdoor training facilities. Indoors, there were people wrestling each other in the sand. On the other side, a group of people were lifting heavy-looking stones, different-sized bags of sand, and logs. In the other area there were several wooden dummies for practice. The whole area smelled like saw dust and sweat.

Master Lucio Coiarelli was cleaning and putting away a few of the wooden practice swords. Andanir noticed that he had a large scar on his left cheek and was missing his pinky and part of the ring finger on his left hand. He noticed the elf looking. "Hello, Ututur. Get a good look, boy. I got lucky, and the three fellows that did this are dead."

"Good to see you, my friend," said Ututur, then turned to Andanir. "He was ambushed at night. My grandfather always said a warrior must practice with his axe so that it can be used at any time."

The sword master smiled. "I got lucky. What's your name?"

"My name is Andanir."

The sword master extended his right hand, and Andanir took it. "I heard you had taken in a little elf boy."

"Yes, he does not wish to go back to his people. Can you train him?"

"Yes, of course. I can't guarantee results, but yes, I can train him."

"I want him to come here every day. How much will you require?" asked Ututur.

"I've waited a long time for a chance to repay you for the many life debts I owe you, my friend. Before I get too old, I will repay them." He looked over the little elf and asked, "How old are you?"

"I have seen nine spring festivals."

"You look a little frail, but we'll train your body with the boulders, ropes, and bags. When can he start?"

Ututur said, "My grandfather used to say it's best to keep little ones busy, so tomorrow."

"Good; be here after breakfast when the monastery bell rings for the second time at sunrise; we'll end at the mid-morning bell."

"Good. Thank you. We're off to see the gnome. The boy needs to learn some letters and numbers."

The sword master smiled and turned to the little boy. "Don't let him turn you into a baby goat."

Andanir tried to look brave. "I won't."

"Goodbye, and I'll have Emiliana or Rolf bring by some cheese and dried sausages," said Ututur.

"Thank you. See you tomorrow, Andanir."

"Goodbye, master."

Their next destination was a large, old, two-story house. The half-orc knocked loudly and walked in through the open door. The first room had several desks and writing implements.

"Who is it? I'll be right out," came a high-pitched voice from another room.

The boy saw an old looking gnome with ears that were even more pointy than his, walk into the room. The gnome was dressed in a fine robe and well-made boots and wore several heavy gold necklaces with many gems. The gnome was not much taller than he.

The old gnome hugged Master Ututur and his head barely came up to the giant half-orc's waist. "It's good to see you, my friend; it's been too long."

Ututur placed his arms gently around the gnome. "It's been only ten days or so, Ovidio."

"Yes, see, too long. Is this the boy you found?"

"How does everyone know I have a boy? His name is Andanir."

The gnome rummaged around his desk, ignored them both. Andanir just looked at the gnome and his master. After many heartbeats the gnome said, "Hold this, Andanir." He placed a small gem into the boy's hand. The red gem felt cool to the touch but began to grow warm in his hand. "I'll teach him. He has some talent, but most importantly, he has no evil in his heart."

The boy gave the gem back quickly and tried to look unafraid.

The gnome took the gem back. "Don't worry boy; I won't eat you or turn you into a chicken."

"How about a baby goat?" the boy asked.

"Have you been talking to Lucio? Don't believe anything he says about me. When will you start?"

Andanir smiled and found the old gnome charming and replied. "I'll be here after the third bell at midmorning."

"Good, see you tomorrow." The old gnome started muttering and went to the other room, barely aware of them.

Ututur turned to the boy and used his head to point to the door. "Let's go see Mistress Ilina."

They walked toward the edge of the city in silence and shortly spotted her in her large garden, her long dark hair tied behind her head. She was tending to some young plants. She stood and waved at them, Ututur waved back with a smile on his face.

The healer put her hand tools away and washed her hands with water from the rain barrel. "Come inside," she said as soon as the half-orc and the boy were near enough to hear. She put a kettle on and prepared to make herbal tea for everyone.

They walked into a cozy cottage with a large living area. One side was filled with different herbs, and there was a side room where Ilina treated people who came to see her. Ututur asked, "How are you? I haven't seen you since you took out the stiches."

"I'm well. I see the boy is still with you. How are you, Andanir?"

Andanir stood still, not sure what to do with himself. "I'm well; Master Ututur has been taking care of me. I'm going to start learning from the sword master and the magical gnome."

"I see. What brings you two out here?"

Ututur took a deep breath, a little afraid that she would reject his request. "I, hmm, I mean we came to ask you a big favor. My grandfather used to say even a stupid orc can kill a warrior with a dull rusty blade, but it is easier to kill your enemy if you aren't stupid, and your blade is sharp and clean."

Both the boy and the healer looked at the giant, slightly confused and not sure how to respond.

"I'm sorry. I think he meant that good training is essential for success. Can you teach the boy about the healing arts and herbs?"

Ilina smiled; she had spoken with Ututur enough that she always expected him to cite his grandfather's wise sayings. She also hoped that this would allow the three of them to spend time together. "I'll be happy to pass on my knowledge. When can he come?"

Andanir spoke up. "I can come every day after my lessons with Master Ovidio. I think his lessons will be over by the fourth bell of the morning."

"Excellent. You can help me prepare herbs, and we'll snack together as well."

Ututur smiled and relished the idea that he had a good excuse to spend more time with her. "I'll send some food with the boy, and I can pay you for your troubles."

Ilina put her hand on the boy's shoulders. "No, I could use the boy's help. Besides, it gets lonely out here, and I need the company."

❈❈❈

The High Priestess' daughter walked back to the Double Boar Inn along the main shopping thoroughfare. It was almost midday and her stomach growled; the eating establishments were beginning to fill with patrons, and the smells coming from the food vendors along the street were making her mouth water. She saw many races mingling together; the streets were filled with conversations and laughter. She passed by a half-orc female grilling chicken on wood skewers, which reminded her of one of the blessed treats that she used to enjoy at the spring festival back home. All of the food was blessed by a priestess of the Huntress. But now her mother forbade anyone in their house from eating any meat. Eithne paused to see the half-orc female expertly grill the tiny skewers. She was selling them by the handful. A young-looking gnome girl bought two handfuls of the snacks. Her mouth watered as the girl looked up, making eye contact with her. "Hello, you look hungry. Want one?" The little gnome offered her one of her ten skewers. She reached out without thinking and took one. "Thank you."

As the young girl walked away, without thinking Eithne ate the chicken; it melted in her mouth. The subtle herbs and spices were delicious. The half-orc called out to her in a deep but pleasant voice, "Would you like to buy some? They are only five coppers for a hand."

She shook her head. "No, thank you," while looking for a way to dispose of the stick.

"I'll take that garbage," said the half-orc vendor.

She handed her skewer to the smiling vendor, turned, and hurried to the inn. By the time she got there her hunger had grown; the little piece of chicken had just encouraged her appetite. She took out a travel cake and opened the windows overlooking the street. She ate the travel cake without relish. It tasted fine, but it was not a real meal. The High Priestess' daughter saw several young couples chatting and walking hand-in-hand. A young handsome elven boy with a human girl were strolling by the inn. They looked happy and stopped to kiss each other as they passed by her window. She felt jealous. *Why can't I have a normal life? I just want to learn and do things with the other elves my age back home. Why does mother forbid me from seeing anyone my age? I feel so alone. This all started around the time she married Andanir's father.* She took another bite of the dry travel cake and threw the rest at the wall in her room. The cake hit the wall with a satisfying thud, breaking into several large pieces.

Joacim Bohm, Manfred's older brother was handsome and had shoulder length blonde hair and short beard which made him look older than his thirty summers. He worked with his father in the family salt business. He was seated next to his father, Timoteus Bohm. Both men were not too upset by the news of his brother's death. Joacim watched his father, who also didn't seem surprised. His family had received the news of his death from the two bodyguards, Hiskia Jensen and Aurelio Tommaso; both had witnessed the judicial combat.

"Mother, the two guards have been with us for years and Goodman Hiskia has been in the family service for over twenty years. I trust their account of the events. Manfred was too much of a hot head for his own good."

"I agree with Joacim; Manfred's ill temper often got the better of him. Hiskia, tell me about the half-orc and the events," said his father.

"My lord, the half-orc was in charge of the baggage train. The Consul had given direct orders to prepare the camp and the meals for the army. Manfred stayed in camp during the battle and was bored. He found the half-orc working in the camp and ordered him to stop doing what he had been ordered to do by the Consul. As a result, when the army returned from the battle, there was no food. The cooks were forced to leave the pigs they had just butchered, and the meat spoiled in the sun."

"Then what happened?" asked Joacim.

Jensen was old enough to know that telling a lie was easy at first but impossible to maintain once people started to investigate. "The Consul and the other captains were angry. The men had fought bravely and had spent the entire day chasing a fleeing enemy. The Consul questioned the half-orc and found out that Manfred had forced him to disobey the Consul's direct orders. Worst of all, Manfred hadn't gone to the battle with the other captains. I told Manfred that he couldn't just sleep and lounge at camp while everyone was off fighting."

"The stupid boy," said the father, anger creeping into his voice. "Goodman Tommaso, do you agree with this account?"

"Yes, my lord. Both of us asked Lord Manfred to dress for battle and fight with the army."

"He never thought things through and didn't appreciate the consequences of his actions. He often did whatever he wished. What can you tell us about the half-orc?" asked the brother, curious how others viewed the fellow.

"I have seen Master Bunour on campaign, and I have spoken with him several times. He's trustworthy and a very skilled warrior, with the strength of several men. Many veterans in the army like working with him, and people in town respect him," replied Jensen.

The father rose from his seat. "You two can leave; we'll find other work for you. My son was foolish, and nothing can be done."

"What do you mean nothing can be done?" shrieked Lady Bohm. Turning to her eldest son she added, "How can you sit there and just let a savage half-orc who killed your brother get away with it?"

"Mother, Manfred was stupid; you can be hanged for dereliction of duty during a battle. He may have just been lazy, not wanting to get out of bed that day, but to others it looked like cowardice.

Everyone must provide for our common defense or Nixland cannot stand. Manfred was the one who became a council member and wanted to play at being a soldier. He should have been willing to act like a soldier and join the battle, but he only wanted to give orders and show his importance. He could have stayed safe in the reserve militia. His own foolishness was what caused his death. The law is clear; any retaliation for a death from a fair trial by combat within a five-year period without cause, is punishable by at least ten years' imprisonment and forfeiture of property. We cannot risk the family fortune when Manfred's actions led to the trial by combat."

"I don't care; they killed my son. I'll have my revenge." The mother pointed to her husband and son. "Neither of you ever liked Manfred. Joacim, you were always jealous of your brother because he was my favorite, and all the girls liked him."

"Enough!" shouted the elder Bohm. "There'll be no retaliation. I know of this Ututur. I have served with him as well, and Goodman Hiskia's assessment of him is accurate. Our son's stupidity and pride got the best of him." The elder Bohm turned to face his wife. "Swear you'll do nothing."

"I can't promise anything." Eleonora replied.

"Sit down, Captain Martel," said Consul Lorenz as he sank back into his large, cushioned chair.

"Thank you, my Lord Consul."

"Just Aldous. May I call you Wilhelm? I asked you here to make sure you understand the importance of Ostheim to Nixland's defense. As you know, we only have four thousand professional men at arms and one thousand mixed cavalry stationed throughout our nation. The bulk of the army is raised from the town militias of the united cantons. Ostheim must hold out for at least ten days for our militias to mobilize and reach the border."

"Yes, my Lord Aldous."

"The council and I agree. We'll send an additional three hundred men at arms and one hundred cavalry from other cantons. You're also authorized to mobilize the Ostheim town militia every ten days for additional training. Make sure the militia can be raised in short notice.

At full strength, how many soldiers will be available to defend Ostheim?"

"With the additional men I'll have five hundred professional men at arms and one hundred and fifty cavalry. The town militia has one hundred heavily armored mounted men and two thousand lightly armored spearmen with shields. There are also about three hundred archers. Additionally, have about fifty experienced hunters and woodsmen to act as scouts on horseback.

"Good, make sure they are prepared to defend the town and scout the border region as often as they can. Are there defensive ditches around the wall?"

"Yes, there is a single ditch, but I will start digging and improving the earthworks and begin stockpiling supplies for a long siege. The council will meet with the town Burgomaster, and you will have his full cooperation. The Burgomaster is also a captain of the town militia and will understand what needs to be done. We'll dig a deeper ditch on the most exposed section of the outer wall. Is that all? I have to pack and some shopping to do before I leave for Ostheim," Wilhelm said.

"Yes, one last thing. You'll escort the elven prisoners to the border."

"Yes, my lord. They can march with our soldiers."

"No, the extra soldiers will march more quickly on their own. They leave tomorrow morning under the command of a Sergeant; you'll need to escort the elves by yourself. We cannot let them know we are increasing the number of soldiers at Ostheim. Oh, I almost forgot. You'll get four of the new ballista. They are smaller and quicker to reload and have almost the same range as the older models. You should be able to reposition them quickly along the town wall. I'll send you more detailed written instructions."

Wilhelm stood and bowed. "If that is all my lord, I need to make preparations before I depart."

Mount Haven was not a fully walled city. It was protected by three fortifications guarding the main approaches to the city. The elven prisoners were being held at the Stonegate Keep. This fortress was built astride a narrow mountain pass leading to Ostheim. The main road passed through the enclosed courtyard. The gates were wide enough for four wagons to pass through together. A tall tower on each side of the road overlooked the entire area. Once the gates were closed no one could move toward Mount Haven without conducting significant siege operations. If an enemy breached the gates, the old part of town had a citadel protected by a defensive wall. The citadel was the original fortress that could protect the entire town's population in an emergency, but it was not large enough to house them long term. Normally, the town watch and the militia kept their weapons and supplies there. Both the militia and professional men-at-arms used the large courtyard for training. More importantly, the Vigiles had their Nixland headquarters there.

Wilhelm rode to Stonegate Keep where the hundred and seven elves were being held prisoner. The elves were brought out from the makeshift holding pens and waited in the courtyard for Colmin, the Second to the Warlord to arrive. He noticed a dark-haired woman tending several wounded elves. "Who is she and what is she doing?" he asked one of the men-at-arms.

"Her name is Mistress Iliana Kuhn; she's a good healer. She sewed my arm up when I got wounded a few years ago. She said an elf paid her to come here and tend to the wounded."

"Hold my horse; I'll be right back after I talk with the lady."

The man-at-arms had noticed the double star on the Wilhelm's cloak and said, "Yes, Lord Captain."

"Hello, my name is Wilhelm."

The healer looked up from tending an elf that had a festering wound on his upper arm which had been pierced by a spear. "Hello, I'm Ilina, can I help you?"

"Can he travel? What about the other wounded?" he asked.

"He has a slight fever but I've cleaned and rebandaged the wound. If this wound had been treated properly, he would be almost healed by now. There is one more badly wounded elf. His leg was crushed, and the bones were not set properly. His leg is useless and needs to be amputated. The other ten wounded seem to be healing well." She tried not to make it sound like an accusation.

"I'm sorry, I just got here. Can you do the amputation?" asked Wilhelm.

"Yes, but Caoimhe doesn't want me to do it."

"What do you need to amputate?"

"I'll need a clean place or a table, boiling water, and more vinegar," said Ilina.

Wilhelm looked around for anyone who could help. He spotted a soldier with a gold band on his upper arm. "Hello, are you the sergeant?"

"Yes, my lord."

"Can you get this woman the supplies she needs to perform surgery?

"Yes, my lord."

The men-at-arms brought out a large table and had a small fire going with a cauldron of water starting to boil. The dark-haired healer had spread out her instruments on a clean white cloth and had a several jugs and bottles lined up on a smaller table next to the big one. Wilhelm noticed Eoin arriving on a wagon full of packages, barrels, and crates. The High Priestess' daughter sat at his side. She was in deep thought and not really paying attention to her surroundings. He waved at the elf and walked quickly to the slowing wagon.

"Eoin, how was your stay in Mount Haven?" asked Wilhelm.

The elven warrior smiled. "It's a large city with many interesting things to see. I bought some supplies for the journey home."

"Good. There are two seriously wounded elves; that lady is tending to them."

"Yes, I asked if she would come and check on them before we start back home. I was worried about the wounded."

The captain stroked his full beard with his right hand. "Look, that one needs his leg amputated. His wound did not heal well, and he has a fever."

"Can she perform the surgery?" the Second asked as he walked toward the healer. He didn't recognize the wounded warrior by sight, but the elf didn't look well; the flesh had become swollen and red around the wound.

Ilina looked up and saw Eoin, who had hired her for five gold pieces. The wounded warrior tried to prop himself up. "Lord Second, please, I can't lose my leg. How will I hunt? What will I do to support my family?"

Eoin knelt down next to the wounded elf. He couldn't remember the warrior's name. Too many names and faces; he couldn't remember them all. "If this continues, you will lose your life."

"Please, Second, I do not wish this surgery. Please let me die with dignity."

The healer sighed and stood looking up at the sky. "If he travels, he'll suffer."

"This is foolish; you should amputate the leg to give this elf a chance at life," said Wilhelm.

Eoin looked at Wilhelm with tears in his eyes. "Yes, but it is also important to respect the wishes of all beings. Do you have anything to help ease the pain?"

Ilina opened her leather bag; she produced a small glass bottle wrapped in a piece of cloth. "This is a potion to help with pain and ease the passing. Once taken there is no turning back. If he waits too long, he will pass out and will not be able to swallow this."

"Please, Eoin ask him; command him to try the surgery," Wilhelm's young face darkened as he pleaded with Eoin.

The healer bent over Caoimhe and held his hand. "Please let me perform the surgery. Life is precious and worth living."

Eithne had approached without being noticed and stood near the human female. "Please Caoimhe, life should not be wasted."

Caoimhe said, "I'm afraid."

"I know, but you'll still be able to help your family," Ilina replied.

Caoimhe moaned in pain and said, "All right, do the surgery."

"I'll need your help." The healer said, looking at the young female elf and Eoin.

The High Priestess' daughter swallowed hard. "I would like to help."

"What's your name?"

"Eithne."

"You can call me Ilina."

Once they placed Caoimhe on the table, Ilina had everyone wash their hands, took out a bottle of cretic potion and poured some into Caoimhe's mouth. "Eoin, hold him steady. Eithne, wash the entire leg with the cooled, boiled water and dry it with a clean cloth. Then wipe the whole leg with the vinegar water." She din't like using the powerful potion derived from the juice of the opium poppy. The powerful drug took effect immediately, and Caoimhe's face relaxed.

Ilina placed two tourniquets on the leg, one above and one below where she would cut. She went to the boiling cauldron and used a hook to take out the instruments she would use and again poured some vinegar on them. "When I start cutting, he'll still feel pain, so hold him down. I'm going to cut between the two tourniquets at the knee joint and create a skin flap to cover the stump."

Caoimhe was still awake, and Ilina gave him more of the cretic potion. "How do you feel?"

"Sleepy and warm."

"Good, don't fight the potion. Just let it take you to sleep."

As Caoimhe fell into a drug-induced sleep Ilina said, "Get ready."

Wilhelm felt uncertain and readied himself. Cutting down an opponent with his axe was easy; surgery was a different story. She used some rope to tie Caoimhe down. Eoin and Eithne came closer and waited for instructions. Ilina hoped that the potion would keep Caoimhe asleep until it was over, but everyone had a different reaction to the powerful drug.

Eithne stood behind Ilina and waited for instructions. She was taken by surprise when Ilina quickly cut the leg below the knee with several expert cuts and used a saw on the bone. She handed Eithne the large bloody knife. "Wash this and put it back into the boiling cauldron." Ilina dropped the amputated leg on the ground and ignored it. Eithne almost vomited. She quickly turned away, washed the bloody knife and saw with clean water, and placed it into the boiling water. On her way back to the table Eithne could not take her eyes off Ilina, admiring her calm. Eithne's own stomach was churning; she continued to gag. By the time she reached the table, Ilina had finished using thread to tie off the places where blood flowed. Then she expertly sewed the skin flap to seal the wound.

Eithne stood behind Ilina and managed not to faint at the sight of the blood. The healer said, "Help me with the bandages after I wash my hands. Eoin, Wilhelm, you don't have to hold him down anymore. Just make sure he doesn't fall off the table," Ilina pointed with her right elbow.

Eithne nodded and waited. Ilina brought a clean bandage out of her bag as well as a bottle of wild honey. She poured some on the bandage and began wrapping the leg. "Eithne, hold the leg up while I wrap the bandage."

Eithne kept focused on her task; when Ilina finished, she let go of the leg and took a step back. Before Eithne could walk away, she got another glimpse of the amputated leg and fainted.

Wilhem's little caravan was ready to head out. Eithne sat beside the two wounded elves on the wagon. He heard the healer talk to the elf girl. "You were brave and did well. Here are some extra bandages; change the dressing in two days and keep the wound dry. Give Caoimhe a little of this cretic potion if he is in severe pain. This is a dangerous thing to keep taking. Many people don't survive amputations, so be prepared. He may pass away during the journey."

"Thank you. I know his chances aren't good. Eoin told me that he wouldn't live to see the Great Forest again." Eithne didn't know what came over her, but she hopped off the wagon and hugged Ilina. "Thank you again." This human was the first person she had met who didn't treat her like a simple child. She also respected the human woman for the gentle way she treated the wounded. This entire trip hadn't gone as she expected.

CHAPTER 7

Caoimhe died on the third day of the journey home. They buried his body in an unmarked grave. Eithne sang a small prayer and keened over the grave. She cried in silence as they approached the forest edge and began to question why elves and humans had to fight and die. Neither the healer Ilina nor Wilhelm were evil like she had been taught. Eithne wondered what their world would be like if everyone adopted Ilina's kind ways.

The elf girl watched Wilhelm sitting still on his horse and waved goodbye to him as the caravan passed into Litauia. He watched them for a while, then rode off to Ostheim. The rest of the journey was uneventful, and the elves felt more cheerful as they walked among the trees of their homeland. They supplemented their store-bought rations with a few successful hunts. Eithne enjoyed having time to think about her own prejudices. The three days went by quickly, without further incident. When they reached Beinn na Callaird, a servant was waiting to fetch Eithne. The High Priestess wanted an immediate report.

"Well child how was the journey?" her mother asked when she arrived. Before she could reply the High Priestess continued, "Did Eoin pay too much ransom?"

"Everything went well. Eoin got the prisoners back." *She didn't even ask about the wounded or how many returned.*

"Nothing else to tell me, child?"

"Nothing unusual happened. One died on the way home."

Her mother waved a dismissive hand. "That's not important."

At that moment she decided not to tell her mother about Andanir and only said, "I'm going to get something to eat before I go to my room."

"All right, you may leave."

The elven girl's heart was beating furiously from lying to her mother. She walked to her room thinking about the way her mother behaved. She was not allowed to associate with other young elves and didn't have any friends her age. She couldn't get Caoimhe's handsome features out of her mind nor the amputation. The warrior died for no reason. Nothing her mother preached was worth the lives of so many elves.

Why was her mother so eager to fight the humans? So many elves died in that needless raid. Why did her mother want her to treat Andanir so badly? Maybe he had been treated too harshly for no reason. And what was her mother doing sneaking around at night and leaving the keep? *Is it my imagination, or did she look younger, the lines on her face were noticeably less?* Eithne put these thoughts aside as she entered the kitchen.

In the three months since Consul Lorenz submitted his recommendation to reorganize the Nixland army, the full council had discussed the changes. The vast majority agreed with the Consul and a group of councilors wrote a new law cementing the plans. Still, he was nervous as the Sergeant-at-Arms read aloud the brief summary of the new law they would vote on.

"Hear ye, hear ye, hear ye! The one true and rightful council of Nixland is now in session. All who have rightful business draw near, give attention, and ye shall be heard by this duly elected body. Please be seated."

After the hall became silent the sergeant read a brief summary of the law. "The new law reorganizes the Nixland Army in the following manner. In brief, the Consul General will retain the command of the entire army and be provided as many aides as he requires. The army will be divided into three units: the vanguard (Vorhut), the center (Gewalthut), and the rearguard (Nachhut). The army will also be divided into groups of one hundred soldiers or five hundred soldiers. The army's size shall be adjusted as needs change. The vanguard will consist of the fastest elements of mounted soldiers. The center will include militia, heavy cavalry, crossbowmen, and heavy war machinery. The rearguard will be made up of the baggage train, healers, skilled artisans as needed (blacksmiths, carpenters, leather workers, animal trainers, herders, hunters, but may include other skilled tradesmen) and will be assigned at least two elements of veteran soldiers who will provide labor and guard the baggage train. Each of the three units of the reorganized army will be under the command of a Captain General who may take command of any other unit in case of emergency. Each unit will have a sergeant and a veteran soldier, or First as an assistant. The sergeant will also designate three senior soldiers who have served over ten years as Seconds to help the First in conducting administrative and logistical duties. All who agree raise their hands and say 'yea,' and those opposed say 'nay' and stand."

The 'yaes' won by a landslide, with only two 'nays'. Lorenz quietly celebrated the victory; the new army should be able to take the field much more quickly. He was sure the army would be more efficient and flexible on the battlefield.

Master Ututur couldn't sit still. "Is something wrong, master?" Andanir asked, worried that he had made a mistake. In the past three months he had finally gotten into a good rhythm. They woke up early, and after breakfast they cleaned the small three-room house on the outskirts of town. He would then go to Master Lucio's training ground for his lessons. He progressed to using wooden practice daggers and had become used to the physical exercise routine designed to strengthen his body and train his gymnastics skills. After the training he would go to Master Ovidio's house where he discussed readings and learn mathematics. After the training and lessons came his favorite part of the day, helping Mistress Ilina's with her garden and other chores.

But today Master Ututur had not eaten his morning meal, which he often said was the most important meal of the day. The half-orc smiled and ruffled the boy's head. "Nothing is wrong, boy. The Consul has asked me to come to the High Council chambers to discuss an important matter. I don't think I did anything wrong, but it makes me nervous. Don't worry, boy."

"Yes, master. I'll finish washing the bowls and go to the training ground."

In the three months the half-orc had noticed how hard the boy worked and how he tried to please him as much as possible. Despite his own initial reticence, Ututur liked having the boy around; it lessened his loneliness. And it gave him an excuse to visit Ilina. "Good, I'll see you later after the meeting."

The half-ork felt bewildered as he held a beautifully woven red sash with a white stripe. He was standing outside of the High Council chambers when Consul Lorenz came up behind him. "The sash will fit you well, Ututur."

"But my Lord, I didn't want to have this rank or responsibility."

"We all must do our part, and it was easy to have you appointed as a captain. It's high time we did a better job of organizing and provisioning the army. We were lucky the elves were disorganized and not well-trained. I'm afraid that the winds of war will blow toward our mountain home. We must be prepared to move quickly. The old ways have worked well enough, but I want to improve the army."

"Yes, my Lord."

"You can call me Aldous. I want you to think of a way for an army of at least 10,000 to move quickly from one end of Nixland to the border outposts to reinforce our regional militia as quickly as possible. I have calculated that if the entire Nixland army were brought together we would have a total force of at least 70,000 soldiers. But, I want a force that can move quickly to any part of our homeland in case of an unexpected attack and buy time for the rest of the army to assemble and march. You have the full backing of the entire council, and on military decisions you will answer only to me. The other captains are your equals in authority."

"Yes. I'll do my best," said Ututur humbled by the honor.

"Good. I want you to provide me with ideas before the fall harvest festival," Consul Lorenz said as he left the council hall.

Master Ututur walked out of the building toward his shop holding the sash like a fragile object, grateful for the faith the Consul had shown him, but anxious to prove himself worthy of that trust.

Master Ovdio noticed that his elven charge was daydreaming, he walked up to him quietly and poked him with a stick he had tucked into his sash. "You must train your mind to focus on the tasks at hand."

"Sorry, I was worried about Master Ututur."

"I know it's difficult but train your mind to worry about things you can control and let the other things just drift away. Come. I'll show you how I meditate and focus the mind. Sit here by the fire, close your eyes, feel all the parts of your body relax, and then focus on a single point behind your closed eyes. Breathe deeply and expand your lungs to their full capacity. You are trying to settle your mind and learn to see the energy in all things." They sat meditating, and the gnome chanted some ancient words. The little elf began to feel warm energy flow into him and before he knew it, the monastery bell rang for midday.

"That's enough for today, Andanir. Make sure you go over the multiplication tables."

"Yes master," he said as he moved to leave. He quickened his pace as he walked toward Mistress Ilina's house. He enjoyed her lessons and her kindness. Today she was going to teach him how to harvest and dry herbs from the garden.

She was already at work. He didn't waste any time and joined her as she picked rosemary. "Remember, all herbs are at their most potent right before they produce flowers. I like to take about eight to ten bunches, tie them with string, and hang them upside down under the porch or in the small barn with drying racks." She showed the boy how to cut herbs using a small, hooked knife. They spent time harvesting the rest of the rosemary until her basket was full; she then led him to the porch where there were two stools and a small table.

"I use some herbs when they are fresh. Others I dry. Here, this is how I tie the herbs," she said showing him how to tie a small bunch with a well-practiced motion.

He did his best but for every one bunch he tied she tied four or five. They were almost finished when they saw Master Ututur coming down the dirt road toward them holding a small basket.

"Hello Ilina, I brought a light meal for both of you."

The healer smiled and fixed her hair. "We can eat right here.

Andanir, can you go fetch plates, cups, and some water?"

"Yes, right away," he said and ran to the house.

As soon as he was inside the giant asked in a low voice, "How is the boy doing?"

"He's doing well. He has a very good memory and is gentle."

"Good, his nightmares haves stopped. I don't know the first thing about raising a child, never mind an elven one. I brought some fresh bread, cheese, and a few slices of roast pork."

"This looks delicious, thank you. All children have the same needs. You have to love them and be patient and teach them how to be good."

The grownups stopped their conversation when the boy returned with the plates, cups, and a pitcher of water. The three enjoyed the outdoor meal like a real family. They sat together enjoying each other's company. After lunch, Ututur stood and said, "I have an announcement. I was appointed a Captain by the High Council today."

Ilina smiled. "That's great. But what does it mean?"

"The army is being reorganized and modernized. I'll be one of the three captains in the field, but I'll be mostly in command of the rearguard and the baggage train. I'll have to travel to the other towns and inspect the borders with the Consul."

"It sounds important," she said and took another bite of the bread and cheese.

"It is important," added Andanir.

"It's nothing, just a fancy title. I'll still be cooking, cleaning, and taking care of the animals." Ututur said with a shy smile as he finished his slice of roasted pork.

Ilina bowed and said, "Yes, Lord Captain. Seriously, it's an honor."

Ututur smiled and looked at Ilina and Andanir; this could be the family he had always wanted. He brushed these thoughts aside and said, "I have to get back to work. I'll see you at the shop. Goodbye Ilina, and thank you again for helping with the boy. I hope he's not too much trouble." He stood and stretched to his full height of twenty hands, easily touching the roof of the porch.

"Andanir is a dear and very helpful," Ilina said as she began cleaning up.

"Do you need any help?" asked Ututur.

"No, we can finish up, and it's not much," she said with a smile.

With that the half-orc turned and began his walk back to his store. Halfway to the small gate he looked back and saw Ilina watching him. He waved, turned around quickly, and hurried his pace.

Ilina waved back and smiled at how awkward he seemed for a fearsome warrior.

"Well done," the voice of the goddess whispered in the High Priestess' ear. "This is one of many tasks that I will require to regain my strength, and as you are a loyal servant, I will grant you the power to fulfill your desires. Now anoint yourself with the life blood."

The High Priestess bowed her head while a small pool of dark, foul-smelling blood appeared at the center of the altar. She dipped her fingers in the small pool, and guided by the voice, began marking her body with ancient symbols she didn't recognize as she began to hear a quiet humming sound. When she drew the last symbol on her stomach; she felt the hum increase. Power rose from the ground into her feet. The symbols began to itch. Her heart raced and her mind filled with more arcane symbols and spells long forgotten by her people. She recognized all of the spells, even ones she had never known, but realized that many were forbidden. The followers of the Huntress believed them to be evil and dangerous. As quickly as the spells entered her mind, they disappeared.

"I can't remember the spells."

"This is a taste of what I can provide you, my child. You must show me how devoted you are."

"Haven't I done enough?"

The light female voice changed, and an ancient voice rumbled, "No."

The Hight Priestess said, "I'll do whatever is necessary, my lady, to restore the glory and power of my people. I'll do anything to restore our lands."

"I'll test you even more in the future; I must make sure your devotion is complete so that my power in the world will grow. Go and increase the number of my followers, and I shall reward you. I have touched others and will guide them to you with my name. Fashion them into an army of believers. Disobey me at your own peril. The future of all Elves rests on you. Do not doom your people. If you deny me, they will disappear and be forgotten by time."

"May I know your name, my goddess?"

"There have been many names, but you may call me Larvanis. Next time I'll require more gifts, my child. Now go, and I'll begin reaching out to others."

Chapter 8

Lady Eleonora Bohm waited in her study for the man who had worked for her and Manfred. She would get revenge for her son even if her husband and other son were too weak to act.

A servant escorted Goodman Klaus Horch into the room and asked, "Should I bring any refreshments?"

"No, and make sure I'm not disturbed," Lady Bohm said as she shooed the servant away.

"I need you to do something for me."

"My Lady, I'm here to serve."

"No, doubt you've heard that the half-orc killed my son."

"Yes." Klaus already didn't like where this was heading.

Lady Bohm looked out the window. "I need you to help me humiliate and destroy this half-orc."

He wrung his hands. "I'm not sure that's such a good idea. He's been promoted to a captain in the army. People trust him, and he's protected by the five-year ban on reprisals."

"I don't care; he must be punished for what he did. Manfred was going to be the head of the High Council one day. He would have led the army. Now he's gone. If you don't help me, I'll turn you over to the Vigiles for all of your crimes."

He was sure Lady Bohm would turn him in for rigging her son's election, among other things he had done for Manfred. "I have to wait five years after the no-reprisal period is over, but I can begin planning now."

"I want to humiliate him and destroy his reputation in this city."

"Yes, my lady, but I don't think we should meet in person again. We need to protect ourselves."

"Yes. You're right. I can't use my other son; he's too much of a do-gooder to help. I'll use my daughter; we can send each other messages through her. She's young and won't suspect anything."

"I'll send you a copper coin when I need to send you a message.

We can use twin sticks to send secure messages."

"How do I use it?"

"You wrap a piece of parchment one finger in width on the stick and write along its length and only a person with the twin stick can unwind and read it. I'll bring it by the end of the week and show you how to use it. I'll need some money up front."

Eleonora hated money grubbing peasants, but this had to be done. She took out a leather pouch from the drawer of her side table, throwing the pouch on the ground. "Here, there are thirty vreneli and twenty silver rappen to start. This is more money than a worker sees in a lifetime, but I'll give you more once we're done. I expect regular reports from you. If I suspect you just ran off with the money, I'll have you killed. Do you understand?"

"Yes, my lady," Klaus said in a deferential tone as he picked up the bag. "I'll return by the end of the week and tell you my plans."

Master Ututur smiled to himself as he walked to the western market square where the long-distance traders stayed to trade and rest. Nixland was a rich hub along the main trade route connecting the western nations and kingdoms of the Land of the Twelve Moons to the far eastern San Empire and Spice Lands. He was headed to a small tavern to meet Master Niccolo Eufrasio, a spice merchant from Palmanova, a city state far south of Nixland, whose family led trade caravans into the San empire and beyond. He had traded with the merchant for more than fifteen summers and was looking forward to seeing him.

Life had returned to normal since the brief skirmish. He established a new routine around the boy and Ilina. They ate lunch together twice a week. Ututur found himself enjoying his life and looking forward to these meals together. This was the first time he hadn't felt lonely since his grandfather had passed away.

The noise of the market grew louder as he neared. Ututur sniffed the air and recognized the spices and herbs from distant lands as he walked to the outdoor seating area of the tavern. Master Eufrasio stood and waved him over to a small table, giving him a hug before they sat down.

"You look well Ututur, or should I call you Lord Captain?"

Ututur's cheeks burned. He was not used to a title or so much public scrutiny. "No, Niccolo just Ututur. It's good to see you again my friend. I know the road can be difficult."

"Yes, I'm planning to let my nephew take over the transportation part of the business soon. I'm planning to send him to the San empire to get his feet wet. I hope I can count on you to help him." The spice merchant signaled a young sever for two more of the ales. He then reached inside his pocket and brought out something wrapped in a piece of plain linen. He unfolded the wrapper and reveled a small clay jar with a cork stopper, carefully pouring the contents onto the piece of linen as the server arrived with two lidded tankards of ale. Ututur saw the tasty treasure pour out: white peppercorns, black peppercorns, pink peppercorns, cinnamon bark, cardamom, and cloves.

"I also have the usual coriander, cumin, and fennel seeds."

"May I?" Ututur pointed to the treasure on the table.

"Sure, go ahead." The merchant was proud of his goods.

The half-orc took a black peppercorn, sniffed at it, and took a small bite. He washed the savory taste from his mouth with the ale. He picked up the cinnamon bark and savored the fragrance. As usual, Niccolo's spices were of excellent quality.

"So, what do you think, my friend?" the merchant asked.

"Not bad, my friend."

"Not bad! These are the best spices from across the great oceans of the south and the plains in the east." Niccolo had come to know this ritual over the years. They had conducted business together like this many times and always treated each other fairly.

"Hmmm, I'll take one sack each of the black peppercorns, white peppercorns, cinnamon, fennel seeds, coriander, cumin, cardamom, and cloves." Each sack weighed about fifty mina. Ututur tried to mentally calculate how much he would need for the rest of the year, using the standard formula of a thousand grain of wheat weight per shekel and ten shekels per mina. "I think I'll take two sacks of the fennel seeds. I need the extra to make the sweet sausages for the midsummer festival and the harvest festival."

Niccolo motioned Ututur to come close. When there was little chance of being overheard, he said, "I'll take twenty-three gold vreneli coins for the lot, and I throw in a small pouch of saffron."

"Done," the half-orc whispered back.

The merchant sat back and winked at Ututur. "Master Bunour, how can I feed my children at these prices? I might as well give my precious goods away!" They shook hands as Niccolo tried to look grumpy.

Ututur smiled, as they both sat back and drank from their tankards. After he finished his ale, Ututur picked up the sack he had brought. "This is something for the journey home. I made the dried sausages using your peppercorns. The dried vegetable soup mix also has some of your spices."

"Thank you, my friend. This will be a very nice treat on our journey home. I plan to come back to Nixland early in the fall before the snow closes the mountain passes. Do you have any special requests?"

"Yes, can you get me more grains of paradise and asafetida? I like using the grains of paradise for special batches of dried sausage and the asafetida for savory stews."

"I'll make sure to bring you at least half a talen weight of the spices this fall. I'll also bring at least five hundred talens of long grain rice for trade. My hope is to buy at least the equal weight in sugar beets to take back to Palmanova. Would you like some rice?"

"Yes, I would like ten one-talen sacks of rice. Will you have time to eat dinner with me today?"

"No, I wish I could. But I must meet with the cheesemakers' and the artificers' guilds. I was entrusted by our City Council to open trade negotiations with them. When I return, we'll have dinner."

"What would you buy from the artificers' guild?"

"People are interested in the small brass and wheel sparkers for fire starting. Many of our artisans are also interested in your tall windup clocks. We have water clocks and sundials, but a windup clock would help manufacturers with their work.

"I have a question, Ututur my friend." Niccolo added in a more serious tone as he looked around. "Is there going to be a war with the eastern elves?"

"We fought a small battle not too long ago. They were poorly equipped and still do not know how to fight as an organized army. Individually they are skilled warriors, but in massed formations they lack discipline, training, and equipment. Many of the captured warriors didn't even have chain mail armor. They wore simple, everyday clothes."

"Well, I hope they don't begin a war they cannot hope to win. Thank you, my friend. Do you think that your council would want to purchase some weapons and armor from the city states?"

"I don't know Niccolo, but you should ask the Consul, Aldous Lorenz. Now I have a question for you. I know you travel here with a small wagon train, but if you buy cheese in quantity, how will you transport them back?"

The merchant rubbed his beard which was dark mixed with grey, with his right hand. I like to use mules in addition to the wagons. Each mule can haul four talens worth of goods. They are sturdy and can travel on any terrain. So, if I had to abandon the wagons because of snow, the mule train can traverse the high mountain passes. Loaded down we can travel at least seventeen double paced miles in one day."

Ututur made a mental note of how much a mule could haul and how far it could travel. "Good luck and have a safe journey home."

"Thank you. I'll have my men drop off the spices later today." They embraced and Ututur left the tavern to look at the different goods at the market. He found a shop selling some boys' clothes and bought three linen shirts and three woolen pants for the boy. He reminded himself to take the boy to the boot maker to get new sandals and boots made before the fall. He also found a weaver who had beautifully woven cloaks, and shawls. He purchased a green woolen shawl for Ilina. He didn't notice a hooded figure with dark hair following him through the market.

Ututur returned to the Iron Cauldron and found Emiliana and her mother Venturi serving customers. He was glad to see them doing well; it had not been easy for those two since Emiliana's father, Cuma died fighting with him in the army. When Ututur opened the Iron Cauldron it was natural for him to offer them a stake in the store. Since the opening they had prospered from the venture. Ututur waved, went to the back of the store, and found Rolf cleaning the equipment.

"Good afternoon, Rolf. How did the morning go?"

"Fine, Master Ututur. I made room in the warehouse storage area for the new herbs and spices and moved the older stock to the front. I also helped Venturi to take stock of our current inventory. The only problem I see is that the elf bought a large quantity of the pocket soups and dried vegetable travel rations and half of our travel bread. So we have to replenish them soon."

"How soon do you think we should buy more vegetables?"

"Right away, master; we need time to prepare them and dry them thoroughly. I already started the broth for the dried soup mix." He pointed to two large cauldrons filled with water and beef bone. "I will attend the soup all night, and by tomorrow we should be able to start the drying process and form small blocks for wrapping."

"Well done. I have a question for you. How long have you been with me, Rolf?"

"I've been here for five years. I started when I was twelve, master."

"This year you must start serving in the militia. Since you're skilled at cooking, I'll ask that you serve with me in the rearguard. I've asked Johan to make you a mail shirt, a regulation round shield, a fighting axe, and a spear. You'll be asked to go to the basic militia training next week. There you'll learn how to use the spear and shield and the basic formations. One more thing, I'm cutting your pay in half when you start serving."

Rolf was confused at first and protested, "But master!"

Ututur held his right hand up. "Listen, I'm going to give you a ten percent share of the Iron Caldron for the cut wages."

Tears of gratitude filled Rolf's eyes. "Thank you master," was all he could say. A ten percent share would at least triple the amount of money he would earn in a year, allow him to have a stable life, and ensure his sister and mother were taken care of. He might even think of starting a family of his own.

The conversation was interrupted by a wagon driver knocking at the side entrance to the warehouse. "I have the spices from Master Eufrasio."

"Great, bring them this way," said Ututur.

"I'll help unload, master," added Rolf as he took off his apron and walked out with the hauler.

As the sacks of spices came in, the half-orc inspected them for any moisture or mold. He used a fruit coring knife took a sample from a sack of white peppercorns and found them in perfect condition.

Once finished the hauler came back with a different small sack. "Master Eufrasio asked me to give this to you." He handed the half-orc the small bag. "These are dried juniper berries."

"Thank you and thank Master Eufrasio for me." He opened the drawstrings, took a deep whiff of the dried berries and inhaled the delicious smell. At that moment Andanir walked into the warehouse after his daily lessons. Ututur motioned for the elf to come and smell the juniper berries.

Andanir smelled the dried berries. "I know this smell. Many grown elves like to put them into their freshly made water of life."

"You mean distilled alcohol?" asked Ututur.

"Yes, the adults use fruit and a copper boiler to make the water of life," Andanir said as he swept the warehouse.

Ututur smiled as he got an idea. He would visit a farmer he knew who also made some of the best grain alcohols in the valley. He looked at the boy at work and thought about Ilina and felt content. He had never thought that life would be so good.

Goodman Klaus Horch had been away from the city for three weeks and now rode along the well-known road back to Mount Haven. He was hired as captain of the guard in charge of protecting a trade caravan from Mount Haven to the dwarven city of Toft in the northern high mountains. The caravan of twenty wagons and sixty men had carried wheat, dried fruit, and fine woolen and silk fabrics from Mount Haven. In return they traded for steel tools, swords, axes, and spearheads of the finest quality as well as for superior armor plates that could be made into the finest brigandine armor.

Their journey was almost over and he relaxed. This close to the capital there was little chance of meeting brigands. His thought returned to Lady Bohm and her desire for revenge. Prior to his departure, he followed the giant half-orc for a week and found nothing of interest. The half-orc was hardworking, respected, and dangerous. He didn't particularly want to tangle with a newly appointed captain. He decided he would have to gladly give the Lady Bohm her money back. He had only gotten involved with that powerful family because Manfred had threatened him and used his gambling debt against him. But how was he going to get out of her clutches? He wanted to be a free man.

Deep in thought, Klaus paid little attention to his surroundings; this trade route was well known and safe. He took his job seriously and as the captain of the guards did his best to make sure the caravan was well-protected. He had sent three of his men ahead to scout potential ambush sites even as they entered the safety of Nixland. But his thoughts still strayed to the half-orc. *How the hell do I get out from under Lady Bohm's feet?*

"Captain, a rider is fast approaching," came a shout from one of the drivers, bringing Klaus' thoughts back to the present. Caravan guards always called the senior guard in charge of security captain. He shook his head to clear his thoughts and saw one of the men on patrol speeding back. He guided his horse into a quick walk and met the guard a few feet away from the caravan.

"Captain, we got to a farm along the route and found there has been a massacre," gasped the guard in hurried tones.

"Calm yourself, get some water, and rest your horse. How far away is it?"

"It's only four double paced miles away."

He was familiar with the Scholz farm. It was a well-known place to stop and trade for food and supplies. The couple had three children, two boys and a girl. He checked his curved sword and made sure his bar mace was secure in the saddle. He pointed to the front rank of the thirty guards. "You three with me. We ride." He yelled back to the caravan master, "You should make camp here away from the farm. Make sure to have your weapons handy, and string your crossbows now."

The caravan master wasted no time in looking for a good spot to camp for the evening and had him organize a patrol to scout the surrounding area.

By the time Klaus arrived at the farmhouse the three scouts had already dug a shallow grave and gathered stones to pile on top. One of the veteran guards signaled him over. The husband had two arrows in his back, and his throat was cut. He also had several stab wounds in his back.

"I didn't touch anything. I wanted you to see this first, captain," Marco said as he knelt over the body.

"Those arrows look like elven arrows with hawk-feather fletching." Klaus dismounted and examined the arrows. He frowned, what were elves doing so far from their home?

"Ay, I think you're right."

"Come, you have to see this," Marco said as he led his way inside. "Prepare yourself. It's not pleasant."

Klaus was surprised at the veteran's words. Before he could see anything, the smell of blood and feces hit his nose. Blood had sprayed all over the interior of the farmhouse. There were runes he didn't recognize written in blood on each of the walls. The wife was naked. Her body was chopped to pieces, and the older boy's body was on the kitchen table, his intestines piled next to the body. He used his sword and looked into the body cavity. The heart, liver, and kidneys were missing. "Where are the other two children?"

"There are no other bodies. We searched at least five hundred paces around the house. We found horse tracks leading into the woods, but no children."

"How many horses?"

"I would say at least five. There are at least ten others on foot. And look." Marco pointed to the floor and the area just outside.

"I see." Klaus looked at the bloody partial footprints of two children next to boot prints of different sizes. "We'll leave the bodies and make sure the other men witness this as well."

"What about the livestock and food?"

"Feed the animals but leave everything. Let the next of kin salvage the rest of the farm. Return to the caravan and double the guards. I'll get the sheriff and the Vigiles, then return as soon as I can." Klaus mounted his horse and took off for Mount Haven. He had never seen an attack like this. He had seen the aftermath of brigand attacks before but never this close to Mount Haven. In all his years of soldiering and spying, he had never seen a body mutilated in such a way before.

❊❊❊

Naked forms danced in the firelight, casting eerie shadows. They had sacred runes painted in white ash mixed with blood all over their bodies. Roisin felt powerful and young again as she stood naked near the fire roasting a human liver. Then she held a human heart and kidneys above her head. In a shrill voice she chanted the new prayers the High Priestess had taught her. She finished the ritual as instructed and ate some of the organs before she fed the dog soldiers.

This was the first time in over a hundred years since these hounds of Larvarnis had hunted. In fact, the hounds of Larvarnis hadn't been seen since the Goblin Wars. She took the roasted liver off the fire, took a bite, and passed the liver among the elves. She could tasted the earthy metallic flavor as power radiated from the ground, up through her loins and into her body. As the last hunter finished the liver, the group was bathed by a harsh glow of power. The ritual would give the elven hunters greater endurance, speed, and strength for days. The hounds didn't need food or water to hunt their prey. The priestess felt energized as the meat washed away her fatigue. She also noticed that the two lightly-wounded elves were healed during the ceremony.

She truly believed that now victory over the humans of Nixland was possible. The ancestral lands in the east and west would return to them forever. All her remaining doubts were gone; victory was a matter of time. As she saw the warriors around the fire she couldn't wait for another raid and the chance to sacrifice more humans to Larvarnis. She looked down at her smooth young hands and cried from sheer ecstasy. She hadn't felt this strong in a long time. Walking among the warriors she blessed them as she satisfied her lust with several of them.

❊❊❊

As news of the massacre had spread throughout Mount Haven, members of the council demanded a thorough investigation. The High Council already sent Sheriff Bastina to take charge. Who immediately sent two men to fetch Ututur and the Vigiles. After getting his travel kit together he rode slowly toward Master Ovidio's house with Goodman Klaus Horch, whom he had asked to come along to provide details of what he had found.

The small group stood outside Ututur's home. The half-orc turned to Ilina and Andanir and spoke quietly. "I'll not be gone too long; three days, a week at most." He pointed to Andanir, "Keep up with your lessons with the weapons master and help Ilina as much as you can. If you have time you can go to the store and help Rolf and Mistress Venturi."

"I'll do my best, master." Andanir was amazed at the size of Ututur's war axe, which was almost as tall as his master.

"Don't worry, he'll be fine. He's a good boy," Ilina said looking down at Andanir.

Andanir recognized Master Ovidio and the female Vigiles but not the others. Master Ovidio smiled and waved to Andanir, who looked like a child going on a picnic in his colorful clothes and red cloak. Master Ututur placed his large single-headed war axe and leather backpack in the gnome's wagon, and adjusted his eating knife and his oversized rondel dagger on his belt before hopping on the wagon to sit next to the small gnome. As the party departed Andanir asked Ilina, "Who are the others?"

"The one riding next to the Vigiles is Sheriff Ateos Bastina, and the dark-skinned young man is Ridolfo Parisi, a newly elevated Vigiles. I don't know the other man; I think he's a merchant guard. And you know Master Ovidio."

"Are they in danger?" asked Andanir.

"I don't know. But they can take care of themselves, and I've heard Master Ovidio can summon lightning and fire." Ilina said as she watched the group ride off. She hoped Ututur would turn to wave goodbye to the boy. She smiled and her heart lightened when the half-orc turned and waved at them both. She waved back and looked at Andanir waving frantically. The boy's face creased with worry.

"Master Ovidio is nice but I'm not sure he can do anything," Andanir said in a worried tone. The gnome was absent minded and often seemed distracted by random things. So far, all Master Ovidio taught him was reading, writing in common, and math. Why was Mistress Ilina and the others certain that he could control lightning and fire? Andanir hoped she was right but doubted it.

Except for Klaus the group had worked together with Sheriff Bastina over the years as part of the militia and in various difficult investigations. Once they were outside of the city, Vigiles Albrecht introduced the group to Klaus Horch the merchant guard, "Tell Ututur and Ovidio what you saw."

Klaus felt a little uncomfortable riding next to the giant half-orc. He didn't like being so close to a mark. "Well, I was hired to be the captain of the guard for a trade caravan. We were on the way back from trading with the Dwarves of the northern Jotunheimen Mountains. I sent scouts ahead of the caravan, and they found the farmer dead facedown."

Ridolfo felt nervous because this was his first investigation since becoming a full Vigiles. "How was he killed?"

"The farmer had two arrow wounds in his back and was stabbed at least three times from behind. Inside the farmhouse the wife looked like she had struggled with the attackers. We found a boy around fourteen on the kitchen table; his organs were taken out."

Ovidio's ears perked up. "What was taken? You have to show me exactly how the body was placed." He hoped it wasn't a dark ritual.

"As far as I could tell they took the boy's heart, liver, and kidneys. We left the bodies as we found them."

"Did your men search the area around the farm?" Ututur asked.

"Yes, we searched all around the farm, and didn't find the two other children. They found nothing else of interest."

The sheriff added, "This is very strange because there hasn't been any brigand activity this close to Mount Haven in a long time."

They traveled in silence for the rest of the journey to the farm. The group arrived around midday, the gnome asked if he could go into the house alone to examine the scene.

Ututur jumped off the small wagon and scouted around the

outside of the house. He looked at the tracks and began circling wider. It was at least two days since the attack and there should still be signs. Once he got near the woods, he noticed that a small band had moved through the brush; there was some dried blood among the broken leaves. The footprints were not fresh but were consistent with a small band on foot accompanied by three horses. The band's tracks were headed toward another farm and not deeper into the woods or toward the elven lands. He ran as fast as he could back to the group.

The Vigiles asked, "What have you found, Ututur?"

"I think the band is headed toward another farm not far from here. The tracks don't go deeper into the woods or toward the elven lands. We should go quickly and check on the farms in that direction. Ututur pointed east.

The gnome tried to remain calm but insisted. "We should go quickly. I've never seen this kind of sacrifice before, but I have read about them. The ancient runes and the body placement is a sacrifice to an evil trickster goddess."

"Are you sure?" the Vigiles asked.

"The runes are very old. They come from a time before the humans settled this area. I thought the worship of this goddess ceased after the followers of Mielki the Huntress destroyed their altars and killed many of her devotees after the goblin wars. It was rumored that a handful of priestesses survived and continued to worship the trickster in secret, but there has been no evidence of them in over a hundred years. The trickster goddess has her roots in the beginning of time when the underworld was created. Many believe that she was responsible for the Goblin Wars."

Vigiles Albrecht feared the worst. "We'll need to move fast. Ovidio, your wagon is too slow, we'll move ahead. Join us as fast as you can."

"I'll be right behind you," said the small gnome with a deep frown on his face.

Klaus asked, "What about the half-orc?"

"Don't concern yourself about Ututur," Albrecht said with a smile. On foot the half-orc could easily keep up with a horse.

The sheriff said, "Let's ride, we're wasting time."

"Lead the way Ateos." The Vigiles urged her horse into a slow trot behind the sheriff.

The entire group headed toward the next farm five miles to the east of their location. As they rode Klaus was surprised to see how easily the half-orc kept up with a horse while holding his large axe.

✳✳✳

Priestess Roisin looked at the mass of bodies near her. The elven warriors hadn't slept for two days. The sexual ritual was almost complete and the warriors had pleasured her and her two young acolytes repeatedly for two days. Sometimes three would tear into one of the young female acolytes at the same time. She felt the excitement at the sight of the brutal sex. It had been four days since the first attack at the farm. She had sent the two young children back with two warriors to meet the High Priestess at the secret camp. The next farm was only a few miles away, and they would attack at dusk. She felt excitement at the prospect of feeling the power of the goddess again. So far this was a success test of their new powers. *Perhaps I'll enjoy being serviced by a couple of the warriors again tonight.*

✳✳✳

It was late in the day when the group slowed their horses as they reached the outskirts of the farm. They were about to round the bend when they heard a distant scream quickly replaced by laughter. Ututur motioned for the group to stop and lowered his voice to address the Vigiles. "Greta, I'll scout ahead. Everyone else keep your eyes sharp."

He ran in a crouch to hide his size. He moved closer to the farm as more screams and mocking laughter filled the air. He hid behind a tree and could see the farmhouse in a small clearing. He saw a figure tied to a fence near the main house where three elves were taking turns throwing knives at the body. A new scream, higher pitched, came from inside the house, and he saw a single elf take a young child in his arms and run toward the eastern edge of the clearing. He could barely make out three hooded figures on horseback. The half-orc ran as silently as possible back to the group.

"The farm is being attacked. There are at least four attackers on foot. I saw one take a child toward three mounted figures waiting by the edge of the woods. If we go now, we can take the ones on foot by surprise."

The sherriff put on his helmet and drew his sword. The others followed his example and readied themselves. The half-orc turned and was surprised to see Ovidio's wagon moving quickly toward their group.

"When we charge, try to capture one alive," the Vigiles said, then turning to the gnome yelled, "Charge."

Ututur ran faster as the horsemen began steady trot. Klaus was surprised again at how fast the half-orc moved. The giant easily kept pace with the horses, and when they were within the final fifty paces of the three elves by the fence, Ututur yelled, "Klaus, come with me to the house, and the rest with the Vigiles."

The elves outside didn't notice the riders until they finally heard the war cries over the screams coming from inside the house; they turned and looked at each other in surprise. Ututur saw the Vigiles, with the other riders, charge at the three elves. She rode past one and ran her sword through his neck almost taking the head off, then used her momentum to free her sword from the falling figure. The sheriff was not as swift but delivered a deep cut to the neck of the second elf, who clutched it as blood fountained from the fatal wound. Ridolfo slowed as his target turned to face him with a drawn sword. He delivered a downward cut, which was blocked by the elf, he used his horse to push the elf off balance and delivered a blow to the elf's head. But before Ridolfo could pull his sword free; the elf fell taking his embedded sword with him.

By the time the third elf hit the ground Ututur had reached the farmhouse doorway. Before he could enter, an elf with a bow ran out. The giant wasted no time; he used his long-bladed, single-headed axe. With his first cut he chopped off the elf's left arm, bashing him in the chest with a thrust with the spike on top of his axe. The dying elf fell backward from the blow knocking back a second elf who was trying to enter the fight.

Two more elves ran out the farmhouse back door, charging Klaus who blocked one attack with his sword. The second elf tackled him and stabbed him in the side with a short dagger, but his vest of plates and chain mail shirt stopped the weapon. The other elf had recovered and was about to stab him in the face when the half-orc hit the elf with the flat of the axe blade, sending the elf staggering backwards. Klaus reversed his position, mounted his attacker, grabbed the elf's dagger with both of his hands, and forced it into the elf's chest. The blade slowly entered and as it went deeper the struggle ended.

The half-orc helped Klaus stand while he kept an eye on the elf that had attacked the human. The elf was out cold and had a bleeding head wound. Both the Vigiles and the sheriff rushed into the house. The half-orc followed while Klaus took a moment to clear his head. Two more elves were waiting with short swords drawn. On the kitchen table lay a young boy, his stomach was cut open but his eyes fluttered; his hands went to cover his stomach only to find that his intestines had spilt onto the floor. A human woman lay unconscious on the ground. As Vigiles Albrecht entered, one elf thrust a short sword at her. She parried and lunged. Her thrust pierced the elf's chest and she recovered to a fighting stance, ready for the counter that never came.

Sheriff Bastina yelled, "Yield!" The elf facing him ran forward slashing wildly with his short sword. The sheriff used his curved blade to ward off the slashes and cut the elf's wrist. The attacker kept coming, and the sheriff used a reverse cut to the neck, slicing open the elf's throat and stepping back. Bastina stayed out of reach because he didn't want an injury from a dying opponent.

Before the elf hit the ground, Ututur pushed past Klaus and ran toward the edge of the forest where four figures, three mounted and one on foot stood staring at the farmhouse. The elf on foot handed a small bundle to one of the mounted figures and began to run toward the charging half-orc. By this time the others had also made it outside and followed the giant.

One of the mounted figures moved forward and began a low chant. A small fire formed above her head and flew straight at them. The fireball moved toward the farmhouse gaining speed as it neared.

Ovidio arrived at the edge of the farm and saw the fireball form. He made quick gestures in the air and also began to chant. Ovdio released a large bolt of electrical energy from his hands. The energy bolt struck the slower moving fireball, detonating it safely before it hit the half-orc or any of the others exiting the farmhouse. However, the explosion lit the entire area around the farmhouse, knocking everyone down. Ututur lay stunned on the ground. He slowly stood as the cloaked figure who had cast the spell rode into the woods and disappeared.

The elf that had charged on foot reached Ututur, who didn't have time to swing his axe. He dropped his axe and tackled the elf, lifting him, off the ground and slamming him down. Before the elf recovered Ututur drew his rondel dagger and stabbed him several times.

By the time the rest of the group came to the half-orc's side, the elves on horseback were gone. Ututur was ready to chase the enemy into the woods when the Vigiles rode up to him. "Easy my friend, we can't chase them in the dark, especially with magic in the air." The others remained silent.

"But they have a child," said Ututur, leaning against the handle of his axe and breathing heavily. "We have to try.'

Vigiles Albrecht reached down and rested her hand on his shoulders. "I'm sorry, my friend. It's getting dark. At first light we'll send word back to the council, get reinforcements, and begin our search. Let's go back to the farmhouse." Ututur reached down and felt for a pulse on the body of the elf at his feet. Not finding one, he kicked it before he walked back to the farm with Vigiles Albrecht at his side. He'd wanted to catch one of the raiders alive to get information.

By the time the entire group got back to the farmhouse the boy had stopped screaming. Albrecht and Ututur found the three others inside.

Ovidio was holding the boy's hand. "I've done all I can. I've taken his pain away, but he'll not live much longer. Too much blood has been lost and his organs are damaged. The woman is alive, but she should not see this."

Klaus and Ridolfo carried her to the bedroom and laid her down. The Vigiles asked, "Are any of the attackers alive?"

Master Ovidio shook his head. "No."

"Did they use magic like you?" Ututur asked.

"No, my friend. It's an older, more primal magic, and the source is not the same. Mine comes from the study of nature and mathematics." The boy let out a long last breath and passed away while they talked. The gnome went to take care of the woman who was still alive, and had only superficial cuts and a bruised head. The others gathered the bodies and decided to burn all of them on a large funeral pyre. They set up camp in the barn, brought out the woman, and laid her to sleep nearby. They sat by the fire and ate their rations in silence.

After the meal Klaus approached the half-orc. "Thank you for saving me earlier."

"No need for thanks. We fight for the same side; we are comrades. You'd have done the same for me."

All Klaus could do was nod in thanks. *I like the half-orc, and I don't like working for the Bohms. I'm going to find a different job far away from Mount Haven and start a new life.*

At first light Ututur went with Ridolfo to the area of the forest to look for tracks but could find none, reporting this back to their companions. At the farm, Ututur found the woman was awake in the wagon but unable to speak. Ovidio was packing his wagon and said, "We'll take the woman back and get her to the monks. They can help take care of her."

"I couldn't find any tracks," Ututur said in frustration.

"I didn't think you would. I need to do more research, but this kind of magic can influence nature and all life forces. I'll know more once I get back to my books."

While Ututur scouted more with Ridolfo, the sheriff left to inform the council of the outcome of the mission, while Klaus returned to his caravan. By the time Ututur and the rest of the companions were close to Mount Haven, the sheriff had already mustered thirty men from the city guard and was riding toward them. Sheriff Bastina signaled for the men to stop, slowing his fresh horse. "Vigiles Albrecht did you find anything of use this morning? How is the woman?"

"Ututur couldn't find any tracks worth following. Master Ovidio thinks the girl is mute from fear."

"The High Council wants to see you and Ututur as soon as you get back," said the sheriff.

The Vigiles said, "Good luck, and be careful, my friend."

"I will and thank you all for your help." He gave a slight bow to everyone before continuing to the farm.

CHAPTER 9

The High Council met with everyone who had been at the two farmhouses.

"Are you sure the same band of elves attacked the Pera and Werner farms?" asked Galdino Di Bartolo. The Head of the High Council looked tired.

Vigiles Albretch placed several arrows on the table. "As you can see, all of the arrows are exactly the same. They are made in the same way, and all use the same hunting point. Also, Ututur tracked the group from the Pera farm to the Werner farm."

Mistress Schwertfeger sat still, rereading the accounts. She turned to the half-orc with a sour face. "Are you positive that you tracked the one group?"

"Yes, there is no doubt that we tracked the group from the Pera farm to the Werner's," said Ututur. Showing no emotion on his face.

"Master Ovidio, it's been generations since anyone has seen or heard of dark magic practiced out in the open. Practitioners of the dark arts are rare and usually practice their foul arts in secret. Are you certain you encountered dark magic at the Werner farm?" Councilor Salce asked in a casual tone. His tone suggested he didn't believe the gnome.

"I'm one of the few now living who was at the last Battle of the High Ridge during the Goblin War. In the distant mountains, humans, dwarves, orcs, and half-orcs stood shoulder to shoulder against the elven led hoard of goblins, giants, ogres, and other foul beings that planned to subdue our world using the dark magic spun from their worship of an evil goddess. I was young then. They outnumbered us, but we achieved a costly victory that day. A few days ago, a single sorcerer stood before us and attacked us with fire the likes of which I haven't seen since that battle many years ago. There is no mistaking the foul stench of the magic powered by ritual sacrifice."

The gnome stood lost in thought.

Astrid Moretto was newly elevated to the high council and had not spoken often. "We cannot sit by and let this happen in our lands. We must respond."

Consul Lorenz agreed. "We'll respond. With the permission of the High Council, I'd like to have Vigiles Albrecht address the entire council and report her findings. I want the militia and the professional soldiers to increase the number of patrols along the Litauia border up to the Jotunheimen Mountains."

The councilors nodded their heads in agreement and Galdino Di Bartolo, as head of the High Council, put in, "Let's adjourn for now. I'll schedule the Vigiles as the first speaker at the next full council meeting in four days."

As everyone was leaving Aldous stood and asked Ututur, "Can you stay a little longer? I have a few questions."

Yes, what can I do'?"

"Have you given any thought to what I asked about?" asked Aldous.

"You mean how to move the army's supply train faster?"

The other members of the High Council were busy conversing with each other, but after hearing Consul Aldous' question, they stopped their individual conversations. Councilor Salce added with a slight smirk, "Yes, we would like to hear the half-orc's thoughts."

Ututur cleared his throat. "Yes, I think the fastest way to move an army of any size in rough terrain is to stop using the slow wagon train as the main supply method. We should have everyone mounted and supported by mule train."

"Will they be able to transport the provisions and war materials? And will we have to train more cavalry?" asked Councilor Salce.

"I think using mule trains to transport supplies will work. The animals can travel through mountains and forests trails without too much difficulty even with a considerable load. Some of the heavy equipment of the baggage train will have to be abandoned or modified, but we should be able to move and supply a large fighting force just with the mules. The mounted men will dismount for combat as infantrymen. In the future, they could be trained for mounted combat. But for now, that's not necessary."

The other councilors looked at Aldous for a reaction. "I like the idea. I want to give it a try with the first patrol of one hundred mounted footmen," he said, stroking his beard. "They will only use mules to transport their supplies, no wagons. The next cavalry patrol along the great east-west highway will also use only mules for their supply."

"We could also use a mix of wagons and mules, with the wagons moving along the roads and providing support," Ututur added.

"Can you write up a short proposal?" asked Councilor Salce. "This is a good idea, overall." He seemed surprised that a half-orc could come up with a workable plan.

Ututur's mouth barely showed his pleased smile. "I'll have a proposal ready by next council meeting.

Priestess Roisin and the two acolytes rode through the night, only slowing to let their horses rest. She used her newfound powers to feed energy to her companions and their horses to continue their flight. As the night wore on the exhausted human baby stopped crying. By the third day the baby was unconscious.

High Priestess Sioban was standing by the altar when the three arrived. "My lady, I was not expecting to see you here," said Roisin as she dismounted.

"Where are my dog soldiers?" the High Priestess asked as she took the child from one of the acolytes. They couldn't afford to lose the dog soldiers. Their hounds were too valuable and not easily replaced. She had used a lot of magical energy infusing the loyal warriors with dark magic.

"We were attacked by a group of warriors and a wizard," Roisin said as she knelt with the two acolytes.

The High Priestess stepped forward and slapped Roisin with her left hand while holding the child with her right. "You were supposed to be careful. We can't be discovered. We have not gathered enough followers or power to stand in the open."

"Yes, my lady. But the goddess granted me power to fight. I was able to wield fire at the enemy."

"What? How? Never mind, I'll use this child now, and we'll find new ways to capture the offerings we need. We must recruit more warriors and acolytes to our righteous cause. For now, come help me."

The High Priestess had everyone remove their clothes as the acolytes held the child. The High Priestess began chanting the sacred words as she slit the child's throat and used the blood to draw the ancient runes on their bodies. She opened the child's belly, removed the organs, and placed them on the altar. As she continued chanting, power began to flow through the naked group.

A voice came to them, "Well done, my children. But I need more. You've tasted but a fraction of what I can do and what you can accomplish with my help. Sioban, as High Priestess, you are my chosen, and must find new bodies to sacrifice to me. You are not strong enough yet to retake your ancestral lands, but someday you will be. I'll guide you to new followers among the humans and other races."

They stood, thanked the goddess, and watched the blood and the organs disappear into the altar. The limp child's body was all that remained. Sioban looked at her hands; the wrinkles that had begun to show were gone, and she felt like a young girl again. She looked at Roisin's breasts in surprise; they no longer sagged from age but looked firm and supple like a young maiden's. "Just as the goddess restores and enriches our bodies, she will restore our ancestral lands and the glory of our people," she exclaimed as she ordered the acolytes to build a fire and tossed the child's remains into it.

Roisin felt strong and looked carefully at the High Priestess whose body was also rejuvenated. "How shall we find more sacrifices?"

"We can buy some slaves from the Thunder Horse clans. Those barbarians will be eager to sell slaves if we help them. We can also kidnap children from Nixland; this will be more difficult now and must be done quietly." The High Priestess stepped in close and kissed Roisin on the lips. "I think we'll also be able to lead humans to worship the goddess."

"Yes, my lady," Roisin replied as she returned the kiss.

High Priestess Sioban bit Roisin's lower lip hard. "Roisin, make another mistake and I will bathe in your blood. Is that understood?"

✳✳✳

The leaves were beginning to change color as Vigiles Albrecht passed farmers and townspeople on her way to the council meeting. Although the fall harvest was near, preparations were subdued by the news of the murders. It hadn't taken long for gossip about the Pera and Werner farm massacres to spread in Mount Haven.

As she entered the chamber, Galdino Di Bartolo waved to her to take an empty seat. "Thank you for coming. As you know, since the attacks this summer, we've been trying to meet with the elves, to no avail. We ask you on behalf of the people of Nixland to take a message to the Chieftain of Litauia and to conduct your own investigation of the events of the summer."

The Vigiles sat back in her seat. "I'll continue my independent and impartial investigation of the massacres. If there are any links to Litauia, I'll report back to you."

"We'll send an escort with you and make sure the elves understand the gravity of the situation. They must be made aware that the free Cantons of Nixland will not tolerate any attacks on our land and will ask our allies to the north, south, and west to help protect our land from the practice of evil magic." Councilor Salce's bald head was covered in sweat, and his hands shook as he addressed everyone in the room. "We don't seek war, but we'll be fighting on their land, not ours."

"I don't want to be hasty, but we do need to get to the bottom of these attacks. People are frightened and demand justice," Councilor Schwertfeger added, not letting any emotion cross her face.

Holding a sealed letter, Consul Lorenz handed it to Vigiles Albrecht. "Here's a letter to Captain Martel. He'll escort you with a hundred mounted men-at-arms under the Vigiles flag across the Litauia border to the gates of Beinn na Callaird. I believe that the original Council of Twelve agreement allows the Vigiles to raise up to a thousand soldiers to aid in their investigations, so the hundred men-at-arms should not be a problem."

The Vigiles took the letter, placed it in an oiled leather letter carrier, and put it back inside her vest. "Even the elves will not impede a Vigiles on official business. I'll ride out today and will send word back to you as soon as I can."

This mission took several months to plan since the elves first attacked Nixland. The first envoys to the elven lands had been met with denials and refusals to grant any meetings with the elven leaders. She wanted this investigation to succeed. Failure could mean another meaningless war. She needed to know if this was the evil act of a single sorcerer or the work of a cabal. She prayed to the creator that it was just one sorcerer. "I shall do my best, but if I fail, others of my order will take up my mantle. I swear this on the oaths taken by all that is holy and good." The High Council stood and bowed as the Vigiles rose, bowing again as she left.

After Albrecht mounted her waiting horse, she asked Parisi. "Did you send the letter I gave you to the Grand Master, Azmi Issawi, at Hold Keep."

"Yes, I sent it via a courier."

"I'm going on another patrol with the sheriff in two days. We'll sweep the main road east and go north to the farms closest to the Eastern border. We must stay vigilant."

On his way from work Master Ututur passed by a children's clothing store and saw a few toys and shirts in the window. He paused for a moment, turned and walked into the store; he had passed it almost every day since he opened his own store over ten years ago but never had the need to go inside. A small, older halfling woman stepped out from the back and smiled at him. "I recognize you," she said.

"I'm Ututur, I own the Iron Caldron with Emiliana and Venturi."

"Yes, I know. I'm Meliore. What can I do for you?"

"I need two new shirts and woolen pants for a small boy. He's nine years old, thin, and about this tall," Ututur gestured.

"I've seen the elf boy running around. Here, let me see what I have."

While she looked behind the counter, Ututur saw a brown, cloth toy horse and picked it up.

"That's a favorite among the children, along with the dragon lizard. It's stuffed with cotton."

"I'll take the horse and the clothes," he said, holding the stuffed horse awkwardly.

"That will be four silvers," Meliore said, tying the bundle with string.

Ututur handed her the coins. "Thank you. I'll need a winter coat for him soon. Can you make one for him?"

"Yes, we can make one to fit him and make it a little bigger so he can wear it for more than one season; boys grow so fast. How about a pair of winter boots? I work with a good boot maker. I can also look into getting him a sheepskin jerkin."

"Yes, some warm boots and a jerkin would be useful."

"Bring him by any time; we're open every day except for the public festival days."

"Thank you."

While waiting for Master Ututur to return, Andanir practiced the gymnastic moves Master Lucio had taught him as well as basic unarmed fighting stances. After going through these drills, he picked up a stick he had found. Andanir practiced all of the moves he had been taught. He moved backward and forward with ease finishing with a lunging thrust. He wanted to progress faster and begin sparing with the other students his age. Many were more advanced and he could only watch as they wrestled and practiced boxing. Some of the older students were allowed to fight with their hands wrapped, and they also used their feet for kicking and tripping with only a few rules for safety. Every student started with the long dagger and smallsword for thrusting. As each student mastered each of the weapons, they were taught other weapons and styles. The students from wealthier families moved to fully armored combat, mounted combat, and dueling.

While Andanir was practicing, Ututur returned and watched. "Nice footwork," he said as Andanir lunged and recovered for a counterattack.

"Thank you, master. I didn't hear you return," said Andanir surprised by Ututur's stealth.

"I bought you some new clothes. We'll go to town after your

lessons tomorrow and get new boots measured before the winter. Here, put them away in your room, and let's get supper going before it gets dark." Ututur handed the tied bundle to Andanir.

"What is this?" Andanir was holding up the horse.

"Umm, It's a toy for you. If you don't like it, I can take it back."

"No, master I'd like to keep it. Thank you." Andanir ran into the house without saying another word, cradling the horse. Ututur could hear the sobs.

He walked to the outdoor fire pit and started a fire for the stew he was going to make for them.

Andanir came out shortly, dry tear tracks on his face. "The stew will be ready soon; go wash your face, boy."

"Yes master."

Ututur was happy to see the boy smile.

Klaus Horch dreaded this meeting, but because of the unfortunate raids at the farms he had been asked by several council members to help provide extra security on several regular trade routes. He'd be busy till the roads closed for the winter. This was the excuse he needed to get away from Eleonora Bohm.

"What have you found?" Lady Bohm asked while sipping her expensive tea from the far western lands across the sea.

"As I told you already, the half-orc is honest and trusted by the people in town; many council members like him. They ask for his opinions on important matters. I've bad news; I can't work for you any longer." He placed her money on the side table.

"What! You can't just quit!" Lady Bohm stood and took a few steps toward him with her hand on a small dagger.

Klaus held up his hands. "Peace my lady, please, I was ordered by the council to work for them. They are adding more security on the regular trade routes because of the elven attacks on the farms. I have no choice but to obey. I'll be patrolling some of the trade routes and along the elven border." He was exaggerating; he had made the suggestion himself to one of the council members, but this allowed him to fulfill his militia service obligations and get him out from under Lady Bohm's thumb. Perhaps turn a new chapter in his life.

Lady Bohm eyed him sideways; she knew about the raids and his involvement in killing the murderous elves at that farm. "I guess I'll have to find someone else."

"I'm sorry my lady, but I think these events will keep me busy for a long time; the senior Vigiles has also asked me to do something for her as soon as she returns from the elven lands."

"Fine, you're dismissed. I appreciate you returning my money." She took out three gold Vreneli and handed them to Klaus. "For your service. Tell me when you are free to work for me again."

"Thank you, and goodbye." He bowed low and took the gold coins and smiled to himself; *I'll never do anything for that family again. I like that half-orc, and now I owe him nothing.* He stood and left the room feeling like a great weight had been lifted off his shoulders. He was going to get a drink and some food maybe even a woman companion for the evening.

Lady Bohm sat back and finished her tea. *There's always more than one way to skin a goblin.* She knew one other man, Rolando Fulvio, who could do the job; he lived in Budenfeld, a northern city some four days journey from Mount Haven. He was a killer and was suspected of having ties with slavers. Her family had used him as a caravan guard and to kill someone who had threatened Manfred after gambling with him in a tavern. Lady Bohm sent her maid servant to fetch Goodman Tommaso and bring him to her at once. Afterwards, she sat at her table and wrote a letter asking Rolando Fulvio to come to Mount Haven to take care of the person who had killed Manfred. She promised him it would be worth his while. She smiled thinking about the half-orc dead.

The soft knock the door to her private study opened and a sleepy-looking Tommaso walked in. "My lady, you asked to see me."

"Why do you look like you've been sleeping?"

He closed the door behind him. "I just returned from a four-day patrol as part of my militia obligation. We rode hard, camped with minimal equipment, and slept under the stars."

This seemed to mollify the Lady Bohm. "I'm going to send you to Budenfeld to give a message to a man named Rolanda Fulvio. Do you know him?"

"Yes, I met him a few times guarding a caravan on the northern route."

"Good, ask him to come avenge Manfred. Give him this letter, and make sure you bring him back with you."

"My lady, I might not be able to return before the winter snow closes the northern road."

"You can stay with our people who run the warehouses there for the winter and bring him back in the spring."

"Yes, my lady, I'll ride out tomorrow after I gather some supplies," said Tommaso as he stood to leave.

"If I don't see you in thirty days, I'll expect you here in the spring."

CHAPTER 10

"I hope your journey was without incident?" asked Wilhelm.

"I saw no one on the road. I think people are too busy with preparations for the fall harvest. Besides it's past peak trade season so there are fewer trade caravans until next spring." Vigiles Albretch warmed her hands by the small wood stove.

"If you are ready, we can begin our journey at sunrise tomorrow."

She turned to Wilhelm, "Captain, the faster we get to the bottom of this, the better it'll be for all concerned. Some in the High Council want to punish the elves for the earlier raid and will use this as an excuse for starting a new war. Many who would vote against a war are afraid of the dark sorcery and when pushed they'll support the call for a war."

Wilhelm stood and poured himself another whiskey from the small barrel. "Would you care for another?"

Feeling tired from the road, she shook her head. "No."

"This talk of dark sorcery, is it true?" asked the captain doing an admirable job of keeping any fear out of his voice.

"Yes, I saw it myself. If it hadn't been for the gnome wizard, we'd all have been killed. When we ride out tomorrow, we'll travel under the Vigiles banner." She went to her saddle bags and took out a green banner with a red hand. "Make sure your men display this and no other colors."

"Yes, I'll see to it," he replied and took the flag. "I fear no elf, but magic is something else." He drained his small cup and stood. "I'll show you to your room then check on the men and the preparations for our journey. I can have a servant bring food to your room if you like."

"Yes, some fruit, cheese, bread, and some wine." She moved slowly from fatigue as he walked down the hall to an open door.

"Here we are. I'll send a servant with your food right away. The toilet is down the hall, and there is a washroom next to it with clean cold water. We don't heat the water till the first snow."

"Thank you, and cold water is fine."

She dropped her saddlebags and took off her sword belt. She rubbed her left side where the leather belt had chafed and took off her travel jacket, mail vest, and boots. She found a bar of soap and a clean towel. She went to the washroom, undressed fully, and used the small bucket from a barrel, poured the cold water over her head. The cold refreshed her. The bergamot scented soap smelled like lime from the distant southern lands with a slight floral note. She washed her shoulder length dark hair to get rid of the grim from the road. As a side benefit of being a Vigiles most people treated her with the utmost courtesy and provided her with the occasional luxury.

After pouring a couple of more buckets on herself, she felt clean and refreshed. Once back in her room, she found a small plate of grapes, sliced apples, and a mild cheese with a small wedge of bread made of oats and rye. She took a few grapes and a bite of cheese, continuing to eat without much thought. After filling her stomach, she laid down in the bed but couldn't clear her mind The possibility of an evil sorcerer in the world troubled her. She shuddered involuntarily as she remembered Ovidio's warning that this kind of evil sorcery was usually fueled by hatred and living sacrifices to an evil deity. If left unchecked, whomever was behind this would become very powerful as they gained the deity's favor. Ovidio had said that he would have been very difficult to interrupt the fire spell that quickly if the sorcerer was more powerful.

Wilhelm rode out with the Vigiles at the front of the column of light cavalry, all of the professionals wore chain mail under coats of plates covered in black leather. All of the soldiers wore the yellow sash of Nixland. They rode with their helmets off, and some wore floppy hats or a thin woolen hood to keep the sun off their faces. Their armor jingled as they rode. They traveled with a train of thirty mules and forty extra mounts. As the group rode closer to the elven border a small, thatched hut marked the official crossing. There, a motley group of seven ill-equipped eleven guards greeted them, some with nocked bows. At the sight of the aggressive behavior the sergeant ordered the mounted men to put on their conical helmets and free their swords. The captain stopped the column and rode forward with Vigiles Albrecht.

An older looking elf walked forward. "What is your business here? No soldiers may cross into our lands without permission from the Chieftain."

Vigiles Albrecht nudged her horse slightly forward. "Good afternoon. My name is Greta Albrecht, I'm the head Vigiles in Nixland." At the mention of the Vigiles the elves began whispering among themselves. "As you can see, we fly the Vigiles flag." She pointed to one of the mounted men with a battle standard. He displayed the green flag with an open red hand. "I demand free passage immediately."

The older elf turned to the others, motioned them to lower their weapons, then called over a younger elf and whispered in his ear. As soon the older elf had finished, the younger one ran to a small horse stall, mounted, and quickly rode off.

The older elf turned back to the Vigiles. "You may pass, but what is this about?"

She had no wish to hide the truth or encourage these elves to start their own rumors. "I'm here on official business. There have been two attacks by elves in Nixland, and there is dark sorcery at work."

The older elf's eyes widened, and he made a sign to ward off evil. "That's not possible. No elf would pray to the dark ones here. Maybe in the distant lands far to the east of the Great Plains, or maybe some of the mountain tribes, but not here in Litauia. We only worship the Huntress and the Goddess of Creation," he said as he spat on the ground.

"Well, that's part of the reason we're here. I've been instructed to find the truth and help administer justice."

"Stay on the main road; you'll pass through my home of Ar d'Tus Chathair on your way to Beinn na Callaird, the capital. Go at a slow pace so the rider I sent ahead can warn the guards of your approach."

Wilhelm noticed how poorly equipped the warriors were and the sad state of their outpost. The older elf wore an ill-fitting chain mail shirt with a worn-out scabbard for his sword. "What's your name?

How long do you stay out at this outpost? Have you seen these arrows before?" He motioned to Vigiles Albrecht to show the elves the arrows from the scene of the massacre.

"I'm Bacstair, the village elder. We're all from Ar d'Tus Chathair, new warriors arrive every four days to take our place." Bacstair came a little closer to looked at the arrows, taking one and examining it closely. "It's not very well made, but it's elven, maybe from the far northern tribes." He took out one of his own arrows and showed it to Albrecht. "Most of us around this area like to use the blue, green, and grey feathers of the green-headed duck or the white feathers of a swan; the nobles use black feathers. This is a hawk feather. If you look at how the fletching is attached, we wind silk around our feathers once we glue them in place. On this one, the thread is very coarse, not silk. Look, the fletching on ours is cut in a wave pattern; this is straight. Look at my warriors' arrows." Bacstair had his elves show their arrow fletching. All of them had blue or white feathers cut in a curved wave pattern. "It's true, though, that we do buy these arrows and sometime use them for practice, but we don't make ours this way." Only one elf had two arrows cut with a rectangular pattern, and he indicated he had bought these from a merchant from the far northeastern part of the elven lands where backwoods tribes lived.

Looking at the way the two arrows were made, the Vigiles could tell the difference. Both were clearly made by elves because of how thin the shafts were compared to human arrows. She could also tell that Bacstair's arrow was of a far superior quality. "Thank you, Master Bacstair, we'll be on our way."

As Bacstair watched the mounted column move past him, he looked at his poorly equipped warriors, he felt shame and jealousy. Many of the young warriors under his command in Ar d'Tus Chathair didn't have armor or a good hand weapon; some only had a small hunting knife and a bow. *These human soldiers are so well equipped, and the five hundred warriors of my town stand no chance against even this small group of well-armed riders.* He shuddered as he thought. *And these aren't even the fully armored Nixland heavy cavalry.*

Eoin the Second was eating an apple and resting after his sword practice when a messenger came running into the training ground. "Lord Second, we have urgent news from the border guards. Mounted soldiers from Nixland are riding across the great road from Ostheim."

"When did they cross and how many soldiers?" asked the Second.

The messenger looked around, "A great host, my Lord Second. They passed Ar d'Tus Chathair three days ago. They should be approaching Beinn na Callaird in the next day. The messengers rode hard to get here before the humans."

"Cadnael, thank the messengers, but next time I need to know exact details."

"I'm sorry, my Lord."

"Get ready to ride out to meet these humans. We'll ride out as soon as possible; send out more scouts and get me accurate information. Now go." Eoin turned to the other warriors in the training arena. "Get your horses and equipment ready and prepare to ride out."

Eoin rode at the head of fifty mounted elven warriors; each had their own equipment, and the only thing they had in common was a brown cloak. Many didn't own any armor. They had been riding for about five double-paced miles when he spotted the calvary riding in two well-formed columns. As soon as the Nixlanders spotted the elves they neatly changed their formation to ten horses across, filling the entire road, and Eoin could see all of the men don their conical helmets and loosen their shields. Their helmets glinted in the morning sun.

Eoin's mouth went dry as he recognized the Vigiles banner. From beside him Cadnael said, "At least they aren't the heavy cavalry, and we aren't here to fight, My Lord."

Eoin nodded as much to himself as an acknowledgement. "Thank the Huntress for that small gift. Look at them. They may be just the light cavalry, but they could cut us down in minutes. I'll go greet our guests. Stay with the warriors."

❄❄❄

Wilhelm recognized the Second right away. "It's the same elf who came to negotiate for the prisoners. I remember him. He seemed like someone with a good head on his shoulders. Let's hold here, Sergeant."

Sergeant Netland gave a command, which was repeated by the first as a bugler played a short flourish to signal a halt.

Wilhelm waited and as soon as the elf was close enough to talk, he raised his hand. "How are you Eoin?"

"I'm well; what brings you and your friends here?"

Vigiles Albrecht waved and said, "Hello Eoin. It's my doing. I need to investigate two massacres in Nixland."

"It's good to see you again, but I'm confused. Why are you here?"

"Elves were responsible for the massacres, and evil sorcery was used," said the Vigiles in a curt tone.

Eoin spat on the ground, "We are followers of the Huntress and the Goddess of Creation. Dark sorcery has always been forbidden. In fact, no one has seen dark magic since the Goblin War. I think the last sorceress was killed over a hundred years ago. What evidence do you have?"

The Vigiles took the arrows out of her saddle bags, handed the arrows over, and added, "I was there and saw the elves and the magic."

"Is there anything else you can tell me?" Eoin asked.

"The elves all were naked or shirtless and had runes painted on their bodies; I didn't recognize any of the runes. A scholar said the runes were very old, and he had only seen them in books never in real life since the end of the Goblin War."

"Can you show me?" Eoin asked as he examined the arrows closer. There was. No doubt that the arrows were made by northern elves.

The Vigiles took out a piece of parchment with copies of the runes and handed it to the elf as she took the arrows back. Eoin kept his facial expression neutral as he looked at the runes. He didn't know what they meant but had seen them on a few abandoned ancient altars in the woods.

Albrecht asked, "Do know the runes? Have you seen them before?"

Eoin didn't answer right away. "I think I have seen them, but I don't know what they mean or where I have seen them exactly." He returned the piece of parchment. "Come; let's continue to Beinn na Callaird. The Warlord is waiting to see you."

Wilhelm turned to Netland, a young newly elevated female sergeant. She had long blonde hair with several braids to keep it out of her face. Although she was young, he had promoted her because of her abilities. "Sergeant, let's move back to a column of two."

Sergeant Netland gave a command to the signaler who sounded the horn. The mounted men reacted quickly and returned to a column formation. The eleven-warrior looked at the sergeant's blonde side braids and fine features and was impressed by how the warriors responded in unison to her commands. "Your soldiers are well trained."

As they started to move forward Wilhelm added, "Yes, we train regularly for combat."

As they moved forward, Sergeant Netland rode up to Wilhelm. "My Lord, may I allow the men to take off their helmets?"

"Yes."

Sargeant Netland yelled out, "Helms off!"

Wilhelm heard the clattering of metal as soldiers took off their helmets along with their mail coifs and stowed their cloth arming caps for travel. Along the column, soldiers relaxed as they sighed in relief. The soldiers were hot even from the brief period of wearing a metal helmet in the sun.

Vigiles Albrecht found the elf's answer a little strange and asked. "You said the Warlord is waiting for us. Is your Chieftain going to be there?"

"Our Chieftain is ill. Perhaps we can arrange a meeting, but it might not be of any use to you."

"Thank you." The Vigiles found it disturbing that she would not be able to speak to the Chieftain. *I wonder who's really in charge.*

❈ ❈ ❈

"Why wasn't I invited to this meeting!" Demanded High Priestess Sioban as she strode into the Warlord's office.

Warlord Eachmhile stood and frowned. "This does not concern you. The Vigiles wanted to ask questions regarding her investigation into killings in Nixland."

The High Priestess walked into the room with her white dress flowing around her and stared at Eoin the Second and Warlord Eachmhile who stood next to each other. "You know that I represent the Chieftain while he's ill."

"This is not a matter that has risen to the level where Chief Noldorin needs to be involved," said Eoin.

"I'll be the judge of that," the High Priestess said as she turned to the human guests. Her haughty demeanor suggested that she should be consulted about everything. "Greetings of the Huntress to you. I'm Clodagh of Clan Sioban, wife of the Chieftain and the High-Priestess of Litauia."

"This is Lady Greta Albrecht, a Vigiles from Nixland," gestured the Second.

Wilhelm stood straighter and said in a clipped tone, "I'm Captain Wilhelm Martel of the United Cantons of Nixland."

"Well, why are you here with so many soldiers?" asked the High Priestess. "It's almost an act of war."

"They are my escort; they ride under my banner," replied the Vigiles quickly. "We're here to investigate any possible links between the recent massacres in Nixland and Litauia. More importantly, we're here to see if you have any knowledge of these events or any information on who could be responsible for the use of evil sorcery in Nixland."

Before the Warlord could speak Lady Sioban said, "That sounds like an accusation. Trying to blame our peaceful people of vile deeds and evil sorcery. Do you have any proof?"

"These are the arrows we took from the dead elves, and I was there personally and witnessed the use of sorcery." Vigiles Albrecht put the arrows from the massacres on the table next to the Warlord.

The High Priestess went to the table and moved the arrows around with her pinky finger. "Yes, cheap arrows that could have been made by elves, but not our warriors. And how do you know it was sorcery and not some cheap halfling illusion? The elves could have been simple rogue brigands."

"We had a master gnome wizard with us; he was forced to use his magic to counter the fire, or I would not be standing here." The Vigiles watched the High Priestess carefully for any reaction. The young face betrayed nothing.

"Well maybe you are right. Eachmhile, this is a matter that you should deal with. If there are any developments let me know," said the High Priestess to the Warlord and turned to leave. "I'll want a full report after they're gone."

"Yes, I'll have a report for the Chieftain," the Warlord replied.

After the meeting the Warlord sat at his desk and looked at the arrows with Eoin. The meeting had not gone well as a result of Lady Sioban's interruption. The news of a sorcerer was disturbing. "We must be more careful. Eoin, Lady Sioban's influence is growing, and she has spies everywhere. We must cooperate with the Vigiles," the Warlord said in frustration.

"We should do more My Lord."

"Yes, I want more patrols along the border. Find the source of these arrows. We can't afford a war with the Nixlanders. Our warriors are brave and skilled but no match for the larger, better trained Nixland army."

"And better equipped," added Eoin quickly.

The Warlord picked up the parchment and looked at the runes. "I'll talk with a priestess of Mieliki. Perhaps the followers of the Huntress will know what these runes mean."

"I didn't tell the Vigiles, but I've seen this before on an old, abandoned altar deep in the woods north of the city," said Eoin.

"What! Send for the priestess of Mieliki right away. Afterwards I want you to take the Vigiles to the site. We can't have the humans think we're hiding something this evil. All of the other races will unite against us. Whatever this is, it must be rooted out. We must know if the northern tribes have turned away from Mieliki and if they have traveled this far south."

❋❋❋

Wilhelm had sent his soldiers back to Ostheim under Sergeant Netland's command because Consul Lorenz wanted to know how fast a large, mounted unit using just horses and mules to carry supplies could move. He wanted to go home with them; instead, he sat on his horse and waited for the Vigiles in front of the stables. They were going to follow the Second to investigate a site that might shed light on the runes drawn on the dead elves.

"Hello, Captain Martel," said the High Priestess' daughter from behind, walking a horse of her own.

Wilhelm turned his horse. "Call me Wilhelm; how have you been, Eithne? What are you doing here?"

"I'm well. I was asked by my mother to go with you and observe the investigation. Is it true that elves killed human children with the help of an evil sorcerer?"

"It sounds like you're well informed. There've been a couple of attacks, and we're here to investigate." He thought he detected a note of concern in the pretty young elf's voice.

The Second, the Vigiles, and an older female elf walked out of the stables with their mounts. The Second noticed Eithne and asked, "Are you joining us?"

"Yes," she said mounting a horse. "I won't get in the way."

"This is Neeiv Bronwen; she is a Priestess of the Huntress and a scholar. She knows many forgotten languages. I've shown her the runes you brought here."

After the introductions, the group moved slowly out of the stable with Eoin and Eithne in the lead. Wilhelm followed and noticed that many of the buildings in the city needed repair. What was once a beautiful city was crumbling around them. As they rode, he slowed his horse to ask the old priestess, "Have you seen the old runes before?"

Before she answered, she made a sign in the air with her right hand. "Yes, I've seen those runes in some of the old histories. They were only used by the followers of Lavarnis, a goddess of the underworld and a trickster. Those were protective runes used on chosen elven warriors who were often called hounds of Larvarnis.

These dog soldiers feel little pain and can march for days with little food or water."

"I thought they were just stories told to frighten children," said Eithne.

"No, my child. Many elves, giants, ogres, humans, and goblins became Larvarnis' followers. They were powerful and feared. The Goblin War ended their terrible reign. During the long war terrible deeds were perpetrated powered by dark magic. Finally, an army of men, elves, gnomes, dwarves, orcs, and half-orcs defeated the followers of Larvarnis at the battle of the Northern Pass. It's been close to two hundred years since these runes were last seen. Even then there weren't many dog soldiers," said Bronwen in a tight voice.

Wilhelm turned to look at the Vigiles; she was lost in thought and didn't seem to be paying attention to the conversation. "Eithne, I've been meaning to ask you. How is that elven warrior with the leg wound?"

Eithne turned back to look at Wilhelm. "Caoimhe died on the road."

"I'm sorry," Wilhelm said. The warrior's death had seemed to have impacted the elven girl.

"Thank you. All this killing must be stopped," said Eithne, giving him a shy smile.

The group rode in silence along the road for about three double-paced miles. Finally, Eoin stopped the group. "We'll continue on foot into the woods."

Once the group dismounted, they walked through the forest along small overgrown game trails. Wilhelm was amazed how the elven warrior guided them through the dense forest. He took this chance to ask Bronwen, "Priestess, what kind of rituals did Larvarnis' followers perform?"

"Please just call me Neeiv. I've read several books on the history of the wars. They differed in some details, but all agreed that Larvarnis was jealous of her sister Mielki who was worshiped by the vast majority of elves and other races of the known world. The Trickster became consumed by her jealousy and used her power to gain more followers. She vowed to cleanse the world of Mielki's followers. There are few records of the actual rituals involved." Neeiv looked around as if someone would overhear them. "I'm a scholar and a priestess. I've never studied dark magic, but what I've deduced is that Larvarnis perverted all of the rituals of the Huntress and the other gods. Instead of the offering animals caught in the fall hunt or fruits of the harvest, Larvarnis demanded her worshipers sacrifice live beings, humans, elves, dwarves for their sadistic rituals. In some of the stories, children were preferred. The dark sorcerers gained their power through the ritual consumption of the offerings. In other stories the followers of Larvanis also perverted the fertility rituals of the Goddess of Creation and performed deviant sexual acts as part of the sacrifice."

"So, all anyone has to do to gain dark magical powers is sacrifice innocent victims?" Vigiles Albrecht was disturbed at the Priestess' answer.

"No, it's not that simple. To gain power you must study all of the texts and all of the rituals and learn the sacred language and the symbols of power. You have to know the proper incantations. Once Larvarnis accepts the offering, the sorcerer may gain some of her divine power. Today, healers channel the divine power of the benevolent gods, gained through prayer and by living a life of charity and love. On the other hand, wizards have some innate affinity to magical energy. They can only tap into this magical energy through decades of studying mathematics, nature, and alchemy. Even then only a few are able channel enough energy for powerful spells. These spells use a combination of incantations, charms, and drawing of elemental symbols to direct the energy present all around us," replied Neeiv.

The Vigiles was digesting what the priestess had said when she bumped into the captain as the group reached a clearing. "Sorry Wilhelm, I wasn't watching where I was going." She entered the clearing and looked at the Second. "There's nothing here."

The elven warrior moved forward and began looking carefully at the clearing. The entire group spread out behind the elf and searched. Soon the Vigiles saw signs of recent activity; the marks on the ground and the broken vegetation indicated something large had been removed from the center of the clearing. There was a large rectangular outline of fresh soil visible in the grass. She examined a stone fire pit filled with ashes from a recent fire.

"This a cursed place," said the elven priestess.

"Look what I found," said Albrecht.

Eithne gave a muffled shriek when she saw a pile of goat heads and decaying remains.

Vigiles Albrecht bent down to examine the carcasses. "From the looks of these, this hasn't been going on too long. Even the oldest set of bones hasn't been out here very long. We're approaching the Full Corn Moon, so the first one must have been killed around the Flower Moon."

"How can you tell?" asked the young elven girl.

"You just take into consideration the weather, time of year and the state and color of the bones. See there some have intact flesh that has not decayed," put in Wilhelm.

"And by the look of things, the latest one is not more than fifty days old." The Vigiles moved the grizzly remnants with a stick she found.

The elven priestess stood looking over Albrecht's shoulder and asked, "Are all the organs intact?"

The Vigiles picked up a new stick and examined the freshest corpse. There was a neat single cut to the neck and a long cut in the abdomen, but the internal cavity was empty with the stomach and intestines left outside. "Looks like the heart, liver, and kidneys are missing. Does that mean anything?

Neeiv made a sign to ward off evil. "According to the old texts, priestesses of Larvaris would perform their rituals each full moon."

"What about humans, elves, and the other races?" asked the Vigiles.

"Yes, children of all races were butchered the same way."

Eoin looked around for any other animal signs. "This is not normal; there are no signs of any scavengers at all."

The group split up to look for clues to where the altar had been taken. Eoin, the Second found a large group of tracks leading toward the river; the trail ended at the water's edge.

Albrecht pointed south. "Beinn na Callaird is downriver from here."

"Yes, but so are several other cities, and a sailboat or a rowed ship can easily go upriver. There is no proof that elves from Beinn na Callaird are involved," said Eoin.

"True enough," said Wilhelm.

Vigiles Albrecht threw the stick she used to inspect the corpses far away. "I've seen enough. Let's go back."

CHAPTER 11

Lady Sioban woke in a sweat from a fevered dream. She dressed quickly and went down the hall to Roisin's room. She entered without knocking and found the priestess naked, in the arms of a female servant. "Get out!"

The naked priestess was surprised by the intrusion. "How may I be of service, my Lady?

Sioban waited till the naked servant was gone. "Roisin, Larvarnis spoke to me again last night. We have to deal with the humans investigating your blunder in Nixland. She told me to throw their scent off your trail and give them something else to chase after."

"Why don't we just kill them?"

"We are not strong enough to emerge from the shadows, and we must spread the word of our goddess. For now, our goal is to rebuild the glory of her temples and gather more followers."

"I'm sorry about Nixland. What can I do, my Lady?" Roisin moved and bowed to the High Priestess before embracing her.

The High Priestess return the hug with a quick kiss. "I was told to use the Northern elven tribes to distract the Nixlanders from what we are building here and use the distraction to extend the goddess's reach into the heart of Nixland and to other parts of the known world. I was also told that there are humans and other races who are willing to submit to Larvarnis. Together, we'll be able to gather more humans and elves for the sacrificial rites. But for now, I'll need a child for the ritual during the Full Corn Moon."

"Yes, My Lady," replied Roisin with another bow.

Catguallaun woke from a dream. The goddess commanded him to lead an army of elves against the invading humans and defend the ancient sacred lands. The goddess promised him a return to the days of glory, dignity, and riches. He dreamt of the fabled elven kingdoms of the past, where his ancestors ruled. When he awoke, he found himself back in his mud-and-thatch hovel. His ancestors had been warlords and chieftains. Now, though Catguallaun was a chief in name he worked hard as a simple farmer all day and hunted by night with other elves to make ends meet. He stood and washed his face. This was the fifth time he had this dream. He looked out of his window. His small village stood in the shadows of a crumbled wall that had once been a mighty fortress. His whole village was poor; he could muster twenty-two warriors at most; they all needed to work hard to prepare for the approaching winter. There was no time to go chasing dreams.

But two things happened that day to change Catguallaun's mind. First, Aoife Sioban, disguised as a trader came to town from Ar d'Tus Chathair and told the villagers that a human Vigiles had come from Nixland. The Vigiles blamed northern elves for killing human children and sacrificing them to an evil god. Later, runners came from surrounding villages and summoned him along with other leaders to a war council. The meeting would take place in three days during the Full Corn Moon. It wasn't difficult to believe that the secular, pleasure-seeking, indolent southern elves blamed them for the killings. The northern tribes had been blamed for every trouble since the southern tribes defeated them and united all the weaker tribes into one elven society after the Goblin War. His people were good and hardworking. It was just like the southern elves to plot against them with humans.

Lady Sioban sat at her table sipping tea when a knock interrupted her. A servant brought the Vigiles into the room. She wanted to throw out the dirty human but calmed herself. After all, she had summoned the human. "Please come in and sit down; would you like some tea?"

"Yes, thank you," Vigiles Albrecht replied as she took a seat opposite the High Priestess.

Lady Sioban poured tea into a small teacup of the finest porcelain. "I must confess, I have no love for the Nixlanders but I also will not condone any kind of evil in this land. The goddess will not abide by false profits and nonbelievers. I have many acolytes throughout Litauia and beyond. Word has come to me that is very delicate in nature and concerns both Nixland and Litauia."

Lady Sioban paused and looked at the Vigiles who took a sip of the tea, surprised by its delicate floral essence. "Please continue."

"My acolyte told me that there are elves of the northern tribes who have been secretly worshiping an evil deity and are preparing a huge raid into our lands and across the border into Nixland." Lady Sioban took a sip of tea before she continued. "I don't know how large a force it will be, but I can tell you that the savages resent us and outnumber us. I don't know how many warriors we can muster in short notice."

"We should have this discussion with Captain Martel, your Warlord and his Second," said the Vigiles.

"We will as soon as we're done here. I wanted to speak to you alone first and make sure you understand that this information came from me, and I want to cooperate as much as possible. I'm only looking out for the best interest of the elves and wish for a closer relationship with Nixland."

The Vigiles couldn't read the calm smooth face of the elven woman. She didn't know what to think about this turn of events. "I'll keep that in mind. Stamping out evil in all forms is part of why my order exists, and our oath is to help all those who cannot help themselves in the pursuit of justice."

Wilhelm sat and listened to Lady Sioban tell the small gathering about the looming attack from elves from the northern tribes, who had turned to worshiping an evil deity. It was difficult to believe such practices existed in this day and age, so long after the wars had ended. But he found his eyes retuning to Kiley Saoirse, the other Second to the Warlord, and taking in her beauty.

"Can we speak with your acolyte? How many warriors are involved? And how soon before we can expect this attack?" asked the human captain with a deep frown on his face. He was looking for enough information to formulate a defensive plan and a counter attack.

"No, she's afraid, and has returned to her village in the north. She told me that she has seen thousands gathered to worship in secret in the northern woods. I'm not sure when they'll attack, but my informant told me that she thinks these evil worshipers will meet during the Full Corn Moon, so sometime after that. If my guess is right, it'll be after the Hunter's Moon because the power of the gods is strongest then. And Warlord Eachmhile, my husband, asks you as his friend to defend the city from this evil using any means necessary," Lady Sioban said, standing before the group.

The Warlord turned to his two subordinates. "I want you both to inspect the city's defenses. Make sure it can withstand an attack. Muster the warriors. We'll counterattack if the opportunity presents itself."

Kiley asked, "Should I set up patrols to the North, my Lord?"

"Yes. Captain Martel and Vigiles Albrecht, I'm officially asking you on behalf of the elves of Litauia to help us."

"You must write to the Council of Nixland and ask them officially for help. As soon as I'm given permission, I'll personally lead the effort to help your people." Wilhelm hated making these promises before the council made a decision but there was no way the council would refuse.

The Vigiles looked around the room and met the gaze of those gathered. "We are not a large military organization but will also support your people against this evil. I'll ask for more assistance from our master at Hold Keep."

"I'll leave as soon as soon as you can have the letters drawn up," added Wilhelm.

Lady Sioban smiled as she rose with her hands clasped in front of her. "I thank you for listening, and the goddess thanks you. If you'll excuse me, I have other duties to attend to."

After the meeting, Lady Sioban went to an old warehouse she had purchased. In the main part of the building workers were busy loading and unloading goods from all over the known world to distribute to merchants who had placed orders with her factors. She walked quickly to the back of the warehouse, entered a private room, locking it behind her. To ensure there were no accidental intrusions, she placed a thick wooden plank across the door. Satisfied, she used an incantation to open a secret door to an underground passage her followers had built. The passage led to a number of connected tunnels. The goddess had shown her the way to the ancient catacombs under the city. This complex was going to serve as the main temple to Larvarnis. The northern elves under her control brought the ancient altar from the woods into the main large chamber through a secret entrance near the river. The catacombs provided a perfect place for her growing army to hide. The area had become a small city in its own right with schools for the young, shops, and work areas for artisans of all kinds. It was also a perfect place for her to perform the rites Larvarnis demanded. The catacombs were vast with ample room to store the sacrificial offerings before they were given to Larvarnis.

Lady Sioban strode through catacombs lit by glowing fungus and smokeless lanterns. The elves guarding the passages bowed. When she neared the main antechamber to the shrine and altar, she pointed to the guards. "Bring two offerings and summon Trahern and Rianor." The guards bowed and ran to fetch her War Chief.

She took off her robes in the antechamber and approached the altar naked, carrying an ornate but sharp curved, ancient dagger. Sioban found the magical dagger with the goddess' help in a secret location in the catacombs. The dagger had not rusted or lost its keen edge while it had remained hidden through the years. The weapon was almost black and had a wavy pattern to its blade; it was made from the remnants of a falling star.

As she began chanting, her followers arrived. Two guards brought the offerings, one a small human seven-year-old boy and the other a young elven girl of not more than thirteen summers.

She motioned for the boy to be placed on the altar and used her knife to swiftly slice open his throat, then opened up his belly. With little care she dumped the intestines onto the floor. She reached into the stomach cavity and cut out the liver and kidneys. Afterward she reached into the chest from the stomach ripping through the thin membrane to find the heart and lungs. She gripped the slippery beating heart while looking at the boy's screaming face. When it stopped beating, she cut it out, offered them to Larvarnis, and threw them into the fire. She then turned to the boy's penis and testicles and cut them off as well and threw them into the cooking fire. The chamber filled with the power of the goddess. Several of her followers looked at the young female elf, and the High Priestess Sioban for approval. They ripped the little girl's clothes off. Her screams ceased after a few moments; all that could be heard was the chanting and yells of the warriors as they raped her. After the boy's organs were taken out of the fire, the High Priestess took a bite of the heart and gave it to the followers who gathered for the worship. She took a bite out of the lungs and passed them around. She motioned for the girl to be brought up to the altar and used the knife again to sacrifice the elven child to Larvarnis. She removed the girl's organs, paying special attention to the uterus, making sure it was taken out in one piece and placed it carefully in the cooking fire.

"Well done," whispered a female voice in the High Priestess' ear. "Now send some of the followers to kill the human envoy."

Lady Sioban nodded and motioned Trahern to step forward. She drew the ancient runes on his bare chest with the blood of the elven girl from the altar. She almost allowed him to take her sexually. She promised herself that next time she would allow herself to enjoy him. "Take thirty of the blessed; kill the human captain and his escort."

Trahern motioned for the first thirty to step forward and receive Sioban's blessing.

The High Priestess drew runes on the thirty warriors kneeling in front of her. "Remember the old ways. Through the will of the Larvarnis and by these deaths she'll give life unto the world. She'll deliver our people from slavery and oblivion. Our people will find their rightful place in this new world forged in sacrifice. We will no longer be ruled by humans, dwarves, orcs, or any other inferior race."

She took a piece of the girl's heart and uterus and left the shrine. She entered the antechamber where two female acolytes cleaned her body and dressed her. Sioban had been keeping an eye on the silver haired beauty who she had been grooming for some time. She turned to the silver haired acolyte and asked, "What's your name?"

"Rianor Enid," replied the girl.

The High Priestess grabbed Rianor and kissed the young female delighting in the surprise of the acolyte. "Nice. I'm going to elevate you to a priestess. You'll go on a mission with Trahern. Here, I brought you some meat from the sacrifice. Feast upon this offering, and I'll teach you to call upon the power of the goddess."

"Yes, mistress," Rianor said as she knelt and took the offering in her cupped hands. After eating the burnt offerings, she kissed Sioban's stomach while holding the naked High Priestess in an adoring embrace.

Wilhelm rechecked the leather document holder inside his vest pocket. He rode at a fast walk next to Kiley. The Warlord insisted that the female Second escort him to the border town. Wilhelm looked at her and couldn't tell how old she was. He decided she had to be young, although with elves it was hard to tell. She had long dark hair, unusual for an elf. Or at least he thought that most elves had blonde or light hair. "So how long have you been a Second to the Warlord?"

She looked at him with an angry expression. "I was appointed only a few moons ago. But I'm capable of doing this job."

"I didn't mean offense. I was just curious." He didn't know what else to say. "Should we go faster along this good stretch of road?" Without replying Kiley spurred her horse to a trot. Surprised, the captain and the ten elven warriors gave chase.

After a quick midday meal of oat cakes and water they resumed their journey. The captain wanted to talk to the elf, but as her demeanor didn't welcome any conversation, he rode in silence to their camp for the night; the elves kept to themselves. After taking care of the horses and taking off his traveling armor, he ate his oat cakes with dried sausage and dried fruit by himself near the fire. After the meal he walked into the woods and relieved himself. He returned to his bedroll, found the earthen jug of brandy from his saddle bags, and took a good swig. The golden liquid warmed him as it went down, although some of the old soldiers always told him not to drink alcoholic drinks if you were stuck out in the cold. The nights were getting colder as the Harvest Moon approached. After another sip he put the jug away, pulled his blanket over his shoulder, turned away from the fire, and let sleep take him.

Wilhelm again rode alone the next day. It was close to mid-morning when elf maiden rode up next to him and said in a neutral tone. "We'll be out of the forest road by the end of the tomorrow, and we'll arrive in Ar d'Tus Chathair."

"Yes, I thought as much. Will you accompany me all the way to Ostheim?"

"Yes. I was told to see you all the way home, wait for a reply, and guide the Nixland forces back. I hope your Council will aid us against the northern elves. In any event, I was told to return home by the Harvest Moon, so we have twenty-two days left." Kiley's eyebrows furrowed as she began to look around.

Wilhelm felt something was amiss and scanned the road. The woods had grown quiet; he could no longer hear any woodland creatures or birds. Even the brown squirrels who had been busily snorting at them during their ride had disappeared. Kiley said, "There's something wrong; be prepared."

A short distance further, the elf maiden halted the column of ten warriors and scanned the woods. The horses became anxious, their whinnies and squeals piercing the silent forest. The human captain looked into the woods but couldn't see anything; however, he felt cold and the air compressed around him. He heard a woosh as something exploded near the ten elven warriors escorting him. The blast almost threw him off his horse.

As soon as he recovered, Wilhelm saw that the middle four riders and horses had been shredded to pieces by shards of ice. His trained warhorse calmed quickly, as he reached back for his helmet. He put it on as fast as he could and tied the leather thong. Next, he unbuckled his spiked war hammer. Scanning the forest, he saw at least twenty naked elven warriors emerge from the tree line. Their bodies were covered with the familiar runes. Another five stood by the edge of the forest and fired arrows at them. He was ready to form a line with the mounted elves and charge the enemy, but to his surprise Kiley and her remaining five warriors dismounted and strung their bows.

"Kiley I mean Saoirse, the enemy is upon us; get ready to fight!" said Wilhelm as he changed his grip on the war hammer to make sure the spike was down. The blunt end worked well against armored soldiers, but the spike would be more effective against naked warriors. He wished he had on his heavy plate battle armor. He almost felt naked wearing just his traveling green gambeson and a short black brigandine vest.

Kiley and her warriors shot their arrows as fast as they could. Six enemy warriors went down, and others slowed their charge. Wilhelm moved his horse to the edge of the fighting and waited for the enemy. He wanted to charge them before they reached the elf maiden and her dismounted warriors. He would get two passes before he would be forced to dismount as well.

On his first deadly pass, he used the spike to hit two elves on the back of the head and as he rode past them, leaving them dead with brains seeping out of small holes in their skulls. He wheeled his warhorse, and on his second pass a warrior stood his ground, waiting for him with a spear. He slowed and prepared to parry the spearhead before striking, but the elf tipped over with an arrow protruding from his chest. The captain changed his target, charged again, and killed two more. He felt an arrow hit his vest, the point digging into the outer fabric layer. He pulled the arrow out of the vest as he looked about. Four elven warriors lay dead, and the other two were wounded. He looked for an escape route, but their horses had run away when the battle started.

Wilhelm rode as fast he could to Kiley. A naked warrior stood in front of her. He hit the elf with his war hammer. He reached down. "Kiley! Here, grab my hand and mount up; we have to make a run for it!"

Kiley's remaining warriors placed themselves in between the enemy and his horse. One turned to the Second and yelled. "We'll hold them here! Go!"

Kiley reached up toward Wilhelm's extended hand but almost pulled away, as she looked at her warriors. "Come; we have to run." He helped her get on his horse. As soon as she sat behind him, he urged his horse to gallop away. As they rode, arrows streaked past them. The sounds of the battle began to fade; after more than three double-paced miles he felt his horse tire and saw red foam come out of the horse's nostril. As soon as he slowed, he felt Kiley's grip loosen as well.

"Are you alright?"

"I'm wounded."

Wilhelm stopped the horse and helped Kiley dismount. When he got off his horse, he knew they were in deep trouble. He helped her sit down and saw two arrows protruding from her back. *Dammed elves; why didn't she have on some kind of armor?* His horse had also been hit by several arrows. Three of the hits were superficial, but one arrow was lodged deep in the right side and looked like it pierced the lung. There was red foam coming from the horses' nostrils, and the animal looked weak.

Kiley sat up and pulled one arrow out of the fleshy part of her shoulder. The other was in her right side. "I don't think it hit anything vital, just fat and skin and not the intestine or an internal organ. But you're going to have to pull it out. Thank the goddess it's not a hunting broadhead," she said as she looked at the bodkin point sticking out of her side. She took off her satchel, looked inside, and said, "Good, I have some honey. Remove the bodkin point, pull the arrow out, and use the warmed honey as a lubricant."

Wilhelm threw his helmet on the ground and searched his saddlebags for the brandy and his leather pouch holding his razor. He doused the razor and his hands with the brandy and offered some to Kiley. After she took a gulp, he used the razor to cut away the bees wax and thread holding the point of the arrow onto the shaft. Kiley winced but didn't speak. Once the point was removed, Wilhelm used his fingers to spread as much honey as possible on the protruding end. "Hold on." He offered her his leather pouch. "Get ready. Do you want me to do it slow or fast?"

"Fast," she replied, putting the leather pouch in her mouth and biting down.

Wilhelm pulled the arrow out in a nice steady motion and thanked the gods when her insides did not protrude out of the wound. Only fresh red blood came out with the arrow.

"I think I got lucky," she said as he examined the wound for any intestinal fluids. "There should be a bandage in my bag."

Wilhelm also had one large bandage and some clean packing material. He dressed the wound while she held her shirt up.

Meanwhile his horse was on the ground, her head down, her breath accompanied by gurgling noises.

Wilhelm looked at the winding road ahead and turned to Kiley. "We have to get moving, and we have to get off the road. We'll try to cut through the woods to Ostheim."

"How far are we?" asked the wounded elf as she got up holding her side.

"From the point of the ambush it was around forty double-paced miles. If we cut through the woods, it might be around thirty-five."

"But we'll be on foot, and I'm injured. We'll be lucky if we can make it in four or five days."

"Can you walk?"

"Yes, let's get going before they catch up to us."

Wilhelm took off his sword but kept his dagger and hunting knife along with his one-handed axe from his horse. The sword would just be a hindrance on foot. After he lay down his equipment Wilhelm walked up to his horse and quickly cut both carotid arteries. He took time to close his eyes and murmured a prayer to the gods. He put Kiley's satchel around his neck, threw his saddle bags over his left shoulder, then helped the wounded elf stand. She helped him get his bearings, and they started walking west.

Rianor stood looking at the aftermath of the ambush. The power she felt when she unleashed the ice shard was like nothing she had ever felt before. She felt the goddess within her when the intoxicating tendrils of power travelled throughout her body. After she released the power, she collapsed to the ground, exhausted. When Trahern helped her rise, she saw that she had missed the target. The ice shards hit the ground in front of the southern elves they were ambushing, but those hit by the shards lay dead with puncture wounds. She had lost eleven warriors, and four others were seriously wounded. The young priestess stood and watched as two escaped her ambush.

Trahern shot at the escaping forms as his dog soldiers killed the last southern elf. "Should I send a few warriors after them?"

"Yes, send four dog soldiers; the others can help the wounded get back to the catacombs." Rianor had expected more from her warriors, but those southern elves were well trained. And the dammed human had killed at least four warriors on his own.

"Yes, Priestess."

She watched as Trahern instructed four warriors and sent them to hunt down the two that escaped.

Rianor looked at the battlefield once again. She craved to feel the power of the goddess once again but she almost fell from fatigue. With the grace of Larvarnis, her people would take back their ancestral lands from the humans, dwarves, and orcs. The humans would be forced to stop looking down on elves and would treat them as equals. Their once great and beautiful cities would be restored to their former glory.

Chapter 12

Andanir lay in his bed playing with Enbarr, the toy horse Ututur had given him. It was a rest day today, and he didn't have to go to the training grounds or to Master Ovidio's. He imagined riding a horse like Enbarr in an open field. Andanir was startled when he heard his master yell commands.

Andanir got up, put his boots on as fast as he could, and raced out to see what was going on. He saw Rolf in a mail shirt, a round helmet with an aventail, a gambeson, a round shield slung on his back, and holding a spear, standing at attention. "Good morning, master."

Ututur turned and waved. "Good morning."

Andanir watched as his master instructed Rolf how to plant his spear for a cavalry charge and how to form a shield wall.

Ututur yelled, "We're practicing with the spear. Want to join us?"

Andanir grabbed the broom leaning against the wall and ran to join them. He stood next to Rolf as Ututur explained the finer points of fighting in a group. "Fighting in formation is very different than fighting in a skirmish line or fighting on your own. "Don't swing the spear or any weapon wildly when you're in formation. Always be aware of everyone around you. Trust the soldiers next to you and behind you in the shield wall. Listen for commands and stay in formation. If the line breaks, everyone is in danger, so fill the gaps as quickly as possible."

It was close to mid-morning; they spent the rest of the morning practicing with the spear. Andanir liked the exercises that Ututur showed them, thrusting with the spear at imaginary enemies. "Remember, the sword is fancy, but nothing beats good spear work," said the half-orc as he showed different thrusts using his own spear which was about eighteen hands long, tipped with a cutting and thrusting blade. Andanir was sweating, and the broom felt heavy in his hands as he tried to follow Ututur's instructions.

"Enough," said his master finally. "Let's break for the day. Both of you did well."

Rolf bowed, thanked the master, gathered his equipment, and headed home.

Andanir also bowed the way Master Lucio Cociarelli had shown him. "Thank you, master." He felt a sense of pride as Ututur gently placed a large hand on his head.

"You did well. Let's get cleaned up and prepare something to eat."

They took off their shirts and washed themselves. While they were drying themselves, Ilina walked up to their cabin with a basket. Andanir saw her first and ran to give a hug. "Hello, mistress. What are you doing here?"

"I thought that on this rest day we could eat something and go to the market afterwards," Ilina said as she walked toward Ututur with Andanir's arms around her waist. She was growing to love the boy and used to spending time with the two.

Ututur still had his shirt off, and Ilina gawked as she saw his bronze skin and muscles as he finished drying himself, she felt herself blush. She turned and waited till he had a clean shirt on. Andanir asked, "What did you bring to eat?"

"Oh, just a vegetable stew with beans and some fresh flat bread," Ilina said as she looked down at him.

"Sounds delicious," added Ututur as he finished dressing.

"I'll go get some bowls, spoons, and mugs," said Andanir as he ran into the house. By the time he returned, his master and Mistress Ilina were seated at the table on the porch of their cabin.

They ate in the shade and looked out into the garden. "Looks like both of you are doing well," said Ilina as she dipped her flat bread into the spicy vegetable stew.

"Yes, Master Ututur has been showing me how to use the spear today."

"A spear? Is it wise to give a boy a spear?" She knew that everyone should be able to defend themselves but the thought of arming the little elf at such a young age disturbed her alittle.

"Well, it's not really a spear," Andanir said between spoonsful of the delicious stew. He loved both Ilina's and Ututur's cooking. The food here had more spices than the bland foods he grew up with.

"It's a broom," said Ututur, finishing his last piece of flat bread.

Ilina smiled as she finished her stew. "It's good to have training, but violence should always be the last resort."

Andanir thought that the half-orc would disagree, but to his surprise Master Ututur did not. "I agree. It's always best to talk and solve problems without fighting. My grandfather would say a warrior who can win by using his mind and words is superior to the warrior who always resorts to the axe. Because it only takes one loss in battle to start the journey to the underworld." Andanir had always been led to believe that orcs and humans were blood-thirsty. Now he wondered if dwarves were really as stupid as he was told. Andanir's beliefs had first been formed by his mother who believed that all beings deserved respect, then his stepmother tried to reform him in a different mold. Living with Master Ututur and learning from humans, he began to question all he had learned in Litauia about the other races and the world.

Ututur stood and stretched. "Come on, boy stop your daydreaming. Let's go to the market before it closes."

"Yes, master," Andanir said smiling at them both and happy that he no longer had the nightmares. For many days after the battle, he dreamt that he couldn't move or breath as a creature stalked him in the darkness.

It was early afternoon and Rolando sat alone at the bar in Budenfeld. The Frozen Cat tavern was large and could hold at least two hundred patrons. It had a raised wooden platform for entertainers. The tavern was empty because it was too early in the workday for the regulars to come in. Budenfeld was a major trading hub near the border to two of the western kingdoms, Al Anikka to the northwest and Riom directly to the west. These two kingdoms touched the western and north-western corners of Nixland. The Cerq River ran from the Jotunheimen Mountains in the north and flowed south past the City States into the Small Ada Sea, separating the Northern Bedu nomadic tribal lands. Rolando was tired from his sixty-day journey. He had guided a major trade caravan from the lands of the Northern

Bedu across Ada and past the City States. The caravan carried grey and white salt from the Bedu tribes. The merchants also bought frankincense, garnets, and rare purple rubies. Rolando sat at the bar drinking whiskey and thinking how he and the other guards did all the work while these fat merchants made so much money. Everywhere he went, these merchants and lords lived in luxury while men like him worked to get barely enough to eat. Being a dirt farmer was no better. They grew all the food but some lord would come and take a large share in taxes. He poured himself another drink of brandy from the bottle he bought.

"Hey, are you Rolando Fulvio?" asked Tommaso.

"Yeah, who's asking," he replied, taking another drink.

"I'm Aurelio Tommaso, and I work for Lady Eleonora Bohm. I was with you in a trade caravan run by Manfred Bohm a few years ago."

"Yeah, the salt merchants."

"Yes, they do trade in salt, but they also have many other business interests."

"What do you want?"

"Lady Bohm wants to hire you to do some work for her. Let's go sit over there in a quiet corner."

Rolando followed Tommaso to a small table and said, "Well?"

"Manfred was killed in a judicial combat. Lady Bohm wants to avenge her son. She wants you could come to Mount Haven and deal with the killer."

Rolando had done this before for Manfred, and the Bohm's paid well. "How much is she willing to pay?"

"She gave me this letter for you."

Rolando took the letter and opened it. The letter promised him two hundred Vreneli gold coins, a huge sum if he could kill Manfred's murderer. With that money he could retire before he got too old to enjoy life. "Fine. I'll go with you, but I need a couple of days rest before I go on the road again. I haven't had decent food and drink for a long time. I could use the services of a woman as well. Do you have some extra money I can have now?"

"Here. I was told to give you four gold coins for your troubles, but we need to leave before the first snowfall."

"Don't worry. We'll get to Mount Haven before the Hunter's Moon."

Tommaso smiled, relieved he didn't have to spend the winter in some warehouse in Budenfeld. He didn't want to anger the Lady Bohm. "Done! We'll leave in two days."

After they shook hands, Tommaso left for his room at a different inn, and Rolando headed to a nearby brothel.

Wilhelm winced as he watched Kiley struggle to walk at a steady pace; by sunset she looked exhausted. He found a small clearing near a creek and prepared a campsite while she rested. In the fading light, she looked pale even for an elf. He prepared a bundle of pine needles as a resting area next to a tree. "Sit here and cover yourself." Wilhelm draped his blanket over her shoulders. "I'll start a smokeless fire in a low pit so it can't be seen."

He dug a deep fire pit to hide their position at night. This might be their last meal for a while. If their enemy were pursuing them, their initial lead would be gone by tomorrow. He couldn't risk a fire or the smells of cooking that would lead the enemy to their position. The water was boiling, and he poured the last two packets of the soup mix into the pot. He searched Kiley's satchel but found no food.

He looked over and saw her resting with her eyes closed. He took the pot off the fire and broke two of the rock-hard biscuits into the pot, creating a thicker soup. He approached the elf. "Eat this before you fall asleep. You'll need your strength for tomorrow."

"Thank you," she opened her eyes and looked at him. "I think our enemy will catch up to us by tomorrow."

"I was thinking the same thing. What should we do?" asked Wilhelm as he fed her a spoonful of the soup.

"We'll never outrun them because of my wounds," she said after eating another spoonful. She raised her eyebrows and said, "This is pretty good for field rations."

Wilhelm smiled and gave her another spoonful. "Yes, this is from a shop in Mount Haven called the Iron Caldron, they also make some of the finest dried sausages and cheese."

"I can't eat anymore. You finish the rest."

Wilhelm couldn't believe how beautiful she was and stopped himself from staring. "How's your wound?"

She lifted her shirt with some difficulty. "The bleeding has mostly stopped. No other fluids came out, so I should be able to recover even without a healer."

Wilhelm asked, "May I look at your shoulder?"

She turned slightly and winced as he examined the bandage. He wasn't sure how far they needed to go before they reached the border. If he had to carry her, he'd be exhausted by the time the enemy caught up to them. "Do you know how many days we have till the Harvest Moon?"

The elf closed her eyes and said, "We have twenty days left. What are you thinking?"

"We can't run from the enemy. They'll catch us. I'll be too tired to fight after another day, and you'll be weaker."

"Are you thinking about fighting them now?"

"Well, maybe we can ambush them here."

"We don't know how many elves are pursuing us," said Kiely as she sat up straighter.

"I figure it can't be that many more left. We killed at least nine of them, and your warriors wounded more. They'll take their wounded back with them."

She smiled. "I like the way you think. It's risky without knowing more, but it'll be a well-deserved victory or a glorious end. I can make a few traps and help you."

"I'll find a good place to hide and we'll take them by surprise." Wilhelm finished the soup and out of habit scrubbed the pot with clean dirt and rinsed it with some water. He refilled the pot with clean water from a small stream and set it on the fire. They were deep in the woods, and he didn't want to risk getting sick from unclean water. He gathered a large number of leaves and made a hiding position facing Kiley, doing his best to sweep away most of his footprints while Kiley created a few traps. Once they finished their preparations, they tried to sleep, but every noise woke him. He also felt cold because he had given her the only blanket and there weren't any rocks he could heat in the fire for warmth. "Are you sleeping?" came Kiley's soft voice.

"No," replied Wilhelm.

"If you're cold, come and share this blanket."

Wilhelm didn't wait for another invitation. He found a spot next to her; her warm body felt pleasant and comforting.

"We're going to die, aren't we?" she asked in a soft voice.

"We still have a chance," he said, trying to put confidence in his tone.

"Do you like music?" she asked, changing the subject as she rested her head on his shoulder and began humming a soft tune.

The four elves sent by the young priestess didn't have any trouble following the two they hunted. Caden, Aodh, Clom, and Maoilios had passed the dead horse by the side of the road yesterday evening and followed the tracks into the woods. One was the human, and the other was an elf. "The wounded one must be getting weak; they are moving slowly," Caden said, looking at the tracks. "We'll catch them soon."

By mid-morning they came to a ridge overlooking a small clearing below them. Caden motioned his party to stop and moved silently forward to observe the campsite. Lying next to a large tree was an elf; she wasn't moving and looked dead. A small fire burned nearby, and there were signs of a hasty abandonment of the camp: a cooking pot lay overturned next to the elf, and a saddlebag was open with its contents on the ground. Caden was cautious and used hand signals to tell the party to wait and observe.

Caden waited for a thousand heartbeats, and seeing no movement in the camp, he whispered, "I can't get a shot with my bow. Let's go check on the elf and make sure she's dead; then, we'll go after the human." The four elves stood and began descending into the camp. They walked carefully and watched for any movement.

Wilhelm was hidden under a pile of leaves near Kiley. He saw the elves on the ridge. As they slowly moved closer, he felt another bite on his neck but tried to ignore the insects. Whatever bit him crawled down his shirt; it bit him again, this time in the middle of his back. Sweat poured down his body, but he kept still and controlled his breathing. Kiley was very still, and Wilhelm began to worry that she had passed out from loss of blood. But as he looked at her, she opened her left eye slightly and winked at him.

He smiled and his mind went over the traps they had set. They used all of his cordage to rig a large wooden stump to fall above Kiley's head, hitting anyone standing over her. They also placed stake traps near her. He hoped someone might leap onto them while trying to avoid the stump swinging at their heads.

The elves moved closer. Two held spears and had daggers sheathed on their belts. The other two had short swords and bows. One stopped and walked toward his saddle bag, telling the others to make sure Kiley was dead.

The two with spears walked toward Kiley, and one poked her in the chest with the spear. As soon as the spear made contact, she grabbed it, shocking the male elf, held it, and triggered the trap. The wooden stump hit the surprised elf in the side of the head and knocked him out. The other elf with the spear dove out of the way and let out a yell as he impaled himself on several sharpened sticks. Kiley released the spear and stabbed the dazed elf in the gut with her hunting knife.

Wilhelm waited for the other two elves to turn away from the saddle bags. He saw that the effort had strained Kiley; she was having difficulty standing. Both of the elves near him turned and began to nock their bows. He roared and charged from under the pile of leaves but the long wait made his right leg stiff. He had difficulty moving fast. He swung his axe with his right hand, lodging it deep in the head of one of the elves who twitched and fell face down onto the ground taking the buried axe with him. The last elf turned to face him. They were too close to each other, and Wilhelm had to abandoned the axe while the elf dropped his bow and drew a short sword.

The elf facing Wilhelm was quick; before he was ready the elf had swung the sword at his chest. Luckily, his gambeson protected him from getting cut. Wilhelm realized he couldn't just trade blows with the elf, who had a longer reach.

Wilhelm circled to his right, staying out of reach. The wounded elf who had fallen on the stakes was beginning to stand. He had to finish this fight fast, or he would face two opponents at once. The elf with the sword looked confident and lunged in for a thrust to Wilhelm's stomach. He sidestepped, grabbing the back of the elf's neck with his left hand and placed his dagger to the inside of the elf's sword hand. The elf's sword was rendered useless; now they grappled with each other. Wilhelm smiled because of his size and weight advantage. Before the elf could create some space between them Wilhelm attacked, thrusting his dagger as fast as he could into the elf's upper body. He lost count of how many times he stabbed the elf, but he could feel him begin to weaken. He stabbed as deeply as he could and held the elf's neck until he felt no more movement.

Wilhelm let the dead elf drop and turned just in time to see the wounded elf limp toward him holding an upraised dagger. The elf's slash was weak, and only the tip penetrated Wilhelm's gambeson. Before he could counter, the shorthaired elf stiffened as a spearpoint sprouted from her chest. Kiley released the spear and sat down, breathing heavily from the exertion. The skewered elf slid backward on the spear shaft as more of the spear protruded from his chest; the dying elf finally fell backward screaming. Silence returned to the camp.

CHAPTER 13

Andanir raced forward to see all the merchants at the market and join the throng of children gathered around the sticky candy man, who was busy winding and pulling taffy. It was an expensive sweet treat, but Andanir felt in his pocket and found the five copper coins his master had given him. The candy man was calling out to all passersby, boasting about how good the candy was, and was selling a long piece for only two coppers. Andanir took out two of his coppers and handed them to the candy man, who cut a piece of spiced toffy about a hand long and gave it to Andanir. He stood there looking at the sweet. The memory of his mother came flooding into back; she loved to eat a sweet honey-based spiced candy during the harvest festival. He felt tears fill his eyes as he walked away from the candy man.

He heard a group of children yelling. "She's stupid and dumb, can't say anything." A tall dark-haired boy stood with two other boys and poked a girl with a long stick. The other two stood by the bully's side laughing at the girl.

Andanir recognized the mute girl Rialta from the training grounds. He walked quickly closer. "Come on, stop it!"

The boys looked at Andanir and laughed. "What are you going to do, puny little elf freak?" The dark-haired boy threw a punch, but Andanir moved his feet and avoided the blow easily. A merchant noticed the group and yelled, "Stop what you are doing and get out of here before I call the watch or the Vigiles."

Rialta grabbed Andanir's hand, and they walked away from the bullies. The girl was crying but gave Andanir a hug and smiled. He said, "You're Rialta. I've seen you at Master Lucio's training ground. I'm new there. My name is Andanir. Want a bite of this?"

She nodded her head. Andanir saw a tear fall off her chin. "Don't cry; they're just bullies." He offered her another bite, and they shared the candy in silence.

"Want to walk with me to go see the other artisans?" Andanir took another bite and gave the rest to Rialta, who nodded yes. They walked down a row of merchants who were selling pottery and cooking implements.

Andanir was looking at the pots and pans when Rialta tugged his hand. She led him to the row of merchants selling jewelry and weapons. They both gawked at the fancy jewelry. They held hands while they moved to an area where merchants sold weapons and armor. They stopped at a merchant selling hunting knives and daggers. Andanir stood and gazed at the bewildering assortment of daggers. He hadn't realized that there were so many different kinds. Some had flat blades, others had triangular profiles, and another was as thick as his forefinger with a flat side and a sharpened edge. They had very different handles and guards; some round, others had no guard.

"These are the best in Nixland. Some come from across the Small Ada Sea, and others are from Riom," said the big bladesmith.

"Master Cociarelli told me never buy a cheap dagger because a good dagger can save your life," replied Andanir.

"I've heard of Master Cociarelli; he is very famous."

"How much are these daggers?" asked Andanir.

"The cheapest is five gold pieces, and the most expensive one I have is the one behind me under the glass case. It's fifty gold pieces," the merchant replied, showing Andanir the blade.

Andanir saw the blade was not shiny but had wavy patterns throughout. "Why is that one so expensive?"

"It's made out of Damascus steel from across the Small Ada Sea. The point will pierce steel armor without breaking while retaining its edge even when struck with a sword."

"There you are, Andanir." Ilina was walking with Master Ututur and looking at the vendors.

"Hi, I was looking around with my friend, Rialta."

"Hello, Rialta. I'm Ilina, and that's Ututur."

Andanir said, "She can't talk but that's all right. She's nice. Is it time to go home, master?"

"Yes, it's time. That's a fine dagger."

"Not many like it this far north," said the merchant.

"Maybe when I need a new one, I'll seek you out."

"My name is Dodek. I come to Mount Haven often."

"I'll keep that in mind. I'm Ututur, and this is Andanir. Good day to you."

"Good day."

Rialta got Andanir's attention, hugged him, used hand gestures to say that she had to go, and waved goodbye.

They walked back to Ilina's house and helped her carry the bundles of herbs and spices she purchased. She asked Ututur, "Do you know that girl?"

"Yes, she's Captain Bianco's niece. Her father died while working on a caravan, and her mother ran away after receiving the news. Since then, the girl hasn't said a word."

Andanir walked holding onto a large bundle of fresh brahmi leaves. "What are these good for?" he asked.

Ilina looked at him. "It's good in a tea. It's also used to relieve stress and can help when you have a stomachache." Turning to Ututur and Andanir she added, "I wish I could do something for her. Do you want to stay for dinner? It's almost vespers and time for supper."

Andanir waited for Ilina to go inside. "Can we stay, master?"

Ututur thought, *she is beautiful and kind.* "Sure, why not."

Ututur woke early next morning but instead of getting up immediately he lay in bed thinking about Ilina, her long dark hair, and how nice she was to the elf boy. It would be nice to have a wife. He shook his head; he had to get his mind focused. This was a busy day. He had to supervise the making of a new batch of dried beef jerky, a new batch of fresh cheese, and begin stocking the root cellar at the store for the winter. He would also meet with the Consul and the three other captains before lunch at sext to discuss the new baggage train and the composition of the army.

He got up, went to Andanir's room, and opened the door. Andanir wasn't there. Ututur went to the kitchen to find the boy already up and heating water for morning oat porridge with dried fruits. "The porridge is almost ready, master."

"You're up early."

"Yes, I can't wait to go to the training ground."

Ututur smiled and knew it must be because of Rialta. "It's good to enjoy training."

Andanir's fair skin couldn't hide his blushing cheeks. "Yes master," and brought out two bowls of porridge with a handful of mixed dried fruit and a small dollop of honey.

❀ ❀ ❀

Andanir ran to the training ground eager to start the day. The run was also a good way to warm up. He was early and saw Rialta going through some gymnastic exercises. He walked up to her, and she looked toward him as she completed her footwork forms. Andanir clapped. "That's great."

She smiled, walked over, and gave him a hug.

"We're here to work, not just hug," came a loud booming voice. Master Lucio walked into the main training area with his grey cape flowing behind him.

"Good morning, master," Andanir said with a low bow. Rialta bowed next to him.

"I think both of you are the same age or close enough. Rialta, I'm assigning you to help Andanir learn the defensive forms, and both of you can practice the basic throws. Remember, always be ready for a hidden knife or dagger. Don't get thrown, but if you do, get up as quickly as possible. Be ready to your vitals while you're down."

They both bowed as the sword master walked away to a smaller room for his first private student. After going through the defensive footwork, Rialta showed him the five basic throws; they practiced tripping and throwing each other with the inside leg sweep and outside leg sweep. After a short water break, they practiced throwing each other over the hip by trapping the head or gripping the clothing. They finished with her throwing him over her shoulders. Andanir got up a little dazed and bowed to her. Afterwards they practiced their dagger thrust attacks on straw dummies. Andanir loved working out with her and when it was time to go, he gave her a hug.

The elf boy smiled and bowed. "Thank you so much for showing me. I'll see you tomorrow. I have to go to my lessons with Master Ovidio."

Rialta bowed back and waved.

Consul Lorenz scanned the report again, facing the other High Council members and the captains. "I've received good news from Ostheim. Captain Martel and Vigiles Albrecht are in Beinn na Callaird. The sergeant's report indicates that by just using extra mounts and the mule train, they were able to cut two full days off the travel time from Ostheim to the elven capital. The sergeant added that they could cut another half day if they started earlier and moved faster on the first day."

Captain Voght was pleasantly surprised at the army's speed. "That's great news, but what about the newly reorganized footmen and crossbowmen? Should we consider having a contingent of mounted footmen?"

Lorenz added, "Yes, if we have to react in a speedy manner this new mobility will help us move our soldiers quickly to any part of the border. Every captain will have to be able to command a fully integrated force of infantry, cavalry, some missile troops, and their supply train."

"This is all fine and good in theory, but who'll attack us? We've been at peace with our neighbors to the north and west. The elves to the east are weak, their warriors were no match for our professional soldiers and trained militia. All of these changes are not free," said High Councilor Salce.

"You have a good point, Councilor Salce. But the safety of the United Cantons must be our primary concern. Even if we spend more money for the upkeep of the mule train and the military, in the long run we'll save money by reducing the number of days the soldiers are out in the field, thus reducing the cost of supplies used and reducing the number of paid days for the militia," said Head Councilor di Bartolo.

Councilor Salce frowned a little, but seemed satisfied with the answer and didn't add any other objections.

Councilor Schwertfeger sat up straighter. "Do you have any more news about the attacks on the farms by those elves, Sheriff Bastina?"

"No, I've traveled to all of the outlying farms within thirty double paced miles from Mount Haven; no other attacks have been reported. I've also traveled to Ostheim to check with their watchmen and soldiers."

"Good, continue your investigations, sheriff. For now, let's continue to reorganize the army and the baggage train. We'll meet again as soon as we've heard back from either Mistress Albretch or Captain Martel." As the meeting ended, the members of the High Council and the captains broke up into small side conversations.

"Captain Bunour, I would like a word with you," said Consul Lorenz.

"Yes, Consul."

"Your system works well. I think we'll reorganize our entire army in this way."

"Even the rearguard?" asked Ututur.

"Yes, there will be no rearguard unless we field our entire army. Captain Pfeiffer's vanguard will be our fastest element comprised of only of light horse and light mounted infantry with spear, shield, and chain mail. They will be accompanied by mounted crossbowmen and a mobile ballista. Master Ovidio has built a smaller mobile ballista. He said we can mount it on a wagon or transport it in sections by mule. Captain Pfeiffer's light force will be able to march even faster," explained Aldous.

"Will I travel with the vanguard?"

"Yes, if they are the only troops deployed. However, if the entire army is deployed, the center will travel with wagons and the traditional baggage train, and the vanguard will travel ahead with their own mule train. I'll make a determination when the time comes where I'll need you."

It sounds like we'll all have independent and flexible commands," noted Ututur. "But I need to learn more about mass infantry and calvary tactics."

"I agree, I'll send you some classic treatises on war from my library. I think the other captains also need to learn more. We'll meet and have simulated battles on a map; I'll act as judge. You must teach the other captains and senior sergeants how to organize the supply train. Everyone must know how much food the army needs on the march," said Lorenz. "Here, start with these." The Consul handed two books, translated into common to Ututur to read.

"Thank you, Aldous," said Ututur. "I'll read them as soon as I get the chance.

On her way out, Captain Bianco touched his arm. "May I have a word?"

"Yes, how may I be of service?"

"Call me Rosanella. I found out that my niece has become friends with your charge. The elf boy."

"Yes, Andanir. They seem to enjoy each other's company."

"Yes, I think they'll be good for one another, she likes him a lot. I just wanted you to know she's a smart girl. It's just she hasn't spoken since her father died, and her mother left. I was worried about her because she has no friends."

"Andanir is very gentle. He also doesn't have many friends here." The half-orc remembered his own lonely childhood with his grandfather and wanted something different for the boy.

"I'll have you both over for dinner one of these days."

"That would be wonderful, thank you," said Ututur as Captain Pfeiffer joined their conversation.

"Captain Bunour, when we have our next training day, can you go over the carrying capacity of the mules and how far they can travel with the sergeants of the vanguard? Some of the soldiers from the city are not familiar with how to work with pack animals."

"Please it's Ututur. Yes, I'll be happy to do so."

"And you can call me Max."

Ututur chatted with other members of the High Council and the other captains a little while longer and left feeling confident that the mule train would be a good supplement to the traditional wagon train. He hoped they wouldn't need to use them soon.

Chapter 14

Wilhelm stumbled from exhaustion; he had discarded all of the unnecessary items and all of his armor. He carried Kiley after their successful ambush. She had fainted right after the fight; while she didn't weigh much carrying her piggyback for the entire day sapped his energy. She faded in and out of consciousness and often moaned in pain. He checked her wounds to make sure she wasn't bleeding. This was not the easy trip back home he had expected. He thought that he was getting close to the secondary road leading to the outskirts of Ostheim. However, he'd never taken this particular hunting trail. At each step he worried that they were lost; it was taking too long to get out of these woods. He had to get back to Ostheim, in order to get word back to the High Council. He needed to warn his people before the attack.

He stopped, set Kiley down, and looked at her weakened form. He wondered if he should abandon her here and run as fast as he could to Ostheim. He could send help to rescue her. He took another sip of water from his water skin and tried to force the half-conscious elf to take a few sips. Looking at the frail elf, he realized he couldn't leave her out here. He took another sip, lifted her on his back, and continued his westward trek. Wilhelm tried to focus on taking one step at a time even as his leg muscles ached.

The sun was high in the sky; the weather was still hot during the day, but the early autumn chill was in the air during the mornings and evenings. Wilhelm lost his footing and almost fell over. He avoided dropping the elf but twisted his right ankle. He stopped in pain and placed her on the ground.

Kiley was awake. "Please, you should leave me and go get help for my people."

"No, we must be close, and I don't want to explain why I left you behind. Here, have some water."

She took a sip and gave back the water skin. Wilhelm's clothes were soaked with sweat from both the heat and the exertion. He got her back on his back and began to walk again. "So, what do you like doing for fun?"

"What?" Kiley asked.

"You know, when you have time to yourself?"

"I like to play music and read stories." She sighed.

"What kind of music? Do you play an instrument, or do you sing?"

Kiley coughed and said, "I play the drums and the lute."

"I think I'm tone deaf. I can't sing or play any instruments, but I do enjoy listening to music."

"I'll play for you sometime when we have the chance."

Wilhelm continued to talk and asked her more questions but soon realized that he was talking to himself. She had fainted again, and he did his best not to jostle her as he limped along. He was beginning to lose hope that they would reach the town today. The sun was setting and the western sky was a beautiful orange. He strained himself to continue despite the pain, scrambling up an embankment. As soon as he reached the top, he felt the ground even out. He saw the road ahead of him and felt relief. With renewed energy he adjusted Kiley on his back and walked toward the setting sun.

"When we have time, I'll take you to dinner, and if you want to you can play for me." Wilhelm continued his one-sided conversation just to keep his mind off his ankle. He realized she was snoring on his back, asleep. She almost sounded like a kitten. His legs and arm muscles burned as he put one foot in front of the other toward Ostheim. The sun had set, as he recognized more landmarks, knew that the city walls were not too much further. He stumbled once again, almost dropping her, recovered. His ankle throbbed with every step; he felt a hole in his left riding boot and was almost tempted to remove both boots. "I'll get you to Ostheim, and I promise to get help for your people," he said to the unconscious elf on his back.

Out of the darkness he heard "Halt! Who goes there! Identify yourself!" He could see armed figures with torches approaching. "It's me, Captain Martel. Help me with this wounded elf."

"Yes, sir," came a startled voice.

"Get me Sergeants Pierluigi and Netland at once and have someone bring some food and water to my quarters. Get her to a healer as fast as you can." Wilhelm let his men take the elf to the Sun Temple hospital run by the priests of Hillin the Protectrice. He walked as quickly as he could as several men escorted him to his room.

"Let the sergeants in as soon as they arrive." He took off all of his dirty clothes and limped to the washroom where he cleaned his body with cold water from the barrel. He used the scented soap to clean his matted hair and greasy beard. His ankle was swollen and discolored. He focused his mind on what he had to do next as he put on some clean woolen pants and a linen shirt.

A loud knock came from his door and Sergeant Biagio Pierluigi, a veteran of twenty-five summers as a professional solider, walked in with a concerned look on his face. Sergeant Ingrid Netland followed close behind. She stood in sharp contrast to the old veteran. She was young and recently promoted. She looked more like a well-mannered lady than a professional soldier. Pierluigi had been Wilhelm's first sergeant when he joined the army as a young soldier and continued to be at Wilhelm's side since his promotion to captain.

Wilhelm dried his hair and hobbled to a chair. "Can someone write a letter for me?"

Sergeant Pierluigi opened the door and asked the guard outside, "Where's the healer?" Turning to the Captain he said, "You don't look good, Wil."

Ingrid sat at the desk and readied a piece of parchment.

"I'm in pain, but we have to act quickly. I want to ride out with the troops tomorrow with as many mules as we need to support the soldiers. Have an experienced veteran take two hundred foot soldiers and make sure the hunting trails through the woods are clear. Tell them to stay on our side of the border."

The older sergeant asked, "Where're we going? Are we going to fight?"

"Biagio we're going toward Beinn na Callaird, but we may find the enemy before we reach the city. We're going to fight alongside the eastern elves against northern tribal elves. These dark elves are responsible for the massacres near Mount Haven. They ambushed us on the way back. Warn the men these northern elves use dark magic."

The old sergeant sat down in a chair, turned to face his captain. "I've never really seen magic but I've heard tales. How can we win? How will our boys know which elves to fight?"

Wilhelm took out the two items he had saved: the elven letter to the council and the drawings of the runes on the dead elves. "Biagio, our enemies will wear these runes on their bodies, but they are not immune to the blade." Meanwhile, the steward brought in a tray of cold roasted chicken, bread, and apples. Wilhelm ate while he dictated a message to the High Council describing the situation. "Ingrid, make sure you tell them this is an emergency. Tell them that we're going into Litauia under the banner of the Vigiles to aid the elves."

Sergeant Pierluigi looked at the runes. "I'll try to prepare the men, but magic!"

Wilhelm looked at both of his sergeants. "Biagio, Ingrid, we'll be fine if we remember our training. Ingrid, send a messenger to deliver both my letter and the letter from the elves to the High Council immediately." Wilhelm limped over to Ingrid and put his seal on the letter she closed with hot wax. As soon as the wax was dry, she ran out of the room to find messengers.

Sergeant Pierluigi stayed behind watching Wilhelm eat. "If we go under the banner of the Vigiles we'll be limited to one thousand men total. That means we'll have to travel light and bring less skilled craftsmen and workers with us in the supply train."

Wilhelm sat back down and propped his leg up. "Speed is of the essence; we should stay on the road as much as possible and bring one of the mobile ballistas."

"Yes, I'll ready one wagon mounted ballista, and we'll take all five hundred professional soldiers and three hundred militiamen who can ride. We'll carry all of the spears and shields on the wagons and mules. I'll make sure to leave behind enough veterans for the city's defense. You need to rest Wil, if you're going to ride with us."

"Right. Where's that damned healer?" he asked trying to get comfortable.

The older man got up to leave and patted the younger man's shoulders and threw a blanket on hm. "Rest easy; I'll take care of the preparations and make the selections. We'll be ready as soon as the sun rises."

As Wilhelm finished his food, a guard knocked and came in. "Lord Captain, three fast messengers left for Mount Haven. They should arrive there by late afternoon tomorrow if all goes well."

Wilhelm finished his wine. "Good. Is the healer coming?"

"I'll go check, My Lord."

The healer from the Sun temple wrapped his foot with bandages and told him to keep it elevated. Nothing was broken. He told Wilhelm that the elven maiden was doing fine. Another healer was tending to her while she rested. The healer insisted that the ankle should stay wrapped for a few days, but how was he going to wear boots? He fell asleep in his chair and woke feeling tired and sore. The sun was rising and he had to take off the wrapping to get his boots on. At least some of the swelling had lessened.

By the time he reached the courtyard the soldiers were prepared to march. Both of his sergeants had worked most of the night and the early hours before sunrise making preparations. A footman brought him a horse. He tried to sit comfortably but still ached from his recent ordeal. He mounted his horse and waited for his soldiers to get ready. "Sergeant Pierluigi, who's the next senior man?"

"It's Abelard; he has been serving for fifteen years and has a good head on his shoulders."

Wilhelm winced in pain when he put too much pressure on his sprained ankle. "Promote him to First and have him lead the foot patrol toward the border. Make sure that path is clear. Afterwards, he'll remain in Ostheim to help organize the militia and make sure they're in fighting condition. When we get back, I'm going to promote you to sub-Captain and promote him to Sergeant."

"Thank you, Lord Captain."

"Let's move out slowly." Wilhelm guided his horse out of the marshaling area at a slow walking pace. His small force consisted of five hundred professional soldiers and two hundred mounted militia with crossbows, supported by one mobile ballista on a wagon with a crew of ten. His rearguard was comprised of one hundred and fifty people leading ten wagons and one hundred mules. He was leaving behind four thousand militiamen to guard the city. They were a mixed group of fully trained soldiers and raw untrained recruits. "By midday I want you to send out ten messengers to make contact with the elves from Beinn na Callaird. I want to know where we should join them for battle. As soon as we cross the border, we'll send out patrols along the road to look for ambushes. Wear this." Wilhelm handed Pierluigi his old captain's red sash.

Pierluigi took the sash and placed it around his waist. "Thank you, Captain. I'll lead one of the patrols myself. I want to see the lay of the land once we cross the border. In all these years, I've never been near Beinn na Callaird. I'll have Sergeant Netland take a troop of fifty horsemen ahead to make sure the road is clear."

"Good! Make it so. I don't think we'll get to visit the city this time, my friend." Wilhelm watched hundreds of people line the streets to say farewell to his soldiers. Some of the small children were weeping while others craned their necks to see their fathers and mothers ride off to an unknown danger. A tall bald priest of Hillin the Protector arrived with five other priests and priestesses from the Sun Temple. They all wore the necklaces with a stylized sun emblem. He was supposed to be the giver of life and creation. Wilhelm walked his horse out of the column and approached the senior priest, recognizable by his ornate staff. "We could use your blessings. We may face an evil and powerful sorcerer soon."

The priest raised his hand, came closer. "We'll do what we can." He walked back and began singing a song of blessing. The other five joined in; the song cut through the morning and a calm came over the marching army.

Wilhelm spurred his horse and went down the line to inspect his soldiers. As the song drifted among his soldiers, he felt a slight tingle run up and down his spine and the pain in his ankle lessened. The professional soldiers looked like they were just going on another patrol. In contrast, the men and women from the militia looked nervous. He spotted a young-looking man who wore his chainmail without his padded shirt. "You there, get out of line and come here," he commanded. The boy looked frightened. Wilhem said, "Calm down. What's your name?"

"Ahren, Lord Captain," the boy replied. "Am I in trouble?"

"No, but you need to take that mail shirt off and wear your regular shirt, never wear the chainmail without your padded shirt. Without the undergarments your skin will be rubbed raw before the day is over, and your sweat is not good for the armor. You can carry the chain mail behind you on the saddle."

A militia sergeant came out of line toward them. "I'm Sergeant Wulfnoth. Is there anything wrong, Captain?"

"No, Sergeant, just making sure the equipment is secure. Carry on," he said as he rode further down the line to check on the rest of the column, finally stopping at the first wagon. The wagon had one of the new mounted mobile ballista which was untested in battle. "What's your name? Have you tested this rig yet?"

"It's Savin, and yes my Lord. We received this about five days ago. My boys and I practiced putting it together. We've test-fired it several times. It's capable of deadly accuracy up to two furlongs, or about four hundred double paces."

Wilhelm considered the ambush he had survived. "On the battlefield I want you to look for anyone who appears to be wielding any kind of magic."

As Wilhelm rode on and continued his impromptu inspection, the wagon driver turned to Savin. "How are we going to tell if it's a magic user?"

"I don't know, Dario. We'll pick targets like we've been taught. We'll hit everyone with a fancy hat. Anyone who looks like they're telling people what to do will get a stick. Right? How many broadheads and extra fletchings did you bring?"

"We have thirty bolts with enough extra points and feathers to make another forty or so, and we have extra rope in case the one we're using breaks," said Dario.

Chapter 15

High Priestess Lady Sioban was furious. "You let two get away?"

Rianor was on her knees, her head bowed. "I sent four warriors after them, and the female elf was wounded."

"But they failed! Get out of my sight; you'll travel with Trahern on another mission. Go and prepare to leave. Pray for redemption."

"Now Trahern, I have a new task for you. The goddess is sending a large war band of northern elves; they are marching and gathering strength as they move south toward Beinn no Callaird. Go meet them; guide them through the woods to the east of the city. Wait there; we want the city elves to think we're going to attack from the east."

Trahern was eager to kill humans and eliminate the weak city elves who had forgotten their heritage and turned their backs on the old ways. "Yes, My Lady. Will we have victory?"

"No, Trahern. The humans and these southern elves are too strong. This will only help weaken them for the future. We'll sacrifice many in the coming days to Larvanis. The goddess will weaken the enemy as we gain strength and power. We'll prepare to strike these weaklings from within. You'll soon go and meet a warrior called Catguallaun; he leads the war band south."

"Yes, my Lady. May the goddess protect us." He bowed low and left thinking about how the humans and the weak southern elves would soon suffer for forsaking their culture.

Catguallaun dreamt every night of the past glories of the northern elves as the goddess showed him the visions of restored elven cities. Many others who joined the war band also had similar visions. They numbered at least ten thousand. He felt proud of these warriors who left everything behind to answer the call of the goddess. He was preparing to sleep for the night when he heard a female voice. "Don't be afraid, Catguallaun. I'll help you save the elves from human influence. I'll help you lift up our people to their former glory. An elf called Trahern is coming with a priestess to guide you. She'll help your warriors fight the humans and the elven traitors. Fight with the bravery of old and soak this sacred land with blood."

Ginevra and the other riders were exhausted by the time they reached Mount Haven. With the help of a city guard, Ginevra rode to the Consul's home while her companions took care of the tired mounts. It was past vespers but not yet compline by the time she knocked on the door.

"Who is it?" asked Consul Lorenz as he opened his door dressed in comfortable pants and a loose linen shirt.

"I'm Ginevra; I have two letters, one for you and the other for the High Council. This is from Captain Wilhelm Martel, and the other is from the elves of Litauia."

"Come in and wait." He opened Captain Martel's letter first and read it twice. He then opened the letter from the elves.

He turned to the city guard. "I want you to send messengers to all of the captain generals and tell them to come to my house immediately. Tell them it's urgent. Inform the High Council I'm calling an emergency meeting tomorrow morning at lauds as the sun rises. Have them ready to call a meeting of the entire council as soon as possible."

"Ginevra, I want you to rest, but first go find other messengers and send them back to Ostheim with my message." The Consul went to his writing desk and quickly wrote a simple message. "Message received. Good luck. We're on our way."

"Yes, my Lord Consul. But I'd rather take the message back myself with my companions."

"As you wish."

Ututur was just finishing dishes from supper while thinking about Ilina and whether he should ask her to go to the fall festival with him. Andanir was playing outside looking for lighting bugs; suddenly, he ran into the house. "Master, a rider is coming. I think it's a soldier."

Ututur washed the last mug and dried his hands on a rag. "Let's see what he wants." They both walked outside and in a few moments they saw a rider with a hooded lantern approach.

"Lord captain, your presence is required at the Consul's house immediately. It's an emergency."

"Right, I'll be there as soon as I can." When he looked down at Andanir, he could see the worry on the little elf's face. "Get a few things; I'm taking you to Ilina's."

"Yes, master." Andanir ran to his room to get Enbarr, his toy horse, and his blanket and place it in an old burlap sack.

"We have to hurry, so get on my back Andanir," said Ututur. When the boy was securely on his back, the half-orc trotted toward Ilina's home. By the time he reached it, night had fallen, but Ututur's vision was almost as good as a dwarf's in the dark. Before he reached for the door, Ututur realized he might have made a mistake; what if she had company or a male visitor? He almost turned away, but the Consul seldom called emergency meetings. He took a long deep breath and knocked on the door. Ututur didn't realize that Andanir had fallen asleep riding on his back. Ilina looked through the small, hinged metal viewer and opened the door as soon as she saw him.

"I'm sorry to ask you, but there's an emergency meeting with the Consul. I didn't want to leave him alone," he said, pointing with his head toward the sleeping form on his huge back.

"It's fine; bring him in and put him on the guest bed in the other room."

Ututur laid Andanir as gently as he could on the small guest bed and turned toward Ilina, who was standing close to him. "I don't know when I'll be done with the meeting."

She said, "Don't worry. Come get him tomorrow; I'll take care of him."

"This may be a call to arms, and I may have to go on campaign."

"Don't worry. I'll be happy to have him stay with me as long as you need."

"Thank you so much," he said as he walked toward the door.

"Good luck. I hope there is not going to be more fighting," said Ilina as she kept the fear out of her voice.

"Thank you for coming," the Consul said as he watched his

captains across the map table. He'd explained the situation and what Captain Martel had done. "We'll utilize the one thousand professional soldiers we have first, but I'll also take two thousand militiamen and reinforce Ostheim. Captain Vogt, you'll remain here and guard the capital; if you need to, you can muster the militia and prepare to defend the city or send more troops to us at Ostheim."

"Yes, my Lord Consul. Has the High Council been notified?" asked Vogt.

"Yes, I sent a messenger to all the members. They've started their own emergency contact chain. Captain Pfeiffer, I want you to take a force of two hundred mounted men and patrol the northern road; make sure no one is crossing the border north of Ostheim. If you have to engage, conduct a fighting withdrawal toward Ostheim and send word."

"How far north should I go?" asked Pfeiffer, looking at the map. On the map, the Consul pointed to the foothills of the Jotunheimen mountains. "Here, where the dwarven lands begin. Captain Rosanella and Captain Ututur, you'll come with me to Ostheim. We'll react to the situation as it develops across the border and wait for news from Wilhelm and the elves. I plan to leave tomorrow afternoon as soon as the militia can be mustered. Now go make your preparations. Ututur and Rosanella, stay for a moment."

After the others had left Aldous said, "I want both of you to move as rapidly as possible to Ostheim with the one thousand professional soldiers. Unlike the militia, they are flexible and are trained as both cavalry and infantry. You'll leave the workers and healers behind travel as lightly as possible."

"Yes, my Lord," replied Rosanella although she didn't like leaving behind most of the healers, armorers, farriers, leather workers, and scribes that were normally part of the baggage train. This would force Ututur and her to take on additional roles, but she understood the need for speed.

"How many crossbows should we take? And how many men from the baggage train should I bring?" asked Ututur.

Consul Lorenz pondered for a moment. "Take a hundred crossbows, and I'll bring two hundred more. I think you'll need at least fifty mules. Take enough people to control the animals. I'll deal with the rest of the baggage train for the militia myself. Do you have someone that's experienced who can help me?"

"Understood, my Lord, and I've an experienced man named Sigmund Pasak and a young woman, Adala Mann. They'll be able to help you organize the rearguard. Sigmund is a veteran footman with experience in the militia and is steady under stress," said Ututur.

"Good. Tell them to report to me and I'll see you both tomorrow morning."

The Chieftain lay in his bed thinking, *I can't remember why I'm in bed. I feel so weak, and why haven't I seen Andanir? I should get out of bed and see what Doireann is up to. Bandit, why do you have a muzzle?* He couldn't remember anything clearly, and when he slid his legs off the bed, he almost collapsed. He looked down, realizing that his leg muscles had atrophied and couldn't even support his own weight. He felt himself falling and could not hold himself up. He stumbled against a table next to his bed and collapsed. The water jug on the table broke into pieces. He tried to rise but could not.

Lady Sioban heard the commotion and ran in. "You stupid old fool! What do you think you're doing out of bed?"

Osin felt confused and looked around the room as Bandit began to growl. "What's going on?" he asked softly.

Lady Sioban raised her hand to hit the dog; Bandit cowered, bared his teeth, and retreated to the corner. "I'll get rid of you both soon." She turned to the weakened chieftain; with her strength magnified by the rituals she had little difficulty in getting him back into bed. Afterwards she went across the room to her dresser and retrieved more of the special potion. She must have forgotten to give him the medicine yesterday. Did the maid forget to remind her? After, she quickly forced the medicine down the old fool's throat she yelled, "Help, the Chieftain has fallen! I need help!"

Without much delay, several servants came running as well as her daughter. They helped clean up the broken shards of pottery on the floor, and she ordered them to bring another jug of water. By the time the servants returned the Chieftain was asleep.

"Thank you; now leave me with my husband," the High Priestess commanded.

Eithne looked back and felt that before the old elf passed out his eyes looked desperate and seemed to be pleading for help. *Why does he need so much medicine?*

Sioban turned and said, "Take that dog with you, Eithne. I don't want to see it again in here. Have a servant get rid of it."

"Yes, Mother. Come here, Bandit." As Eithne walked Bandit out of the room she saw him look back and bare his teeth. She handed him off to a waiting servant.

As soon as she heard the door shut, Lady Sioban bent close to the Chieftain's face. "Don't cause any more trouble or I'll make you feel tremendous pain. Do you understand?" She punched him as hard as she could in the stomach.

Osin Noldorin, once a proud warrior and a renown hunter let out a weak gasp. He nodded his head and began to feel his consciousness fade again into darkness.

Lady Sioban stood and looked at her face in the mirror and smiled. The goddess had restored her health and some of her youth. Then the voice whispered, "There'll be battle soon. But the northern elves have become degenerates and are weak. They've little chance of winning against the humans. Whether they win this battle or not, you'll form an alliance with the humans and gain more followers. I've begun to identify more willing followers among the humans and other races. They'll help us restore balance to the world and rebuild my strength."

"Can't you help the northern elves gain victory?"

"I can, but they're weak and do not deserve victory. I can give you power, but success depends on your own strength and cunning. I need you to prepare a sacrifice for the harvest moon."

"Yes, my Lady."

CHAPTER 16

Grand Master Azmi Issawi of the Vigiles sat in his private office leaning back in his comfortable chair away from his desk. He reread Greta Albrecht's letter three times. The news was disturbing. He sent for Master Harun Faheem, an experienced scholar and investigator, then looked again at the letter without reading it, just gazing at the runes depicted in the letter.

Harun knocked once and walked in wearing his loose clothing and blue turban. "Good morning, Azmi."

"Come in, Harun. I know you were planning to step down from the Vigiles this winter, but I have to ask you to investigate something for me. This is urgent."

Harun stood there for a moment before sitting down. "My friend, I'm old and…"

Azmi stopped Harun mid-sentence with a raised hand. "Sit, my friend. I know, but you're one of the few active members of our order who has experience investigating evil magic. Over the centuries our order has lost a lot of knowledge of how to fight dark magic." Harun had rooted out a group of evil magicians in the southern city states and in the dwarven lands years ago. The magicians weren't powerful and were easy to track down and kill before they could gain power. Otherwise, there had been no reports of dark magic since the Goblin Wars. Dark magic always involved the sacrifice of living beings, and over the centuries the Vigiles helped destroy this dark threat in the civilized world. "We may have a dark sorceress coming out in the open among the elves of Litauia." The Grand Master handed his friend Albrecht's letter.

Harun stroked his greying beard while he read the letter. "If this report was accurate, we must warn everyone. Dark sorcery spreads quickly like a wildfire blown by an evil dry wind. You must look for some of the old relics and books in this keep."

"I've already sent messengers to the three western kingdoms and to the southern city states. I've sent instructions to everyone in our order to investigate any strange incidents and missing persons. I'm even sending a mission to the dwarven and orcish lands to the north. A mission will be sent across the Ada Sea to warn the northern Bedu tribes and beyond. I'm tempted to send a mission across to the Thunder Horse nomadic clans of the eastern steppe to warn people of this rising evil."

Harun stroked his long grey beard. "If you are going to send a mission that far east, you should also try to warn the San Empire and the Kingdom of Cinam."

"Perhaps. Will you help me investigate this evil?"

"Yes, I'll do it for our friendship. When should I go?" asked the aging Vigiles.

"You should leave before the mountain passes close for the winter. You'll have help from two full members of our order in Mount Haven. I can send more help next spring. But for now, go undercover and only let other Vigiles know your identity."

Harun nodded. "I'll be ready to leave after the midday meal. I believe that I should be able to join one of the last trade caravans going east, posing as a traveling scholar studying plants and flowers of Nixland."

"Thank you, and go with the gods, my friend," said Azmi, as he embraced his old friend and kissed him on both cheeks. "I'll have some of the scholars look into the old stored relics used in the past to fight dark sorcerers."

Harun left the meeting and walked to his chambers thinking, *I'm getting too old for this. This will be my last mission, and as soon as this is done, I'm going to retire to the southern city sates and spend my time drinking wine and researching plants and flowers.*

Consul Lorenz gazed at the soldiers slowly marching past him with Rosanella and Ututur by his side. Family members stood waving goodbye to their loved ones while several priests and priestesses from the different temples blessed the troops as they rode out.

Ututur asked, "Why is this happening? Do you think there'll be any fighting?"

"I hope not. The eastern city elves are not well-equipped, and they haven't adopted modern ways of fighting. It depends how many northern elves attack and where they strike. Captain Pfeiffer left at first light taking the northern road and he'll conduct a reconnaissance in force. I'll march toward Ostheim with the militia. I want you to move beyond Ostheim as fast as you can; send scouts to Wilhelm and let him know where you are and that we're on the way. Make sure the enemy doesn't attack his rear. I want you and Rosanella to help find and fix the enemy's position."

"We'll do our best," she said. "By your leave, my Lord Consul, I'm going to check on the soldiers."

"Good luck," he replied. "This is serious business. I asked Master Ovidio if he could help, but he told me he's busy doing research on the runes from the massacre sites and didn't want to leave. However, he did give me this crystal necklace. He said that this will provide some protection. Rosanella, you take it. Excuse me, I have to see how the militia is doing."

Rosanella took the crystal necklace and put it in her inner vest pocket. "Thank you. With any luck, the elves will be able to work this out among themselves."

"I hope so." Muttered the half-orc worried. Ututur moved near the huge draft horse he would ride and waited for the column to pass.

"Master," came a high-pitched voice.

Ututur turned and saw Ilina and Andanir walking toward him. "Thank you, Ilina, for taking care of Andanir while I'm gone."

"You're welcome, and don't worry; we'll be fine," she said.

"Master, are you going to fight?" asked Andanir with a worried expression. He was stilled troubled by the battle he had experienced and didn't want to lose anyone else he cared about. He didn't have the nightmares every night since staying with Ututur but he had one last night.

"I don't think so; we're just going to make sure we aren't attacked." Ututur squatted down. "Don't worry; like my grandfather used to say; fear not death for none may escape it, so live life to the fullest while you breathe. I'll be back soon."

Ilina hugged him when he stood and gave him a bundle. "Here, take these bandages; and the mixture of wild honey and herbs to prevent putrification of wounds."

Ututur saw tears form in both Ilina's and Andanir's eyes. "I have to get going. I'll be fine; this is probably nothing."

Andanir tugged at his shirt and held out the gold torc he wore around his neck. "This was my mother's; it'll help protect you."

"I can't take it," said Ututur.

"You can give it back when you return."

Ututur took it and placed it around his wrist. He thought the torc felt unusually warm. *It's probably because it has been around Andanir's neck.* He mounted the huge horse, waved good-bye, and urged the horse forward as they watched him ride off with the rest of the soldiers.

Wilhelm sent small groups on patrols as his column of eight hundred rode toward Ar d'Tus Chathair. He was going to make camp to the east of the town and wait for word from Eoin. As his army approached the elven border town, Bacstair was waiting for him with around thirty elven warriors at the border. Wilhelm halted the column. "Hello, Bacstair."

"Hello, I was told to expect soldiers, but so many? What's going on?" the old elven leader asked.

"We might be at war soon with some northern elves. Your Warlord is not sure where the enemy will strike," Wilhelm replied.

"Our warriors have not seen anything unusual."

"I see. I want to take my soldiers and make camp east of your town."

"Good, I'll send word to the capital of your approach," said Bacstair as he came closer to Wilhelm.

"I'm expecting more soldiers from Nixland; please tell them where I'm camped and help any of the scouts or messengers that may ride through. I'll send some of my soldiers to buy fresh provisions from your town."

"I'll have the farmers ready to give you what they can spare and sell you the goods you need. We'll have the supplies at the big barn near the stable at the center of town. Good luck, Captain," said the older elven leader.

"Thank you." Wilhelm bowed from his saddle. He signaled his troops to move forward, and they rode through the center of town while elves gathered and gawked at the human army.

Eoin was worried about Kiley, the newly elevated Second; his scouts had discovered the ambush site and brought the dead warriors back for their funeral rites. However, Kiley's and Wilhelm's bodies weren't among the recovered. He just hoped they were safe. He could only send out a small search party because a scouting party had just returned from the north with bad news. They had discovered a large force of dark eves from the north, "My lord Eachmhile, we may not receive any aid from Nixland in time," he said.

The elven Warlord frowned and gazed at the map. "We'll call all of the warriors nearby; we have to prepare to defend the capital."

The Second looked at the map and pointed north of Beinn na Callaird. "Vigiles, my scouts have spotted a huge army that is marching south. They saw at least 10,000. These dark elves had only one banner bearing an ancient rune like the ones you showed us with a crescent moon over a tree."

Vigiles Albrecht had run into a dead end in her search for the evil sorceress, but the northern elves marching south couldn't be a coincidence. "Did your scouts see anything else unusual?"

The Second replied, "No. I just don't know why this is happening. We've never really had any problems like this with the northern tribes."

The Warlord looked up from studying his map. "They've never united like this before, at least not since the Goblin War. Without more information we can't deploy our warriors. Eoin, send out more scouts; we must know where these elves are headed."

The Second pointed to the map. "I've already sent out three more scouting parties along this area. We'll find them soon. At least no goblins have been sighted."

Vigiles said, "I would like to stay here. I'm curious how these northern elves come to fly the ancient rune as their banner."

While his soldiers made camp three double-paced miles outside of Ar d'Tus Chathair, Wilhelm rested on a blanket and studied his map with his Sergeants Wulfnoth and Pierluigi. He had been at camp for two days and waited for a response from Eoin to his message.

"Riders approaching!" a sentry cried out.

Pierluigi said, "I'll go see what it is."

A few moments later he escorted an elf messenger to his captain. The elf bowed. "I have a letter from Eoin, the Second. He also told me to thank you and that he received your message. He said to make sure to stay to the west of Beinn na Callaird because we don't know where the enemy is headed yet."

Wilhelm took the letter and opened it. It showed a rough map of the enemy east of the elven capital.

The elven messenger asked, "Do you have a return message?

"Bring me a quill and some parchment."

Pierluigi brought him a small wooden writing box.

The captain wrote out a simple message and said, "Tell your Second and your Warlord that we'll wait here for more troops from Nixland."

The messenger bowed and ran back to his horse.

"Well, I guess we'll be here a while, make sure to post sentries and send out regular patrols. Did Sergeant Netland return yet?"

"Not yet. I think she intended to get close to the elven capital before swinging north and turning back," replied Pierluigi.

"Thank you, I'm going to rest a little. Wake me if there is any news." Wilhelm was still tired from carrying Kiley on his back, and his ankle throbbed when he walked. Sergeant Wulfnoth stood to leave. "Captain, will I have time to do some extra training with the militia?"

"Yes, but don't work them too hard."

"As you command my Lord," replied the militia sergeant.

On the second day out of Mount Haven the half-orc found himself walking his horse often. He had never been a great rider because he learned how to ride as an adult. In fact, Orcs didn't keep horses in the mountains and would trade or eat any they captured. In contrast, Rosanella seemed comfortable riding all day. Ututur was about to remount his horse when a rider came from the east. The column continued forward and met the rider. Rosanella gave the order to halt while they talked to the messenger.

"Captain Martel sent me. He's moving east and would like to know how fast he can expect you," the rider said.

Rosanella turned to Ututur. "What do you think?"

"I think we'll be able to reach Ostheim by the end of the day tomorrow," he replied.

"Have you seen the enemy yet?" she asked the rider.

The messenger took a drink of water from his water skin. "No, but Captain Martel was attacked by northern elves led by a magic user. He was carrying a wounded elf girl, who we left recovering in Ostheim. He asks that you come as fast as you can."

After doing some calculations in his head Ututur said, "We could move faster and get beyond Ostheim if we don't rest for too long during the middle of the day."

Rosanella said, "Yes, tell Captain Martel we'll move as fast as we can."

"Thank you."

"Do you need anything?" asked Ututur, looking at the dust-covered man.

"May I have a fresh horse?"

"Yes, take one of our spare horses and take yours so you can change mounts as you travel. Good luck."

"Well, I guess we didn't need the Vigiles to find out who's responsible for the dark sorcery," said Rosanella as the messenger left.

"Maybe, but we still don't know where it began. We only know that the northern elves are involved. Let's have the men eat and rest now. That way we don't have to rest later."

"I'll see to it," said Rosanella.

Eoin rushed into Warlord's map room. A patrol had spotted the bulk of the northern elves moving to the east of the Beinn na Callaird where they would have open ground. He ran into the main chamber and said, "My Lord," stopping when he saw the High Priestess speaking. Lady Sioban was there with several attendants.

"If you have news, don't stop on my account," Lady Sioban said in a smooth, silky voice. Was it his imagination, or did she look younger? The youthful glow of her skin was undeniable.

"A scouting party has spotted the dark elves approaching the city from the northeast."

"How many?" asked the Warlord.

"No less than ten thousand, my Lord, perhaps up to fifteen thousand. A group of scouts are shadowing their movements and trying to get a better count. They're two days' march away from the open plains to our east."

"We'll keep our warriors behind the city walls and prepare for a siege. Did the scouts notice any siege weapons or any large wagon train?" asked Warlord Eachmhile.

"No, my Lord; they're all on foot," the Second said. "I've received word from the humans; a column of soldiers has camped outside of Ar d'Tus Chathair and is ready to support us. Both Captain Martel and Saoirse the Second are alive. He's leading the human column."

"Excuse me," Lady Sioban interrupted. "If the dark elves are coming to attack our city from the east, shouldn't we keep all of our soldiers here to defend the walls, and if they don't have siege weapons, we won't even need the help of humans."

The Warlord continued to study his large map. "If the scouts' information is trustworthy, then you have a point High Priestess. We don't have to fight outside these walls." Turning to his Second he added, "Make additional preparations for a siege and send word to the humans to remain where they are and wait for further developments."

Eoin didn't like this. Why would they even try to conduct a siege without siege engines of any kind? Even in the stories from the old Goblin Wars, armies with access to magic still used siege engines against fortified towns and castles. "Yes, my Lord, I'll check the preparations." Eoin bowed slightly before leaving. "Good day my Lord, High Priestess."

❊❊❊

Lady Sioban left the meeting with a smile on her face. If the elves stayed in the city, she could send the northern elves to defeat the humans who were camped west, then turn and attack the city from the west. They could weaken or even defeat the humans out in the open. Her army would have a chance at victory. It wasn't necessary, but it would be nice. She hurried to leave the Warlord's office and took her attendants to the warehouse where all her acolytes, followers of Larvanis, waited. She had purged the sisterhood of the followers of the Huntress. She smiled knowing only two days remained till the harvest moon.

The three walked into the cavern and Lady Sioban saw Roisin in the antechamber, with a young skinny brown-haired acolyte on her lap. The priestess had her hand under the girl's dress. "Leave us; we have some work to do."

"Yes, my Lady," said the acolyte.

Roisin asked, "How did the meeting go with the Warlord?"

"If we can hold the city elves here, we might be able to destroy the humans and turn our dog soldiers loose on the weak southern elves. This will help us gain more power," said Sioban. "Fetch Rianor and bring another sacrifice to the altar."

The High Priestess undressed and chanted incantations as her acolytes looked on. Rianor and Trahern followed Roisin into the large sacrificial chamber, already undressed. Word spread, and more elves gathered for the sacrificial rite. Two acolytes placed a small human child on the altar where High Priestess Sioban chanted and offered the child to the goddess. After the blood rites, Sioban rested in the antechamber and waited for Rianor, Trahern, and Roisin to finish feasting and having sex.

"Avar Trahern and Rianor Enid, I have a mission for you. You'll go to Catguallaun's camp northeast of the city. Tell him to attack the humans camped to the west of Beinn na Callaird. After defeating the humans, he can turn the dog soldiers toward the east and attack Beinn na Callaird. Instruct him to continue to march south for another day, and on the second day march all day and night to the west to take the humans by surprise. These city elves will not be able to react because they will be too busy cowering behind the walls waiting for an attack."

"Our warriors will be too tired to attack after marching all day and night," said Trahern.

Sioban smiled. "No Rianor, they will have the power of the goddess with them. I'll teach them how to use magic to give Catgullaun's army some of the powers of dog soldiers. They'll have strength and stamina to march all night. I'll also beseech the goddess for success. Before the battle, I'll offer more sacrifices. Come Rianor, I'll instruct you on what you need to do."

Chapter 17

Ututur and Rosanella joined Wilhelm at the makeshift camp to discuss what they should do in the coming days. The half-orc was tired from the march but noted that their current position was wide open to attack from all sides. "Wilhelm, if we are going to be here a while, we should look for a more defensible spot and build a defensive encampment. I've also received word that Consul Aldous is now two days' march behind us."

Wilhelm cleared a spot on the ground and began drawing with a stick. "I agree. I thought we would be joining the main elven army to take the fight to the enemy. However, the dark elves have already moved south quickly, and their main army is on the eastern side of the elven capital." He drew the relative positions of the capital and the enemy force. "We're here, west of the city. I found a good spot three miles further east. The great East West Road curves there and has a drop off on the right side of the road. On the left there is a hill, and beyond it the land opens up to a large field. Beyond the open field is the Great Forest."

Ututur looked at Wilhelm's drawing and saw an excellent strategy to defend the entire area. "That's a great place." They nodded to each other.

"I don't understand," Rosanella said.

Ututur took the offered stick and squatted near the drawing. "If we construct a fortified encampment across the narrow stretch of land with the hill to our left and the valley to our right, any enemy attack will be forced into a narrow front, and they will not be able to use their numerical advantage against us." Ututur pointed with the stick.

"And there we can't be outflanked, and the open ground will let us charge with our cavalry if we have the opportunity," finished Rosanella.

"Exactly, and we can sortie out from there, harass the enemy and prevent an encirclement of the elven capital," Wilhelm added, pointing to the proposed sortie location. "The elven capital is less than a day's ride from there."

"Do we have enough tools to build a fortification?" asked Ututur.

Wilhelm said, "I'm going to see the head elf, Bacstair, tomorrow. I'll ask him for help with the construction, see if they can spare some laborers and tools. Tomorrow, can you two take the soldiers there and begin building the fortified encampment? I'll have Sergeant Pierluigi guide you to the location. If you'll excuse me, I'll turn in and get some rest."

Each of the captains returned to their own sleeping area. As Ututur lay down his mind turned to Andanir and Ilina, and he touched the torc the boy had given him to wear. He smiled; he missed them both. He forced himself to think about how to build an encampment. Ututur had taken his promotion seriously and read several treatises on warfare. In *The Art of Real War*, a scholar from a distant land had stressed the importance of defensive encampments with clean latrines and wash areas, and other works from the western kingdoms described how field encampments were constructed by large mobile armies. All of the works stressed the importance of keeping everything clean for illness prevention. He was eager to test these ideas himself.

The combined army moved to the new, more defensible location and began building their camp. Ututur bent down and used a long string to mark out ten double paces with the help of Sergeant Netland who was assigned to help him build the camp. Meanwhile Captain Bianco took fifty mounted troops to scout the road and the surrounding area. At the same time, Wilhelm took one hundred men to Ar d'Tus Chathair to bring back supplies.

As the half-orc marked out the land with sticks, Sergeant Netland directed a hundred soldiers with shovels to start digging a ditch three double-paces wide and three double-paces deep. He made sure the soldiers put all of the dirt on the western side of the ditch making it more difficult for anyone to climb to their defensive palisade. Ututur had two hundred men fell small trees for wood and then build them into sections that were waist high so that it would be easy for his men to shoot and fight over. However, from the bottom of the ditch, it was a difficult climb to reach the top of the wall. Ututur instructed a separate crew to build a small tower and a movable wooden wall across the road. He also relocated the mobile ballista on the wagon to the center of their position with a good view of the entire front. The soldiers built up the earthen mound to give the wagon an unobstructed view.

By the time Wilhelm returned with extra supplies and two hundred elven workers, the outline of the encampment was clearly visible. It was easily over two hundred double paces long. Behind the construction soldiers were busy organizing the camp and building several makeshift stable areas for the horses, as well as latrines and cooking areas. With additional tools and workers, they finished the main earthwork before supper.

As the sun set Ututur climbed the tall earthen mound next to the mobile ballista and was rewarded with a clear view of the entire area in front of their encampment.

"You've done well, Ututur," said Wilhelm from below as he began climbing up to join the half-orc. They both looked at the field in front of them and saw Rosanella's troop emerge from the eastern edge of the road.

"Wilhelm, do you think the ballista can hit something that far?" asked Ututur.

"I think so. Master Sevin would you be able to hit something that far away?" Wilhelm asked as he looked down from the raised wagon.

"Not as far as the horses, but see where that pine tree is by the road? It's about one two hundred double paces." Sevin pointed at the tree. "This will shoot accurately up to that tree; further range is possible, but the shot won't be guaranteed to hit an individual at that distance. I'll be placing distance markers soon."

The next morning Bacstair returned to the fortified encampment. The elves from his town brought with them several thousand arrows ready to be cut down for the human crossbows and fresh food for the soldiers. The arrow shafts were thinner but would work in the crossbows. Not long after, Consul Lorenz rode into the encampment with fifty mounted bodyguards.

The Consul walked with the captains into a single large tent with a map table and some chairs. "The camp looks good. Whose idea was it to create such an encampment? It's different from the way we usually do things with just earthen berms."

"It was Ututur's idea," Wilhelm said.

"But Wilhelm chose this site," added the half-orc, proud of the acknowledgement.

"Where is Rosanella?" asked Aldous.

"She didn't want to wait around, so she led another patrol to the north," the half-orc answered.

Aldous' tone turned more informal once the small group was out of earshot from the rest of the army. He had Wilhelm and Ututur sit down and fill him in on the situation. After the briefing Aldous said, "I'll carry on to the elven capital with my bodyguards. I need to talk to their Warlord and his Second."

"Yes, my Lord," Wilhelm and Ututur said as they followed Aldous out of the tent.

Wilhelm asked, "Do you know how the elf maiden, Kiley, is doing?"

Aldous turned to Wilhelm and smiled. "She's doing well; the healers from the Sun temple say that she should fully recover. She wanted to travel with me, but I ordered her to stay and rest. I don't know if she'll listen to me."

"Thank you," answered Wilhelm, feeling relieved and picturing her face and long, silver-blonde hair.

"When will the rest of the soldiers arrive?" Ututur asked.

The Consul reached his horse, and his personal guards quickly stopped their conversation and mounted their horses. "The rest of the army should arrive by midday tomorrow. I put Sergeant Szymon in charge. I'll return as soon as I can after I talk with the elven Warlord. Good luck," the Consul said as he signaled for his mounted guard to move.

Kiley still felt weak, even though her wounds had closed and she didn't have a fever. The healers had done good work mending her wounds. The human warlord had ordered her to stay behind, but he wasn't her commander. So as soon as he had left, she convinced a nurse and several guards to let her go. She had to wear borrowed clothes and was given a horse and saddle bags filled with supplies. They even gave her an eating dagger and what the humans called a *langes messer*, a single-edged long knife about two forearms in length. One human soldier also gave her a travel cloak which dragged on the ground when she walked but would be perfect to sleep under.

She rode quickly and urged the horse into a trot. She had to catch up to the human army that had just passed through. She wanted to hurt those northern elves who had killed her warriors, and she wanted to thank Wil. She was surprised that she felt something for the human. *Probably because he saved me. And he is not displeasing to the eye.*

Rolando rode in silence next to Lady Bohm's messenger, Tommaso. His back used to hurt only when he rode long distances, now just a short morning ride caused pain. He felt old; he had only seen thirty-eight summers, but on the last caravan he suffered from constant severe back pain. *If I can't ride anymore, what am I going to do? How will I live?* Since he began his journey with Tommaso, he remembered dreaming of a woman's voice, it was sultry and full vague promises. As hard as he tried, he couldn't remember them clearly. But today his back pain was worse, and both of his legs hurt "Hey, let's take a break. I need to piss."

Tommaso stopped his horse. "Sure, I'll go as well. We can have something to eat and let the horses graze here a little."

After relieving himself, Rolando felt dizzy, and his cock felt numb. He heard a soft female voice. "If you follow me and pledge your loyalty, I'll reward you."

"What good is money if I can't even ride or walk without pain," he said in a low whisper. *I can't believe I'm talking to myself.*

"I can heal you."

I must be going crazy, Rolando thought as he returned to his horse.

"What can I do for you to believe?"

"Heal my body," he said with growing frustration and anger.

Tommaso was getting some cheese and two apples form his saddle bag. "Did you say something?"

"No, just talking to myself. My back hurts from all the riding."

After eating half the apple and some cheese Rolando gave the rest of his apple to his horse. He was reluctant to mount his horse knowing how much that would hurt his back. He gritted his teeth and swung his leg over. To his amazement, his back and legs had stopped hurting.

"See, I can heal you if I choose," said the silky-smooth voice.

Rolando couldn't remember how long it had been since he didn't have pain. "Thank you," he whispered.

"Pray to me Rolando and obey. Help my followers gain strength, and I'll reward you."

"I'll think on it."

The Lady Eleonora Bohm sat at her dressing table and looked at her hands. They were wrinkled with age and felt like rough leather. She looked carefully in the mirror and noticed more lines on her face and neck. There was even another discolored spot on her cheek. She knew her breasts sagged, and her buttocks were no longer full and firm.

Last night she had another beguiling dream; she was young again and could feel her body move with youthful energy. She had these dreams many times in the past year, but last night's dream was so vivid she could feel the smoothness of her young skin and see a younger face reflected in the mirror.

"I can make that dream a reality," came a soft voice.

Startled, Eleonora dropped her hairbrush and turned. She felt a presence but she was alone in her room.

"I can make you young again."

"Who is this? If you're playing a joke on me, you'll be sorry."

"I'm the one you pray to. I know you don't trust easily, so I'll show you. Look at your hands."

Eleonora looked at her hands. As she stared, the wrinkles disappeared and her skin became smooth. She gasped her hands felt smooth. "What sorcery is this?"

"This is my power. Your prayers will be answered if you are loyal and devoted."

Before Eleonora could reply the presence was gone and her hands felt rough again.

Andanir was ready to turn in for the evening when he asked Ilina, "Will Master Ututur be all right? Is he going to die in battle against the bad people?"

"I don't know, Andanir. But he is strong and a good warrior."

"I don't want him to get hurt."

"Do you want to say a prayer? We can light a candle, and I'll burn some sage while we pray."

"All right."

Ilina lit a candle and a bundle of sage in front of the hearth and prayed to Beavi, goddess of life, to keep Ututur safc.

"I asked the Mielki the Huntress to protect Master Ututur till he comes home."

"Off to bed now; you have a long day tomorrow. Didn't you say Master Cociarelli is going to let you handle a real dagger?"

"Yes, mistress."

"I told you to stop that; just call me Ilina," she said and kissed him on his head.

The elven Warlord Eachmhile examined the map and marked the position of the fortified human encampment west of their city with a black stone. He pointed to the map on the table covered with red stones and black stones. "Look Lorenz, the dark elves are here." He pointed to the red stones to the east of the capital. "They have no siege engines and rush forward in no particular formation. We'll be fine behind our walls."

Eoin added, "As far as we can tell, the dark ones do not travel with any wagons or other supplies. That army cannot sustain itself long in the field without a tail. They'll be thirsty and hungry before long and will be gone from our walls. I give them three days at most."

"I think you're right," Consul Lorenz said, sitting down and taking a sip of pale summer ale. The two elves joined him in drinking from their cups. There was a knock at the door. High Priestess Sioban walked in with Roisin following behind.

"Please remain seated. How's the battle plan going?" Sioban asked.

"It's going well, High Priestess," replied the Warlord. He stood and gestured to the map. Was it the ale or did she look younger, more desirable. "We'll defend ourselves here inside the walls, and our human allies won't have to fight at all. The dark elves cannot move their army without our knowing. They don't have the means to breach our walls, nor the supplies to stay in the field for a prolonged period."

The High Priestess turned to Consul Lorenz. "Looks like you and your men wasted your time coming here."

"No, anyone wielding evil magic must be rooted out," Lorenz said taking another sip of ale.

"Where is the Vigiles by the way?" asked the High Priestess.

Eoin said, "She went out to look for more clues. She's trying to identify the sorcerer and find her location."

Lady Sioban kept her face neutral. "It's getting late. I'll retire for the evening; good luck and blessings of the true goddess be with you. Please keep me informed."

It was the day before the harvest moon. As the sun set, a low moan reverberated throughout the woods. In the woods northeast of Beinn na Callaird, the northern elves began to dance as they chanted. Twenty thousand elven voices took up Rianor's chant. Before her, elves held down a male elf boy. Rianor took off her clothes and faced the rising moon. She began chanting the incantations as she had been instructed. Dark power filled the gathering as the dancers fell into a stupor.

As the throng danced their heartbeats merged and beat in rhythm with each other. She smiled as she cut open the screaming boy's stomach and scooped out his insides and searched for the liver and kidneys. Four warriors held her sacrifice down as she threw the organs at the dancers. They fought over the meat like animals and devoured it in seconds. She reached into the dying boy's body and looked at the pain on his face as she pulled out his heart and bit into it. The heart quivered when she chewed and savored each bite. She let the warriors have the rest.

At the same time, in the caverns below Beinn na Callaird, High Priestess Sioban stood naked with Roisin at her side. They chanted together in front of ten elven children with their hands and feet bound on the floor, five boys and five girls. As they chanted, the buildup of magic filled the cavern with power. Miles away in the forest Rianor also felt the power being generated by her High Priestess. All of the gathered elves in the caverns and in the woods felt Larvanis' power. The High Priestess went from child to child, slitting their throats and letting the blood spill to the ground while Roisin gathered some of the blood in a bowl made from a skull and began painting Sioban's body with the sacred runes. Meanwhile acolytes butchered the sacrificial meat.

In the woods, Rianor cut the throat of another offering and painted her body with the sacred blood. At both locations the victims' bodies were defiled, the organs removed and eaten as part of the ritual.

The goddess commanded the dark elf hoard to run and attack the humans west of Beinn na Callaird the next day. Normally it would take a rider almost two days to travel from the eastern part of the Great Forest to the western edge where the humans were camped. However, dark magic flowed into the gathered hoard giving them unnatural energy and stamina. The dog soldiers began to move at tremendous speed through the woods, howling as they ran.

Vigiles Albrecht searched the area where the altar had stood, well west of the northern eleven army's known position. After a wasted morning, she found a well-established trail from the site going north. Bare dirt was clearly visible, and no stray vegetation grew along the path. It was easy to follow, almost like a garden path, and her horse didn't have difficulty walking on it. She followed the path till evening but found nothing. She decided to stay in the forest for the night so she could see where the path led in the morning. She made a hasty camp away from the trail and ate some trail rations.

A distant noise woke her from a restless sleep. At first, she thought it might be a pack of coyotes or some other nocturnal animal. But as she lay still a dread came over her, and she realized that she didn't hear any of the usual nighttime creatures. A low rumble reverberated through the woods; she felt the earth vibrate. She heard hoots and howls, but not from any animal she knew.

As the noise grew clearer, she could make out individual cries and words. "Kill them! Cut out their hearts!"

The forest was too dark to allow her to ride safely. Her legs trembled from fear as she put on her mail shirt and sword belt. She tossed her saddle bags over her right shoulder and moved as fast as she could away from the cries. She had to scramble on her hands and knees at times to get to a ridge that overlooked her campsite for a better vantage point. When she reached the top, she no longer heard the noise heading toward her, so she paused and found a good spot to observe the area below.

Initially, the Vigiles didn't understand what she was seeing. The air was still humming; the hairs on her arms rose as her body became covered in goose bumps. In the distance below the trees, the ground was undulating like an ant hill. As she watched, she understood. Below her a mass of elves ran at great speed, west toward the border. She heard screaming, and in the distance someone shouted, "Find the rider!" Immediately her horse screamed in pain.

Before the screams ended, she found her bearings and headed quickly towards Beinn na Callaird. In the darkness she fell several times because she couldn't see clearly. Her initial lead was dwindling, the pursuers could see better in the darkness and were running at full speed. Her knees were bruised from falling. Somewhere in the darkness she lost her saddle bags. As she struggled to maintain her speed, the hunters moved closer. She wasn't sure how far she was from the city, but the moon was beginning to set. In the distance she heard a voice call out, "Stop! Let's go back and join the priestess." She heard the majority of the pursuers turn back to rejoin the hoard. With most of her pursuers gone, she slowed down, got her bearings, and continued her journey.

After traveling several more double-paced miles the Vigiles began to relax. As the sun rose, the woods began to thin and as she continued downhill, she saw the road ahead. She sighed in relief as she stepped onto the familiar road. Just as she relaxed, she heard a twig snap behind her. She froze in fear and strained to locate the source of the noise. The Vigiles drew her short sword and spike dagger. A figure emerged from the woods; a naked male elf armed with a sword.

Because she was focused on the figure closing in on her, she didn't see the other elf but she heard movement from above. She managed to glimpse the second elf about to jump on top of her. All she could do was bring up her sword. He fell on her, knocking the wind out of her, but years of training took over as she let go of her sword. She grappled with her right hand, stabbing the elf in the side with her dagger. The elf wasn't well trained and just tried to out muscle her; he was already dying from the deep stab wounds to his liver. She struggled out from under him and scrambled to her feet, grabbing the dying elf's sword.

The other attacker came running toward her, but she gained her feet and took a defensive stance; he slowed. Vigiles Albrecht took several deep breaths and tried to get a feel for the unfamiliar sword. As the elf approached, she noticed the runes covering his body. She let him close the distance and examined her attacker. She noticed his awkward flat-footed stance and his hesitation; this attacker also had little training.

She changed her stance in which she led with the dagger and pulled the sword back to lure the attacker in. She let him attack first. The elf swung the sword in a wild ark aimed for her head. She let it swing past, stepped in, and stabbed his neck with the sword, then followed with a deep stab to the abdomen with her dagger. She withdrew the dagger, took two steps back, and waited. The elf grabbed his bleeding neck and charged wildly forward, swinging his sword left and right. She kept him out of range extending the sword forward and waited for him to bleed to death; there was no need to attack any further. The elf finally weakened and fell to the ground gasping. She dropped the unfamiliar sword and retrieved her own. After she cleaned her dagger with dirt she ran toward the elven capital.

❊❊❊

Rianor and Trahern followed the elven hoard on their horses. Rianor was still energized after the ritual; she had felt the enormous power of the goddess flow through her and into the hoard. After the offerings, Catguallaun allowed Rianor to feed him and draw the sacred runes on his body. The power of the goddess flowed through him also, and he felt strength flow into his arms and legs. His hunger and thirst were gone.

Afterwards, Rianor and Trahern told Catguallaun about the gathered human army. Before the majority of the hoard began its impetuous march, Catguallaun ordered two thousand warriors to remain east of Beinn na Callaird and create a distraction. Tranhern believed that this would convince the city elves that the attack would still come from the east and prevent the warlord from supporting the humans. Ever since the end of the ritual Rianor had an ecstatic smile on her face as she rode across the Great Forest at an impossible pace. She couldn't wait for the hoard to catch the human army west of the city by surprise.

Chapter 18

Exhausted, Vigiles Albrecht reached the elven city gates covered in dirt and sweat. She demanded to see Consul Lorenz, the elven Warlord, and his Second. The elven guards hesitated for a moment then took her to the Warlord's meeting room and gave her water and a plate of fall fruits. She took bites from a persimmon and drank water from the cup.

Eoin was the first to arrive. The Vigiles explained her story as fast as she could. "We have to send soldiers to help the human army. The elven hoard marched west last night. They moved with great speed through the woods."

"Let's wait until the Consul and Warlord arrive."

"What's the meaning of this?" asked the Warlord, who was not at all pleased to have someone wake him so early.

Vigiles Albrecht told her story again. "We have to help the human army."

The Warlord frowned. "Even if what you say is true, it'll take them two days on foot to reach them. We'll scout the northern and eastern parts of the Great Forest for the dark elves to confirm your story."

The Vigiles felt panic rise realizing that the Nixland army might be doomed. "But they're moving so fast, faster than it should be possible."

Eoin looked worried and added, "Even if what you say is true, we have to make sure this isn't a ruse to draw our army from the city; there's plenty of time to march west against the dark elves. No one can march across the Great Forest in less than three days."

"I agree, normally it would take several days to march such a large group but I'm afraid that things aren't normal. I'm going to rejoin the Nixland army," said Consul Lorenz.

Vigiles Albrecht stood frustrated. "I'll go with you. But I'll need a new horse."

"Warlord, with your permission I would like to take some warriors and scout the western part of the forest." The Second frowned with growing concern at the seriousness of the situation. Who knew what dark magic could do. If the Vigiles were to be believed, the dark elves could overrun the small human force then turn east and attack Beinn na Callaird.

The Elven Warlord didn't know what to believe. "Take all of the scouts we have in the city and patrol the area near the human camp. Report back as fast as you can. Maybe you'll find them exhausted from the night's march."

The Vigiles listened to the discussions and kept her doubts to herself. She remembered the undulating primal mass she had seen and felt in the darkness. Their speed was unnatural, and the malevolence she felt during the night was like nothing she had ever experienced. It wasn't her imagination; the earth had vibrated with power, evil power. She didn't think the dark elves would take long to reach the human camp in the west.

Ututur woke with a sore back; he splashed water on his face and went out to inspect the defenses one more time. He also wanted to make sure the workers had dug the latrines as he had instructed.

"Good morning, Ututur," came from Rosanella.

"Good morning."

"Do you think I should go out on patrol again today?" she asked drinking a hot mug of tea.

"Maybe later in the day. Can I ask you something?" asked Ututur as he looked out over the wooden palisades.

Rosanella said, "Of course."

"Should we build defensive earthworks behind us and completely enclose the encampment?"

"It'll be good practice for the soldiers," replied Rosanella as she finished her tea. "May I ask you something personal?"

Ututur nodded his head.

"I wanted to ask if your ward Andanir can come and keep Rialta company regularly."

"I think he'll like that. When he's done with his lessons and chores it would be a good idea for him to have a friend his age. Perhaps she could join him at Master Ovidio's for some lessons."

Rosanella smiled. "That would be wonderful for my niece. I'll tell Wilhelm and get Sergeants, Pierluigi and Wulfnoth to start working on the earthworks after breakfast."

Sevin liked the new, more mobile ballista. It was lighter than the older models and slightly smaller. It also had a maximum range of five hundred paces. He set up a man-size target twenty paces away and another out at two hundred double-paces. He moved well out of the way, signaled his crew to arm the ballista. He ran back to the wagon, used the moveable nail front sight and rear notch to aim, and fired the ballista at the closer target. The bolt went wide of the man-size target. He heard snickers from the soldiers on guard around him. Sevin adjusted the rear sight and directed Dario to reload thc ballista. The second shot hit the left side of the target. Sevin made fine adjustments to the sight, fired another bolt, this time the fifteen-hands-long bolt struck the target in the middle of the chest. He switched to the further target. After four tires he hit it in the center. Sevin marked elevation on the rear sight with charcoal. "That's enough for today; release the rope tension. Daio, go recover the bolts and mark the distances."

Sergeant Szymon let the men sleep in; they were tired from the long march. There was no need to hurry anymore. A messenger had arrived yesterday evening notifying him that the northern elven army was far away to the east of the elven capital. They could take their time. His troops would reach the encampment after midday today.

The sun had not yet risen as Consul Lorenz, the Vigiles Albrecht, and Eoin rode at the head of the hastily-put-together column of three hundred elven warriors. Eoin mustered all the available mounted warriors to scout the area near the human camp and ride to the Great Forest in order to locate the northern elves. The group rode out without planning or support. Most of the gathered southern elven army still manned the eastern walls. They were encamped on the eastern side of the city.

The small group alternated between a trot and a canter to preserve the horses. They traveled about three double-paced miles when a surge of dark elves charged them from the forested hill to their right. The column was showered with arrows as the elves on foot closed the distance rapidly. The Consul ordered the mounted warriors to ride as fast as they could before the hoard cut the road off and trapped them. As they galloped, many fell from their mounts with arrow wounds. Because of the time required for the rear of the column to start galloping, the last forty riders were dragged off their horses and killed. The dark elves tore the warriors and horses to shreds and feasted on them. They had escaped the encirclement of the elven capital. As soon as they lost their pursuers, the Consul ordered the column to slow down. They had lost more than half of their small group.

❊❊❊

Rosanella was inspecting the gate across the road when she heard a guard yell out. "Riders! Riders are approaching!"

She climbed the small, raised tower and looked out. The riders were galloping toward the gate. They were at least one double-paced mile away and moving fast. She was about to climb down when a guard tugged her sleeve. "Look, Captain," he said, and pointed to the edge of the Great Forest behind the riders. The forest edge itself seemed to pulse. She strained her eyes and used her hand to block out the sun's glare. The edge of the forest was moving forward, and she spotted two new riders on horseback waiting at the edge.

❊❊❊❊

"Rianor, I need your help; we can't let all of those soldiers get back to the camp. One of them is the human leader," Trahern said as he drew his bow.

"I'll see what I can do," Rianor lowered her head and chanted. When she completed her chant, she moved closer to touch his bow and quiver. Trahern could feel the power of the goddess radiate from his bow to his arm. From the corner of his eye, he saw Rianor slump in her saddle from the exertion.

He ignored her and drew an arrow. He didn't know what to

expect but aimed the bow high and targeted the front rider. When he released the arrow, it shot straight into the sky and didn't drop. He was amazed, and quickly nocked another arrow. This time he aimed flat even though the riders were at least two hundred double paces away. He picked out a target who he hoped was the human leader, and released. The arrow flew straight and fast. The arrow hit a rider that got in the way. The enchanted arrow passed through the armored body as the rider fell from his horse and hit another human rider.

Trahern looked at his quiver and saw that he only had six more arrows. He quickly looked for the human leader again. The man was in the lead with his war banner flying from a rider at his side. He took aim and released. The arrow flew straight, but again another rider got in the way. However, the enchantment allowed the arrow to pass through the rider and hit the older human in the leg.

Captain Bianco watched as the Consul's group neared the gate, wincing as she watched an arrow pierce one rider who fell from his horse and hit Aldous, burying itself deep in his right leg. Before he fell from his horse, an elven warrior steadied Aldous and helped him stay mounted.

"Open the gates! Get a healer up here right now!" she commanded as she climbed down from the tower.

After making sure that the cooks would be able to provide a hot breakfast for the army, Ututur took two hundred soldiers to improve the defensive trench protecting the rear of their encampment. "Looks like we should be able to finish this before midday, Sergeant Wulfnoth."

"I think you're right." Any further comment from Wulfnoth was interrupted by cries from the gate. "Do you want me to go and check on the front gate?"

"No, you continue here, and make sure to rotate the men so they don't get too tired," said the half-orc as he jogged back to the gate.

By the time Ututur reached the main area, the entire camp was in an uproar as men ran about trying to don their gear while others shouted, "To arms! We're under attack!"

Ututur walked to the large command tent. When he got closer, he saw Sergeant Pierluigi and Rosanella dispersing the men. Sergeant Pierluigi yelled out, "Calm yourselves! Get your armor on and go to the walls!"

Inside the tent he saw Consul Lorenz on the ground surrounded by people. They removed his armor, and a healer cut his trousers away, exposing an arrow embedded deep in his right thigh. The wound must have been serious because a lot of blood flowed continuously.

"Wilhelm, what's going on?" asked Ututur.

"The enemy is here in force."

"How can that be? Rosanella scouted the Great Forest yesterday."

"Come. I'll show you."

The two of them went to the raised ballista platform and looked out. Ututur couldn't believe what he saw; in front of them elves had emerged from the woods en masse. This should've been impossible; no normal army could march that fast.

"Captain Bunour!" cried Sergeant Wulfnoth. "Should I have the men stop working on the ditch?"

"No, finish the defensive ditch behind us as fast as possible and start building a wooden palisade there as well. Get the rest of the men armed and ready. Make sure the men that are making extra crossbow bolts continue. We'll need every single one."

As the sergeant ran to carry out Ututur's orders, Wilhelm came up to him with an elf by his side. "This is Eoin Clomin; he's one of the elven Warlord's Seconds. He rode in with the Consul and Vigiles Albrecht."

Ututur said, "We've met before. What happened? We were told these dark elves were east of your capital."

"They were there when we left the capital. My scouts confirmed the position of these dark elves yesterday afternoon," said the Second.

The half-orc considered for a moment. "Is it possible that this is part of a different group?"

The elf frowned and said, "It's possible, but not likely."

The Vigiles joined the small group. "Yesterday, I was in the woods north of the city searching for clues to locate the evil sorceress. After sunset I woke to find myself in the midst of these elves; the ground throbbed, and the air vibrated with dark power. I saw them move with impossible speed in the dark."

"So, do you think a dark magic user is with his army?" asked Wilhelm.

"Yes, I'm sure there is an evil presence here. It may not be the sorceress we seek, but someone wielded powerful magic yesterday and ensorcelled an entire army. The arrow that hit the Consul was unnatural. It must have flown at least three hundred paces in a straight line," she added.

Wilhelm looked out and tried to estimate the number of enemy soldiers gathering in front of them. "They clearly outnumber us. Should we consider retreating?"

"It's already too late. They'll run us down," said the half-orc. "We're better off behind these earthworks."

The half-orc captain noticed Sevin and his crew constructing a makeshift pavise. "Hey there! Can you and your men make more of those?"

"Yes, sir, I think we've enough wood to make at least twenty more," answered Sevin.

"Ututur why did they stop their advance?" asked Rosanella.

"I don't know," he replied. It just didn't make sense.

"I think we should send messengers west, contact the militia, and order them to force march here to reach us faster," said Wilhelm.

Ututur looked at the elves on the field; they were standing as a disorganized hoard, not arrayed in any formation, while many swayed for side to side in a stupor. He saw no camp fires or supply wagons like a regular army. "Can we get any aid from the city, Eoin?" asked Ututur.

"No, the road is cut. But I can go to the border town of Ar d'Tus Chathair and get help," said the elf as he climbed down from the platform.

Catguallaun hungered for blood. "Let's attack now before the humans are ready. The warriors are beginning to tire."

"No, we have to wait," said Trahern. He pointed to Rianor, who was resting under a tree. "We need the priestess' help. She needs time to recover."

"But the warriors need food and water," said Catguallaun who sensed that the power he had gained last night was already waning. "We can't wait too long. Should we try to encircle this camp?"

"No, I don't think we need to. I've looked at their camp, and I don't see many human warriors," Trahern said from under the shade of a large tree.

Eoin and four riders left the human encampment and headed toward Ar d'Tus Chathair. He pushed the horses hard and arrived to see Bacstair organizing three wagonloads of food for the human camp. Eoin quickly told Bacstair the situation and asked him to muster as many warriors as he could. By the time Bacstair had organized three hundred warriors, the human militia had reached the border town. Eoin explained the situation to Sergeant Szymon. The two groups joined forces and marched together toward the beleaguered human encampment.

"We'll double time the last three double-paced miles," said Szymon. "And how is the Consul?"

"I didn't see his wound," said Eoin. "But he was shot in the leg, and healers were attending to him."

The three captains stood together to study the massed enemy. Wilhelm asked, "Ututur why aren't they attacking? If they rush us now, they'll overwhelm us."

"Maybe they aren't ready and need to rest from the night's march," answered Ututur. "I don't see any ladders or other equipment to breach our earthworks."

"We should rest our men. They shouldn't stand in the sun too long," added Rosanella. "We should also place men on the hill to our left flank to make sure the elves do not attack us from that direction."

Wilhelm nodded, "Yes, let's rotate the men through; we'll keep five hundred on the wall at all times. Let the others rest in the shade and eat. Rosanella, take two hundred men with some crossbows and get up there. Prepare the area for defense. Make sure to take water and food with you."

"I'll get right on it."

"Wilhelm, I'm going to check the defensive ditch in the rear and see if it's complete," Ututur said. The half-orc leaped off the ballista emplacement, which had become the de facto command post. Sevin and his crew had constructed dozens of impromptu pavise shields to protect the camp from the inevitable elven arrow barrage. Wilhelm nodded with approval as Rosanella organized the soldiers. Five hundred soldiers remained on the wall as men came off the line, they marched to the rear to rest. The professional soldiers were well trained and flexible in their organization. Although they were usually organized around fighting groups of one hundred soldiers, they were comfortable in forming larger or smaller fighting blocks. The militia was not as good as these professionals, but they were trained and disciplined. The citizens wouldn't break easily because they knew they were fighting for their homes and families. Wilhelm looked out at the elven hoard and tried to imagine how these elves would attack them. He saw no siege engines, and the elves weren't constructing ladders. The northern elves would have to get through the open killing ground to reach the ditch, then cross the ditch then climb the earthworks to enter the encampment. A frontal assault would be suicide.

Ututur jogged toward the rear. Seeing Wulfnoth, he ordered, "Make sure the soldiers are rested. They need to stay ready to reinforce the wall on short notice."

He didn't wait for an answer and hurried on. When he reached the rear of their encampment, the men and women had already finished the basic outline of the ditch while crews took turns deepening the trench. He also saw a crew on top of the ditch packing the dirt down to create a defensive mound. They used stones and wood to create shooting positions for the crossbowmen. He was pleased with the progress. The defensive ditch would be completed by midday. Even now it would provide adequate protection.

The half-orc had been too busy to put on his armor. He returned to his sleeping area, put on his black gambeson, chainmail coat, and aventail with a chainmail flap that could be closed to protect his mouth and nose. Next, he donned his mail coif padded with linen and cotton. Then fastened his steel gorget around his neck before putting on his dark blue brigandine coat. After checking his armor he retrieved his round helmet, gauntlets, put on his war belt, and tied his dagger to his left side. He also tied the pouch with Ilina's bandages to his belt. He grabbed his small hand axe and stuck it in his belt loop. As he mentally readied himself, he retrieved his main weapon, a pole axe sixteen hands long with flat axe blade and a hammer. The top of the pole axe ended in a sharp spike three hands long. Tucking his helmet under his left arm and gripping the pole axe with his right he walked towards the ballista platform. He grabbed another big chopping axe as he passed by a pile of wood; men watched him pass and quickly got out of his way.

Wilhelm turned to see what was causing the commotion and, seeing Ututur marching towards him, he was glad Ututur was not his opponent.

"Wil, you should get your armor on and check on the Consul," Ututur said as he rested his pole axe and chopping axe against the makeshift pavise.

Wilhelm got down from the platform. "I'll be back soon," he said and walked quickly to his tent to don his armor.

Albrecht joined the other captains on the platform overlooking the battlefield. The mid-morning sun was already hot, and Ututur was sweating. He drank some of the apple cider vinegar mixed with water to quench his thirst. The Vigiles informed the giant that the healers had stabilized Aldous. The Consul had lost a lot of blood but would survive. Ututur said, "Greta, you must return to Mount Haven with one of the captains. We must evacuate the Consul; there is no need for the Consul and three captains of Nixland to fall here."

Vigiles Albrecht nodded. "You're right; let's wait for Wilhelm."

Wilhelm, now in his battle armor of chain mail and breastplate joined the Vigiles and the half-orc. The Vigiles explained the idea of evacuating the Consul and a captain back to Mount Haven. When

Wilhelm agreed Albrecht said, "We'll draw straws to see who'll go. The short straw leaves. I'll hold the straws and draw for Rosanella." The two captains drew the long straws and Albrecht drew the short straw for Rosanella.

"Sergeant Pierluigi, tell Captain Bianco to come here quickly; you'll take command of the two hundred men on the hill," said Wilhelm.

"Yes, sir," Pierluigi replied.

In a few short moments, Rosanella raced down from the hilltop. "What is it? I had the soldiers create some barricades with brush and wood."

Ututur looked at and said, "Ahhh, we drew straws and … ummm. Wil?"

Wilhelm looked at Rosanella and said, "What we're trying to say is that decisions had to be made. You know…"

The Vigiles sighed in exasperation. "What these brave warriors are trying to say is that you will retire from the battle and escort the Consul back to Nixland." Before Rosanella could protest the Vigiles added, "I drew the straws; it was fair."

"If we lose here, we cannot have the Consul and three captains fall," Ututur said. "Can you tell Ilina and Andanir," Ututur searched for words. "Tell them of our situation here."

Rosanella looked at the three of them and said, "I'll do it, but I don't like it. Here Ututur, you take this crystal necklace that Master Ovidio loaned to me."

Ututur said, "Thank you." He placed the crystal around his neck. He made sure to tuck it under his gorget, he didn't want to lose his friend's gem.

"Safe travels and let the council know what's happening here," Wilhelm added. "We'll send a messenger as soon as we can," said Ututur.

Both Wilhelm and Ututur looked out in silence over the wooden wall. Well, I guess it's up to you and me," said Ututur turning to Wilhelm.

"Those dark elves will be sorry before the day is done," replied Wilhelm with his teeth clenched.

CHAPTER 19

Captain Rosanella Bianco and the Vigiles rode in silence. The captain hated leaving the army behind, but she understood the half-orc's reasoning and couldn't blame him. She was sweating from the sun, and as their group rounded the corner of the curving mountain road, she saw the column of soldiers with the Consul's black banner bearing a single white star. "I'll be back," said Captain Bianco as she spurred her horse into a gallop.

Rosanella described to Sergeant Szymon and Eoin how the elven hoard appeared seemingly from thin air. After hearing this, Eoin got off his horse and ordered his elves to run toward the encampment. With the Second in the lead, the elves moved quickly with no armor to hinder their movement and quickly pulled ahead of the human column. Sergeant Szymon bid his farewell and continued his quick march toward the camp.

Kiley kept the horse moving at a fast pace. Her shoulder was better, but she still felt pain in her side from the arrow wound. The elves at Ar d'Tús told her that the human army was not too far ahead. She urged the horse into a fast trot. After a short while she saw a group of riders and a wagon.

As she approached the riders she said, "I'm Kiley Saoirse, Second to Warlord. I know Captain Wilhelm Martel."

Rosanella said, "Well met. Wilhelm and Ututur are in a fortified position, and your other Second, Eoin, is marching there with warriors from Ar d'Tus Chathair. There's also a group of soldiers from Nixland marching close behind."

"If you hurry, you can catch up to them," added Vigiles Albrecht.

"Thank you," Kiley said as she spurred her horse.

It was approaching sext. The sun was at its apex the half-orc captain knew that the soldiers had to be hot in their armor. They had waited for half a day for the northern dark elves to attack. Finally, a sentry cried out, "They're moving!" he signaled the drummer and trumpeter to sound the alarm. As the drum beat a fast rhythm, the horn blasted three notes. All of the soldiers who had been resting ran to the walls. One hundred armored soldiers moved to the gate to form a shield wall in case the attackers breached the gate. Wilhelm was resting when he heard the drums and the horn. He asked Sergeant Netland to help him put his armor back on. Once he had donned his plate armor he secured his dagger and sword. He walked with a limp out of the tent with his sallet helmet under his left arm and grabbed his two-handed, spiked war hammer in his right hand. He reached the ballista platform with Sergeant Netland at his side.

"They move without any discipline," Ututur said as he pointed to the ragged group moving forward. As more elves poured out of the woods, two riders emerged. One was cloaked, and the other had long white silver hair and carried a bow. The half-orc watched and tried to count the enemy when someone cried, "Enemy in our rear! Alarm!"

Although Wilhelm reacted first, he grimaced after jumping off the platform and grabbing his hammer. The half-orc didn't want the human to injure his leg anymore. "I'll go check. Wilhelm, stay here with Sergeant Netland."

Ututur reached the rear gate and found it already closed and the soldiers prepared for an assault. There were only fifty soldiers and around one hundred workers there. He peeked over the wooden fence and saw some elves running at full speed toward them. Ututur relaxed immediately when he recognized Eoin leading the group. "Relax men. They're our allies. Open the gate."

Ututur stood and waited for Eoin. "Good. You've arrived in time for the fun."

The elf was out of breath but managed to gasp, "Your own soldiers are not far behind us."

"Let our militia through as soon as they arrive and tell the sergeant to marshal the troops in the center and rest in the shade til they're needed." Turning to the elven commander, he said, "Come with me."

Eoin positioned the elves behind the ballista to give them time to catch their breath and drink some water. He wanted them rested before they were needed. The two climbed the platform. Eoin gawked at the mass of dark elves. "Well met again Wilhelm. How many are there?"

"Eoin, good to see you, my friend. Not sure, but at least twenty thousand. How many warriors did you bring?"

"Three hundred archers," Eoin said in a quiet voice.

"They can move up to the wall and shoot in volleys as soon as the enemy is in range," the half-orc said in a steady voice. He continued looking at the massed hoard of thousands moving slowly forward. He hoped his disappointment in the small number of reinforcements did not come through.

"Rianor, look, do you see the small group on that raised platform?" asked Trahern, pointing at the platform where armored figures were clearly visible.

"Yes." Rianor replied.

"Can you use your power on them?"

"I'll try," the Priestess said and began chanting. She had not fully recovered from the previous night and from blessing Trahern's bow and arrows. She was uncertain how far she could project her power. The last time she used it, the victims were close; this time they were very far away.

Trahern drew his bow; they were easily over four hundred double paces, much farther than any normal bow shot could be expected to reach in a straight line. As Rianor chanted, he drew the bow. Before he could release the air around him grew cold and he heard a tremendous woosh. Although everyone gasped at the power of the spectacular blast, the resulting crater fell short of the human encampment. "What happened?" Trahern asked, swearing under his breath.

"I think I'm too far away," replied Rianor, rubbing her temples.

"Next time wait until you're in range!"

"Yes, I'll wait, but I don't know what happened. Something is making it difficult to focus on the target." Rianor sounded weaker from her exertion. "My power is not as strong as I thought it would be. I'm drained from last night's efforts."

Trahern swore and drew his bow again, aiming for the armored figures on the raised platform in the center of the human line. He released the arrow which flew straight and true. Nonetheless the distance caused the arrow to lose its momentum and miss. He had only two more arrows. He waited for the fully armored figure on the platform to stop pacing. *Stand still, my friend*, Trahern thought as he waited.

Ututur felt Andanir's torc grow warm around his right wrist as the hooded figure had released powerful magic from her raised, glowing hands. There was a large crater in the ground in front of their trench. Everyone on the platform instinctively took cover. Many of the soldiers huddled behind the wooden palisade.

Wilhelm recalled the blessing his soldiers had received as they marched out of town; he hummed the song to himself. As he continued to hum he felt calm. He looked at the shaken soldiers on the wall. One arrow flew past his head; then, as he turned, another arrow hit the inside edge of his helmet, breaking the bodkin, ricocheting, and piercing his left eye. If his head had not been turned, the arrow would have pierced his brain. He screamed in agony as Ututur helped steady him.

Ututur and Sergeant Netland helped Wilhelm down from the platform and ordered several soldiers to take him to the healers. Ututur climbed back onto the platform then donned his own helmet. "Sevin, do you see that female elf on the horse?"

Sevin moved the pavise to better cover the platform and climbed up. "Yes, I see her."

"Can you hit her from here?" the half-orc asked while using the pavise as a shield.

"Not yet. Once she passes the boulder I placed on the field as a marker she'll be in range."

Ututur looked for the boulder, he wasn't paying attention to the mounted archer. Andanir's gold torc suddenly grew hot again, causing him to glance at it. The gnome's blood red ruby crystal gave off a bright light blinding him for a heartbeat. He didn't know what was happening but hoped it was a sign of good luck.

Trahern swore as something bright blinded him as he released his last enchanted arrow at the giant monster. He chunked his last shot and swore. "Lucky bastard."

Although he appeared to be no more than a balding goat farmer, Sergeant Szymon was a veteran militia man with several campaigns under his belt. He estimated that his column was about three double-paced miles from their allies' camp. He swore under his breath and ordered, "Double time march!" *I'm getting too old for this kind of marching.*

By the time the militia had covered two miles, the column was strung out with some soldiers lagging far behind. Szymon slowed the pace and reorganized his soldiers. By the time a coherent column reformed, he saw the encampment and ordered the standard-bearer to unfurl their colors, the yellow and black banner of Nixland. The column continued toward the camp but the militia men faltered when they heard the loud explosion. Szymon shouted, "Steady men! Steady! Get back in line."

The half-orc found the ranging boulder. He also noticed the mounted archer near the sorcerer put his bow away. The sorcerer was still out of the ballista's range. Sergeant Netland returned to his side with an out-of-breath Sergeant Szymon.

"Sergeant Szymon reporting with two thousand men of the Nixland militia," he said, taking deep breaths.

"Rest your men for the moment but get them prepared to fight as soon as possible. How many crossbows did you bring?" Ututur asked.

"We have two hundred, my Lord Captain," answered Szymon.

Ututur thought for a few moments. "I want all of the crossbowmen positioned to the right of the tower. Tell them to stay out of sight under cover of the wall until the order to open fire. Take charge of the crossbowmen and organize them in groups of one hundred. Make sure to distribute the extra crossbow bolts." Both sergeants left to carry out his orders. At least the explosion hadn't breached the defensive wall, the half-orc reflected. He had four hundred crossbows massed with another hundred on top of the hill. The exchange of missiles would begin soon.

From below he heard Sevin clear his throat. "Captain, the white-haired female is about to move into range."

Ututur made room for Sevin's crew. They loaded the ballista with a bolt thicker than his thumb; ten-hands-long, it was tipped with a four-bladed iron barb. The crew cranked the ballista; once it was locked, two men moved the pavise out of the way as Sevin took aim at the sorcerer and fired. The first shot missed by less than an arm's length. The massive bolt hit one of the elves next to the sorcerer, skewering him to the ground.

The two men put the pavise back in place as the experienced crew quickly reloaded the ballista. When it was ready, Sevin ordered, "Move the pavise. Get ready." He took careful aim and ignoring the mayhem surrounding the skewered elf, he took slow and steady breaths. The female elf's horse was agitated by the screaming; his target was moving. The elf raised her hands in the air; she looked like she was chanting. Sevin thought he saw her hands glow slightly. He said a short prayer, held his breath, steadied himself, and adjusted his aim. Before he could fire, the elf released the energy she had built up, this time hitting a section of the wooden palisades and blasting a hole in the earthworks. The crater created by the explosion enlarged the ditch in front of the mound. As the ground exploded, Sevin flinched, losing his target. He quickly took aim again. His target was now slumped on her horse. He ignored the screams of the wounded around him and pressed the release mechanism as smoothly as possible without moving the ballista. The bolt released with a thunk and the barbed bolt hit her in the chest, unhorsing her and traveling halfway through her torso. The elf's fine-featured face was twisted in pain and shock as she looked down at the bolt in her chest. She fell off her horse, the bolt pinning her to the ground. The entire camp heard her unnatural screams.

Ututur commanded in a loud voice. "Sevin, shoot anyone else who looks like they're giving orders."

❈❈❈

When Kiley reached the human encampment, the men had closed the gate; she faced men with crossbows aimed at her. "Stop, who are you?"

"I'm Kiley Saoirse. I'm with Eoin and the other elves. I know Captain Martel."

"Dismount. Some men will escort you, and if you're not who you say you are, you'll regret it."

Two human soldiers escorted her to Eoin, who vouched for her. After the humans left, he told her the situation. "Wilhelm got hit by an arrow and is in the large tent over there. Ututur the half-orc captain is in charge."

"I want to go see Wilhelm; I'll help you afterward," she told him fighting back more sadness than she expected.

Eoin said, "Hurry back. I'm going to see what's going on and ask what the half-orc plans." The Second was also curious about how the humans used the ballista.

Kiley walked into the tent and saw Wilhelm lying on a blanket on the ground. With one side of his head was bandaged he was clearly in pain. She felt shocked, and a mixture of emotions ran through her as she walked towards Wil, who had saved her life.

"Hello, captain," she said.

He opened his right eye and grimaced in pain. "Why are you here? You should be resting and healing."

"I'm fine."

A healer came up to Wilhem and gave him a potion for the pain, saying "He'll be asleep soon. Let him rest. I was able to take the metal shards out, but he lost that eye."

"Yes," she said, and watched him drink the cretic solution.

The potion worked quickly. Kiley could see that Wil was becoming drowsy, she kissed him on the lips quickly, and left. She wondered why she had done that as she ran quickly to where Eoin was standing near the giant half-orc.

Ututur reacted quickly and ordered the men and women from the baggage train to fill in the gap in their earthworks with dirt as fast as possible. Next, he ordered a large section of a mobile pavise to cover the gap in the wall. Sergeant Netland waited patiently at his side. "What do you think sergeant?"

"I think we have to worry about the enemy trying to widen the breach. The gate is another weak point."

"Thank you."

Before committing his soldiers, Ututur wanted more ideas and he invited Eoin to join him to observe the battlefield. Eoin was accompanied by a dark-haired female elven warrior. Both gasped as they saw the huge numbers of dark elves surging closer to their position. Ututur asked, "What do you think?"

Eoin replied, "I'll place the archers right behind your crossbowmen on the right, and mass our fire. We must drive the hoard away from the gate; I don't want them breaking through that point."

The female elf added, "You must fill the gap on your wall."

Ututur listened to the sound advice and was grateful that the sorceress hadn't used her power against the wooden gate. If they had breached the gate, it would have become impossible to defend the encampment.

"Excuse me, captain, I want to swing the ballista around to cover the gap in the earthworks," Sevin said.

"Yes, we'll get out of your way." Ututur jumped off the platform and grabbed his weapons, moving to take his place near the breach on the wall.

"I'll prepare my warriors," said Eoin, leaving the half-orc.

"I'm Kiley. If I may, I'll stay with you and act as your runner."

Ututur nodded. "Sergeant Netland, take personal command of five hundred soldiers from the militia and reinforce this broken section of the palisade. Hold the other men ready for any other breakthroughs. Have Sergeant Szymon take personal command of the soldiers at the gate. I'll send Kiley with any new orders. Now go."

Kiley pointed to the large number of dark elves who had stopped. "Captain, I think the enemy is going to fire a volley."

The half-orc nodded and yelled, "Take cover and prepare to receive arrows!" Most of the soldiers took cover behind the palisade or their pavises. The men standing on the wall raised their shields, peeking over the tops to gauge the distance for their own archers and crossbowmen. The hoard moved in an undisciplined line; after firing one volley they advanced in fits and starts as individual dark elves stopped to shoot their bows. Their barrage had little effect; most of the arrows hit the wooden protective barriers or fell into the dirt.

Ututur peeked around the pavise and pointed his pole axe at the crossbowmen and signaled the elves under Eoin's command. They released a massed volley of arrows and bolts toward their right flank. Hundreds of unarmored naked dark elves fell.

Sergeant Pierluigi saw the missile attack and ordered his crossbows to fire from the hill on the left flank of the elven hoard. The plan worked; the hoard began to funnel itself toward the center of the well-prepared Nixlander line.

Meanwhile Sevin tried to shoot at the mounted elven archer, but his target kept out of range at the edge of the tree line. The mounted elf had the body of the female draped over the back of his horse. Sevin swore and looked for other targets, but when his men cranked the ballista for another shot, one of tension ropes broke, breaking the left arm of the weapon. He told the half-orc. "Captain, the ballista is done for the day. It'll take me half a day to take it apart and repair it."

He looked back at the weapon and saw the crew trying to dismantle the broken machine. "That's all right. Organize your crew and help carry the wounded back to the healers."

"Yes, my Lord," Sevin said, returning to his position.

Catguallaun saw the situation from a different perspective. Standing near the front, he felt the power of the goddess as the elven warriors began moving toward the human camp. The first explosion surprised everyone but it was a strong demonstration of the goddess's power. As they approached the encampment, he noticed the humans hiding behind a wooden wall. *Cowards.* He wasn't close enough to see the trench. As the hoard pushed closer, he saw men uncover a large war machine and shoot a spear at them. He heard screaming behind him but urged the warriors forward.

Catguallaun felt the power of the goddess surge again; this time, a section of the wooden wall blew apart in an icy blast leaving many humans wounded by the shards. Emboldened, his warriors cheered and screamed the old battle cry of "Uboo! uboo! uboo! The sound was overwhelming as they surged forward.

However, when the priestess died, Catguallaun felt the power the of the goddess fade. He heard more screams behind him. His arms and legs felt weary from running all night. "The priestess is dead!" Around him elves faltered. The sense of certain victory disappeared, quickly replaced by fear. Catguallaun yelled, "Steady! Glory to the goddess! Do not fear these wicked humans." He felt the warriors around him hesitate, the archers in the hoard fired arrows as they marched forward.

Suddenly humans appeared from behind the wooden wall and fired their crossbows. From behind the earthworks came arrows from the traitorous southern elves. Countless warriors fell screaming from the massed missile attack. A moment later more crossbow bolts flew from the top of the hill, mowing down warriors like a scythe reaping through a field of hay. Catguallaun thought, *we need to get just a little closer, and we'll be able to charge the humans at full speed. Just a little closer.*

Ututur grimaced as arrows and crossbow bolts killed and maimed thousands. The elves on his right flank stopped advancing and pushed into the center, survivors looked for a way to get out of the rain of arrows and bolts.

"Looks like your plan to keep the dark elves away from the gate is working," said Kiley.

"Yes, what a waste of lives," said Ututur. The hoard was now close enough for him to make out the faces of individual elves. Most of the dark elves wore rags or nothing at all, their bodies were painted with runes. They were poorly armed; some had a staff while others carried simple bows and a few arrows. None wore armor. He estimated that before the hoard could charge, his missiles would kill or wound thousands more, and without any siege equipment the hoard would never breach the trench or the palisade wall. "Kiley, go tell Eoin to have half of the archers shoot at the center now."

"Yes, captain."

Ututur took time to look around him and saw two frightened

young soldiers near him. One held a bugle and the other the Nixland flag. He motioned them to come closer. "What are your names?"

The standard bearer said, "I'm Noe, my Lord." The other young man pointed to his bugle. "My name is Ahern. I'm the bugler."

"Noe, plant the standard here. We aren't going to retreat. Run to the rear and ask the sergeant for a situation report. I want to make sure no one is behind us and report back to me. Ahern stay close and get your bugle ready."

The magic of the goddess that had filled Catguallaun with strength and courage was almost gone. His body felt exhausted. He hadn't slept for two days. He was thirsty and hungry. When he started this foolish journey, he had visions of elves marching forward to battle evil monsters. In his mind his army looked like noble elves of old, wearing shining armor and wielding fabled weapons forged by dwarven masters. The illusion was broken, now he saw the reality of his ill equipped and poverty-stricken northern brothers and sisters stumbling toward death. He looked ahead and saw a monster standing beside the black and yellow flag. Catguallaun cursed the goddess and was angry at being deceived by the priestess. All he could do was run toward this orcish monster, not seeing the trench over which the hoard must pass to reach the earthen mound with the wooden wall.

The half-orc was still shocked when the hoard began their charge at about forty double paces, even though he expected it. He ordered Ahern to signal the men to stand ready.

Ahern stood and blew his horn for a fast call to arms. All along the wall the soldiers rose with their shields and spears. Meanwhile the crossbowmen continued their deadly barrage.

The front of the hoard hit the trench. Some elves fell in while others jumped in; many more were pushed in from behind as the mass of elves surged forward in a deadly stampede. Some broke bones while others were trampled. Screams filled the air, growing louder as the stampede progressed. The momentum of the crowd pushed more dark elves to their deaths. Those few who were able to climb out of the ditch were stopped by the fence. As the dark elves struggled to climb up, they were speared in the face, throat, and chest by Nixland soldiers who fought from the safety of their wall. The steep embankment was difficult to climb and as the battle raged the ground became soaked with blood and gore. The attackers slipped on the muddy surface, falling on top of others trying to climb up.

The half-orc saw Kiley crying while shooting her bow at any elf who managed to climb out of the trench. The attackers broke like a wave on an unmovable rock. The dark elves never had a chance. Ututur almost wanted to call an end to the killing but a tall elf scrambled out and made it to the top.

Catguallaun couldn't believe the size of the orc standing next to the evil human flag. *If I kill him, we can defeat these monsters.* He delivered a blow to the human standing in his way and pushed him aside. He faced the ugly beast and thanked the goddess for the chance to kill an enemy of his people.

The half-orc roared and used his poleaxe to spear the crazed elf with the spike end, lifting him off the ground. The hammer and axe prevented the impaled elf's body from sliding down the shaft of his poleaxe. He dumped the flailing elf back into the trench, where his bleeding body mingled with other trampled corpses.

Catguallaun's chest exploded with pain as his feet left the ground. The world swirled around him as he flew backward into the ditch and was swallowed by the writhing mass of dead and wounded elves. He thought he heard a woman laugh in the distance as his glorious visions of the past disappeared; he sank into the mass and suffocated. The spell that griped the dark elves broke completely as Catguallaun took his last breath. Far away, those elves who had gathered around the eastern edge of Beinn na Callaird melted back to into the woods toward their northern villages.

The half-orc had to stop himself from letting his blood lust take over. He held himself back and stopped the charge downhill. Instead, he stepped back to see how his soldiers were faring. More elves made it out of the trench but were too close for the crossbowmen to shoot. Instead, they fought with their swords and spears, pushing the elves back down away from the wall. Ututur stood tall and observed the entire battlefield. They had stopped the attack. He felt relieved for victory was almost certain. He saw Ahern bleeding but holding his position. He quickly used one of Ilina's bandages in his hip pouch on the lad. "Can you use your horn?"

"Yes, my lord," Ahern replied.

"Signal Sergeants Netland and Szymon."

When Ahern blew his horn, Sergeant Netland organized fresh troops on the wall. As soon as the fresh soldiers took up their positions the frontline fighters began an orderly withdrawal. "Now go tell Sergeant Pierluigi to bring his men down and go to the gate."

The half-orc looked as the trench filled with the dead and dying, the hoard's momentum pushed more of the elves to their deaths. They were dying for no reason; they didn't have a chance. He could see the back of the hoard. He smiled when he saw many elves running away. Another crazed elf made it to the top of the wall where he was standing; he roared and caved in the elf's head with the hammer part of his poleaxe. Blonde hair and pieces of brain were stuck to his weapon as the dead elf slid back into the trench. Ututur took a step back as fresh soldiers arrived to take his place. Too focused on the battle, he failed to notice the mounted archer with the dead priestess as they fled into the forest.

As he watched the carnage, he asked himself. *Why did so many have to die? What made these elves attack? This made no sense.*

Sergeant Netland approached. "Captain, I left the men under the command of the First; it looks like we'll carry the day."

"Yes, we're lucky they were unprepared."

"Should I order soldiers to give chase?" she asked.

"Yes, get five hundred mounted and ready. Don't chase them into the woods. One or two passes should break them."

As the battle continued, fewer elves reached the top of the earthworks. Sergeant Netland's light calvary waited by the gate in silence for his signal. The half-orc turned reluctantly to Ahern.

"Signal the calvary to move forward."

"Yes, my Lord." As soon as Ahern's bugle started another bugler with the calvary joined in the music.

Ututur watched the gate open as the cavalry rode out. Once on the road, five hundred mounted soldiers formed a single line facing the field. They held their round, black and yellow shields, spears pointed to the sky. At Netland's command a bugler played the notes to signal the march forward. The line of armored soldiers started walking their horses forward.

The sound of the bugle cut through the battlefield. Many of the dark elves heard the music and pointed at the massed cavalry. Growing screams of fear came from the doomed hoard.

At about fifty double paces the cavalry leveled their spears. At forty double paces they increased speed and charged the hoard as the bugler played. The shock of the cavalry charge completed the route. The Nixland light calvary ran through the fleeing enemy. Wheeling for another pass, they closed ranks, and some of the mounted warriors who lost their spears unsheathed their swords. They cut down more of the enemy as they rode through the fleeing mass. Sergeant Netland led the calvary back through the gate, leaving the dead and dying on the field.

The half-orc put down his poleaxe and relaxed. All around, the Nixland soldiers laid down their weapons, sat down exhausted, and removed their helmets. The sergeants and firsts walked among the soldiers checking on them while keeping an eye on the retreating enemy.

Ututur finally took off his helmet and filled his lungs with fresh air. He noticed an arrow buried in his side armor and pulled it out. The point hadn't penetrated far. He turned to Ahern. "Sound the recall and get your wound treated. Afterwards stand by the colors and sound the alarm if you see any movement out there." He turned and began his walk through the encampment. After a quick inspection, he turned to the large tent where the wounded were gathered. As he walked to the tent, Sergeant Netland joined him. Before they entered the tent, he heard several voices yell. "Cheers to our Captain! Hurah! Hurah! Hurah!"

CHAPTER 20

Lady Sioban stood by her husband's bedside, looking down at the pitiful Chieftain in anger. *Why won't you die?* As she gave him a double dose of the potion, she continued digesting Trahern's news about the battle. She ordered him to place Rianor's body into an empty chamber. The humans hadn't simply won; they had routed her army. The only benefit was the northern refugees would come in droves to the cities, becoming easy converts to her goddess. As she spooned the inky liquid into her husband's mouth, a soft voice whispered, "The battle is done. The flow of blood has given me strength, and I give you permission to elevate more acolytes into full priestesses. The northern elves lost, which was expected. This defeat will bring more followers. You'll travel to the human lands where you'll spread the word of my coming and teach new followers how to worship me."

Lady Sioban smiled as she gave her weakened husband another spoonful of the thick slimy liquid. Looking at the empty brown glass bottle, she grew angry. *Now that the battle is over, I'm not going to make more of this. Rianor's death should throw the meddling Vigiles off the trail. This time you'll not see another sunrise, Osin.*

She walked to her potion room which was locked and guarded by a simple but deadly magical spell. The room was filled with hundreds of glass jars, bottles, earthen jugs, and jute bags filled with ingredients. Some were common items transformed through the dark rituals she had learned from the ancient tomes. She had learned from Larvanis, the most potent potions were the ones transformed with the addition of blood from the sacrificial rites.

Kiley rode next to the wagon carrying Wilhelm and a few other badly wounded human soldiers. None of elves who were with Eoin were wounded, but the death toll among the dark elves was horrendous. Thousands filled the trench, and thousands more lay on the field. Eoin ordered the captured dark elves to pull wounded elves from the trench. After the living were cleared from the trench, they filled in the makeshift mass grave. Kiley glanced at Wilhelm, asleep from the potion he had taken. The bleeding had stopped; his wound was covered with a bandage soaked in wild honey, and a clean bandage wrapped his head. The healer told her that the arrowhead did not pierce the brain, giving him a good chance of surviving.

Kiley couldn't comprehend why the dark elves would attack. But what disturbed her was the presence of the dark sorceress. Wilhelm opened his right eye. "Kiley, what happened?" he asked as he used his right hand to gently touch the bandage wrapped around his head.

"Wil, be careful; an arrow pierced your eye."

"What about the battle?"

"The half-orc captain took command and led us to an overwhelming victory. We killed the dark sorceress but didn't recover the body. I'm glad you don't have a fever from the wound; you'll recover fully," she said with a smile.

"Kiley, you should be in bed recovering," he replied weakly. "How far are you going?"

Kiley smiled; she liked the way he said her name. "You need rest more than me. I'm going all the way back to Ostheim. I want to make sure you get home safely. Your sergeant has been waiting to speak to you." She turned her horse toward the back to allow Sergeant Pierluigi privacy.

❋❋❋

Wilhelm lay back in relief at the news of their victory. *I think she kissed me, or is my mind clouded by the potion?* He glanced at her youthful face and sighed. He should be thinking about his soldiers and not about a woman, especially an elven one. He knew few elven women who liked human men. He sat up, saw Sergeant Pierluigi, and waved him forward. "Sergeant, how many men did we lose?"

"Thirty-four killed and twenty-eight wounded in total. Only four are seriously wounded, including you, my Lord. I'm glad you're doing well."

"And the enemy?"

"They were routed; I would say over ten thousand were slain, and thousands were wounded."

Wilhelm sat contemplating the magnitude of the victory. "Any word about the Consul?"

"No, but Captain Bunour the half-orc sent messengers to Mount Haven as soon as the battle was over. Sergeant Netland rode ahead with the mounted soldiers from Ostheim. We're moving slower while we travel with the infantry from Mount Haven."

"Thank you," Wilhelm said, resting more comfortably. He offered a prayer to the creator for such a victory.

"Can you call Captain Bunour for me?"

"Yes, My Lord."

Wilhelm was sitting up and drinking from a skin filled with a mix of water, apple vinegar, and honey. He saw the half-orc approach, an imposing figure mounted on a giant draft horse.

"Congratulations, Ututur, on a great victory. The soldiers are calling it the battle of the Great Forest," Wilhelm said.

"You chose a good piece of ground to defend. The rest was the soldiers' doing. It was senseless slaughter, not a great victory. The dark elves were poorly led and without proper equipment. They had no chance once they charged our defensive position. I fear that most of them who survived the battle will die from their wounds or starvation. They came from the north with no supplies," said Ututur.

"That was stupid on their part. But the victory is yours. What happened to the survivors?" asked Wilhelm.

"Thank you. Clomin and his elves searched the woods and let many escape north. While he took as many of the walking wounded as he could back to their capital for treatment, he left the severely wounded on the battlefield. He promised them that he would send help as soon as possible. I left them food and medical supplies but I don't know how many will survive."

"Ututur, we should be rejoicing. Why do you look troubled?" asked Wilhelm.

"I hope you're right. I was attacked by the sorceress back in Nixland." Ututur paused.

"And?"

"The one that attacked me in Nixland wielded fire and had shoulder-length blonde hair. This one wielded ice and looked younger and she had very long silver hair," Ututur said.

"That is disturbing news. People saw her get killed by the ballista."

Ututur nodded. "Yes, we saw her go down. However, as soon as the battle ended, I sent scouts to look for her body."

"Go on," said Wilhelm sitting up trying not to show his concern.

The half-orc lowered his voice. "We didn't find it. We should keep that to ourselves for now. I want to discuss this with the Consul, and the Vigiles."

Wilhelm lay back and tried to rest but the disappearance of the sorcerer's body was an ill omen he did not want to contemplate.

Eithne lay in a deep sleep. In her dream she walked through a familiar, beautiful garden. The plants and flowers bloomed, and the scented air was pleasing. As she walked, she felt she was being watched. When she looked around, her eyes found a darkness enveloping the garden; plants began to wither and die as the blackness touched them. The High Priestess' daughter's heart filled with dread. Her terror froze her limbs; she stood waiting for the darkness to take her.

Suddenly she felt a reassuring hand grip her shoulder, pulling her away from the darkness. Without the help she knew she would be dead. She looked at the person helping her. Eithne didn't recognize the women right away but she had a familiar face with reddish blonde hair she looked like Andanir's mother. She woke up sweating. The room was dark, but she could see moon beams shining through her window. Her heart was beating so fast it felt as if it would burst. When her heart finally stopped pounding, she thought heard noises coming from the chieftain's room. Her own mother often slept in a different room since her stepfather became ill.

She carefully left her room toward the noise. When she didn't hear anything else she was almost ready go back to her room then she heard her mother's unmistakable voice. "Hold him down. We don't need him anymore."

Eithne peeked into the large private chamber decorated with tapestries flanked by fine wooden furniture. She spied her mother, brother, and Roisin standing at the foot of her stepfather's bed. "I'll wake him and make him sign and seal these documents," her mother said. "Hold his head up, Aoife."

Eithne heard her mother chant a few incomprehensible words and saw her feed the Chieftain a liquid from a small bottle. In moments, the old elf stirred and opened his eyes. "What's happening?" he asked in a weak voice.

"Nothing, my husband. I have some documents you must sign." Her mother brought a small tray holding documents and a quill. She put the quill in the Chieftain's hand and helped him sign. Roisin stood by with wax and used a candle to melt it under the signatures. Her mother took the Chieftain's signet ring and sealed the documents.

"Well done, my husband. Now I don't need you anymore. Aoife, kill him."

Eithne let out a small gasp and quickly covered her mouth with her left hand as she watched her brother smother her stepfather with a pillow. She saw her stepfather struggle. Roisin and her mother leaped into action, using their bodies to hold the old elf down as her brother killed him.

Eithne's heart pounded; her mouth was dry. She backed away from the door and tiptoed back to her room. As she closed the door, she heard footsteps just outside her room. She quickly got back into bed and lay there facing away from her door. She shut her eyes tight and clung to her blanket. *Did my door just open?* She heard a slight creak. She opened her eyes slightly and looked at the wall as light from the hallway appeared. Eithne bit back a scream. The door creaked again, and the light from the hallway disappeared. Eithne let out her breath. Shaking with fear, she tried to comprehend what she had witnessed. She lay there unable to fall back asleep. When it was almost dawn, she heard servants yelling in the hallway. "The Chieftain is dead! Help!"

Over the next few days events moved quickly. Lady Sioban produced several documents, one naming her brother Aoife as the adopted son and true heir to the chieftain, another document expanded the power of the High Priestess and created religious courts to root out heretics and sorcerers. These courts held the power to punish anyone with imprisonment or death. A third document allowed the High Priestess to use at least one tenth of the taxes collected by the council for any purpose.

Eithne remained silent, she kept to herself during this transition. Her mother acted quickly; in a matter of days she anointed her brother as the new chieftain. She used her judicial power to conduct secret trials of the dark elven prisoners and sentenced all of them to death for using dark magic. Everyone but Eithne was surprised by her mother's revival of the most gruesome ancient practice. She said that as the High Priestess she had the power to dictate the manner of the execution and burning of sorcerers was the only way to cleanse the world of dark magic. She revived the practice of death by burning in the holy tree.

Her mother had her acolytes build ten sacred hollow trees out of wattle and wood in the center of Beinn na Callaird next to the temple of the Huntress. Each holy tree measured at least twenty double paces tall. One tree could fit about fifty dark elves found guilty of dark magic. One night all of the holy trees were set on fire and over five hundred dark elves were burned alive. Her mother and her brother made everyone in Beinn na Callaird witness the cleansing. Eithne almost fainted from the gruesome screams that came from the burning trees and thought she saw a slender female dance in the flames. Fear of dark magic gripped the city and no one dared oppose her mother or brother lest they be accused.

Other dark elves were beheaded in public, their heads taken to the forest near the site where the ancient altar had stood, ostensibly to act as a warning to anyone who would follow such an evil path.

Her mother also arrested several prominent council members, accusing them of heresy, practicing dark sorcery, and helping the dark elves foment a revolt. The religious court tried and executed them the same day. They too became fuel for another burning holy tree. By the fourth day of her brother's reign only three of the twenty council members remained alive. Her mother's grip on her brother and on

Litauia was complete.

When Trahern returned with Rianor's body, High Priestess Sioban had him placed the corpse in a small chamber in the catacombs on cleansed soil, circling the body with pure gold powder. Once the perfect circle was completed, she chanted over the body as she wrote ancient runes in powdered silver suspended in human fat on the dead body. She poured mercury into the dead elf's mouth. Once the drawings were finished, she ordered the acolytes to bring two young elves to the room. Sioban exulted in the bloody sacrifice and feasted on the raw heart with her acolytes and used the blood to write more runes on the naked dead body. The acolytes chanted beside the body as Larvarnis revived Rianor, returning her soul from the underworld.

Exhausted, the High Priestess instructed her acolytes, "Leave her body here to recover. Get me another sacrifice so I can restore my strength before resting."

"I want you to begin negotiations with the Nixlanders immediately. I want peace between our peoples. I'll open trade and create a joint force of humans and elves to patrol together," demanded the High Priestess. She sat straight and gazed at the remaining three members of the council. Knowing that all those who opposed her were eliminated. "The new chieftain is asking the Warlord for the same thing as we speak. I wanted you to hear it from me. Now prepare to make these changes. Fine replacements for the empty seats on the council. I have many other matters to attend to." She stood and left the room without waiting for a response.

"I don't understand this," Eoin said. "There must be some sort of mistake."

"Yes, the proposals aren't what I expected. I thought she would prepare for war." The Warlord was disgusted by the revival of the five-hundred-year-old holy tree ritual. According to written records, even back then it was not a common practice. In fact, the practice was only reserved for sorcerers and not their followers.

"Maybe she has realized that our warriors are no match for a better equipped and trained Nixland force," offered Kiley.

"Let's wait and see what the Council decides," Eoin said as he sat back in his chair thinking. With so many of the old guard gone the Council was powerless.

"They'll do as she asks; they are afraid of her. The replacement councilors were all handpicked by the High Priestess," said the Warlord. He knew the new chieftain was weak-minded. Their entire society was devolving into something no one in the room recognized. Never in the long history of his people had so many elves been killed in such a short period of time and dark magic was once again being practiced. "Care for a dwarven brandy?" he asked the Warlord.

Ututur had been home only a single day when the High Council ordered the militia to assemble at the main training ground. He knew it was important to acknowledge the bravery of the soldiers but he didn't like to attend the ceremonies. The half-orc felt shy in large gatherings. When he walked through the training ground gates, he saw the councilors and the large crowd that had gathered to watch the proceedings. He approached Consul Lorenz, "Hello, how are you feeling?"

"I'm well. I can walk with the cane without much pain. Congratulations on your victory. I haven't seen you since I was carried off." Lorenz was proud of Ututur's accomplishment, it was vindication of his patronage of the giant. Unlike the kingdoms to their west talent was rewarded. Birthright mattered less in Nixland.

"Thank you, my Lord. The men did the fighting."

"Don't be modest Ututur; you deserve the credit," Lorenz said as he held the half-orc by the shoulder. "We'll be handing out seven medals, based on your recommendations. Soon, I want you to plan an inspection mission to the other border towns and their garrisons."

All the other captains and council members joined other dignitaries on the steps of the main indoor training ground facing the open field and the gathered throng. When the Consul signaled, the buglers sounded a long flourish and drums tapped out a steady beat as the soldiers who had participated in the battle of the Great Forest marched forward. The soldiers wore armor and marched with precision, carrying the flag of Nixland beside Consul Lorenz's personal flag. The sun felt hot and cut through the cool fall morning.

Ututur couldn't focus on the ceremony; his thoughts were on Ilina, Andanir and work. However, his attention returned to the last man getting the bronze medal for bravery. Ututur smiled as Ahern received the medal from Aldous. The boy had stood his ground and continued to fight even after being wounded.

The Head of the High Council, Galdino di Bartolo came forward. "Thank you, citizens, of Nixland. Your bravery and dedication form the foundation of our republic. Now, I want to award a special commendation to Captain Ututur Bunour. The council would like to present the victorious Captain with a gold medal of service and his own battle standard which is to be displayed when he is in command; this standard will fly beside Nixland's banner." As Di Bartolo finished speaking a new standard was unfurled next to the two other banners. It was deep blue with two large silver pole axes crossed in the center and the golden Nixland star in the top right.

The half-orc stood there not knowing what to do until a gentle push from behind by Captain Bianco unfroze him. She whispered, "Congratulations! Don't just stand there; go get the medal."

"Ummm, thank you," the giant mumbled and walked woodenly to face Councilor di Bartolo. He received a small gold star that would be incorporated into his ceremonial sword scabbard, already decorated with multiple awards he earned over years of service. "Thank you, my Lord," he said as he faced the gathered soldiers.

The soldiers cheered loudly for their victorious Captain before marching out. Ututur stood watching the marching soldiers and spotted Ilina, Andanir, Lucio, and Ovidio in the crowd, all waving. He returned their greetings, surprised at the burst of happiness he felt. It brought back happy memories of when his grandfather gave Ututur his own favorite axe. His grandfather honored him after Ututur had become a scout in their tribe's warband, the Sword Breakers.

After the army dispersed, Aldous came up to Ututur and said, "I read your report and suggestions for improving the army. I like your idea of having three permanent subordinates for each Sergeant. We'll officially call them first alternate. We should have a sub-captain as an aid for each captain. I also support creating an element in our military dedicated to construction, engineering, and animal husbandry. I'm afraid the days of simple soldiering are over; the importance of these additional elements cannot be ignored. We'll talk more on this, but congratulations. Enjoy this day."

"Thank you, Aldous, I'll enjoy the fall festivals more this year," Ututur replied.

"I wish I could attend the festival events; I must meet the elven delegation along with the other council members. The elves are eager to forge a new relationship in the aftermath of the battle."

✸✸✸

Ovidio was dressed in another bright multicolored jacket. With a smile on his face, he guided the group to a large tent where local brewers, vintners, and distillers were selling their seasonal drinks. Ovidio's exuberance was contagious. His enthusiasm spread to the rest of the group as he ordered a pitcher of spiced ale and a pitcher of wheat beer for their table. "I love the fall festival; each year the ales get better," Ovidio said.

"Here is a toast to our Captain Ututur," said Lucio raising his mug of ale. "To the best captain this side of the Great Forest!"

Ilina joined in the toast; Ututur raised his mug as well, and even Andanir joined in, raising his glass of watered-down ale. Ovidio was in a generous mood and ordered a plate of fall delicacies for the group. They enjoyed the platter of grilled sausages, mixed salad greens, and grilled root vegetables seasoned with herbs. While the rest of the group ate, Ovidio took Ututur aside and moved them to the other end of their long table, "May I ask you some questions? I've heard several accounts of your battle, and I'm curious."

Ututur leaned forward to talk to his friend. "I'll try to answer your questions. But first here is your necklace. I've been meaning to return it to you." He wasn't sure if the gem did anything at all.

"Thank you. I hope it helped you. The sorceress you first faced used fire?"

"Yes."

"But by accounts, the one you faced in the battle used ice." The gnome stroked his clean-shaven chin.

"Yes. Where are you heading?" asked Ututur.

"I think we may face a greater danger than we first believed," Ovidio said, taking another pull from his mug. "I need to do more research to give you a full answer, but my guess is that we are facing more than one sorcerer."

"What are you saying?" the half-orc tried to keep his voice down. He kept his growing anger from getting the better of him.

"We have to worry about a master sorcerer. Only a master can train others and wield all the different elements with equal power. All the other sorcerers have a preferred elemental power."

"You should tell the Vigiles and Aldous," Ututur said.

"I plan to when we meet this evening. One more question about the dark elves. Did they seem drugged and not fully in control of themselves?" asked Ovidio.

"Yes. From what I understand they ran all night without food or water. When they attacked, they were disorganized and rushed forward into the trench without a battle plan. When the sorceress fell, I sensed a heaviness lift from the battlefield. Soon afterwards the elven hoard faltered, many stopped attacking and fled. Some others just continued their attack even though the battle was lost." Ututur remembered the trench filled with writhing bodies.

Ovidio noticed the sadness in Ututur's eyes and said, "Come, let's join the others and we'll get some sweets for Ilina and the boy afterwards." The little gnome reached out and grasped Ututur's large hand and led him back to the gathered friends.

CHAPTER 21

Sergio Salce was a successful banker and a member of the High Council. Despite his wealth and other accomplishments, people didn't respect him. He was growing older and didn't have an heir that would inherit his wealth; he would never be head of the High Council. His hands and knees ached when the weather was damp or cold. The other members of the High Council slighted him because he'd never been a successful military commander. The voice in his dreams understood his feelings; this morning after waking from his dreams of power he heard a soft voice fill his bed chamber. "I can help you. I can make you powerful and destroy your enemies. I'll provide you with many females who'll produce strong heirs."

"Who is this?" he asked looking around his large, well-decorated room.

"I'm the one who can give you power and help you bend others to your will. Look at your hands," the voice commanded.

As he looked at his bent, bony, stiff hands, his fingers straightened. He flexed his fingers, moving them without pain for the first time in over twenty winters. "I can give you much, much more."

"What must I do?" Salce didn't have to think twice to know a good deal when he saw one.

"Worship me; then I can answer your prayers. A new age is coming, and you can stand with me in power or oppose me and be ground to dust alongside the weak."

Salce had experienced these dreams before, but never like this. In the past the dreams had reminded him of his weakness and loneliness. He often prayed for more power and health. Was the goddess finally answering his prayers? "Yes, I am ready; just say the word."

The soft voice grew louder and rang in his head, "Once you accept my power, there is no turning back!"

"Yes," he screamed in fear and joy. There was no answer; the voice was gone. He lay in bed, not sure if the voice had been real or a nightmare. But he looked at his hands again, his fingers were straight. He opened and closed his fist without pain and the swelling around his knuckles was gone. He rose and found that his knees and back did not ache and his penis was erect for the first time in years. Whatever the price, he would gladly pay it.

Rolando reached Mount Haven as the fall festival was just beginning; people were celebrating the great victory over the dark elves. Tommaso found him lodgings at the Golden Rooster Inn and left. Rolando decided to enjoy the festival while he waited for Elenora to contact him. After the voice talked to him, he continued to walk and ride pain-free. He didn't remember when his body had felt this strong. The voice spoke to him on the street, "Are you ready to obey me?"

"That depends," Rolando answered. He was no fool and wasn't going to agree to anything without more proof. The moment the thought went through his mind and the words escaped his lips, a searing pain wracked his body, spreading from the middle of his back to his arms and legs. After a few gasping breaths he fell on his side as the pain spread to his fingertips and toes. Even his eyes hurt. "This is what you can look forward to. Either you obey, or you will die in pain in a ditch, forgotten." The voice grew harsh. "It matters not to me if you die broken and useless."

"No, please. I'll obey," Rolando begged, and the pain ceased as quickly as it had begun. Some of the people around him were staring, and an old man asked if he was well. The mercenary nodded and stood; he dusted himself off and hurried to the nearest ale tent.

Eleonora didn't know what she was looking for in the woods northeast of Mount Haven, but the voice told her to search for a large stone altar. After dismounting, she led her horse deep into the woods, Entering the clearing, she felt an odd sensation flow through her body. "Yes, this is it," came the soft, beguiling feminine voice. "You did well. I'll have additional tasks for you and Rolando."

"Yes, she whispered." *How did the voice know about Rolando?*

"I know your thoughts; you can't hide from me," giggled Larvarnis in a childlike voice.

Eufrasio led the caravan towards Mount Haven. The city leaders of Palmanova received word from other travelers and merchant's message network of the growing tension between Nixland and Litauia. He had worked for the city state's government for as long as he could remember, but rumors of dark sorcery frightened him. He would have to talk to Ututur and other prominent members of Nixland society. He glanced back at the sixty-eight wagons behind him, trying to calculate the profits he would make on this trip.

Ututur worked furiously preparing the five hundred small clay pots he had purchased. "The last group of trade caravans is due to arrive any day now," he said as he soaked them in strong vinegar.

"Maybe we should make more potted meats," Rolf said soaking each of the pots in boiling water. Afterwards, these pots would be filled with cooked spiced beef or trout cooked in dried herbs then covered with clarified butter. "I think you're right, Rolf. We need to make more. I promised Eufrasio two hundred of the potted meats as well as a hundred lengths of dried spiced sausage with three hundred packets of soup mix. Since winter is coming, we'll keep a hundred for ourselves. We'll sell the rest at the store or at the market. The potter promised me another five hundred small and medium sized clay pots by the end of the week."

"I'll also go around to our regular customers to collect the empties and clean them for reuse," said Rolf as he used iron tongs to remove the pots and their lids from the boiling water.

"Emiliana told me that the store's doing well. It was a great idea to have your mother and sister work in the store with them. Make sure you pay Tilda and Mariken a fair wage."

"Yes, Master," Rolf said, arranging the clay pots and their lids on a drying rack.

Rolf looked at Ututur with a sad smile. "I wanted to serve under you during the battle but was ordered to stay behind. All we did was guard the walls, drill, and patrol the city."

"Count your blessings and hope you'll never have to use your equipment or your training," said Ututur. "War is not all glory, and your family depends on you." He knew all too well the desire for adventure and sympathized with the young man. It was difficult when so many soldiers had been in battle while you stayed behind.

"Yes, Master Ututur," Rolf said, his tone unconvinced.

"Now, let's heat the clarified butter, and I'll start ladling the meats into the pots," Ututur said.

After the battle of the Great Forest, Aoife as the new chieftain. He was reanointed by his mother is a private ceremony with the blood of the innocent. The new chieftain quickly consolidated his power with his mother's help. He ordered the council to sue for peace and negotiate a new treaty with Nixland. His mother also helped him pick out new replacement council members. After the exchange of letters between the two lands, an informal understanding was reached in record time. Soon it was announced that a delegation of elves led by Warlord Eachmhile would travel with the high priestess to Mount Haven and begin direct negotiations before winter. A smaller group would stay until a treaty was completed. Eachmhile was also charged with creating a permanent elven mission to the United Cantons. So far, the Warlord was one of the few that had escaped the High Priestess' purge. Many wondered how long the Warlord would keep his position.

Chapter 22

Lady Sioban rested in her room in Mount Haven and planned a special gathering for those who had heard the voice of Larvanis. She had brought with her two newly elevated acolytes, Balor Ayden and Bodicca Fiadl, who would spread the word of the goddess here and beyond. Both had shown great promise. While the Warlord and Eoin negotiated with the Nixland council members, Lady Sioban purchased a small, fortified building with a cellar and a hidden chamber where they could practice their sacred ritual sacrifices. The building would serve as the embassy and as a temple to Larvanis. It was on the outskirts of the city with easy access to the main city. Tonight, she would consecrate this ground with blood and spread Larvanis's power. "Ayden, Fiadl, I want you to help me consecrate this ground tonight. I'll sacrifice two of the children we brought." Ayden and Fiadl both lowered their heads and bowed. "Yes, Highness, I'll prepare the altar."

Sioban replied, "Good, now leave me."

Tonight would be important. As evening fell Ayden and Fiadl took the drugged elven children they had smuggled into Nixland from the trunks where they had been hidden and brought them down into the cellar's secret chamber. The locked wooden door was hidden behind a stone wall.

The chamber was hidden within the wine storage cellar. The space could hold at least two hundred people; it was almost empty except for few hundred bottles of wine stored in the corner. They placed eight children along the wall near the altar. Afterward, Ayden and Fiadl tied a male and a female child on the makeshift wooden altar and cut away their clothes. They lit sacred candles made of elven and human tallow and undressed. They kissed each other, chanted the prayer the High Priestess taught them. Lady Sioban came down from her room, smiled in approval, and undressed. She first cast a spell that would hide the temple from prying eyes and from magic. At the same time in Beinn na Callaird, Priestess Roisin Heenan stood naked and prepared to sacrifice one of the captured dark elves. Lady Sioban had hidden a hundred prisoners in the underground temple before the rest were burned alive in the holy trees.

A soft voice spoke into Sioban's left ear. It felt as if someone was standing next to her; she even felt a hot breath on her cheek. "Get ready; the time approaches." She joined in the chanting and watched the children squirm on the altar. As the chanting reached a climax, the voice whispered to Sioban and Roisin at the same time. "Now! I'm ready to receive your offering." Sioban and Roisin plunged their knives into their victims at precisely the same time. They expertly cut open the bodies and removed the organs. As the victims' bodies drained of life, Larvarnis's power flowed.

In Mount Haven, power flowed like a mist throughout the city, searching for potential followers. The goddess searched for anyone who could easily be tempted; the old wards and protections that had been placed during the Goblin War had grown weak. Moreover, they weren't designed to stop an intrusion coming from within the city walls. Larvarnis would find weaknesses in individuals and tempt them into her clutches. She probed each insecurity, jealousy, greed, thirst for power, or sadistic longing, and used these failings to corrupt the weak.

Eleonora Bohm awoke with heart pounding. The voice whispered, "Are you willing to submit and follow my commands?"

"Yes," she replied, energy surging through her body. Her skin tingled as her muscles tightened. Running her right hand over her arm, she found that her skin was smooth and supple like a young girl's. She rose from the bed, lit a lantern, and looked in the mirror. The lines on her face which she pretended not to notice had faded; the skin around her mouth and neck appeared smoother.

"If you worship me, this is but a small taste of what I'll do for you. However, you must be willing to obey," the voice ordered. "If you go against me, I'll punish you and take away all I have given. Do you understand?"

Lady Bohm replied without hesitation, "I'm willing to obey."

Rolando enjoyed the local brothel. He couldn't remember the last time he had enjoyed the company of two women as his manhood had failed him many times as he grew older. Afterwards he walked around the festival tents sampling the special beers and foods. He returned to his small room at the inn, feeling pleased. He fell asleep, surprised at how his body had performed with the two young women. The soft voice woke him. "Do you believe? Are you willing to follow me? Or do you want your life to revert to how things were this morning?"

Rolando woke and got his bearings. "I'll follow you."

"I can save you from becoming a crippled beggar for the rest of your life. You must be willing to obey every command."

Rolando thought about the promises the voice had made him. At first, he thought he was going mad, but if this goddess could cure him, he would gladly follow. *Following her would be no worse than anything I've already done.*

Since the voice had spoken to him, councilor Salce had become more aware of how people ignored his advice. He went through the day, noticing how many people disrespected him. He was angry and jealous of the half-orc who had received his own battle standard and a gold medal for just doing his job; anyone could have done what the stupid orc did during the battle. Councilor Salce lay in bed wishing for more money, power, and appreciation. He felt old and lonely, *I don't want to grow old and die alone.*

"Sergio Salce, I can help you gain the respect and power you deserve. I can help you take all the women you want; you'll never be alone again."

"This is trickery. Go away! This is nonsense." Even as he spoke these words, he felt his hands. Somehow, she had healed his swollen joints. *But what else could this voice actually do?*

The voice grew sharp. "Or I can kill you if you wish!"

He lay still, unable to breathe. As hard as he tried, he could not fill his lungs with air.

"Stop testing my power! Are you willing to listen?"

He nodded and then he could breathe.

"I can give you all you want; and all you must do is follow and obey. If you lie or try to deceive me, you'll wish you were dead. Now rise and gaze upon your new body."

Salce did as she commanded, sliding his leg onto the floor expecting his knees to ache. He stood without pain and walked over to the mirror.

"Take your clothes off."

Tears filled Salce's eyes. In the mirror stood a young, well-formed man. His crooked back was straight for the first time in his life. He saw a well-muscled body, like he had never before staring back at him. "How is this possible?"

"Will you obey your goddess?"

Councilor Salce knelt and wept. "Yes!"

Aoife felt strength course through his body as he watched the sacrifice. In private, Roisin fed him burnt offerings from the sacred fire. She sat naked on his lap with her hand moving playfully inside his pants, but all he could think about was his desire for his sister, Eithne. The voice came to him. "Such a naughty boy. You'll have to force yourself on her; I can't make her come to you. You should forget her and take any other. She'll resist you."

He pushed Roisin off him, bent her over the small table, loosened his pants, and used his saliva to make sure she was wet enough for him to penetrate her. As he used her, he promised himself that he would take Eithne soon, meanwhile reaching and grabbing a fistful of Roisin's hair, pulling it hard as he thrust into her.

Larvarnis tried to peer into Ututur's and Andanir's minds, but her intrusion into their house was blocked; she passed by their cabin filled with frustration. But two weak mortals were of no consequence she thought as she moved to tempt others. Ututur woke feeling unrested the next morning and prepared for the day. He washed his face, walked outside, took his poleaxe, and began practicing his forms. Afterwards he used some boulders he placed around his cabin to exercise. *I should get some small boulders for Andanir, and I'll give him the torc back.*

Andanir woke up from a bad night's sleep, looked out the window, and watched his master exercise, amazed once more at his strength and speed. *He must be as strong as a giant. One day I hope I'll be half as strong as him.*

He got up, found the dwarven fire box and started a fire for breakfast. While he waited for the fire to grow, Andanir exercised and practiced his footwork like Master Lucio had taught him.

Ilina woke with a start and heard a soft voice. "I can help you gain knowledge and give you the power to heal any wound or ailment. I can also ease your loneliness."

Ilina simply said, "Stop lying to me and leave."

Larvarnis felt angry that she could not tempt this simple girl. She could feel Ilina was lonely but unable to get a foothold in the healer's mind; she left. She encountered the same problem at Ovidio's. In fact, the little gnome grew downright rude and tried to use his pitiful magic on her.

Larvarnis' strength had been renewed by the blood spilt in the recent battle. However, she had only gained but a small fraction of her lost power. She had been weakened through time by loss of followers and the lack of sacrifices. Now she extended her power throughout Nixland and Litauia. The recent sacrifices gave her fuel to extend her reach, but she quickly grew tired from the exertion. She still hadn't recovered her full strength. The people's abandonment of the gods continued to block her full potential. That night many people resisted her call, but some minds were receptive to the beguiling promises of wealth, youth, power, and fame.

After traveling for days through the mountain passes staying in small towns and villages, Harun felt tired. His knees were aching; perhaps a snowstorm was on the way. He had been scanning the sky for storm clouds but saw none. He scratched his beard; at this altitude it was difficult to predict the weather. *I hope I can make it to the next town before the storm hits.*

Before midday the clouds quickly rolled in from the North and sleet began to fall. Harun wrapped his cloak tighter around his body and pulled his hood over his blue turban. He urged the horse forward at a faster pace. The sky grew grey and visibility decreased as the sleet gave way to wind-blown snow. The old Vigiles continue to ride forward, barely able to see the road ahead. He hoped this was not a sign of things to come.

Harun didn't stop to eat; he just drank from his water skin and chewed on a piece of spicy beef jerky. As the afternoon wore on the snow stopped, and he dismounted to give the horse a rest and offer her a few handfuls of oats, then let her graze on the grass by the side of the road. He opened his saddle bags, found a cloth filled with dried apricots, and took a bite. He took out a map from his inner pocket and estimated another four or five days of travel before he reached Mount Haven if the weather didn't worsen, and no other delays slowed his journey.

The negotiations between the High Council and the elven delegation led by Warlord Eachmhile progressed rapidly; the group drafted a letter of understanding, and a provisional nonaggression treaty. They even drafted a new trade agreement. One of the provisions mandated a joint patrol of the Great Forest by a combined group of soldiers from Nixland and Litauia. With help from the Vigiles, humans and elves would cooperate to root out practitioners of dark sorcery. There was an understanding that the Vigiles would help spread this kind of cooperation with the elves to the other human kingdoms and to the other races. After this historic agreement, Eachmhile and the majority of the elven delegation prepared to return to Beinn na Callaird. Eoin and a few others would remain to iron out further details and establish a permanent embassy. In order to celebrate this historic event, Lady Sioban insisted that a feast be held at the embassy. She also insisted that the elves pay for all the beer, ale, and food for a full day of the fall festival.

Ostensibly Ututur came to talk about how Andanir was adjusting to his new life, but he really wanted to just talk with Ilina and to invite her to the elven embassy party. "What should I wear? I don't have anything fancy," said the half-orc with his eyes down cast.

"I'll help you get something from Meliore. I'm sure she'll have something appropriate," Ilina said. She looked at Ututur and saw him look a little sheepish. "Is there anything else?"

"Umm, yes, will you accompany me to the party at the embassy?" he asked.

Ilina was pleasantly surprised. "Of course, I'll go with you, but I don't want to stay too long."

"By the way, have you seen Andanir?" asked Ututur. "He hides after his lessons and chores."

"No, I haven't seen him. Let's go to Meliore's store, I'll find both of us something to wear," said Ilina.

As soon as Andanir found out that an elven delegation was in town, he began wearing a brown woolen cowl over his tunic. He thanked the goddess for cool weather, otherwise, his winter clothing would have stood out in the crowd. He heard that his stepmother had arrived as the High Priestess. *If she sees me, she'll take me back and punish me.* Andanir lived in fear and made it a point to do his work at the Iron Caldron and go straight to the training ground for additional training with Rialta. Afterwards, he would run as fast as he could to the cabin taking the long way to avoid any contact. He stayed by his new home and trained more on his own using his wooden practice dagger. He also trained using the small boulders master Ututur had gathered for him. He did everything possible to stay away from the elves lest they recognize him.

Larvanis's voice whispered in Lady Sioban's ear, "You'll meet with three humans north of Mount Haven at another ancient altar. You'll consecrate the altar and initiate the humans into our inner circle."

"Yes, I'll obey," Sioban said, smiling at the prospect of gaining more followers.

Three nights prior to the party at the embassy Larvanis guided Lady Eleonora Bohm, Rolando, and Master Salce to the ancient altar. The High Priestess arrived early to cleanse the altar with fresh animal blood. She stood in the clearing as the humans arrived separately. They all wore masks to hide their identity.

Sioban said, "Come and join me. I know you've been chosen. All of you have been called to serve the goddess."

Even with the cloth masks, Eleonora recognized Rolando right away and nodded. She had meant to speak to him but had been too busy. "Rolando, I'm glad to see you. I need to talk to you soon."

Rolando smiled and said, "Yes, my lady."

Master Salce recognized Eleonora Bohm and felt apprehensive, but he nodded to her and said, "Hello, I'm surprised to see you here."

"As am I to see you," replied Eleonora.

The High Priestess greeted the prospective initiates. "Come closer, my friends. I can promise you'll be given what was promised you and more. But the price is high, my friends. You must obey the goddess without question." She removed a few items from her satchel and placed them on the altar. "If you want to continue, remove your masks and reveal yourselves. I'll perform a short ritual and ask the goddess to instruct and reward us." She opened a bottle of special wine and poured some of the contents onto the altar. The liquid was a mixture of blood from the recent sacrifices, bile, honey, and red wine. She chanted and prayed, pouring some of the liquid into an earthen cup. Afterwards she lit the candle made from human and elf tallow, and scented with a mixture of frankincense and myrrh. As she chanted, the woods became silent.

"Kneel!" Larvanis ordered. The power of her voice struck those gathered there.

"I'm pleased that you've come. Will you pledge your lives to me? Your souls? Now undress; bear witness to my power."

While Sioban undressed quickly, the humans did so reluctantly. The High Priestess approached the altar, began chanting again, and took out a covered clay pot of cooked meats. Larvarnis spoke to her new followers. "Come to the sacred altar; rejoice in my power and prepare to receive my gifts. Although you are not worthy, I will accept you."

One by one the humans stood, walked to the altar, and allowed Sioban to feed them a piece of meat; afterwards, each took a sip of the wine. As the High Priestess chanted, Larvanis transformed each of their bodies. Eleonora Bohm became again a young maiden with full firm breasts. Rolando Fulvio's battle scars disappeared; his muscles strengthened. Sergio Salce's body completed its change from a worn-out old man into a young, muscular athlete.

"This is but a tiny part of my power," Larvanis said as the ground vibrated with magical energy. "Examine yourselves. This change will become permanent if you continue to follow me. If not, I will return you to your former state, ravaged by time. The blood and flesh of your enemies make this possible. If you have any qualms about destroying your enemies, leave now. There is no turning back for those who remain."

Each of the new followers understood the goddess's meaning, but the desire for power, youth, and wealth held them in the clearing. "Will you obey and follow me?" asked Larvanis. Cries of affirmation broke the silence of the forest. Sioban smiled with pleasure as she watched the three humans enjoy using each other's young bodies sexually.

Ututur was awed by Ilina's beauty. She wore a green silk dress with natural ease while he felt uncomfortable in his black pants and fine maroon tunic. He wore a new silk captain's sash around his waist, tied like a cummerbund. He still had Andanir's gold torc, his only adornment, which he tightened around his wrist.

As the odd couple mingled, they found themselves in front of the elven Warlord and the High Priestess. The Warlord gestured to the beautiful young elf woman beside him, saying, "This is Lady Sioban, the High Priestess of Litauia. She's responsible for this new treaty between our people."

Lady Sioban said, "You must be Captain Bunour. I've heard much about you from Eoin. You were responsible for the great victory."

"Yes, I was fortunate enough to have command during the battle," the half-orc replied.

Ututur turned to Ilina, "I'm pleased to meet you, my lady. This is Mistress Kuhn, she's a gifted healer."

Sioban grasped the half-orc's hand, causing the torc to send a small jolt up his arm. He tried not to flinch from her touch.

"I'm pleased to meet the one responsible for the destruction of the dark elves." As soon as the High Priestess touched him, she flinched slightly from a painful sensation from the half-orc's arm.

The half-orc noticed the High Priestess' discomfort and asked, "Are you feeling unwell?"

"No, I'm tired from working all day," Sioban stammered. She quickly put on a smile and pulled the Warlord away to talk to more guests.

When the High Priestess and the Warlord had moved away, Ilina asked, "Are you feeling well? You look pale."

"I think so. I felt something when the High Priestess touched me. Maybe I drank too much; I should leave."

"I'll go with you," said Ilina as she held Ututur's left arm.

"You can stay here longer if you would like," Ututur added as he began to look for the way out.

"No."

The two had taken only a few steps toward the main door when Eleonora intercepted them. "Leaving so soon?" she asked.

Ututur didn't recognize the young woman in front of him. "Yes, I have a full day of work tomorrow."

Eleonora was pleased that the half-orc failed to recognize her new younger self. "I'm Eleonora Bohm. You killed my son. Don't you recognize me?"

"I'm sorry," Ututur said quickly.

"We do have to leave," said Ilina, trying to disengage from the woman.

"I'm not going to forget about you," Eleonora said as she grasped Ututur's right arm. Immediately she let him go, gasping loudly from a painful jolt.

Ututur felt a mild, warm sensation from the torc and said, "Please excuse us, we must get going." He guided Ilina to the door and left the party.

"What happened in there?" asked Ilina.

"I don't know. I have a bad feeling about the High Priestess and

Lady Bohm," Ututur said.

"They seemed unpleasant," said Ilina, holding Ututur's arm tighter and moving closer to him as they walked back to her cabin.

Lady Sioban smiled as she drank her tea in the small sitting room. "Our trip has been a success. Both of you will remain here and send me reports regularly."

Ayden and Fiadl bowed their heads.

"I'll instruct you and learn where your magical affinity lies. Come closer, Fiadl." The young female knelt in front of the High Priestess, who put her right hand on her long, wavy strawberry-blonde hair. Sioban recited the chant of the four elements. She drew the four symbols of earth, wind, fire, and water in the air with her left hand above Fiadl's head. As she continued to chant, the symbol for air, an isosceles triangle with a horizontal line in the middle, shimmered in the air and disappeared into Fiadl's head. "Rise my child."

When she stood, Sioban embraced her and whispered words of power into the young elf's ear. Fiadl shuddered as the power of the goddess surged through her body.

The High Priestess released the girl and motioned for Ayden to come forward and kneel. She repeated the process and found that Ayden's affinity was for the earth element. She taught them the basic methods for calling upon the goddess and channeling that power through their element. "Once you finish the chant, you must use your mind to focus the power and envision what you are trying to do. I'll send you each a basic book of sorcery once copies are made. You must practice your chants and mental control before you can use any of these powers effectively. As you gain in power you should be able to use the other elements as well. Now watch me." As Larvanis' high priestess Lady Sioban could wield all four of the elements; moreover, she had read all of the books on sorcery found in the libraries of Litauia and others she had recovered in the catacombs. As Ayden and Fiadl watched, she produced a small ball of wind in her left outstretched palm and in her right constructed a small ball of dirt from the floor.

Ayden asked, "But what can you do with a small ball of dirt?"

Sioban furrowed her eyebrows, "I'm disappointed, Ayden. You must use your imagination." She glanced at a pile of firewood next to the fireplace. "Watch!" She focused and compressed the small ball of dirt until it shrank to half its size, launching it at a log. The ball passed through one large log, leaving behind a perfect circular hole. "Imagine if that was the head of an enemy. For now, if you chant and focus your energy, the magic you cast will be in its most basic form, but once you begin to master the power, you'll be able to use it in many more ways. Additionally, your mind's ability to influence weak individuals will also grow. As you gain mastery, other powers will manifest depending on your natural gifts and the generosity of the goddess, thus you'll be able to cast other spells. The more you devote yourself to the goddess, the more she will reward you. Continue to strengthen this new temple and bring the stone altar here. I'll have a mission for you soon."

"Yes, mistress," they said as they bowed and left Sioban to finish her tea.

Ayden was bored and wanted to gain more power for himself. He didn't understand Sioban's and Fiadl's timidity. *We have the power of the goddess. I don't want to hide and sneak around.* He couldn't hold back his inner desires and wanted to taste the power that flowed through him. He didn't wait for anyone's permission to experiment. He snuck out in the middle of the night to hunt. He reached the center of Mount Haven and found only the taverns, brothels, and gambling dens open.

Ayden hid in the shadows and found that the goddess had given him the power to see better at night. The need to kill was like a hunger that took over his mind and body. He waited in an alley near a tavern; while he was thinking about what he should do, a drunk walked into the alley and started to piss against the wall. Ayden moved quickly, chanting. He cupped the mouth of the drunk with his left hand, and plunged his dagger quickly into the man's back, then laid him on the ground. He continued his chant and used the dagger to cut his throat. Ayden felt energized by the killing, but he didn't feel the power that he felt when the High Priestess performed the ritual on the children.

As he snuck out of the alley he thought, *what am I doing wrong? What must I do to gain power?*

A soft female voice whispered, *"To receive the full effect of a true sacrifice, you must complete the full ritual; otherwise, you'll gain only a fraction of the power. It's good to kill but I warn you now, don't become careless. I'll punish you if you disrupt my plans."*

"Yes, my Lady," replied Ayden, but the thrill of killing was too great. He could feel the hunger growing again.

Andanir loved learning from Master Ovidio and was always amazed at how much the gnome knew. He was even happier when Rialta joined the lessons on some days. The master allowed him to use the vast library in his house. Andanir was adept at mathematics and loved learning about geometry. He was sitting at his desk looking at triangles and some of their properties when his attention strayed to Ovidio, who was reading a particularly old-looking book. "What are you doing, master?" Andanir repeated his question, for the gnome didn't hear him the first time.

"Oh, I am reading a first-hand account of a very old Vigiles named Belen. He lived a long time ago. He wrote that most sorcerers can only wield one element, with which they have a strong affinity. Other books say the same."

"So why is Belen's account so interesting?" asked Andanir.

"Good question, my boy. Belen's account suggests that even if a sorcerer is able to wield multiple elements, they usually prefer to attack with one type."

Andanir kept his ears open and knowing that the first sorcerer had used fire, but Master Ututur said that the one he faced in battle used ice, meaning the water element. "So, master, there must be more than one sorcerer."

"I'm afraid so. According to Belen, a high priestess usually can wield all of the elements, and the two we know about didn't seem powerful enough to be the master," said Ovidio, glancing at Andanir.

"So logically, there must be at least one more. How do they get their power?"

Ovidio walked to Andanir and stood beside him. "It's simple.

First, you must be born with the ability to wield magic. Then, the gods must help you channel the power. Once you have an affinity with the four elements, you must study. The sorcerers we know of must be gaining their strength through sacrificing living beings."

"How can anyone stand up to such evil power?"

"Do you follow Mielki, the Huntress?" asked Ovidio.

"Yes, Master."

"If you are sincere and keep your faith, she will help you. If you have any affinity with magic, you can learn how to use the forces of nature through sacred geometry and incantations. Your studies will allow you to see magical threads." Ovidio sensed that the boy had potential but many with potential could not progress any further. He put a reassuring hand on the young elf's shoulder.

"Can I wield magic?" Andanir was eager to find out.

"You must leave childhood behind and become a young adult before I can test you further. For elves, I'd say around thirteen winters or so. Now, enough about magic. Finish the problems I gave you." The gnome smiled and returned to his book and hoped that the boy had the will to master his mind.

CHAPTER 23

The High Priestess watched as human workers carried the stone altar she had consecrated in the woods. They brought the ancient stone down to the basement by creating a large hole in the side of the wall. These workers were also hired to construct a larger hidden entrance to the basement.

As the evening approached after the workers had left, Lady Sioban returned to the basement with Ayden and Fiadl. Away from the others she chanted and magically moved the altar stone into the hidden chamber where a wooden base waited to hold it. Once inside and the door closed, the two other elves joined in the chanting. She gathered her powers and told the two acolytes to continue to chant. She cast a shadow over her form to make her nearly invisible; anyone looking at her would become confused and quickly forget what they had seen.

As the sorcerers continued their chanting, Sioban ran unnaturally fast out of the embassy, leaving no trace in the dark. She quickly found the home of the head of the Nixland High Council. Although a few people were about, her magic masked her from all prying eyes. She found the main door and knocked. An old man opened the door and looked at her in confusion; he didn't recognize her. "It's late. What can I do for you?"

"May I come in?" she asked.

"Yes," he said.

As soon as she closed the door, she reached out and touched the old man's back, discharging the magical electrical energy she carried within her. Several blood vessels in Galdino's heart burst; he fell, gripping his chest. Before his body hit the floor Sioban turned and ran out of the house, skipping into the night and laughing gleefully. Now she could return home and strengthen her grip from Litauia. As she moved silently in the night, her thoughts returned to the disturbing incident with that half-orc. When she had touched the beast, she felt an odd protective ward that actually caused her pain. She should have someone keep an eye on that one. But what can one savage do?

Galdino's sudden death shocked the city, and the council of Nixland met in an emergency secession to appoint a new member to the high council. Even though many members had already left Mount Haven for their respective cantons, enough were present to form a quorum. The election concluded quickly with the experienced council member Birger Dybdahl, a dwarven master weapons smith and armorer, was elevated to the High Council. At the same time Sergio Salce was appointed as the head of the ruling body.

Since Galdino di Bartolo was one of the representatives from Mount Haven in the Ostkreis canton, an emergency election was organized to fill the seat. To vote a person would have to obtain a minimum of one hundred witnessed signatures or marks to be eligible to run for election within a week. Additionally, the candidate had to be a recognized resident of Nixland through birth or keep a permanent home in the area. Once the candidates were approved, an election would take place ten days later with one public debate conducted in the open militia training ground or the council meeting hall.

Master Ovidio was shocked and saddened by his friend's sudden death. He went to see his old friend one last time before his burial. The body was laid out in a wooden casket in the main council hall guarded by soldiers; many of Galdino's supporters and friends had come to say their farewells. As Ovidio walked close the body, he felt his large ruby crystal grow warm; his vision blurred, and by the time he stood next to the open casket, he could see black tendrils of dark magical energy radiating out from Galdino's chest. The magical energy looked like black smoke. Some of the dark tendrils rose and touched some of the others gathered in the room. One tendril reached for him. Ovidio used all of his mental discipline to smooth his face, he thanked the goddess and focused his mind. He used his finger to draw a perfect circle in the air. No one else in the room could see what he was doing and just chalked it up to eccentric behavior of a gnome. He continued and drew six smaller, perfect intersecting circles inside the larger circle, creating the seed of life. The gnome saw the black tendrils draw back from this sacred shape floating in the air above his dead friend. To banish the darkness forever, Master Ovidio continued his weave and replicated the seed of life pattern nineteen times and completed a flower of life pattern. He only drew a simplified flower of life which was a large circle containing thirteen smaller intersecting circles perfectly spaced apart. His work became fully charged with power and absorbed all of the dark energy inside his dead friend's body. Satisfied, Master Ovidio erased the flower of life. *Someone murdered my friend with dark magic.* He remained calm, offered a prayer to the goddess, and walked quickly out of the hall.

It was midday and Master Harun Faheem was tired from his journey. He asked the guards for directions to the Vigiles headquarters. The city was bustling as people went about their daily chores. He found soldiers on guard at the fortress gate and was directed to leave his horse by the stable. The old Vigiles dismounted and gave the stable boy four coppers to take care of the mare while he talked with the two Vigiles.

Vigiles Albrecht invited Harun into the apartments. She had met the old scholar when she visited Hold Keep many years ago. "Would you join me for breakfast?" she asked.

"Yes, please," Harun responded, sitting near the fire in the kitchen. "Where's Ridolfo? I would like to meet the young man."

She poured hot water into the pot. "He is out on patrol with the local sheriff."

Harun accepted the tea as Albrecht placed some large sugar crystals on a plate in the center of the table. She served up some fresh bread delivered that morning with butter and some cheese.

Harun placed a sugar crystal in his mouth and sipped the hot tea. "This is delicious. I have a letter from the Grand Master; you can read it at your leisure. I was sent here to help you and to begin my own investigation into the sorcerers. While I'm here, I would like my identity as a Vigiles kept secret."

"I understand. I'll tell people that you are a visiting scholar. But

I would like you to stay and participate in a meeting after breakfast with some trusted friends." Vigiles Albrecht sipped her tea, letting the warm liquid drive away the morning chill. She was glad the Grand Master took this matter seriously and sent the scholar to help.

"Where should I stay while I'm here?" asked Harun, taking a piece of bread and dipping it in some soft butter.

"Let me think about it," she replied.

Ututur brought some cookies spiced with cardamom, ginger, cinnamon, and cloves to the meeting. He sat at the large table across from Harun and Vigiles Albrecht. Master Ovidio chewed on one cookie while his hand hovered over the clay jar looking for a perfect one. The Vigiles cleared her throat. "Ahem, Master Ovidio, if you can tell us why you requested this meeting."

"Yes, yes. Hold on," he said as he looked at the cookies one by one. "Ahh, this one will do."

"As you were saying, Master Ovidio," the Vigiles urged impatiently.

"Yes," he said as he started eating the chosen cookie. "This is delicious, Ututur. You've outdone yourself this time. Where was I?"

"You were about to tell us why you asked for this emergency meeting," Ututur said, smiling at the gnome scholar.

"Yes, I think we're all in grave danger. I don't know whom I can trust." Ovidio held his red ruby crystal in his right hand and closed his eyes. "I feel nothing here."

"Why are we in danger?" asked Albrecht.

Ovidio started chanting and began to draw something in the air. Only the gnome could see the perfect silver circle surrounded by six perfect non intersecting circles encased in a square. The egg of life didn't take long to complete as he instilled it with his thoughts and desires for a protective ward. When the gnome finished, no one knew what had happened but a feeling of wellness permeated the gathering. "I'm afraid that the evil has spread to Mount Haven like a plague. My friend Galdino was murdered by someone who wielded dark magic to kill him. He did not die of a chest distress; the attack was deliberate."

"How do you know?" Albrecht asked with a frown on her face,

glancing at Harun to gauge his reaction.

"I detected the dark energy still lingering in Galdino's body. I just tried to detect the presence of dark magic here and cast a spell protecting us from evil. Although I can detect dark magic's evil residue, I'm not sure I can detect a person capable of using dark magic unless they have cast spells on their body."

Ututur questioned, "I thought we killed the dark sorceress?"

"Yes, one was killed in your battle, but here is the problem. Most magic users have an affinity to one of the sacred elements. The one we faced at the farm wielded fire, but the sorceress you killed used water," Ovidio said.

"She used ice," Ututur said.

"A sorcerer can control their element and use it in any form turn water into ice or into steam, or channel magical energy for other kinds of spells. A true master who can wield all the elements will have many apprentices who have an affinity to one of the elements," added Ovidio. "The apprentices are generally weaker so while they can use all of the elements, they just focus on one due to their limited ability."

Vigiles Albrecht said, "The magic user must've come with the elven delegation. We should be able to find her easily."

"Yes, yes. But this is like the plague. This cannot be stopped. It's almost like the way mice reproduce and spread. Dark magic is insidious and will take hold in an unsuspecting population. I've read ancient texts where entire cities and kingdoms succumbed to the evil in months once it reached them," Ovidio said, reaching for another cookie.

"We must warn others," Ututur said.

"I'll take this to the High Council," Greta added.

Ovidio turned and said, "No! We must be very careful how we proceed here; dark sorcery's power comes through its followers and the sacrifice of living beings. It doesn't matter if you were born with ability or simply trained. Galdino's murder confirms the presence of the followers. They spread their evil by enticing those susceptible to its guiles and paralyzing the weak with fear. Once the fear and hysteria spreads, people who have nothing to do with dark magic will look for scapegoats to kill in the name of justice."

Albrecht stood and said, "Master Harun, because of this new information I'm going to tell my friends about your mission."

Harun nodded he took out an old amulet from a pocket in his jacket. He used it to detect the presence of evil while he kept a casual hand on his dagger. He relaxed when he didn't detect anything. "Yes, I think that would be for the best. I've studied such events from the past. In one city in the Kingdom of Al-Anikka people suspected that a young girl's disappearance was a result of a dark sorcerer. Without any proof they blamed an old herbalist who lived alone in the woods of sorcery. They began to accuse people of sorcery, had them tortured and executed. This was led by a seemingly well-meaning magistrate. Out of fear, good people burned, and many were tortured. The magistrate rounded up anyone denounced by their neighbors and burned them as well. When the hysteria was over five hundred people had been unjustly burned as sorcerers. The Vigiles arrived too late to save them but quickly put an end to the hysteria. They found the body of the missing girl in the basement of the magistrate who was abusing her."

The group listened with a growing sense of dread. "Master Harun is a member of Vigiles and was sent here by our Grand Master to help us investigate the situation," Albrecht said. "I'm going to include Ridolfo and Sheriff Bastina when they get back. Otherwise, we should tell no one. We need to keep an eye on the elves and try to identify the magic user."

Ovidio finished his third cookie. "We must pay particular attention to any reports of missing persons. The sheriff can't ignore any reports of vagrants or beggars that go missing."

"Master Ovidio, can Master Harun use your library to do some research while he's here?" Albretch asked. "I'll let the sheriff know of your caution. Meanwhile, all of you keep your eyes open. We should meet again in a few days and review our findings."

"He's welcome to use the library. I could use the help going through the books and scrolls. He can even stay in the library in one of several spare rooms," Ovidio said as he looked for one last perfect cookie.

Harun smiled. "Thank you. I'll take you up on your generous

offer. We must find the dark ones before they expand their powers."

✵✵✵

Rianor woke feeling as if her body was on fire. She tried to move but couldn't; her last memory was of pain as a long arrow hit her chest, throwing her off the horse. As her vision blurred, elves around her rubbed ointment into her chest, and she lost consciousness. If there was an afterlife, she remembered nothing of it, all she felt was never-ending pain.

✵✵✵

Lady Sioban returned to Beinn na Callaird with the Warlord, leaving Eoin, Ayden, and Fiadl with ten servants. She said little to Eachmhile on their journey back but was pleased with how the situation had progressed in Mount Haven. Now the path was clear for them to recruit more followers and continue spreading Larvanis's power. She parted ways with the Warlord and guided her horse to the warehouse, entering the underground catacombs. Acolytes and followers bowed to her; the High Priestess walked to the room where Rianor's body lay. She ordered her acolytes to bring two more elven captives to the chamber.

The golden circle was unbroken, and the silver runes' edges were still sharp, but the runes on Rianor's body had faded. Sioban felt Rianor's body for signs of life and smiled when she found a shallow pulse. Six acolytes entered the room. The High Priestess stood, undressed, handed her clothes to a servant, and began chanting.

She immediately heard the voice of the goddess. *"Well done. I can now begin searching for more followers to the west beyond Nixland. Remember, this will be a long struggle."*

When Sioban finished chanting, she took a dagger from a waiting acolyte, cut open the major artery along the neck of both victims, and let the blood flow onto the floor. She washed her hands in the flow and wrote runes on her body. Afterward, she chanted as she drew fresh runes on Rianor's body. Dark smokey power filled the room and the air shimmered above Rianor's head. The emaciated body began to fill out, fullness returning to the gaunt face. After a few moments Rianor opened her eyes with a hoarse scream.

Sioban smiled, broke the gold and silver circles, and ordered the acolytes, "Take her to a warm room. Feed her some of the sacrificial meat and give her plenty to drink." Sioban turned and walked to the bath, followed by an acolyte with her clothes while two others began butchering the sacrificial meat. After placing the garments on a table, the acolyte followed her into the large bath and washed away the bloody runes with the warm, lavender-scented water.

When Ututur awoke, he lay gathering his thoughts. The cabin was cold this morning. He needed to move into town before the winter. The cabin did not have enough storage space for food and would get snowed in. As he rested, he planned his workday.

He would go to several farms to arrange for food deliveries to the Iron Caldron so that they could start preserving more food for the shop and for personal consumption. Next, he would go to the last market being held in the square and check if Eufrasio had brought his order of spices and rice. *Don't be lazy; the day is waiting*, he thought as he swung his legs over the side of the bed. Andanir was already awake, and they ate their breakfast of cooked oats and dried fruit in silence. When he finished, Ututur rose to wash the bowl and said, "We'll move into town for the winter in five days, so get your things ready."

"Yes, Master. Where will we stay? Do we have to move the furniture and other things?" Andanir asked, finishing his porridge.

"No, I only take my clothes, weapons, and hunting gear. We'll stay above the Iron Caldron's warehouse. You've seen the rooms. There are three bedrooms, a bathing room, and a cooking area." After tidying up, the two left the cabin to start their day.

After arranging for produce deliveries, Ututur walked to the market square and found Eufrasio in a tent with three guards. He stood and hugged Ututur. "Come and sit, my friend." He told his guards, "Leave us. I don't want to be disturbed." The guards closed the tent flaps behind them. "I've some questions for you, my friend, and I need answers from you as a captain of Nixland."

Ututur was surprised but nodded.

"Here, have a sweetened lemon water," Eufrasio offered as he poured a glass. When Ututur took the glass, Eufrasio asked, "What happened at the battle against the dark elves? Are the rumors of dark magic true?"

Ututur took a sip of the water. "Yes, we think there were at least two dark sorceresses at work. We killed one in the battle. I saw a ballista bolt pierce her chest."

"Thank you for telling me. I must warn my people. We've not seen dark magic in generations. I don't know if any of the current so-called magic users are a match against true wielders of dark magic. So much knowledge of the arcane arts have been lost."

"I think you need to talk to Master Ovidio. He's a gnome scholar and knows magic. He can tell you more about dark magic users. I'll have him give you a visit."

"Thank you, my friend, and by next spring I hope you'll have good news to tell me about the dark ones," Eufrasio said as he finished his lemon water. "I have your special spices and the long-grain rice. I'll have my men deliver them to your warehouse later today. We can't let this spread."

Ututur stood and returned the empty glass. "You're right. I hope we'll have good news by the time you return next year. Thank you and have a safe journey back." As Ututur walked around the market, he passed by a row of bladesmiths. The torc on his wrist felt warm as he wandered to a table where a familiar merchant displayed exquisite daggers. Ututur's eyes, however, were drawn to a wooden box holding a long, slender blade.

"I remember you. You're Captain Bunour. I'm Dodek," said the bladesmith. "I make most of these but the one you're looking at comes from across the Ada Sea. It's fifty gold pieces, but I'll let you have it for thirty gold pieces if you tell your men about the quality of my goods."

"You can call me Ututur." The half-orc was drawn to the fine dagger. When Ututur took hold of the dagger, the Damascus steel blade felt alive in his hand. It was a little small for him but would be perfect for the elf boy. "Yes, I do remember you. I'll give you forty gold if you throw in that hunting knife for me and sheaths for both." The dagger would be a perfect gift for the elf boy.

"Done," said Dodek as they shook hands. The merchant picked

out a double-bladed dagger with an armor-piercing point and two well-crafted leather sheaths, handed them to Ututur.

Ututur slid both knives into his belt. "I'll send someone with the gold by the end of the market day."

"Thank you, Master Ututur."

"You're welcome." Ututur headed back to his store and prepared himself for another meeting. He hated the idea that a dark magic user was on the loose in Mount Haven. It would be easier if he could just fight them with his axe. He was lost in his thoughts when bumped into an elf.

"Excuse me, I'm sorry," Ututur said.

"That's all right," said Eoin. "How are you? I've been meaning to visit your store but there's been too much work to do."

"I'm well. How are the negotiations going?"

"They are going well. I'm surprised at how fast things are moving. We'll be done with the new treaty by the spring thaw," said Eoin.

"I hope we can have peace and that we end the scourge of dark magic from our lands." *I don't know if I can trust him. Does he follow the dark one?*

"But we killed the sorceress in battle; you were there," Eoin said, tilting his head sideways like a confused cat.

Ututur wasn't sure how to answer this. He wanted to trust Eoin, who had fought with him. "I've heard that dark magic users have an affinity to one of the sacred elements; the one we killed used water."

"Yes, that is what I was told by our scholars before I came on this mission."

"I fought one before the battle; she used fire."

Eoin's smooth features began to change as open anger filled his visage. "You mean there's one more still out there?"

"Yes, at least one more," added Ututur.

"Thank you. We must talk again and help each other battle this evil. It can't be allowed to grow. I'm going to send word back to my Warlord today."

Ayden stood nearby keeping an eye on Eoin; seeing him speak to the giant half-orc moron, he decided to learn more.

�֍ �֍ ✷

Wilhelm lay in his bed deep in misery. *What good is a one-eyed soldier. What good is a one-eyed man?* Although he had recovered physically, he stayed in his room, filled with self-pity. In dreams a woman's voice promised him the return of his eyesight, and more. The voice promised him power, riches, and women. He shook the crazed thoughts from his mind, drinking wine and ale at first but moving on to strong brandy. He woke up with a headache that did not dissipate, he took a dirty, empty cup and poured out some of the brandy, drinking it down in one burning gulp.

A loud knock at his door made him wince. "Go away!"

More knocks came and the door opened. Kiley walked in and wrinkled her nose at the stench in the room. "It has been nearly thirty days since the battle. They tell me you are healed; I need to talk to you." She closed the door behind her and nodded to sub-Captain Pierluigi, who had taken over Wilhelm's daily duties since the injury. Kiley went to the window, drew back the curtains, and opened the windows wide, bringing fresh air and light into the room.

Wilhelm winced again and sat up. "What are you doing here? I'm not well."

"I came because I was told to talk to the commander here in Ostheim and start joint patrols into the neutral territory and the far north. These joint patrols are supposed to help our people get along with one another and build trust."

Wilhelm looked up at her standing in front of him with the window light behind her. Her long dark hair, unusual for an elf, accentuated her fine features. He remembered how much he had missed her; even when he was recovering from his wound. "I see," was all he was able to say.

"If you're able, I want to go on patrol with you," she said and smiled. "But if you're unwell, then I suppose I must go alone."

"Do you want to spend time with a man with just one eye?"

"Yes, and I have something for you," she said, handing him a leather-and-silk eye patch. She placed it next to him on the bed and kissed his forehead. "I'll be here for two more days. I'll arrange things with Pierluigi for now. I want to spend time with you before I leave."

"Thank you," Wilhelm said as he picked up the eye patch, looked at her back as she walked out of his room and closed the door behind her. *Stop feeling sorry for yourself.* He reached out for the remaining brandy, hesitated, then stopped himself from drinking.

❈ ❈ ❈

"Master Harun, I think I found something," said Ovidio from behind a stack of old tombs. There were three large tables in the library. His table was filled with scrolls strewn across the top, and there were stacks of books on the floor.

"I think I found some information as well," replied Harun from another large table at the opposite end of Ovidio's large library.

They met at the middle table with writing implements and parchment. "I'll take notes," said Ovidio. "Tell me what you found."

"We know that sorcerers and sorceresses are born with magical ability while wizards and witches learn magic by studying nature and math. But, according to Ebus the Eldest, those that use the dark magic are usually motivated by dark emotions and desires. Whether born with ability or trained, they must sacrifice living beings to their gods and use their life force to empower their spells. Once they begin using these powers, they always turn some of their magic for personal vanity. "I believe that means they use magic to appear younger."

"Not only to appear younger; a fragment from a partially burnt book says that they use their powers to restore their health and vitality. The changes are not purely cosmetic," added Ovidio.

"I found a commentary by Ebus the Young, the grandson of Ebus the Eldest. He noted that all dark magic flows through a malevolent or trickster deity. Sacrifices of intelligent beings empower the deity and the magic user," Harun said, pointing to a marked page in a decaying book. "And as the cabal grows in power, they require more sacrifices."

"This differs widely from the magic I was taught."

"What do you mean?" asked Harun, eyeing Ovidio with some suspicion.

"Well, first you must be tested for magical ability and affinity. Second, you study nature and mathematics and practice mental focus so that you can draw power from nature and from within. However, once on this path, you cannot take an intelligent creature's life without cause or use magic for self-profit."

"What happens if you do?"

"Simple. Your magical ability weakens and eventually disappears. Only the evil path of dark magic remain open. All my life I have studied magic, and until we faced the dark sorceress at the farm, I had never wielded it for combat. Even during the great war, I was only a helper to a scholar who was a great healer. The same is true for wizards and witches with no inborn talent; they must train for decades to cast any spell. That is why human wizards and witches must always have some inborn ability. If they didn't, they would be eighty years old before they could learn enough to cast the simplest of spells. Some dwarves, elves, and gnomes have no inborn ability but live long enough to learn magic. I was also taught that defensive magic can be stronger than the attacking magic if the user is blessed by a deity."

"That's interesting," said Harun, running back to his pile of books, picking up one, and searching for a particular passage. "Here, this didn't make sense at first, but in these collected tales an old scholar who had exhibited little magical ability became a powerful wizard and killed a cabal of five. It doesn't say how he did this, but his power was directly proportional to the dark magic he opposed. Once attacked, the scholar's counter-magic killed the dark sorcerers. It was noted that the scholar was noted for his kindness and generosity. Apparently, he also had an amulet of some kind. The book also describes how in each cabal, there's always one leader who can wield all of the elements and followers who can only wield one of the sacred elements.

"So, I suppose when faced with evil, a good wizard or sorcerer can use their power defensively," Ovidio mused, continuing to take notes. "Anyone who uses magic to kill without provocation will not be able to empower their spells unless they turn to evil."

"I also read in several places that those with training can see or smell dark magic," added Harun.

"Yes, that is how I learned that Galdino didn't die of natural causes. I could see the remnants of dark magic although thinking back on it, I think I did notice a foul odor," Ovidio said as he wrote more on his parchment. "I found another interesting passage from a book by Lady Gisela of the Woods. She said that evil always comes to call upon those with dark desires, sometimes in dreams. Once the person accepts the dream vision, the evil deity will talk directly to them while they're awake."

Ovidio continued, "We need to tell our comrades what we found, and I'm going to find a way to protect people during their sleep."

"Yes, you go ahead. I'm going to look through more of these books. I think I saw a passage with some mention how people protected themselves in their dreams," Harun said and returned to his pile of old tombs.

"I'll be back with something for us to eat," Ovidio said. Despite the danger they faced, Harun's presence helped the gnome feel less lonely.

❈❈❈

The room stank of urine and uncontrolled defecation, but Sioban's face remained placid as she stood waiting for Trahern. Rianor was alive again, but she sat in the corner of the room. She looked haggard and had not said a word since her reawakening. She was fed by acolytes who did their best to clean her. The goddess whispered in Sioban's ear, *"Don't worry; it takes some time for the person to come back fully. You need more offerings if you want her to recover more quickly."*

"I must be careful," the High Priestess said as she tapped her foot. *Where is Trahern?* "Someone come clean this room and wash her again!" Sioban felt her frustration grow as she waited and walked out of Rianor's room as their acolytes began cleaning Rianor and the floor around her with scented water.

Trahern ran in as the High Priestess took a seat in an alcove near the main worship area. "My Lady, I rushed here as soon as I was able."

"Good, I have a new mission for you. I want you to travel to the west to Mount Haven and take Fiadl with you to the Southern City states. I want you to begin the process of befriending the people there so we can establish an embassy in each of the five city-states and spread the power of our true goddess. I also want you to make contact with slave traders from the three western kingdoms and from across the Small Ada Sea. We need a steady supply of offerings for the goddess. I had planned to send Rianor, but she hasn't fully recovered. I'll elevate a human woman to a priestess in Mount Haven and use her to spread our power there."

"Yes, my lady," Trahern said, eager to please his mistress. She had given him back his youth and promised to restore the glory of Litauia. Although Trahern looked barely fifty, he was four hundred years old. He remembered when the Elves of Litauia lived in luxury and ruled a mighty empire. Now they barely managed to feed themselves and made trinkets for human traders. He was ashamed of the fact that elven women were now prized as entertainers or courtesans throughout the human lands. For two hundred years, rulers and chieftains had done nothing to improve the situation. He would gladly sacrifice hundreds, even thousands of lives to bring back the honor the elves deserved and restore their rightful place among the races.

Later that evening in her bed chambers, Sioban held Roisin in her arms, using her fingers to move the blonde hair out of Roisin's smooth face. She kissed her once more before getting up. "I have a task for you."

"Yes, my Lady," Roisin said as she sat up in bed.

"Trahern is leaving for the west tomorrow. I want you to go east to make contact with the Thunder Horse clans and restore the Silver Wolf Clan chieftain's health. He'll obey the goddess after she helps him unite the clans under his banner. Afterwards you'll be able to send me slaves on a regular basis. I'm going to build an encampment in the northern woods near the river to hold the slave and sacrifice them when I need. We'll use these barbarians to conquer the human kingdoms beyond Nixland."

"Even with the addition of the barbarians, will we have enough followers to do all of this and raise another army?" asked Roisin, getting up and holding Sioban's naked body from behind.

"Since their defeat, the northern dark elves have become easier to recruit; our influence is growing by the day. They are eager for revenge, which makes them receptive to Larvanis' message. We can also use the soldiers from the horse clans. They are always eager to fight and plunder and Larvarnis will help us weaken the enemy. We will rise to greatness once again."

CHAPTER 24

Eleonora Bohm stood blindfolded inside a cabin in the woods north of Mount Haven. She was met by Ayden and Fiadl, who had blindfolded her and guided her inside. Eleonora could feel others around her. She stood in dark discomfort while the room filled. She could smell woodsmoke from a fire.

Fiadl spoke. "You are here to join in the power of Larvanis. Once you remove your blindfold, there can be no return. If you betray the goddess, your gifts will disappear."

Eleonora Bohm understood that she could not retreat. She also knew a sacrifice would be offered.

Fiadl stood in front of the gathered crowd. "Remove your blindfolds!"

Eleonora stood at the front of a large crowd; she knew most of the faces gathered. She noticed Fulvio and Salce near her along with other humans as well as dwarves, halflings, and some city elves.

"Kneel and prepare yourselves," said Fiadl as she began chanting.

A naked Ayden brought out a young elven girl and undressed her.

As Fiadl continued her chanting, she undressed and laid her robe on a nearby table. As the priestess completed her chants, Ayden brought the girl forward. Fiadl slit the girl's throat and used the blood to draw runes on her own body. Ayden laid the dying girl down and quickly cut out her organs. "You'll receive these gifts even though you're not worthy," he told the crowd.

Fiadl drew runes on Ayden's naked body with the warm blood. Afterwards both continued the ritual, placing the offerings on the cooking fire. Once the meats were roasted Fiadl said, "Come forward and except these gifts."

At this point, a dwarven woman in the crowd stood and attempted to escape. As she reached the door, Ayden chanted, causing four earthen spheres to appear and shoot through the woman's head and chest, leaving her dead. Eleonora Bohm stood naked before Fiadl, took the offering, and fought not to gag as she chewed. Fiadl drew runes on Eleonora's body who felt power course within her. The priestess moved and gave the offerings to the others. Midway through the ritual another human woman jumped up, screaming "This is evil. I can't do this!" Salce and Rolando grabbed her and held her down while Ayden sliced open her stomach and used his bloody hand to rip out her organs and still-beating heart. He took a bite out of the heart and threw it into the fire as an additional offering.

Eleonora Bohm felt drunk with power as the whole cabin vibrated. After all those gathered had eaten the flesh of the offering, another young man rebelled but was quickly ripped apart by the group and his organs added to the feast. As the rest of the group ended their ritual with a wild sexual orgy, Fiadl held Eleonora's naked, bloody body and kissed her neck. "The goddess has blessed you. You're to be elevated to become the first human priestess of Larvanis."

Eleonora smiled and turned her head and kissed Fiadl's lips. "I'll do my best to serve Larvanis and spread her will." As the two watched the orgy unfold, they heard the delighted laughter of their goddess.

Four days had passed since their last meeting when Ututur found himself in Ovidio's library again. All he could think about was Andanir's happy face as he stared at his fall festival gifts this morning. *Andanir's hand is a little small for the two daggers, but he'll grow.* "Ututur, are you listening?" asked Ovidio. The gnome had explained something important.

"Yes, yes. Please continue." The half-orc felt a little embarrassed. He listened while Ovidio and Harun explained what they learned about how to identify evil sorcerers.

Ovidio stressed, "Most importantly, once we kill anyone who can wield dark magic, we must cut off their heads and burn the body. The head must be buried on holy ground and a cleansing ritual must be performed. Otherwise, the sorcerer can be resurrected."

Ututur was shocked and looked at the small group gathered in the library. Since the first meeting, the group had grown to include Ilina, Sheriff Bastina and Vigiles Ridolfo. How were they to fight such a powerful enemy hidden within their midst?

Despite Ututur's misgivings, the plan came together quickly. The group would investigate each of the elves stationed at the new embassy and try to identify the evil magic users. Once identified, Greta would use the power of her office as a Vigiles to arrest and question them. Before they left, Ovidio gave each person six small pieces of parchment inscribed with an intricate geometric drawing. "Harun found the design for protection wards in his research and I modified it. When you return home place one facing each cardinal direction, including one on the ceiling, and one on the floor. This will ward your dwelling against dream intrusions."

"Master, look, we received a large order from the Elven embassy," Rolf said as he waved a large piece of parchment at Ututur.

"Good, let me look at the list. Gather the items and make arrangements with our suppliers to purchase replacements. I'll take the delivery to their embassy myself this afternoon."

It took Rialta a couple of days to gather her courage and write a note to Andanir inviting him to pick some wild grapes with her after his lesson with Mistress Ilina. Andanir couldn't concentrate while he helped Ilina bundle the dried herbs. "Looks like your mind is elsewhere, Andanir."

"Yes, Rialta asked me to pick wild grapes with her."

"They are delicious," Ilina smiled. *I'm glad those two are friends; they're good for one another.*

When Andanir finished he hugged Ilina and ran into the woods beaming. He carried a cloth sack in his left hand, and with his right hand he held the Damascus dagger in place so it wouldn't slap against his thigh. He also wore his mother's torc, which Ututur had returned, around his neck. Andanir made Ututur promise to wear it if he went to war again.

Ututur led the one-horse wagon to the Elven embassy and knocked on the front door. Several servants came out to unload the wagon. He asked a servant, "Where is Eoin?"

The male servant answered, "The Lord Second is attending a meeting with your High Council."

Ututur was waiting for the servants to unload the wagon when he saw two elves exit the mansion. One was the female he had seen the other night, and the other was a male he had never seen before. As soon as he tried to watch the female, he found he could not focus on her features. Ututur shook his head and rubbed his eyes. He walked closer to the female. "Hello."

Fiadl glanced at the half-orc. "What is it you want?"

"My name is…"

She interrupted, "I don't care what your name is. I have nothing to say to an orc."

The venom in her tone shocked Ututur. He bowed and said, "I beg your pardon, my Lady. Your Highness."

Trahern brought out five horses packed for travel and cried out. "Fiadl! What are you doing with that half-wit? We have a long way to travel before nightfall."

As Fiadl pushed past Ututur, a distinctive aroma of musty decay emanated from her. Ututur almost gagged and looked carefully at the two elves. He went to the wagon, took out a small bag of dried apples, and walked with his head down toward the two mounted elves. "My Lord, how far are you traveling? Here is a bag of dried apples for your journey."

Trahern said, "Good, this will help; we're going to the city states."

"Stop your jabbering!" Fiadl spurred her horse, almost knocking Ututur down.

Ututur helped the servants unload the wagon as quickly as possible, then went to the Vigiles' keep. When he arrived, he found no one there, so he turned toward Ovidio's home.

Ayden walked through the woods toward the cabin. *I can't believe I have to stay in this place while Fiadl is allowed to travel and use her powers. She can kill with impunity while on the road. I'm forced to stay here and watch over a bunch of humans.* He heard something ahead and stopped, stooping low and moving quietly as only an elf could. After a dozen double paces, he saw a young human girl with long dark brown hair walking in the woods.

Ayden's mouth watered. His hunger had grown since the night of the sacrifice. His last kill had not satisfied his urgent need. He stalked the child, thinking, *Fiadl is going to be gone, and in five more days there'll be another full moon. I can conduct an empowering ritual myself. Thank you, my goddess.* He snuck up behind the girl and grabbed her. As he whisked her away, she dropped the cloth bag which she had brought to gather wild grapes.

Andanir waited at the agreed location. His grew concerned because Rialta was never late. Finally, as vespers approached, he entered the woods, walking toward an ancient oak tree. Starting from the base of the tree he walked in a circular pattern, searching the ground for any sign that Rialta had been there. The sun was beginning to dip below the horizon, but he still could see. He had walked about a mile from the base of the tree when he found a small cloth bag. The sun had almost, set and he could barely make out any footprints. He fought the growing panic while he raced towards his cabin. *Surely Master Ututur will know what to do.*

Kiley was disappointed as she rode ahead of the joint human and elf column. They had left Ostheim two days ago, but Wil did not present himself for the patrol. Sub-captain Pierluigi remained behind to command the human soldiers. Although Wil had been too weak to ride, she felt a surge of hope when the human sergeant explained that Wil had been exercising since her visit. She rode in silence in the cool fall weather. *I want to spend time with him, talk, and get to know him better. At least he's not drinking.* She had known many elves who wasted away from drinking, using it to escape the misery of poverty and lack of meaning in their lives. *I'll go see him when we return,* she vowed.

After the night of the Chieftain's murder, Eithne had lived in fear. She stayed out of sight and busied herself, going for long rides, anything to stay away from her family. Exhausted, she planned her escape. She had packed a small satchel for a stay at the hunting cabin in the western woods. As she walked out, she passed her mother and brother talking in hushed tones over a table in the meeting hall. Maps and pieces of parchment covered the table. She had almost reached the door when they stopped talking. "Where are you going?" asked her mother.

Eithne began to sweat, feeling a wet bead roll down her back and moisture covered her forehead. "I was going to the hunting lodge. I want to stay there a few days and enjoy the woods in autumn."

"I don't see you much lately," her mother said, coolly regarding her.

"I don't see you much either, little sister," said Aoife. *I want to kiss her and feel her naked underneath me,* he thought as he glanced at her perfect, young face.

"Since there has been so much change and work demanding both of your attention, I wanted to stay out of the way," Eithne said, displaying as little emotion as possible.

Lady Sioban turned back to the parchment, dismissing her with a wave of her hand.

Eithne turned toward the entrance and continued toward the stable but she stiffened as she heard footsteps running after her.

"Wait for me," said Aoife. He caught up to her and put his arm around her as they continued to the stable.

By the time they reached it, Eithne's heart was beating like a frightened rabbit. Aoife talked but she didn't hear a word. When they entered the stables, he grabbed her and turned her to face him. "Listen to me. I love you."

Eithne replied, "I love you too, brother." Her fear grew when she realized they were alone. She began to back away, trying to escape his grip. "You're hurting me."

Aoife grinned and pushed her onto a pile of hay. "I know you like that," he said with a wild grin on his face.

She fell, gasping as he threw himself on top of her, pulled her skirt up, and reached under her shirt to feel her breast. She screamed, "Help! Help! Someone help me!" He shut her mouth with his hand as he opened her legs further.

A young stable girl came in. "What's going on? Stop, or I'll call the guards!"

Aoife turned to look at her and saw the fear and recognition in the girl's face. He stood and marched toward her. "You'll do no such thing!"

Eithne grabbed her satchel, ran outside through the opposite entrance, and finding a few horses tethered there she untied and mounted the closest one, then rode out of the stable yard.

Blinded by rage, Aoife grabbed the stable girl as he turned and saw Eithne ride away. In his fit of rage, he began strangling her and pulled her dress up and raped her. When he was finished, she had stopped breathing. He pulled his pants back up, straightened his clothes, and yelled, "Guards! Guards! I need help. Someone is hurt." Aoife looked at the dead body and felt the intoxicating pleasure of the kill.

Eithne rode quickly out of the southern gate. Before she knew it, she was heading west. Tears streamed down her face; her mouth was so dry she couldn't swallow. She couldn't take a full breath. *I hope they still think I'm going to the hunting lodge.* After several double-paced miles, she slowed the horse and stopped. She took out her hooded riding cloak, put it on, and walked beside the horse, which was sweating and out of breath. Eithne drank from her water skin and rubbed the horse's neck to calm her. She had no plan. She knew only that she must escape her mother and brother.

CHAPTER 25

Andanir ran to the Iron Caldron as fast as he could. "Rolf, have you seen Master Ututur? It's an emergency."

"No, he hasn't returned from making deliveries."

Before he could say more Andanir ran out of the shop toward Master Ovidio's. *He'll know what to do.*

When Andanir reached Master Ovidio's house, he saw Master Ututur's wagon and several horses outside. He knocked and rushed in, seeing a small crowd gathered "Master! Master! You have to help! There has been a kidnapping!"

"What is it, Andanir?" asked Ututur.

"It's Rialta. Something has happened to her!" Andanir showed the bag he found on the trail and explained how she never arrived.

"Andanir, Go fetch Captain Rosanella and bring her here," Ututur directed.

Andanir immediately turned and ran out.

"Now what are we going to do about the two elves that already left?" asked Ututur.

"Ridolfo can go after them and get help from other Vigiles. I'll send word to the Grand Master," Vigiles Albrecht said.

"I'll tell my friend Eufrasio about the dark elves and let him know they are headed south to the city-states," Ututur added. "I'll start the search for the missing girl. I know the area Andanir described."

"I'll go with you," Ovidio said, grabbing his cloak.

"I'll alert the sheriff and wait for Captain Bianco. Then I'll search the Elven embassy. Let's meet back at Master Ovidio's after vespers," Albrecht said.

Ridolfo stood. "I'll get packed and go after them now."

Ovidio warned, "Be careful. You're following at least one dark mage."

"How can I help?" asked Harun.

"Can you fetch Mistress Ilina in case we need a healer? I'll give you directions," Ututur said.

"I couldn't find anything; the trail is difficult to follow in the dark," Ututur said to Andanir, who joined him in the dark after he delivered the message to Rosanella. The half-orc was worried and felt his anger grow but remained calm for the boy. He remembered how his grandfather encouraged him on his first patrol as a full member of the tribal warband. "I don't know if this helps but my grandfather used to say that while everyone is afraid, those who are courageous will keep going despite their fear."

Andanir remained silent, tears falling down his face. "I can't see anything. What should we do?"

Ututur laid a gentle hand on the boy's head. "We'll return to Master Ovidio's. See if the others have news and take up the search before sunrise."

Sherriff Bastina and ten guards searched the city. Rosanella went to their home in town, searched the neighborhood, and gathered thirty soldiers to search the area from her house to the place where Rialta's bag was found.

Vigiles Albrecht went to the Elven embassy. After searching the grounds, she convinced the servants to allow her to search all of the rooms. She left after finding nothing and made her way to Ovidio's.

By the time the Vigiles entered, Ovidio's large common room was filled with voices, and hopeful faces turned to her as she entered the room. "I found nothing at the embassy." A collective moan rose as she shut the door. "We'll start searching again first thing in the morning. Let's eat and rest for the evening."

Eoin returned after dark to find the embassy servants sullen and frightened. One older elf approached him. "May I speak with you, My Lord? I'm Brighid."

Tired from sitting at the meeting all day, Eoin threw his cloak at the servant. "What is it?"

"The female Vigilies was here earlier this evening."

He looked at the gathered elves who stood with bowed heads,

seeming apprehensive. "What did she want? And where are Ayden and Fiadl?" *They are supposed to be in charge while I'm out.*

Brighid stood wringing his hands. "My Lord, Lady Fiadl and Trahern left for the southern city states on official business, and Lord Ayden hasn't been seen all day." The old elf paused, reluctant to continue.

"Well, what did the Vigiles want?"

"She was looking for a missing human child. I don't know why she would think we would have a child."

Eoin felt his heart sink and stood wondering. *Is the evil real, and is one of my people involved?* "Get me a fresh horse!"

He made his way into town and headed in the direction of the Vigiles' keep. A guard told him that the Vigiles had gone out to search for the missing girl. He left a message with the night watchman and returned to the embassy.

Lady Sioban slapped Aoife. "What happened, you imbecile? What did you do?"

"Nothing, mother. All I was trying to do was talk some sense into Eithne. I think she suspects us," replied Aoife.

"What about the child? Did you kill her?"

Aoife knew better than to lie to his mother. "Yes, but it was an accident."

"Was raping her an accident? Stay out of the way, and don't do anything else foolish. There is a time and place to fulfill your dark desires, but you must think before you act. Guards!"

Two guards ran into the private meeting hall and bowed. The High Priestess took several deep calming breaths. "I want you to organize a search party. When you find my daughter, arrest her for the murder of the young child, Iona."

"Start the search at the family hunting cabin," added Aoife with a smile. When he got his hands on her she would suffer for a very long time and he would enjoy using her.

Eithne rode west, tears in her eyes. As the sun set for vespers she dismounted and walked her horse a hundred paces off the main road in case she was followed. To further avoid discovery, she didn't light a fire. She leaned against a tree as the autumn coolness seeped into her body, drinking a little water and eating some of the food. *At least I have food for three days, five if I stretch it out,* she thought as she wrapped the blanket over her traveling cloak, shivering as the temperature continued to drop after the sun set. *But where can I go?*

Eithne dozed, but fear kept her from staying asleep. *I can't believe he tried to rape me. I have to get far away.*

❊❊❊

Albrecht found the note Eoin had left for her when she returned to the keep. She sent a reply to Eoin asking him to meet her tomorrow at the keep or at the search area. She asked a stable boy to deliver the message and tossed him a silver coin.

The Vigiles didn't sleep well and left her quarters as soon as the sun peaked over the horizon. When she arrived at Ilina's, the healer told her that the sheriff went to search the area around her cabin and work his way back toward the city. The healer also said, "Ovidio and Harun are searching the city again with the help of a few of the town guards. Rosanella took fifty soldiers into the woods and is walking the entire area where the bag was found. Andanir and Ututur went with her to track Rialta now that it's light."

"Thank you. I'll search the area from here to Rosanella's house. Watch for the elven emissary and send him my way. Let's meet at Ovidio's tonight," the Vigiles said from the doorway as she left.

❊❊❊

Ututur, Andanir, and Rosanella had no difficulty finding where the girl had dropped the cloth sack. Rosanella joined the soldiers, forming a line and searching for a double-paced mile farther west, away from the spot. Ututur examined Rialta's foot prints; in the day light he found a set of large male boot prints nearby. However, after the two prints merged a few paces away, their tracks disappeared. "What if we don't find more prints? How are we going to save her?" Andanir asked, his eyebrows furrowed.

"My grandfather used to say, "If the warrior can master patience, then he can master any foe," replied Ututur. "We've just begun to search for her. We'll spiral out from here and look for signs."

"But what if she was taken and hurt?" Andanir questioned.

"Let's not let darkness overwhelm our thoughts before we know something for sure. Let's focus on finding her first."

"Yes, master."

Lady Sioban sat drinking tea with Roisin. At first glance they appeared to be young female friends having tea in the gardens around the temple but neither were young nor their conversations light. "I think we need a new Warlord," Sioban mused, sipping her mint tea.

Roisin nibbled on small almond pastry. "Yes, then we can remove other recalcitrant noble families. The next purge will start soon."

"Have you visited Rianor?" Lady Sioban asked.

"Yes, she is improving. I used another captive as a sacrifice. Rianor is able to care for herself now though she still can't speak. I think a few more private offerings will fully restore her," Roisin answered. "If she recovers, we can send her east and spread the word of the goddess among the Thunder Horse Clans."

"Good, but we have more problems. Eithne ran away. Aoife is becoming unstable. I'll place a control spell on him so he can master his lust," Sioban added with a sigh of resignation.

"Here, have something to eat and drink," Ayden said as he placed a piece of dry brown bread and a mug of water in front of Rialta.

Her long brown hair was matted, and her face was bruised from his blows. Rialta pushed the bread away with her feet.

"When I leave here, I'm going to chain you up with this manacle and leg iron. No one will hear you, so scream all you want."

Along with the mansion, the elves had purchased some land and a cabin. Now he would use this place to expand his own powers by making private offerings to Larvanis. He grabbed Rialta and locked her in place. "I have business back in town. I'll leave you the bowl of porridge and the bucket of water. Here is another bucket if you have to relieve yourself. I'll be back soon, so don't try to escape. If you do, I'll follow you and kill everyone you love," added Ayden.

As soon as the elf left Rialta sat down on the floor, used her hands to eat the oat porridge, and drank some water. Afterwards she got up and pulled on the leg iron fastened around her right ankle, trying to loosen it from the floor. The chain would not budge. She tried using her legs to pull, but the iron cut into her, and she started to bleed from the scrapes.

Feeling frustrated and frightened, she sat back down and started to cry silently.

By midday Ututur couldn't believe that they had found no further signs of the missing girl. They were searching in the knee-high grass when in the distance he saw Ilina approaching wearing her forest green pants and brown tunic. "You keep looking. I'm going to see what Mistress Ilina has to say."

"I hope Rialta is all right; it's been two days now. Andanir didn't sleep last night from worry," the half-orc said in a quiet voice so that only Ilina could hear.

"We aren't going to give up." Ilina kept any doubts to herself. "Andanir come here! Let's eat something." She set up a picnic blanket, opened the basket, and set out some meat pies and some watered-down ale.

"Thank you," Ututur said as he accepted the pie.

"How is the search going?" she asked.

"Not well. We found the initial signs, but we haven't had luck finding additional tracks," said Andanir "Rosanella is with the men. I don't think they've found anything either."

"It's like they've been erased," added Ututur.

"Perhaps Master Ovidio could help if the signs have been magically erased," said Ilina.

Ututur hadn't considered the use of magic and felt angry for not having realized the possibility. "You're right. I should've thought of that sooner. Can you fetch Master Ovidio as quickly as possible?"

Ilina finished her pie in two bites, stood, and washed it down with her ale. "I'll go fetch him."

"Thank you, and the food was delicious," said Ututur.

Andanir was still chewing on the second pie and mumbled, "Thank you," waving good-bye. They watched as she jogged to the gnome's house.

Vigiles Albrecht heard a knock and opened the door to find Eoin. The elf had tracked her to Ovidio's house. She couldn't believe her luck. "Come in," she said. "We're having some ale before we continue our search. This is Master Ovidio."

"Good afternoon," Ovidio said, extending his right hand in greeting while holding his red gem with his left hand in his pocket.

"Hello, Master Ovidio. I'm afraid I have to be blunt. Why did you come to the embassy looking for a missing child?"

The Vigiles rested her hand on the hilt of her dagger and looked at Ovidio. "A child went missing. "We're worried about dark magic, and unfortunately, elves have been involved in every recent instance of the use of dark magic," Albrecht replied.

Eoin stood in silence and nodded, "Did you find anything?"

Ovidio turned to the Vigiles. "I sense nothing; I think we must trust him."

"Yes, tell him what we know," she agreed.

Ovidio kept his left hand on his red gem and rubbed his beard with his right. "I've detected dark magic at work here in Mount Haven since your mission's arrival. Not long ago one of our comrades detected dark magic residue emanating from one of your people. On top of that, the head of our High Council was killed using dark magic."

"Who?" asked Eoin.

"I believe it was your priestess," Ovidio waited, looking for any reaction or any sign of dark magic from Eoin.

Eoin sighed. "Strange things have been happening back home. Since the death of our chieftain, the High Priestess has gained much power and installed her son as the new chieftain. I'm leaving for home in a few days with a set of proposals for the final treaty between our peoples. I can investigate the priestess while I'm in Litauia," Eoin said, feeling ashamed that his people were implicated in this evil. "I don't know how much I can do. The High Priestess has many followers and no one can challenge her. Some of our council members have tried and paid with their lives. I'll do what I can but for now I've to get back to the negotiations. Thank you for informing me."

As soon as Eoin departed, Albrecht turned to Ovidio and asked, "So what do you think?"

"I detected nothing from him. From what Harun and I have found, only the practitioners of dark magic can be detected. Simple followers do not give off emanations, but we can look for other signs," Ovidio said. "This is extremely difficult; two centuries have passed since the practice of dark magic was common, and my knowledge is limited. All of the great scholars, wizards, and witches who knew about the subject are long dead and most of their works have perished. Even my own teacher was only a minor scholar who could only teach me the basics."

Ovidio and Albrecht sat resting and trying to think about what more they could do when Ilina knocked and entered. "Master Ovidio, Ututur needs help in tracking Rialta and another set of footprints. He says that magic may have been used to mask their trail. Ututur and Andanir don't know what else to do."

Ovidio sat and scratched his head. "I could use this crystal and a detection spell to enhance my vision. Can you get my cart ready for me? I want to review a few books to see if I can find anything specific on tracking."

Lady Sioban walked in silence to the underground temple, carrying one of Eithne's old dresses. When she entered the antechamber, she disrobed, cleansed herself with water, and focused her senses using the scent of aloeswood incense. She planned to attempt two different kinds of magic before the Hunter's Moon. She would use one sacrifice to summon a black hound from the underworld to track and return Eithne. Afterwards she would kill the meddlesome Warlord.

As acolytes brought three captives to the altar, she raised her knife and chanted. The victims, weakened by drugs and spells, knelt before her with their throats exposed. The High Priestess's knife strokes were quick and efficient. Her hands didn't shake, and in moments the three were bleeding out. The entire chamber hummed with dark power. The acolytes captured the blood and brought the bowls to Sioban. She used the blood to create a summoning circle, then ashes mixed with pure gold powder from the sacrifices to create a holding circle. The acolytes finished butchering the victims. Sioban used the chant she had learned from the ancient books; as she finished her incantations a large misty form began to coalesce within the circle. A dog began to take shape. It was as large as a bull with black fur highlighted with blue and purple tints. It looked a little like a wolf with grey eyes. The High Priestess broke through the two circles. An acolyte handed her a human heart which she fed the beast. She stroked the broad head and spoke to it in the ancient tongue. Sioban gave the beast Eithne's dress to smell. "Bring this girl back to me, but do not harm her."

One chore down, she thought. *Now all that is left is to kill that bothersome old fool, Eachmhile. I'll also need to brew a potion to make sure Aoife controls himself.* Sioban gathered the power and drew runes on her arms with some of the blood on the floor. She prepared the death spell much like the one she had use to kill the councilor in Mount Haven. This time she would burst the blood vessels in Warlord Eachmhile's brain. *This will be a pleasure to witness.*

Eithne continued to travel away from the main road. *I don't know where to go. Maybe the human captain in Ostheim can help, or that woman healer in Mount Haven.* She continued the westward trek while she ate the last bit of the dried fruit and drank the last of her water. *I'm going to have to get more water and forage for food. The horse can graze, and I still have half a bag of oats left.*

She climbed onto the horse, urged it to a slow walk. She checked again and made sure no other riders were on the road.

By the time Albrecht got a small cart prepared, Ovidio was ready to leave with Harun at his side. The two made an odd couple; Ovidio was small, white haired, delicate, with pale skin and wore a colorful red cloak and matching hat. Unlike the flamboyant gnome Harun dressed in muted colors of black, blue, and white. He was very tall with a perfectly trimmed, grey streaked dark beard. Ovidio jumped up and down and waved. "Mistress Albrecht, Harun found an old story of a princess lost in a deep unnatural sleep. The court mage used a spell to detect the sorcery and dispel it. There was enough information on the spell itself that I think I can cast it to track someone. Perhaps I can also use it to detect magical residues on followers of the sorcerer."

"Wonderful!" Vigiles Albrecht exclaimed. *I hope we can find her before it's too late.*

Rosanella returned to Ututur and Andanir on horseback. "Any luck?"

"No," Ututur said.

"I sent the men north and told them to return to the barracks after they went another five double-paced miles. I'm going back to the city to check the house again and retrace her steps from there."

"I'll stay here and see if I can find anything," Ututur said.

"We'll find her," Andanir said with tears forming in his eyes.

Rosanella couldn't respond; she just nodded, reached down from the horse, touched Andanir on his head, and patted Ututur's shoulder before heading back to town.

Before long Vigiles Albrecht, Ovidio, and Harun arrived. Ovidio jumped lightly off the cart, ran over to Andanir, and hugged him. "Master Harun and I found a spell we can use. Take me to the place where you found the bag and footprints."

Andanir held Ovidio's hand and led him to the spot. Ututur approached from behind while Harun and Greta waited. Ovidio pushed Andanir slightly back and produced his red crystal necklace. He chanted, knelt, and placed the gem in a circle of white sand he had brought. The gnome used his gem to draw a perfect circle in the air. All of the others only saw the gnome making gestures in the air. Andanir's torc became warm and the boy could see the silvery circle appear in midair. Ovidio smiled at the boy and marked a dot in the center of the circle. With a flourish the gnome drew three equidistant lines through the center. He finished the sacred shape by drawing six ellipses using the three diameters as the center. The shape glowed brighter as black smoky tendrils became visible to Ovidio and

Andanir. "Come. Follow me."

"I can see the shape." Andanir wondered in amazement at his gnome master's power.

Ututur was confused but remained silent. Master Ovidio smiled with pride. "Good, the meditations we've been doing and your innate ability has opened your eyes. Once you can draw these symbols your mind must be focused to instill them with power and what you want to do."

Albrecht tied her horse to the cart, grabbed her saddle bags, and followed. Ututur stayed close behind Ovidio and kept a lookout for any danger. *I should have brought my axe.* He reached down and found the hilt of his knife, a curved single-edged blade three hands long, a small sword for humans. The handle felt reassuring in his hand. Ovidio led them south for nearly two double-paced miles, in the opposite direction from the previous searches. Suddenly stopping, Master Ovidio, motioned everyone to get down and stay silent. Ututur moved beside Ovidio and noticed Andanir touching the torc around his neck; this made him feel safe somehow. They were near a small cabin with a soft light shining through the closed windows.

Ayden planned to spend the night in the cabin during the full moon and use the girl for a sexual ritual before he sacrificed her. He was resting on the couch when a soft voice hissed in his ear. "You stupid fool. The enemy is approaching. They are going to take the girl from you and kill you. Set a trap and run; there are too many for you to fight alone," said Larvarnis who had been distracted by other events to keep an eye on the fool.

"What kind of trap?" Ayden asked frantically.

"Listen carefully; I'll speak the words and guide your hand," the voice hissed. "Ahh, I recognize one of them. The big one was at the battle and was responsible for the death of many of my followers. I'll enjoy this."

Without thinking, Ayden prepared the spell as he was guided. He hadn't tried using his magic on a large scale yet. He followed the goddess's instructions and used his own blood. He poured magical energy into the earth beneath him and set a perimeter arc in front of the house. If anyone crossed the magical line, the ground would explode.

❋ ❋ ❋

Andanir waited at the edge of the clearing while Ututur led the group with Vigiles Albrecht, Master Ovidio, and Master Harun bringing up the rear. The torc around his neck grew warmer; he felt a slight buzz coming from his mother's jewelry. As the group neared the cabin, a tremendous explosion knocked the entire group backwards. Andanir's body and face were covered in dirt. He was dizzy, his ears rang from the explosion. He sat up when his vision cleared, all of his friends were on the ground. He tried to get to his knees but fell back from the dizziness.

As Andanir sat there steadying himself, he saw the cabin door open. A hooded figure walked out holding a short sword in his hand. Andanir watched helplessly as the figure stumbled slightly toward Vigiles Albrecht. He rose and tried to call out a warning but managed only a croak. As Andanir watched, the hooded figure knelt over the Vigiles and stabbed her in the stomach. The little boy gathered his strength and ran out of the woods screaming. The figure stood and kicked the prone Vigiles. The tall figure stopped what he was doing and fixed his gaze on Andanir.

Andanir ran forward yelling, "Stop!"

The hooded figure moved closer to Ututur and removed his hood. It was a male elf with golden eyes and dark blonde hair that fell below his shoulders. He looked weak and unsteady and stared at Andanir and stopped. "Well, what have we here? A dirty little elf."

Andanir never stopped running, the figure hovered over his Master.

Fortunately for Ututur, the attacker misjudged Andanir's speed; he stabbed the half-orc once in the stomach and before he could stab again the boy was upon him. Andanir raced toward the tall elf and drew the dagger from his side. The tall elf sneered and pointed the sword in the boy's direction. Andanir realized that the grown elf had a big reach advantage and couldn't deliver a lunge without exposing himself. The tall elf smiled, waved his sword, and prepared to attack. At that moment the half-orc reached out and grabbed the elf's ankle.

The surprised elf tried to shake his leg free, but Ututur's grip was too strong. Andanir used the distraction to thrust his dagger into the attacker. The hooded figure was wearing chainmail, but Andanir's training paid off, the boy executed a perfect lunge while leaning to the right side and thrust his dagger upwards into the enemy. The elf screamed when the dagger pierced the armor. The wounded elf tried to counterattack but the boy had already recovered into a balanced fighting stance out of reach of the short sword.

Andanir crouched, guarding his fallen master. The wounded elf waved his sword in front of him and started to circle. Andanir made sure he kept a good distance away from the adult's longer weapon. When the giant half-orc began to rise and took out his own hunting knife, the wounded elf turned and ran. Andanir followed.

"Stop boy!" Ututur ordered. "He'll kill you if you catch him."

When Andanir looked back, his master had already lain back down.

Andanir wiped his dagger on the grass sheathed it and walked back to the giant half-orc's prone form. "What should I do?"

"Calm yourself and help me get up." Ututur said as he held his side with his left hand.

Andanir noticed the blood seeping out form his master's hand. "Are you badly hurt?"

"It's not too serious," Ututur replied although he felt dizzy and almost fainted when he sat up. He breathed deeply, gathered himself, stood, and started toward the fallen Vigiles. "Go check on Master Ovidio!" Ututur could tell that the Vigiles was gravely wounded. Her breath was shallow, and the ground around her was soaked with blood. He tore part of her cloak to staunch the wound.

Andanir ran over to Master Ovdio. He did not see any obvious wounds, and the gnome was breathing. He tried to recall the things Mistress Ilina had said about basic care for the wounded. Since he didn't see any bleeding and Master Ovidio was breathing, he left him and ran to Master Harun. As he approached, he heard a horse gallop away from the back of the cabin. The hooded figure rode slumped over.

Master Harun lay motionless, bleeding from several small

wounds. Andanir examined the man carefully for any major bleeding, but none of the wounds seemed serious. However, his right arm and shoulder lay at an odd angle. He returned to Ututur. "Master Ovidio is not bleeding; he's breathing but unconscious. Master Harun has several small cuts, and I think something is wrong with his shoulder."

"Let's go check the cabin." It was twenty paces away at most, but Ututur's strength failed, and he fell to one knee.

Andanir's heart pounded in his chest. "Master!" He reached out and held Ututur steady.

Andanir felt his mouth go dry. He tried to form some saliva as he took a step toward the cabin with Ututur at his side. He took another step, and his hands shook. Nonetheless, he focused on his friend Rialta; his mother's torc warmed and calmed him.

Andanir opened the door and helped Ututur through inside. The cabin was empty except for a large table near where Rialta was chained to the floor crying. The boy ignored the dark magical smoke pooled on the cabin floor, he rushed over and hugged her; she returned his hug with relief on her face.

"Here, we'll use my knife to pry the nails holding down the chain," said Ututur, handing Andanir his knife.

The knife was almost as think as his finger, he placed it under the nails and with Ututur's help they loosened them. They gripped the chain together, and pulled until it came free. Andanir handed the freed chain to Rialta. "Let's go outside and see how everyone else is doing.

Ututur walked out of the cabin holding his side while Andanir helped Rialta walk. Master Ovidio was up and next to Harun. Ovidio's cloak was enchanted and had prevented the rocks thrown by the explosion from piercing his skin. While Andanir and Rialta helped Master Ututur lift the Vigiles onto the cart; the gnome left the group to examine the cabin. He returned with a grimace and climbed onto the cart. "Much evil magic has been performed there. Too bad the sorcerer escaped."

Andanir walked beside the cart on their way to Ilina's. As they got closer Andanir said, "I'll run ahead and let Mistress Ilina know what to expect."

Ovidio said, "Good thinking."

Andanir quickly reached the cabin and found Ilina working in the herb garden. "Ilina!" he gasped.

"Slow down and catch your breath," Ilina said as she walked out of the garden.

"Ilina, we found Rialta, but Master Ututur, Mistress Albrecht, and Master Harun… Everyone is injured."

"Where are they?" The healer took three deep breaths and calmed herself.

"They're on their way here," said the boy between breaths with tears in his eyes.

"Let's go and wash our hands; you can help me." Ilina took out her prepared leather case of potions, bandages, her sewing kit, and other clean instruments. Her hands shook when she imagined Ututur being wounded. She had Andanir boil more water while she prayed and mentally prepared herself to receive the wounded.

Master Ovidio sat against the wall and watched Ilina stop the Vigiles' bleeding and stabilize her. She quickly sewed the wound closed and bandaged her. Afterward, she cleaned and examined the wound in Ututur's side. "You have a small piece of stone in the wound. I'm going to use these grippers to remove it. It's going to hurt," Ilina said as she rinsed her bloody hands.

Ututur frowned and through gritted teeth said, "I'm ready; go ahead."

Ilina carefully probed the wound with the metal tool, used the gripper, and extracted the stone. She cleaned the wound carefully, using her finger to probe further, making sure nothing else had entered. She checked for any ruptures in the intestine. Ilina's face relaxed when she found no internal damage. "Looks clean, and nothing internal is torn. I'll sew your wound."

Master Ovidio noticed wisps of white magical energy flow from Ilina's fingers onto the silk thread as she sewed the wound closed. She sealed the wound with honey and put on a bandage with mold scrapings from bread. He smiled and thanked the goddess. "You are blessed, mistress. I can see you have been gifted with healing powers."

Ilina stood and moved to the next patient. "I just heal as best I can. Harun's cuts are not serious, but his left shoulder is dislocated. Ilina gave Harun a potion to relax his muscles and dull the pain. She had Master Harun lie flat on his stomach on the dining table. She reached under him, pulled on his hand, and pushed the ball back into the joint. Andanir also saw white wisps of magic flow from Ilina's hands. They were so fortunate to have Ilina as their friend.

CHAPTER 26

Wilhelm left his room and went for a ride after training with his axe. With only one eye his sense of depth perception was off; even mounting his horse was difficult. He felt ashamed of his disability. He wore the eye patch Kiley had given him and rode eastward to clear his head. The outdoor air took his pain away and cleared his mind. He must train harder and be fit enough to go on patrol with Kiley. She had kissed him, leaving him hopeful that she did not despise him, and with at least two more joint patrols before winter, there was the chance that he could prove himself worthy of her interest. *I'm going to stop feeling sorry for myself and pull myself together,* he thought as he rode. In the distance he saw a hooded figure on horseback and urged his horse to move faster toward the rider.

After sighting him, the figure slowed and looked around before continuing slowly. When he got closer, Wilhelm raised his hand. "Hello."

The figure removed the hood, exposing Eithne's face. "Hello, Captain."

"What are you doing here?" he asked.

She didn't know how to respond and simply sat without moving. Before she could answer, Wilhelm unleashed his small axe. Eithne's eyes widened, not understanding his reaction. "What's the meaning of this?"

Wilhelm gestured her to be quiet, rode past her, and scanned the wooded area behind her. He saw nothing and turned his horse around. "Come. Let's begone from here." Before they had ridden far, they heard a growl and Wilhelm glimpsed a huge black creature leap out of the woods. In a few heartbeats, it was upon them. The beast knocked Eithne's horse over, breaking one of its hind legs. The girl was thrown clear and lay in a heap on the ground. The creature rebounded and bit Wilhelm's horse's rear leg tearing a large chunk of it off. Wilhelm jumped clear of his horse as it reared up and fell over.

Wilhelm fell flat dropping his axe. The beast looked like a wolf but was the size of a large bull. It continued its attack on his horse, knocking it down and biting repeatedly with a bone-crunching sound. Wilhelm found his axe, scrambled to his feet and drew his dagger. Eithne, on the ground, moaned from the fall.

The beast's fur was so dark it looked almost blue. Wilhelm saw fangs that were almost as long as his dagger when it turned and faced him. The eyes glowed and seemed to change color as he looked into them. The beast tried to make its way to Eithne. "Hey! Get away from her!" Wilhelm yelled, waving his axe at the beast.

The beast looked at Eithne and then back at him as if it was considering what to do. Then it faced him and began to walk slowly toward him. It lunged at him without warning. Wilhelm used the flat of the axe to slap the beast's muzzle. It leaped back, let out a yelp like a wounded puppy, and snarled. The black fur became a blur as it ran to Wilhelm's left, pivoted, and lunged at his face. He couldn't react in time, and the weight of the dog knocked him down. Then he dropped his axe pulled on the neck fur to prevent the dog from biting his face. It was incredibly strong and Wilhelm could barely keep it from biting him. The animal bit down on his shoulder; Wilhelm screamed in pain but continued to hold the beast away from his face. His right hand found the scruff of its neck and gripped tightly.

Wilhelm realized he would not last long in this fight; the weeks in bed had weakened his body. He cleared his mind and used the dagger in his left hand to stab the beast. After several shallow cuts, he plunged the dagger into the beast's right eye, driving it deep into its brain. The dog let his shoulder go and yelped as its body stiffened. If this had been a natural beast, it would have died instantly, but it was a creature of the dark, summoned with magical energy. The beast looked at Wilhelm one last time, then dissolved into a misty form and melted without leaving a trace of its existence. He looked over and saw Eithne still struggling to sit up. He ran over and helped her get to her feet. His horse was dead; the girl's horse was crippled.

Wilhelm watched as tears coursed down her cheeks and forced himself to gather what meager supplies he could scrounge. He cut a small part of the saddle blanket and covered his wound. He took his dagger and his coin purse with five gold coins. He freed her saddlebags and her water skin. "We must return to my city, but we'll travel through the woods and keep out of sight. There might be others after you."

She stood and watched him put her wounded horse out of its misery. "I'm frightened. Let's get away from here."

❉❉❉

Lady Sioban was bored, but she sat still in the meeting hall with the Warlord and several representatives from high-ranking noble families. They discussed what they should do about the northern tribal elves. Since the battle of the Great Eastern Forest, the nobles were divided on how to deal with the uncouth and backwards northern tribes. Many, including the Warlord wanted to send a military force to investigate the existence of dark magic among the groups and root it out. Others were skeptical and believed that the humans had made up the tale of an evil magic wielder to further encroach into elven lands. Sioban suggested sending missionaries and warriors to observe and investigate the rumors of dark magic. As the meeting progressed a soft voice whispered in her left ear. *"I have bad tidings."*

Lady Sioban looked around, stood, and excused herself from the table. She walked toward a side table where she poured herself some fruit-infused water. Turning her back to the group, she asked, "What has happened?"

"Your hound was killed, and your daughter is running west. You should kill the Warlord."

"Yes, mistress." Sioban frowned at the news. She took a sip of the drink, placed the goblet down, and gestured toward the Warlord. The prepared spell empowered with dark energy poured out of the High Priestess's hands and penetrated the Warlord's head.

The result was immediate. The victim couldn't speak, and the right side of his face stopped moving. As the others looked on helplessly, the Warlord fell to the ground. One of the attendees rushed to help. "It looks like he's having an apoplexy. Call for a healer." Sioban rushed to Eachmhile's side and helped to ease the struggling elf to the ground. She waited in silence as the guards carried the Warlord to a healer. The gathered lords stood whispering among themselves.

Trahern would have preferred to take the shorter southern pass to the City States, but this late in the season the human merchants told him there was a chance they would be trapped by snow. Instead, he led Fiadl toward the western pass which connected Nixland with the Al-Anikka kingdom. From there they would turn south to the city-states. The two elves didn't talk much to each other and often ate in silence. As Trahern chewed on a piece of dried beef for lunch he heard the soft, beguiling voice. *"You are being followed by one human; he's a day's ride behind you. He cannot be allowed to interfere with my plans."*

Trahern opened his mouth to warn Fiadl, but her eyes were rolled back in her head and her mouth was fixed with a wild grin. He waited for her to return to herself. "Someone is pursuing us."

"I know," she replied. "The goddess told me as well. She instructed me to enchant two of your arrows and then to call up a storm to close the pass."

Trahern returned with his quiver and bow. "This is as good a spot as any; we can remain hidden among these trees. I'll have an unobstructed view of the road for more than a double-paced mile." He looked at her in fascination as she held the two arrows and chanted over them. He could see a slight vibration emanating from the wood and metal. Afterwards, she lifted her hands to the sky and chanted. When she was done, she closed her eyes in obvious fatigue. As soon as Trahern picked up the two arrows, he could feel magical energy coursing through them. The enchanted arrows seemed normal but when he looked closely, he saw that the shafts were straighter and stiffer. He tested the arrowhead which was sharper.

"I need to rest," Fiadl said and walked unsteadily to her bed roll. She collapsed and closed her eyes. She knew that without more blood sacrifice it would take longer for her to recover her strength.

Trahern found a good position overlooking the road. He gathered local vegetation and created a blind, using leaves to disguise his cloak. Satisfied with his efforts at blending in, Trahern made himself comfortable for the long wait.

The sun climbed higher as midday approached. Trahern breathed deeply and made sure to flex his muscles so they wouldn't cramp when he had to shoot his bow. In the distance he saw a lone horseman. He knocked one of the enchanted arrows, his thoughts returning to the battle where he had used Rianor's enchanted arrows. He decided to wait till the target came a little closer. The anticipation excited the hunter in Trahern, and he calmed himself with deep breaths, willing his heartbeat to slow. He flexed his fingers and tried to loosen his arms and shoulders as the rider closed.

At five hundred paces Trahern readied himself and tried to gauge the wind by the movement of the smaller bushes and tree branches. He rose slowly, making sure his body was hidden by the blind, and took aim. Before he released, he heard a noise behind him. It was Fiadl waking up from her sleep. She was walking noisily toward him. The rider was now less than three hundred paces away. As soon as the rider saw Fiadl he tried to the stop his horse.

Trahern swore under his breath, "Stupid girl." He stood, aimed again, and released his arrow. Although it was a poor shot, he must have hit the rider, who fell off his horse. Trahern nocked the other arrow and shot the man's horse in the chest, hitting the animal in the lungs and piercing the heart. The horse ran a dozen paces forward and fell as its heart stopped beating.

"You stupid girl," Trahern said as he turned to face Fiadl. "You almost ruined the ambush."

Fiadl was angry. "How dare you speak to a priestess like that?"

"I dare because I'm not your servant! Let's get moving; we've lost half a day here." He quickly glanced at the prone figure lying on the road and turned to their own horses.

As the two elves rode away, Ridolfo regained consciousness from his fall. He was in a great deal of pain with an arrow protruding from his left hip.

Roisin rode east alone because Rianor had not recovered from being raised from the dead. Larvarnis had told the irked priestess that allies waited for her there. She had been ordered to find the Silver Wolf Clan, one of the many independent clans of the Thunder Horse peoples, in their winter pastures. Larvanis claimed they would provide slaves for sacrifice; in return, Roisin would perform magical rituals for the clan's chieftain and restore his youth. She would help him unite the Thunder Horse clans under his Silver Wolf banner in return and help spread the goddess's power and aid the High Priestess.

CHAPTER 27

Inside Ovidio's house a small party was underway. Ututur looked at the gathering of his friends. Harun's arm was in a sling; he planned to stay in Mount Haven and continue to help the Vigiles and Master Ovidio with their investigations. Rosanella and Rialta brought spiced cakes for the party. Sheriff Bastina brought a small cask of fortified wine. Master Cociarelli had ordered a roasted pig to give thanks to the gods for a good harvest. The atmosphere inside the home was festive even though they all knew that evil lurked. Sheriff Bastina and Rosanella had searched for the wounded sorcerer for three days without any luck. Master Ovidio helped, using his magic, also without any luck. The gnome returned to the Elven embassy with Vigiles Albrecht to search for the dark magic user and found none although he sensed something. The first snow had fallen, and the search for the wounded sorcerer was called off.

Rolf helped Andanir move their belongings from Ututur's cabin into the half-orc's place in town for the winter. Everyone was amazed at how fast the Vigiles' and Ututur's wounds had healed. Master Ovidio told him that it was Ilina's healing magic that saved the Vigiles from certain death.

Andanir had nightmares for days after the fight with the sorcerer. He dreamed that he was lost in an unfamiliar forest, being chased by a large black creature. But as the days passed, so did his nightmares.

❈❈❈

Ututur stood by the platter of fresh and aged cheese he brought for the party, talking with Ilina. "I meant to thank you for taking care of me and the boy."

"It was nothing; try the cheese with these tomatoes and some fresh basil. Make sure to dip it in the honey then vinegar," said Ilina as she stepped closer to Ututur. "Do you think this is over?"

"I don't know. I think we killed at least one dark magic user, and Ridolfo is pursuing the other sorceress. With any luck we'll end the evil menace before next summer.

Ilina put her arm around the half-orc. "I hope this all ends soon."

Ututur tried to relax as he felt her arm go around him and noticed Andanir smiling with Rialta at his side. Ovidio and Harun made an odd pair, but they were happy working together in the huge library. The peace with the elves seemed to be holding, and Eoin promised to return in the spring with news.

"Now make the cut like I showed you in your dream. Good, now collect the blood in a bowl. Ignore the screaming. Cut the boy's stomach open and cut the genitals off. Reach in, scoop out the intestines and just thrown them on the floor. Reach into the chest cavity and grab the beating heart. Pull as hard as you can. If you need to use the knife to cut it free and bite into it while its beating. Good, well-done Eleonora. Draw the sacred runes on your body. Now you are ready to perform this ritual for my followers." Said Larvanis. She was pleased with her newest priestess and the growing number of human followers.

Eleonora felt the power course through her body. She would call Rolando to service her sexually later. For now, she danced in the moonlight naked with the dead boy's heart in her hands.

Acknowledgements

This endeavor would not have been possible without support from my wife Jane. From reading early drafts to helping me with the map, she was there from its inception to the end.

I would like to also thank Karen Hodges Miller my editor for working with me on everything and staying with me as I continue my journey as a writer.

Thank you, Emily from Emily's World of Design, for the wonderful cover and artwork.

About the Author

John Park was born is Seoul, South Korea. He received his BA in Economics and Ancient History from Franklin and Marshall College. He also completed coursework for a Ph.D. in Political Science at the University of Pennsylvania and received his J.D. from Cardozo School of Law. He has received a commendation from the Senate and General Assembly of New Jersey and a Congressional Certificate of Recognition for his work in public service. He lives with his wife in Wyoming.

John writes both fantasy and science fiction. The second book in his sci-fi series, The Enemy, will be published in early 2024. The first book in the series. *Message to Arecibo*, can be found on Amazon and at other bookstores.

Connect with John at his websites, sciwriterPark.com, and theauthorwebsite.com/johnpark. And on Facebook and on Twitter.

www.ingramcontent.com/pod-product-compliance
Lightning Source LLC
Chambersburg PA
CBHW071247300726
48975CB00002B/585